# MODEL

™

# ALSO AVAILABLE FROM ⊙TOKYOPOP®

03.03.04T

# ALSO AVAILABLE FROM  TOKYOPOP®

PLANETES
PRIEST
PRINCESS AI
PSYCHIC ACADEMY
RAGNAROK
RAVE MASTER
REALITY CHECK
REBIRTH
REBOUND
REMOTE
RISING STARS OF MANGA
SABER MARIONETTE J
SAILOR MOON
SAINT TAIL
SAIYUKI
SAMURAI DEEPER KYO
SAMURAI GIRL REAL BOUT HIGH SCHOOL
SCRYED
SEIKAI TRILOGY, THE
SGT. FROG
SHAOLIN SISTERS
SHIRAHIME-SYO: SNOW GODDESS TALES
SHUTTERBOX
SKULL MAN, THE
SMUGGLER
SNOW DROP
SORCERER HUNTERS
STONE
SUIKODEN III
SUKI
THREADS OF TIME
TOKYO BABYLON
TOKYO MEW MEW
TOKYO TRIBES
TRAMPS LIKE US
UNDER THE GLASS MOON
VAMPIRE GAME
VISION OF ESCAFLOWNE, THE
WARRIORS OF TAO
WILD ACT
WISH
WORLD OF HARTZ
X-DAY
ZODIAC P.I.

## MANGA NOVELS

CLAMP SCHOOL PARANORMAL INVESTIGATORS
KARMA CLUB
SAILOR MOON
SLAYERS

## ART BOOKS

ART OF CARDCAPTOR SAKURA
ART OF MAGIC KNIGHT RAYEARTH, THE
PEACH: MIWA UEDA ILLUSTRATIONS

## ANIME GUIDES

COWBOY BEBOP
GUNDAM TECHNICAL MANUALS
SAILOR MOON SCOUT GUIDES

## TOKYOPOP KIDS

STRAY SHEEP

## CINE-MANGA™

ALADDIN
ASTRO BOY
CARDCAPTORS
CONFESSIONS OF A TEENAGE DRAMA QUEEN
DUEL MASTERS
FAIRLY ODDPARENTS, THE
FAMILY GUY
FINDING NEMO
G.I. JOE SPY TROOPS
JACKIE CHAN ADVENTURES
JIMMY NEUTRON: BOY GENIUS, THE ADVENTURES OF
KIM POSSIBLE
LILO & STITCH
LIZZIE MCGUIRE
LIZZIE MCGUIRE MOVIE, THE
MALCOLM IN THE MIDDLE
POWER RANGERS: NINJA STORM
SHREK 2
SPONGEBOB SQUAREPANTS
SPY KIDS 2
SPY KIDS 3-D: GAME OVER
TEENAGE MUTANT NINJA TURTLES
THAT'S SO RAVEN
TRANSFORMERS: ARMADA
TRANSFORMERS: ENERGON

# For more
# information visit
# www.TOKYOPOP.com

03.03.04T

Translator - Lauren Na
English Adaptation - Sam Stormcrow Hayes
Retouch and Lettering - Caren McCaleb
Cover Layout - Anna Kernbaum
Graphic Designer - Mona Lisa de Asis

Editor - Bryce P. Coleman
Digital Imaging Manager - Chris Buford
Pre-Press Manager - Antonio DePietro
Production Managers - Jennifer Miller, Mutsumi Miyazaki
Art Director - Matt Alford
Managing Editor - Jill Freshney
VP of Production - Ron Klamert
President & C.O.O. - John Parker
Publisher & C.E.O. - Stuart Levy

E-mail: info@TOKYOPOP.com
Come visit us online at www.TOKYOPOP.com

A  Manga

TOKYOPOP Inc.
5900 Wilshire Blvd. Suite 2000
Los Angeles, CA 90036

*Model Vol. 1*

ISBN: 1-59182-711-6

First TOKYOPOP printing: May 2004

10 9 8 7 6 5 4 3 2 1

Printed in the USA

# MODEL™

## VOLUME ONE

## BY
## LEE SO-YOUNG

TOKYOPOP®

LOS ANGELES • TOKYO • LONDON

# MODEL: ONE

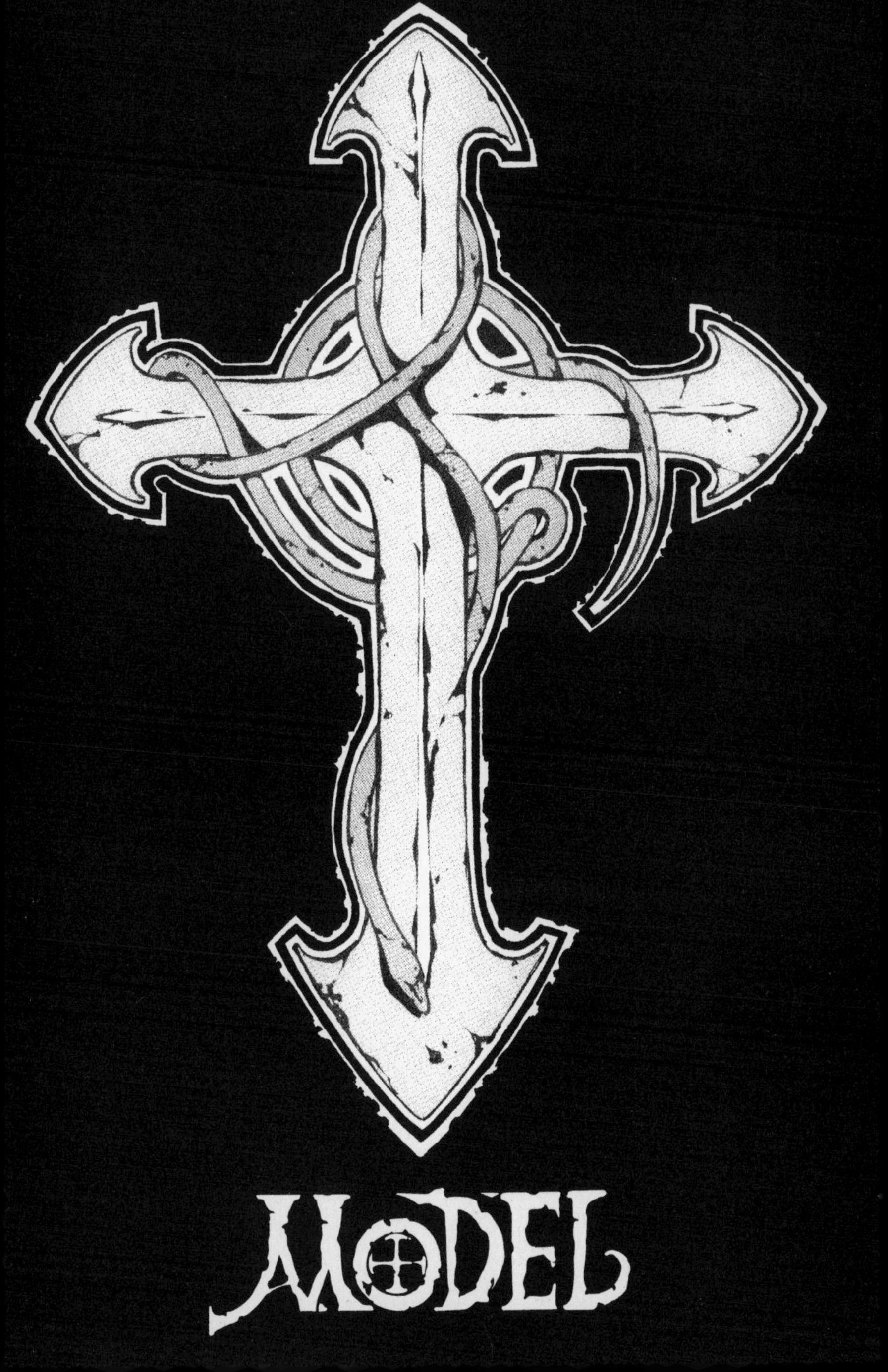

# MODEL

# PROLOGUE

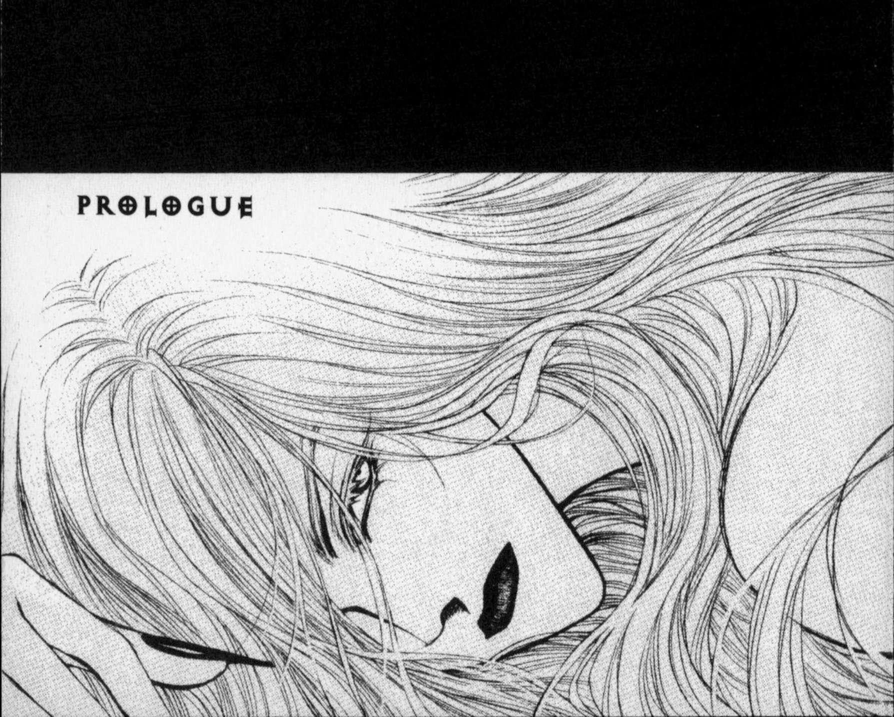

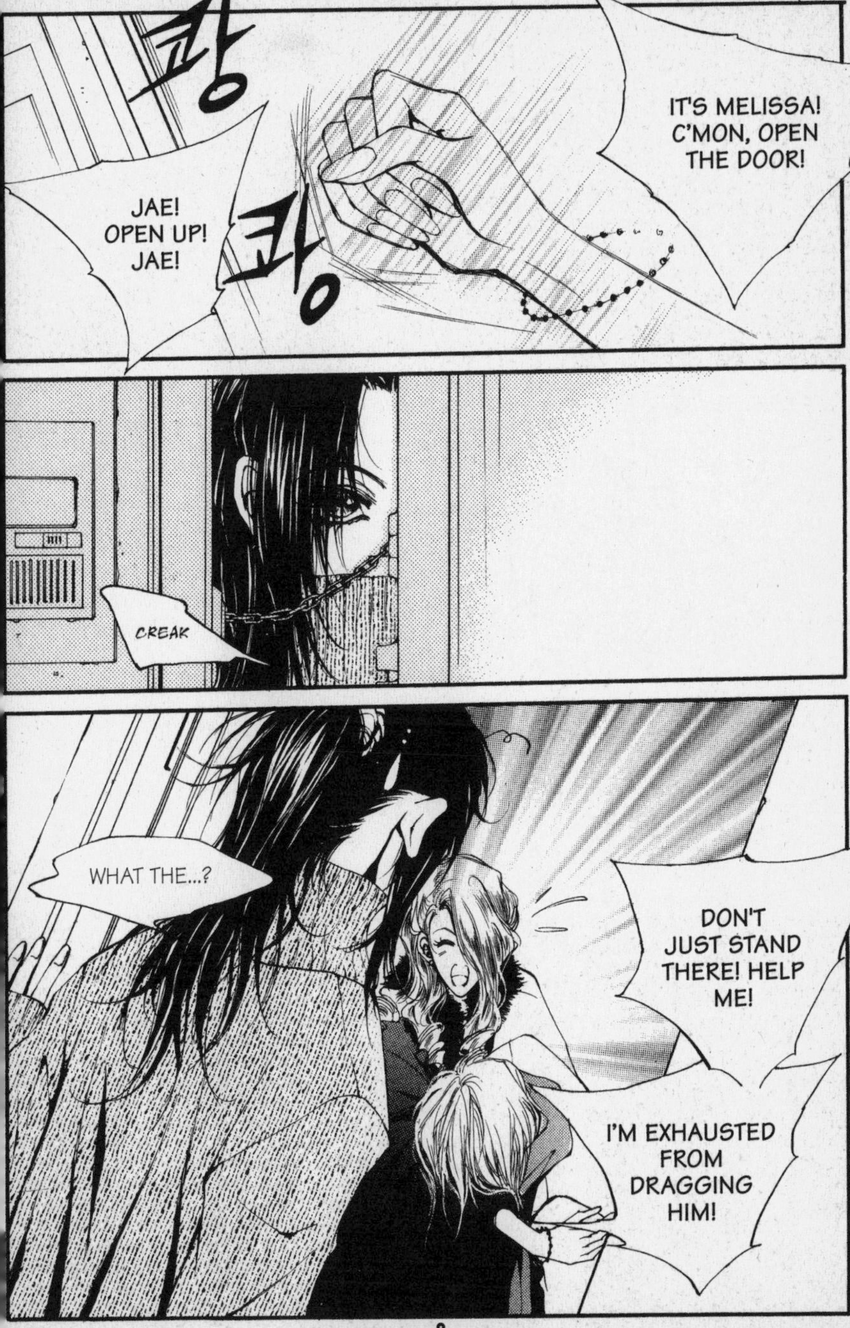
쾅
JAE! OPEN UP! JAE!
쾅
IT'S MELISSA! C'MON, OPEN THE DOOR!
CREAK
WHAT THE...?
DON'T JUST STAND THERE! HELP ME!
I'M EXHAUSTED FROM DRAGGING HIM!

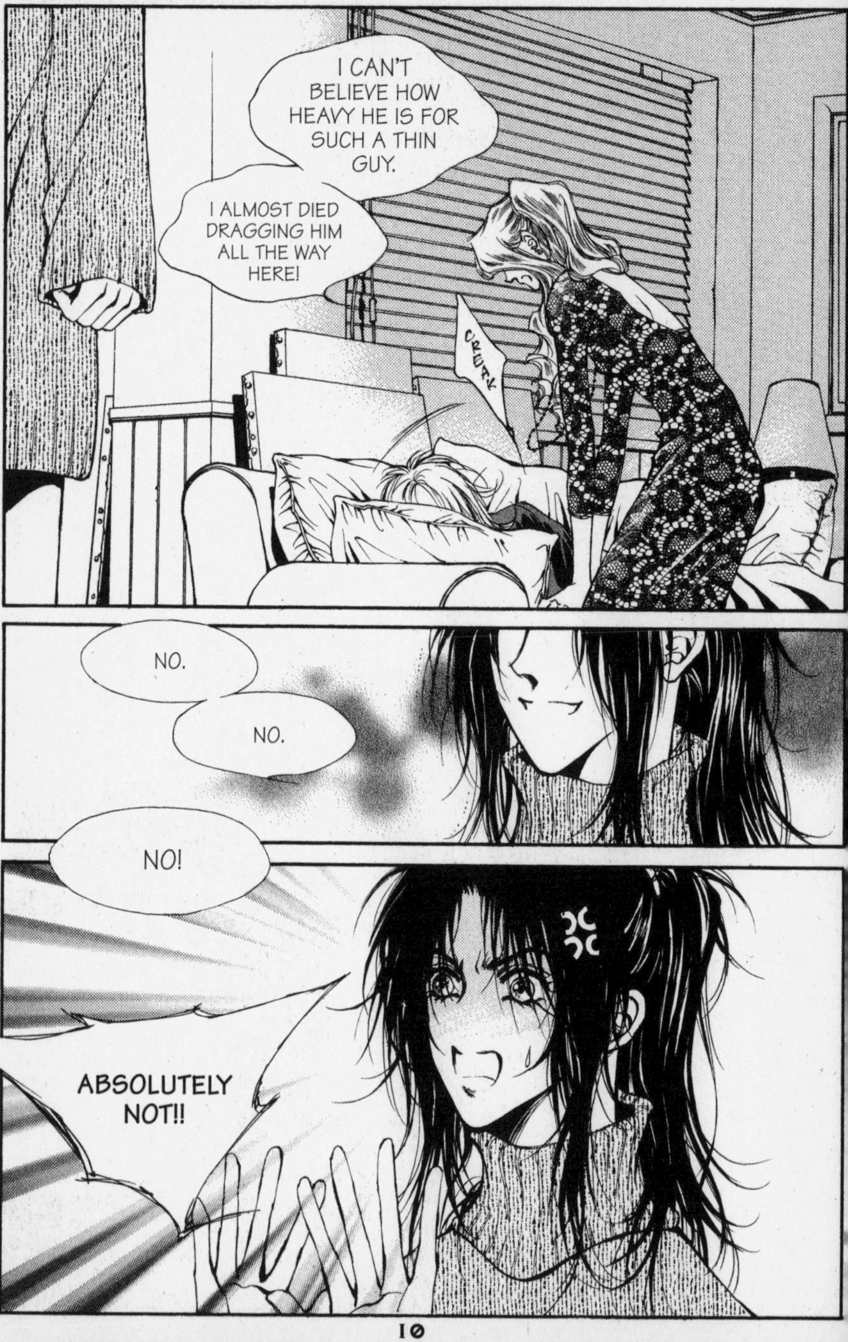

I CAN'T BELIEVE HOW HEAVY HE IS FOR SUCH A THIN GUY.
I ALMOST DIED DRAGGING HIM ALL THE WAY HERE!
CREAK
NO.
NO.
NO!
ABSOLUTELY NOT!!

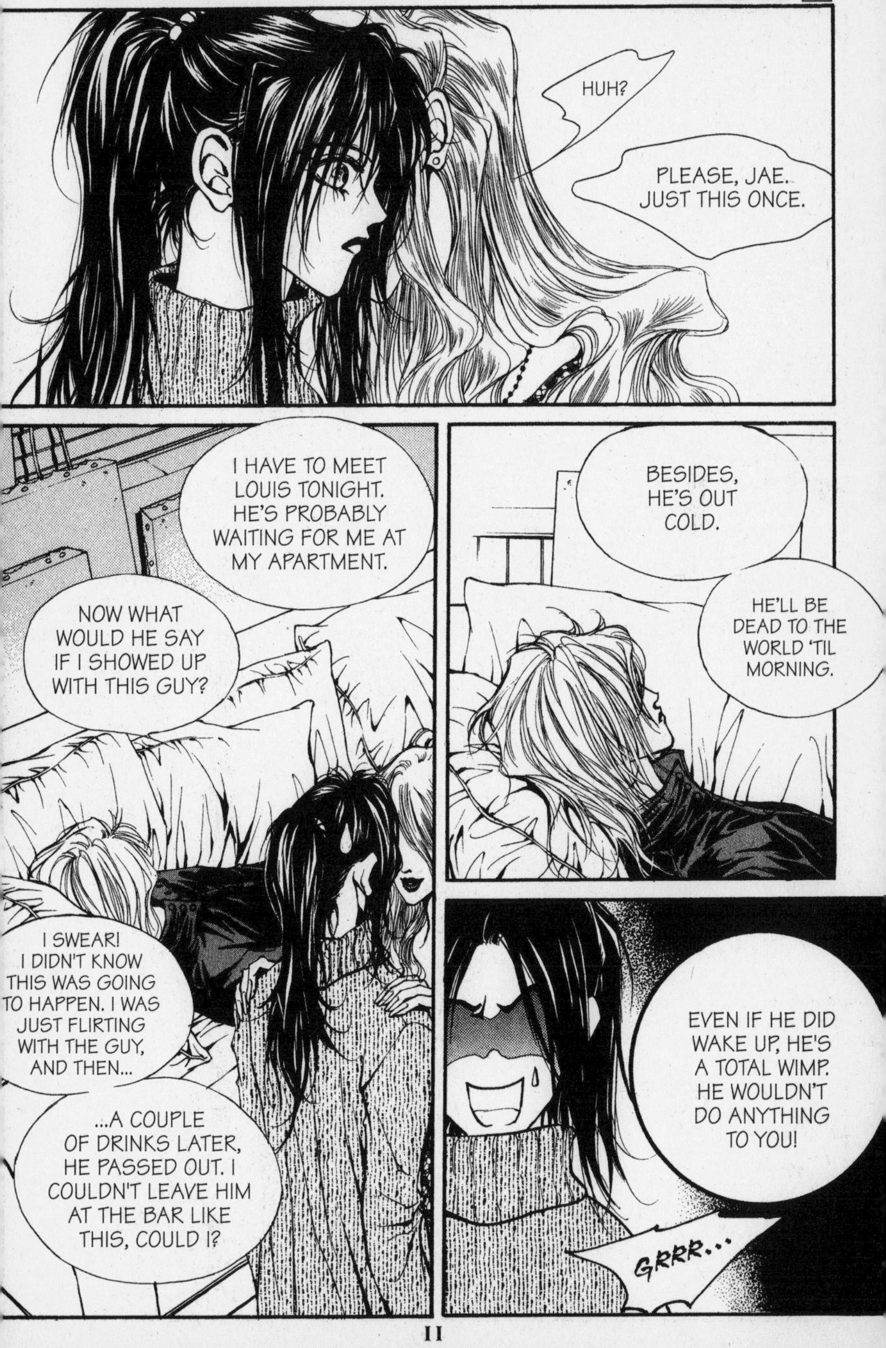
HUH?
PLEASE, JAE. JUST THIS ONCE.
I HAVE TO MEET LOUIS TONIGHT. HE'S PROBABLY WAITING FOR ME AT MY APARTMENT.
NOW WHAT WOULD HE SAY IF I SHOWED UP WITH THIS GUY?
I SWEAR! I DIDN'T KNOW THIS WAS GOING TO HAPPEN. I WAS JUST FLIRTING WITH THE GUY, AND THEN...
...A COUPLE OF DRINKS LATER, HE PASSED OUT. I COULDN'T LEAVE HIM AT THE BAR LIKE THIS, COULD I?
BESIDES, HE'S OUT COLD.
HE'LL BE DEAD TO THE WORLD 'TIL MORNING.
EVEN IF HE DID WAKE UP, HE'S A TOTAL WIMP. HE WOULDN'T DO ANYTHING TO YOU!
GRRR...

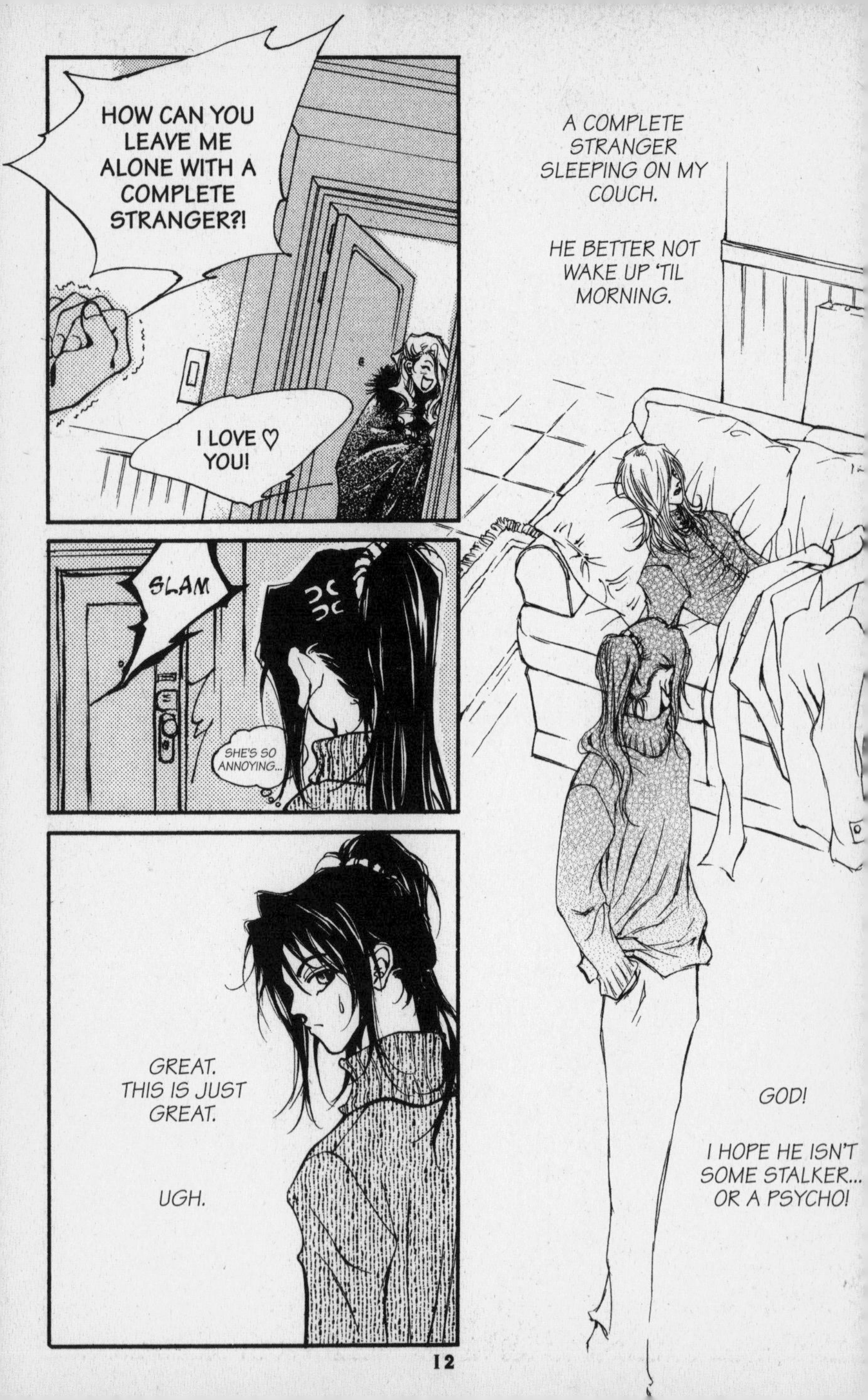
HOW CAN YOU LEAVE ME ALONE WITH A COMPLETE STRANGER?!
I LOVE ♡ YOU!
SLAM
SHE'S SO ANNOYING...
GREAT. THIS IS JUST GREAT.
UGH.
A COMPLETE STRANGER SLEEPING ON MY COUCH.
HE BETTER NOT WAKE UP 'TIL MORNING.
GOD!
I HOPE HE ISN'T SOME STALKER... OR A PSYCHO!

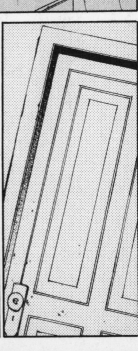

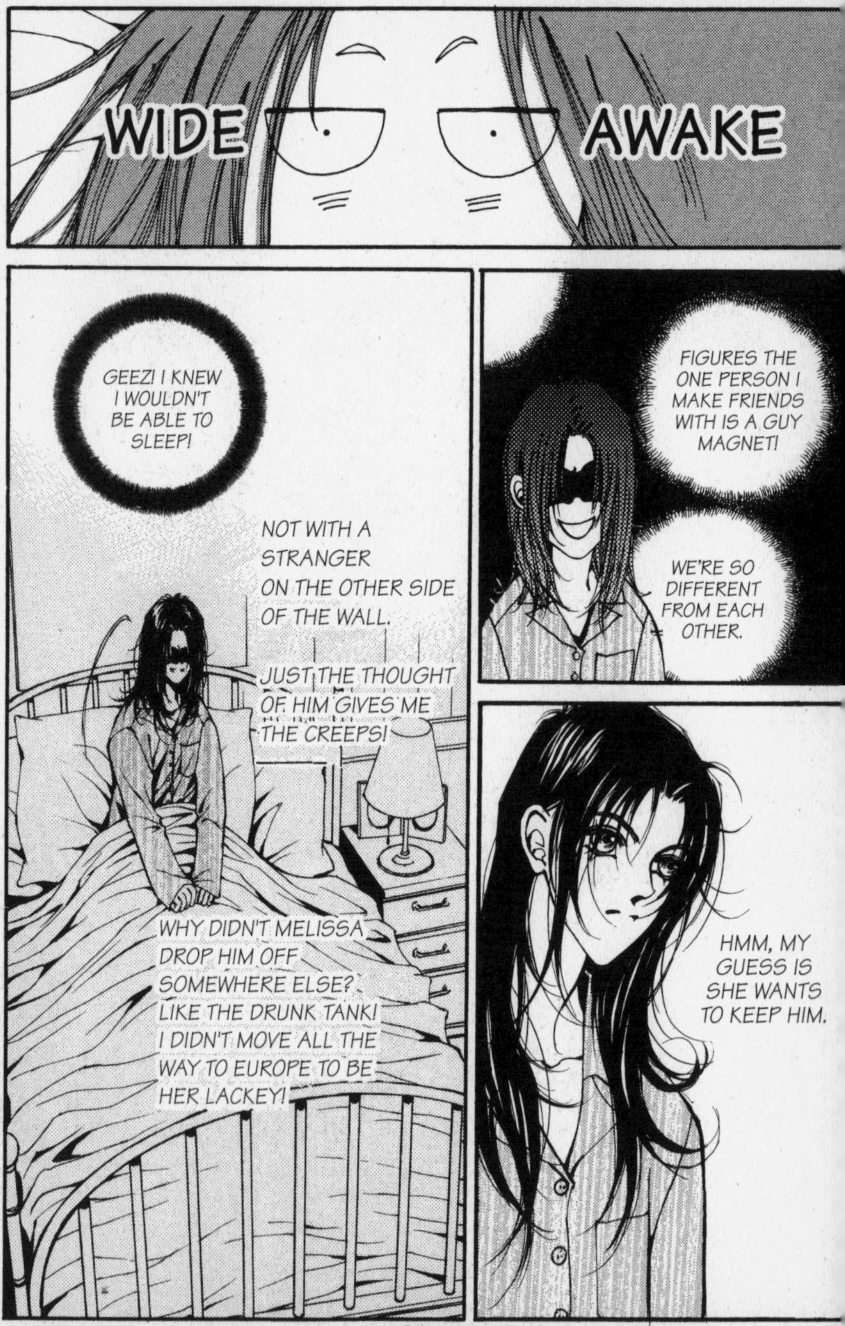
WIDE
AWAKE
GEEZ! I KNEW I WOULDN'T BE ABLE TO SLEEP!
NOT WITH A STRANGER ON THE OTHER SIDE OF THE WALL.
JUST THE THOUGHT OF HIM GIVES ME THE CREEPS!
WHY DIDN'T MELISSA DROP HIM OFF SOMEWHERE ELSE? LIKE THE DRUNK TANK! I DIDN'T MOVE ALL THE WAY TO EUROPE TO BE HER LACKEY!
FIGURES THE ONE PERSON I MAKE FRIENDS WITH IS A GUY MAGNET!
WE'RE SO DIFFERENT FROM EACH OTHER.
HMM, MY GUESS IS SHE WANTS TO KEEP HIM.

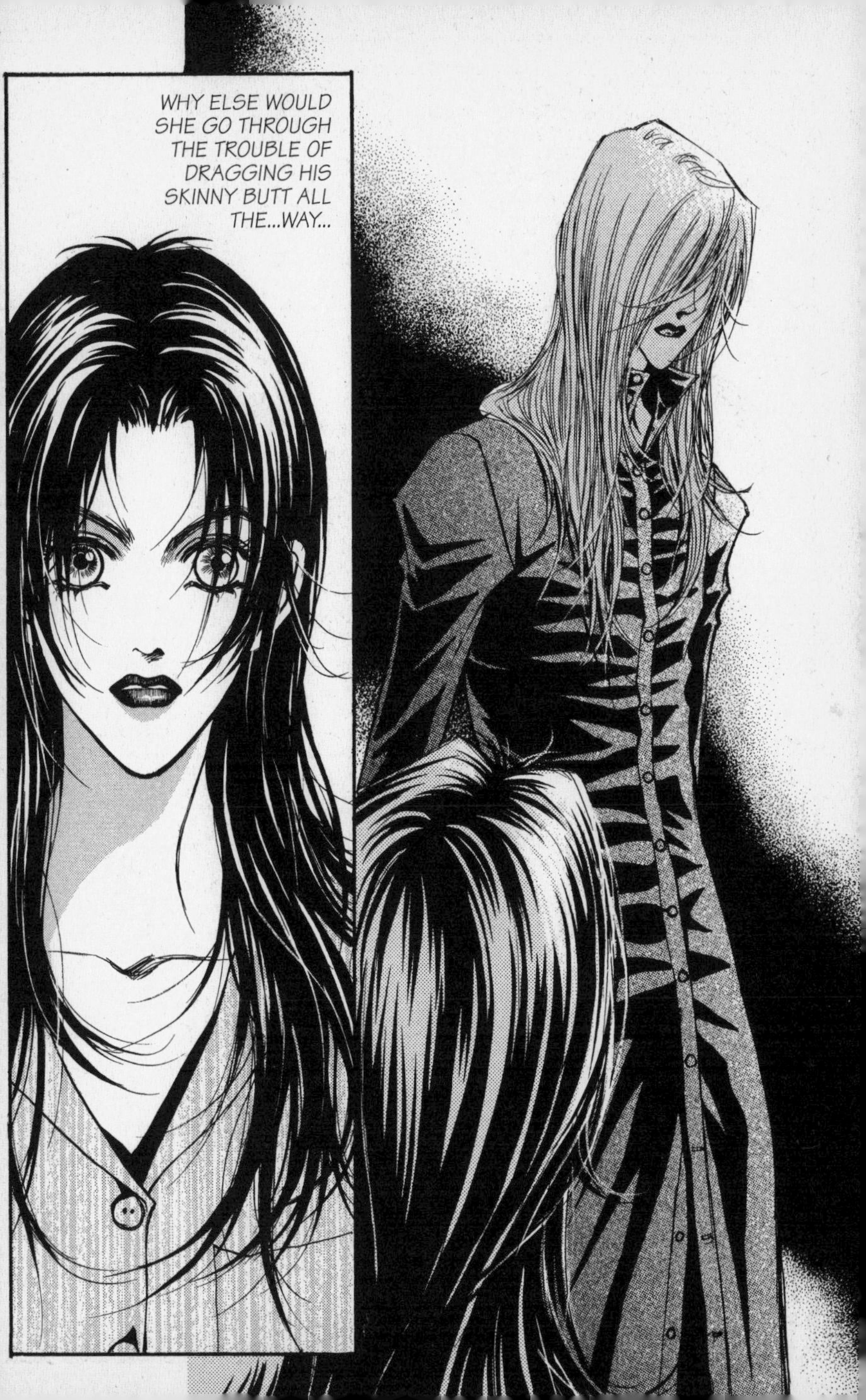
WHY ELSE WOULD SHE GO THROUGH THE TROUBLE OF DRAGGING HIS SKINNY BUTT ALL THE...WAY...

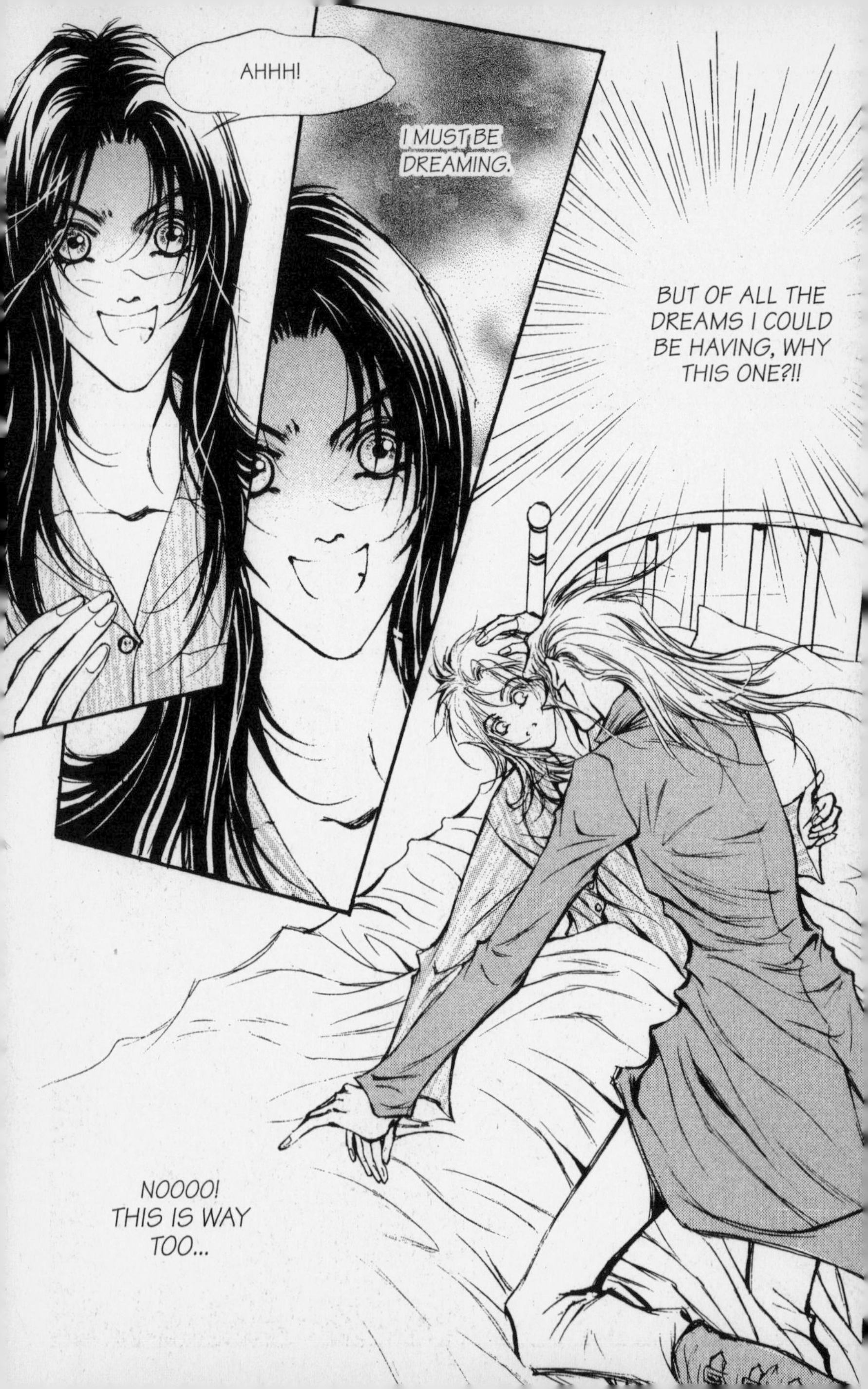
AHHH!
I MUST BE DREAMING.
BUT OF ALL THE DREAMS I COULD BE HAVING, WHY THIS ONE?!!
NOOOO! THIS IS WAY TOO...

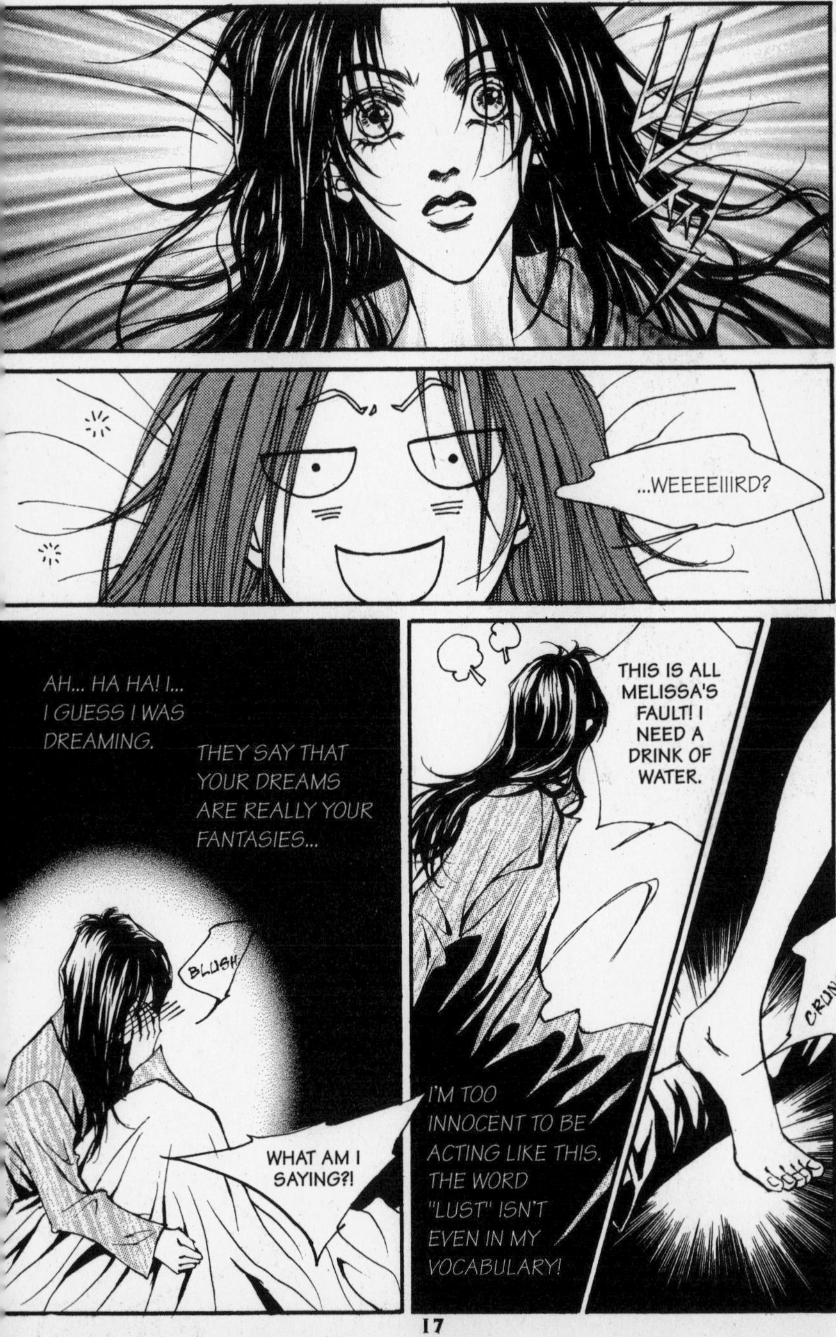
...WEEEEIIIRD?
AH... HA HA! I... I GUESS I WAS DREAMING.
THEY SAY THAT YOUR DREAMS ARE REALLY YOUR FANTASIES...
BLUSH
WHAT AM I SAYING?!
THIS IS ALL MELISSA'S FAULT! I NEED A DRINK OF WATER.
I'M TOO INNOCENT TO BE ACTING LIKE THIS. THE WORD "LUST" ISN'T EVEN IN MY VOCABULARY!
CRUNCH

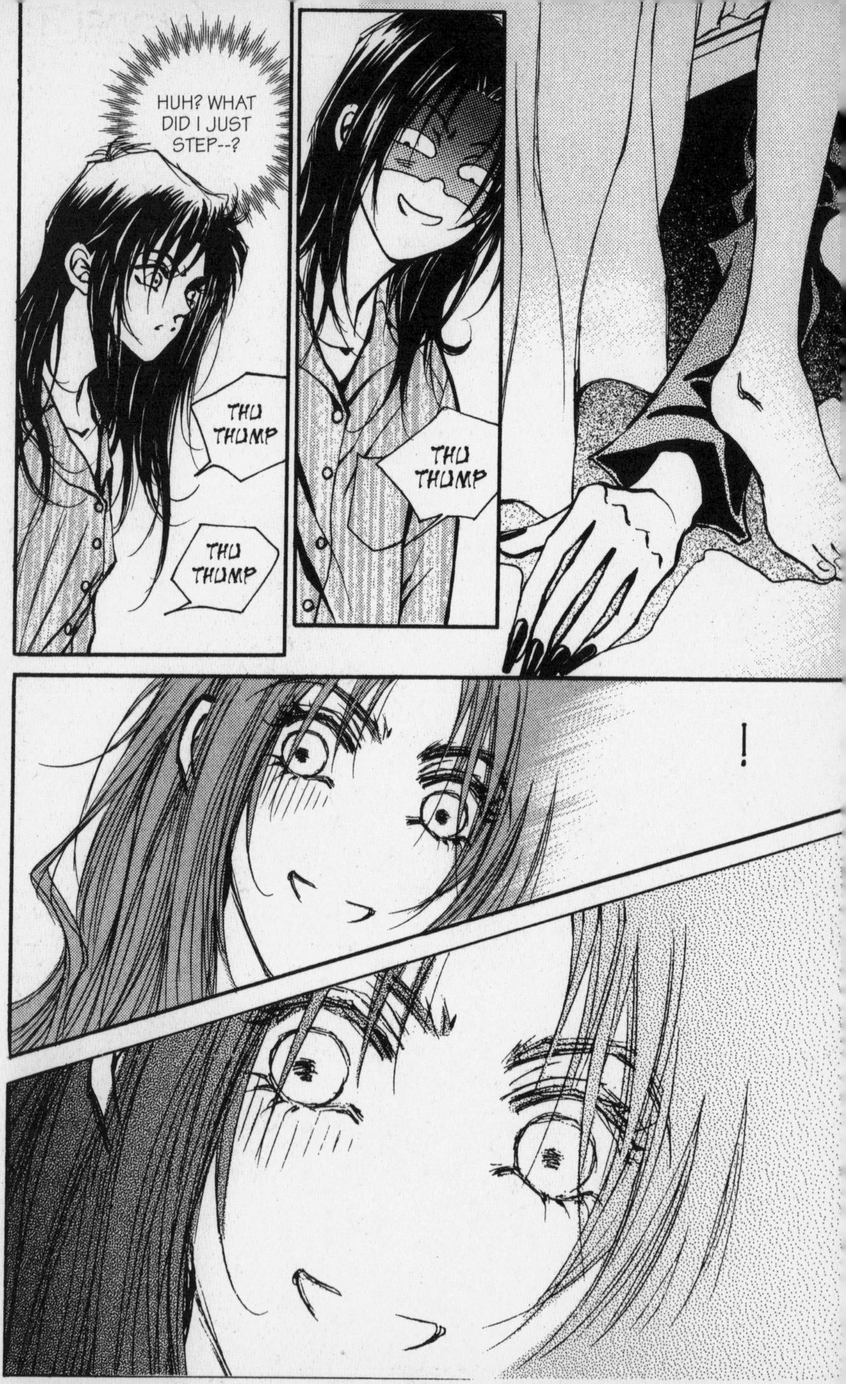

HUH? WHAT DID I JUST STEP--?
THU THUMP
THU THUMP
THU THUMP
!

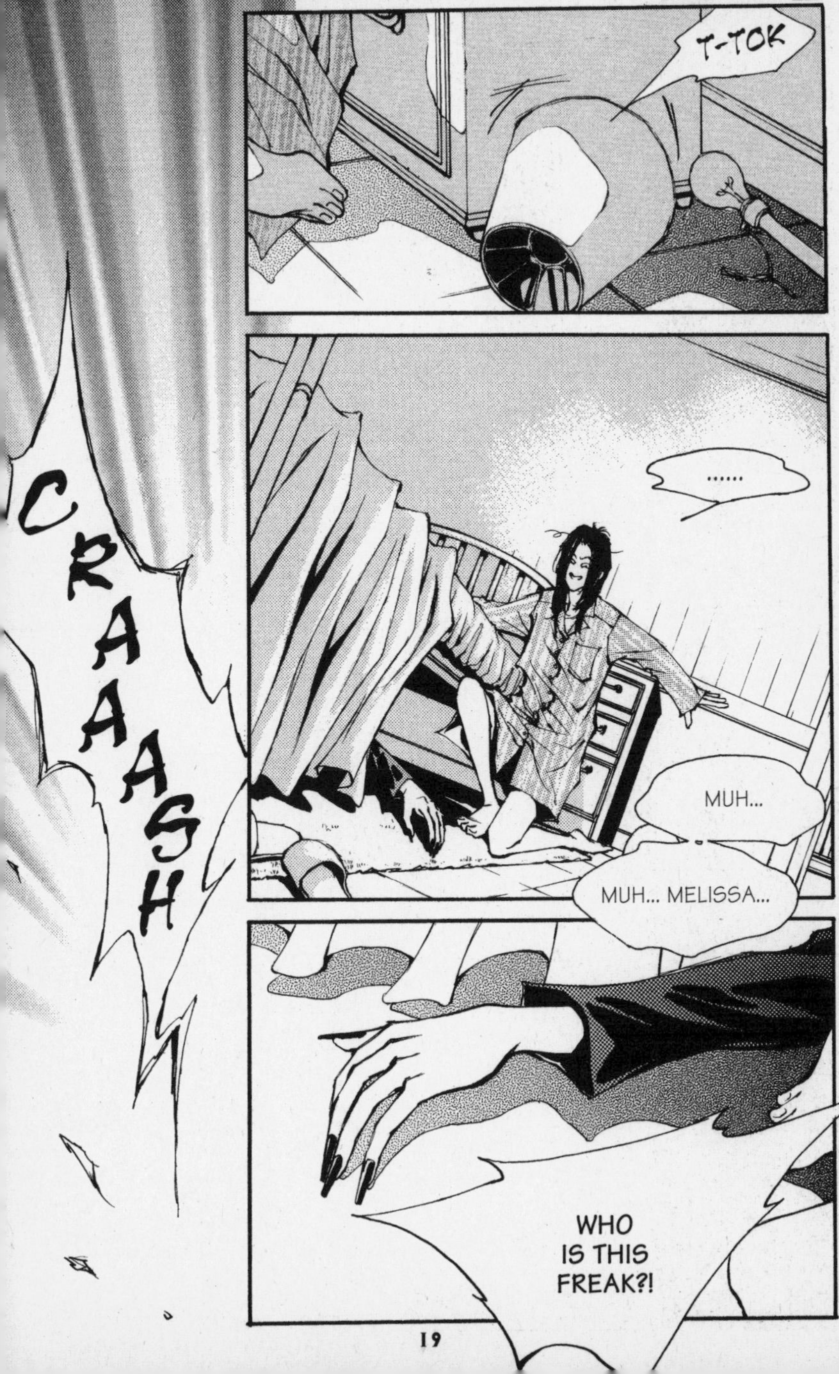
CRAAAASH
T-TOK
......
MUH...
MUH... MELISSA...
WHO IS THIS FREAK?!

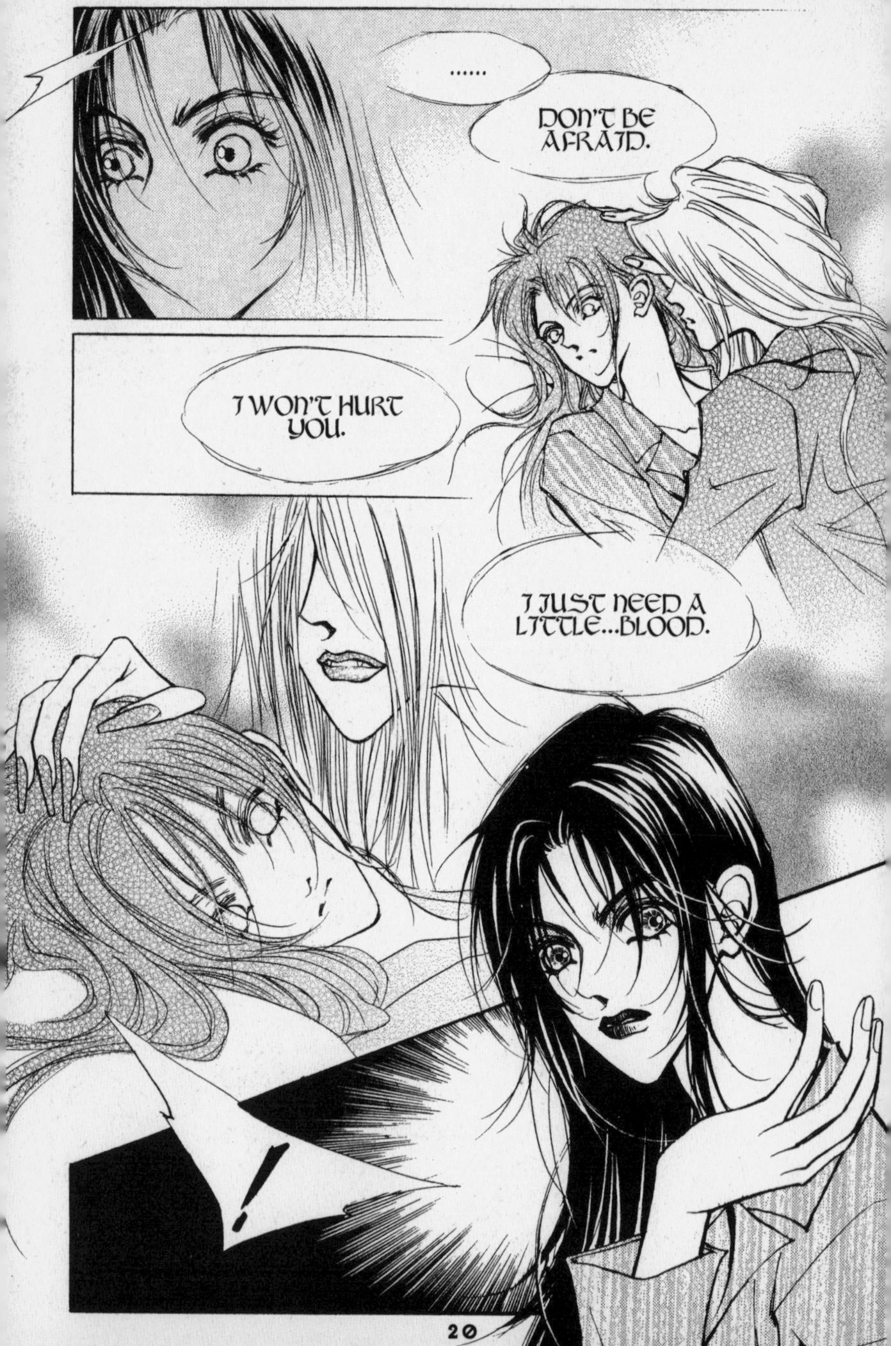
......
DON'T BE AFRAID.
I WON'T HURT YOU.
I JUST NEED A LITTLE...BLOOD.
!

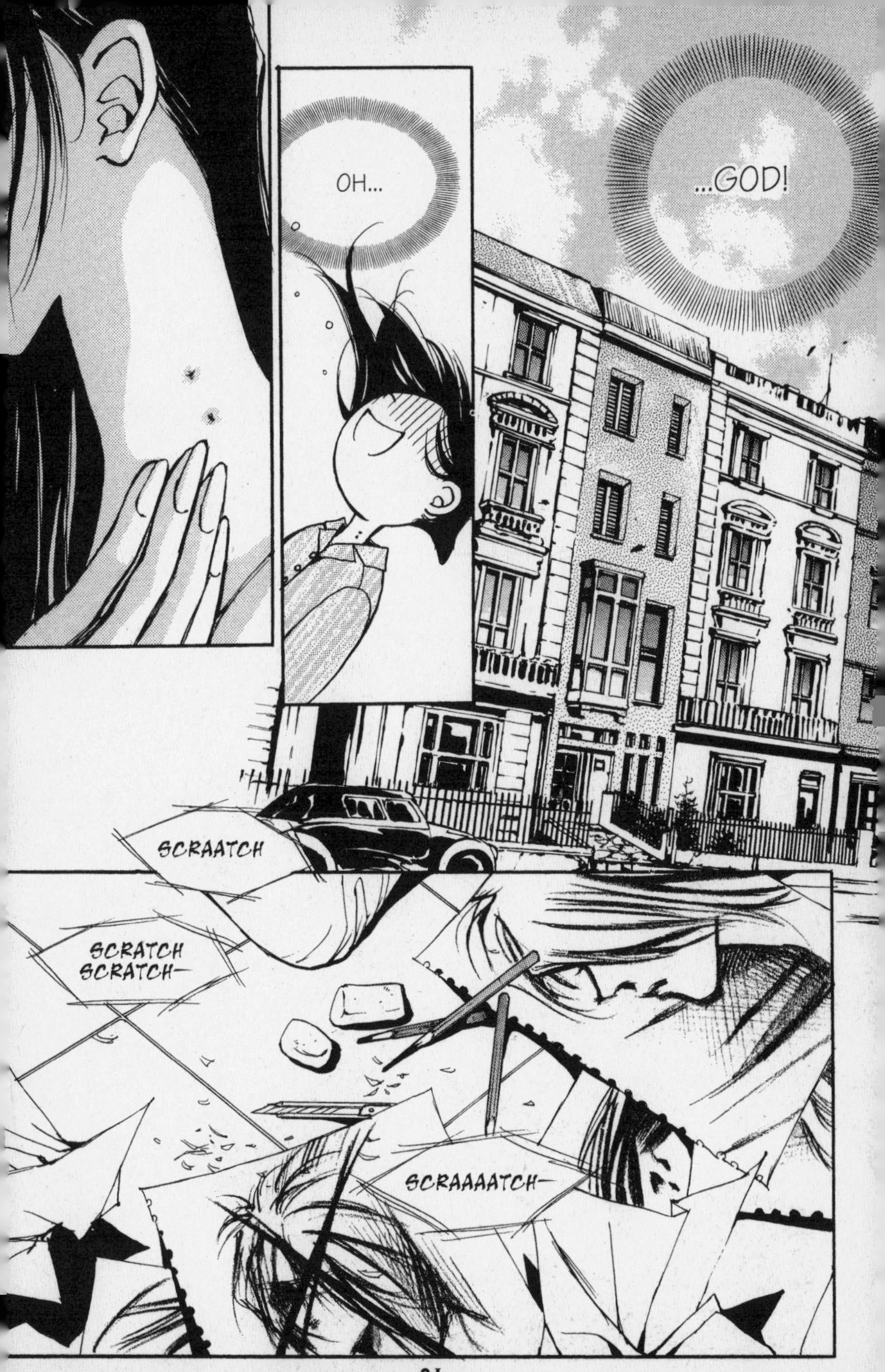
OH...
...GOD!
SCRAATCH
SCRATCH SCRATCH—
SCRAAAATCH—

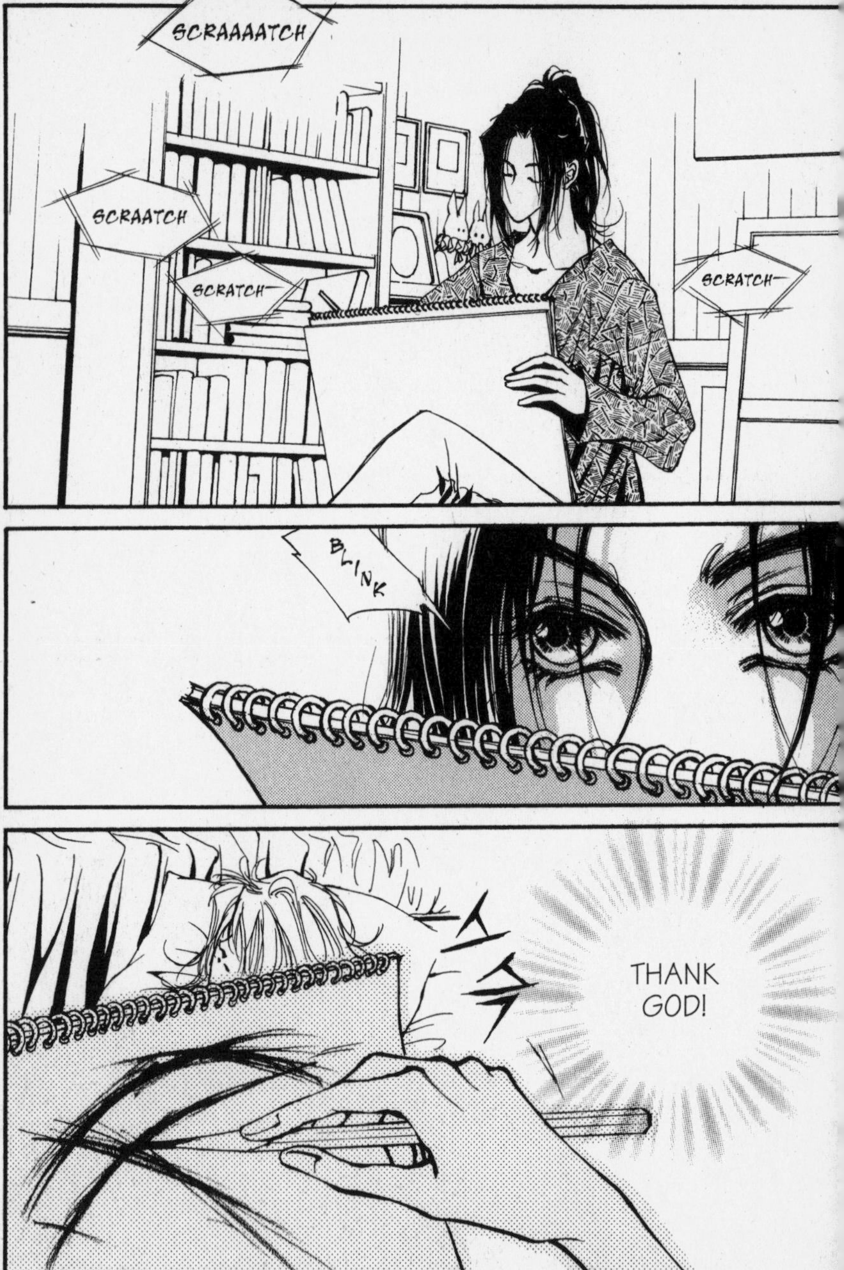
SCRAAAATCH
SCRAATCH
SCRATCH—
SCRATCH—
BLINK
THANK GOD!

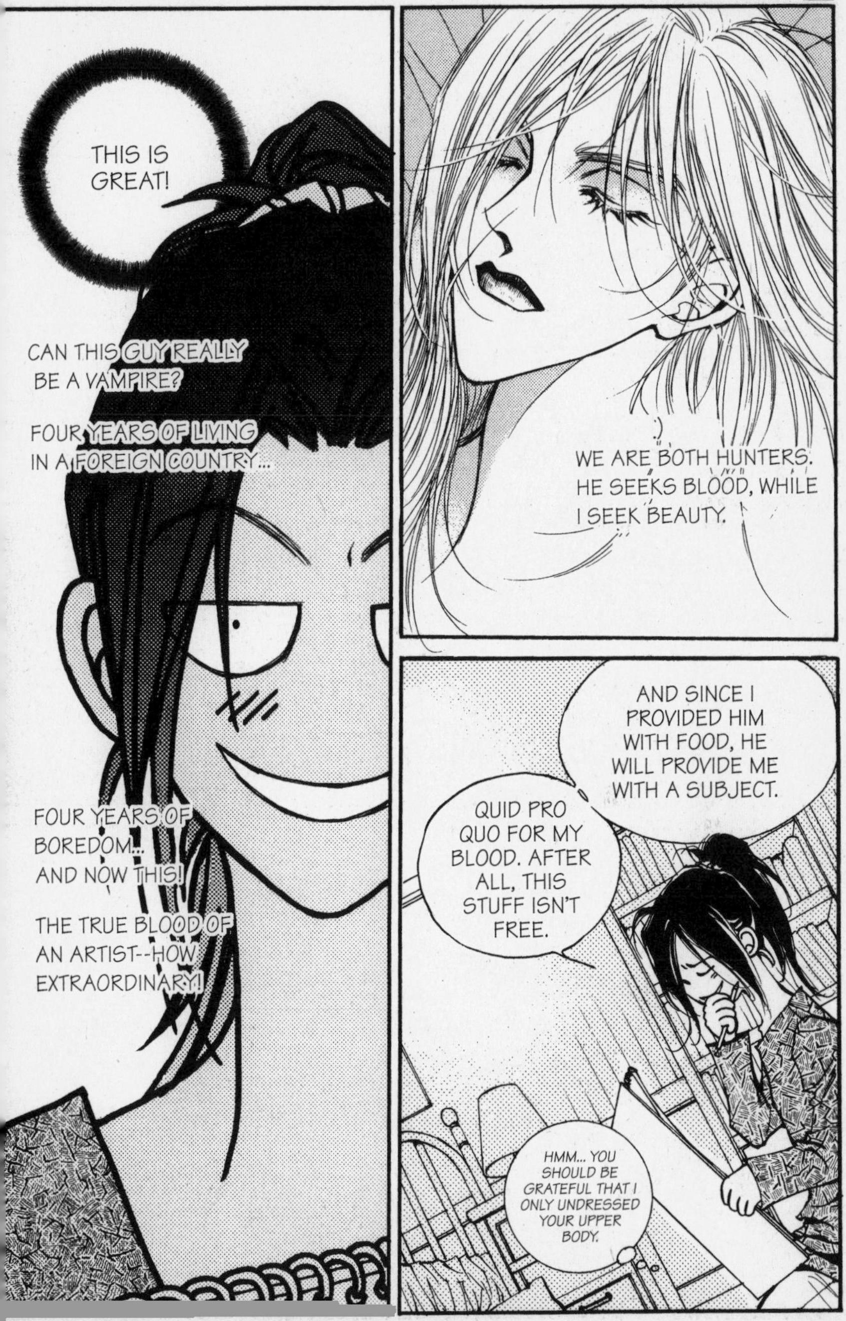
THIS IS GREAT!
CAN THIS GUY REALLY BE A VAMPIRE?
FOUR YEARS OF LIVING IN A FOREIGN COUNTRY...
FOUR YEARS OF BOREDOM... AND NOW THIS!
THE TRUE BLOOD OF AN ARTIST--HOW EXTRAORDINARY!
WE ARE BOTH HUNTERS. HE SEEKS BLOOD, WHILE I SEEK BEAUTY.
AND SINCE I PROVIDED HIM WITH FOOD, HE WILL PROVIDE ME WITH A SUBJECT.
QUID PRO QUO FOR MY BLOOD. AFTER ALL, THIS STUFF ISN'T FREE.
HMM... YOU SHOULD BE GRATEFUL THAT I ONLY UNDRESSED YOUR UPPER BODY.

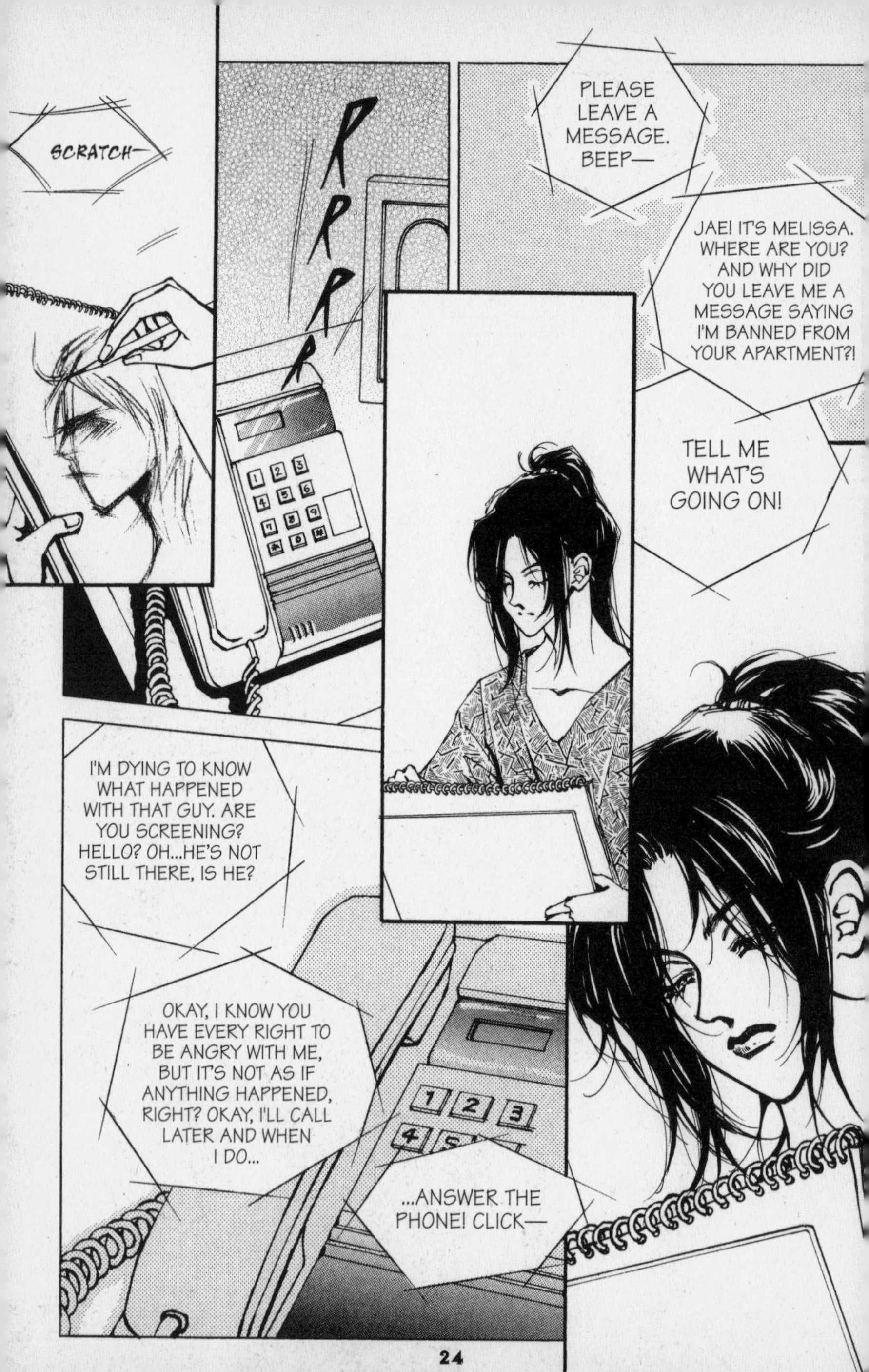
SCRATCH—
RRRRR
PLEASE LEAVE A MESSAGE. BEEP—
JAE! IT'S MELISSA. WHERE ARE YOU? AND WHY DID YOU LEAVE ME A MESSAGE SAYING I'M BANNED FROM YOUR APARTMENT?!
TELL ME WHAT'S GOING ON!
I'M DYING TO KNOW WHAT HAPPENED WITH THAT GUY. ARE YOU SCREENING? HELLO? OH...HE'S NOT STILL THERE, IS HE?
OKAY, I KNOW YOU HAVE EVERY RIGHT TO BE ANGRY WITH ME, BUT IT'S NOT AS IF ANYTHING HAPPENED, RIGHT? OKAY, I'LL CALL LATER AND WHEN I DO...
...ANSWER THE PHONE! CLICK—

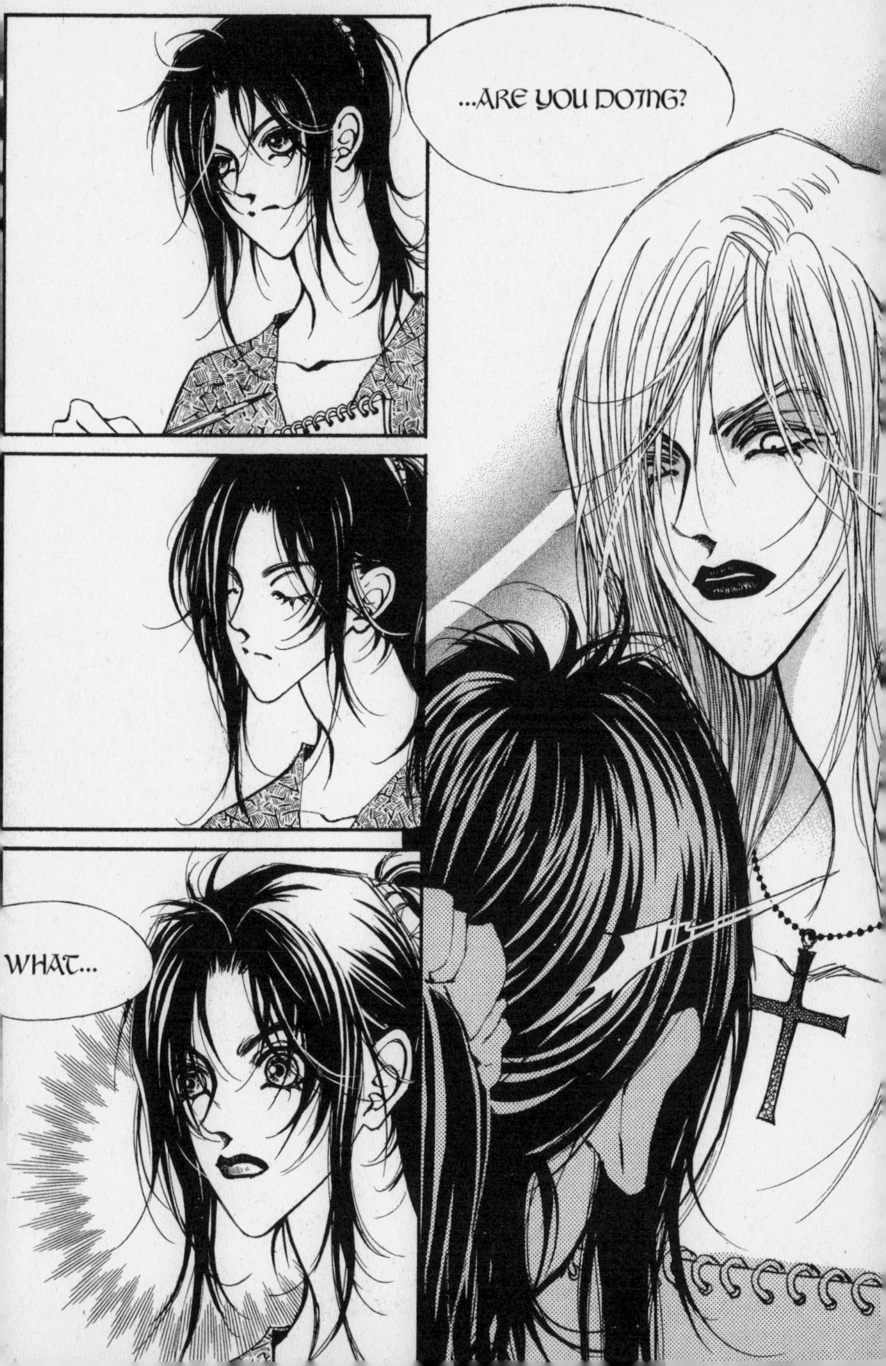
WHAT...
...ARE YOU DOING?

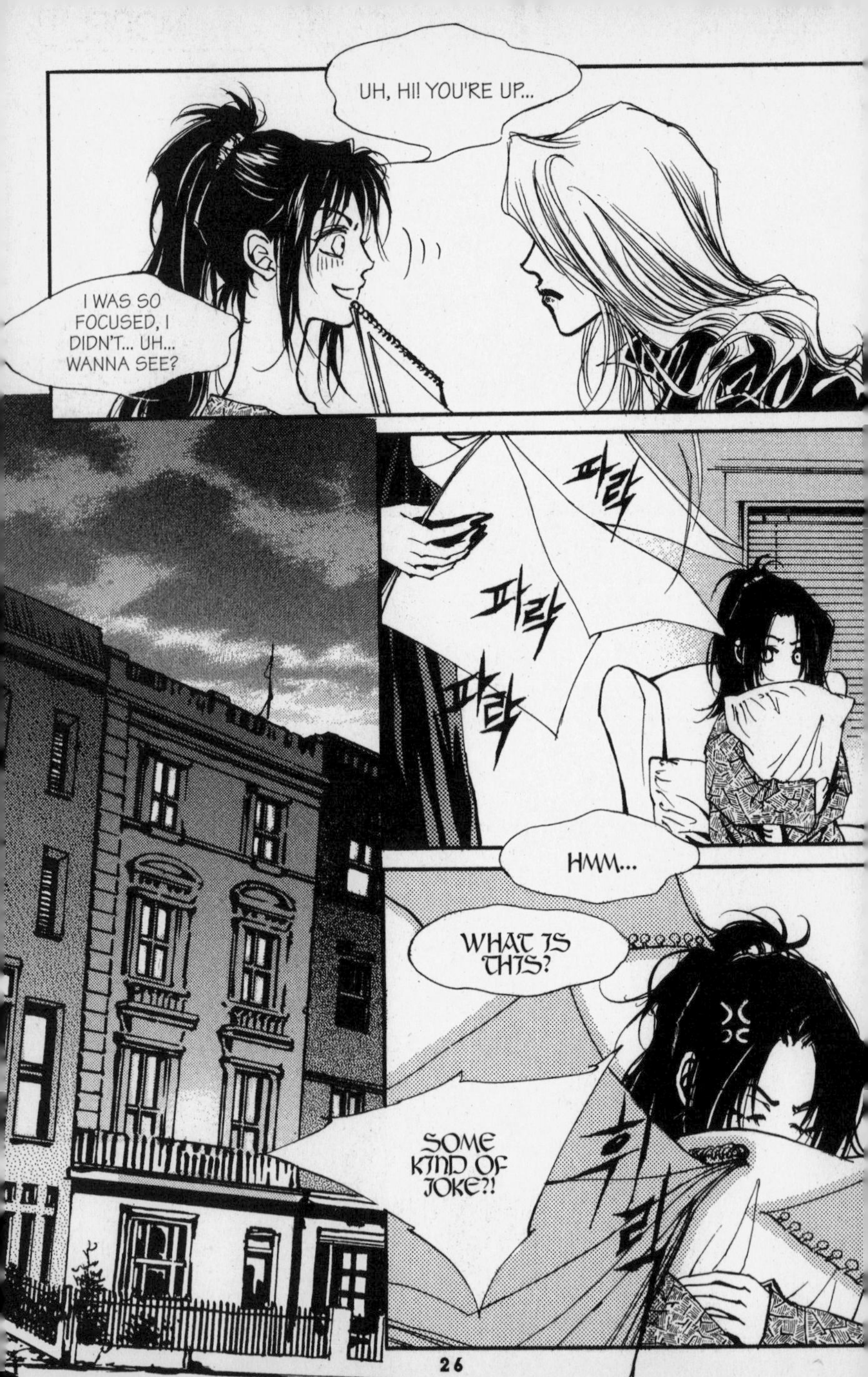
UH, HI! YOU'RE UP...
I WAS SO FOCUSED, I DIDN'T... UH... WANNA SEE?
파락
파락
파락
HMM...
WHAT IS THIS?
SOME KIND OF JOKE?!
후
라

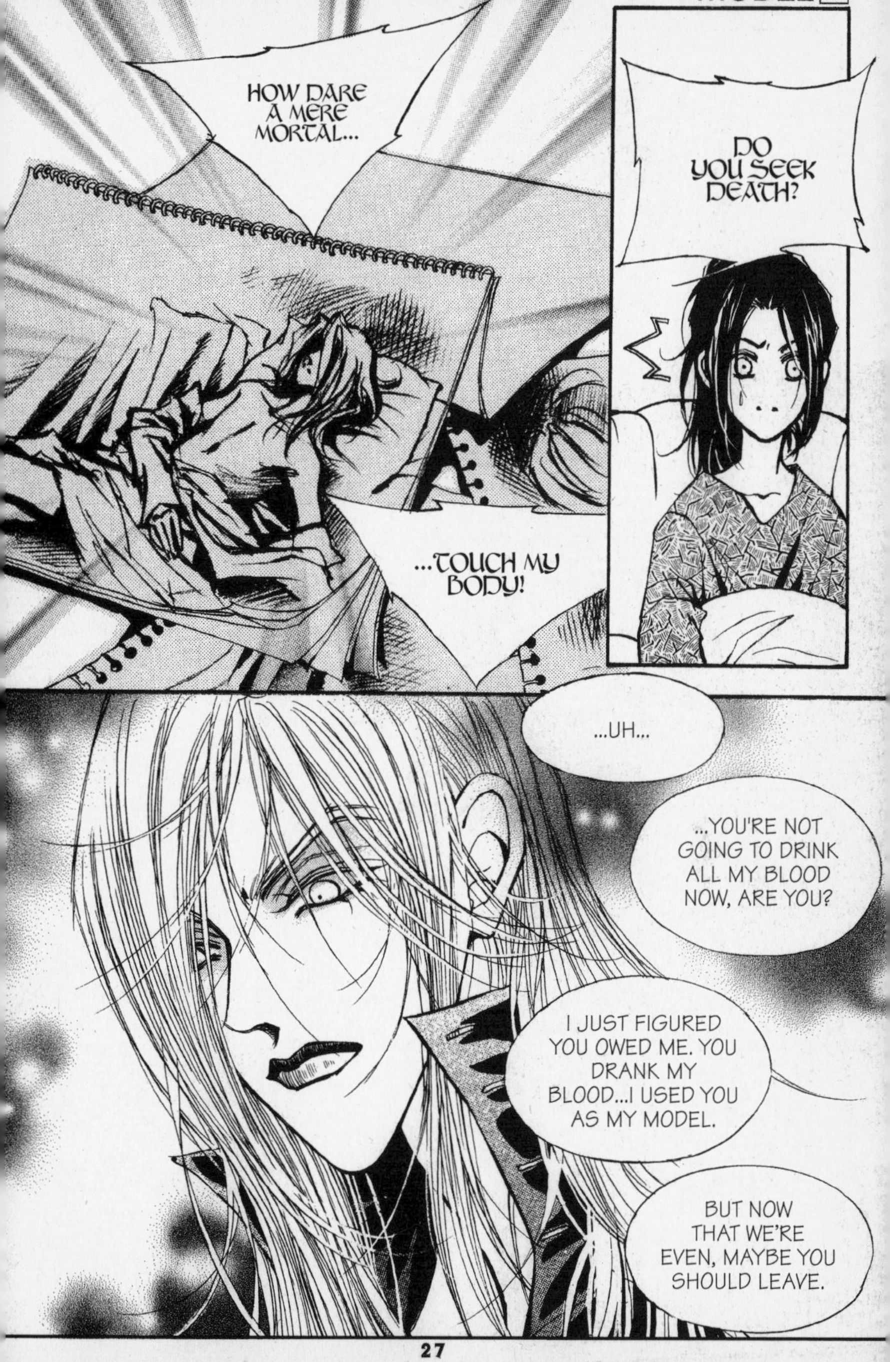
HOW DARE A MERE MORTAL...
...TOUCH MY BODY!
DO YOU SEEK DEATH?
...UH...
...YOU'RE NOT GOING TO DRINK ALL MY BLOOD NOW, ARE YOU?
I JUST FIGURED YOU OWED ME. YOU DRANK MY BLOOD...I USED YOU AS MY MODEL.
BUT NOW THAT WE'RE EVEN, MAYBE YOU SHOULD LEAVE.

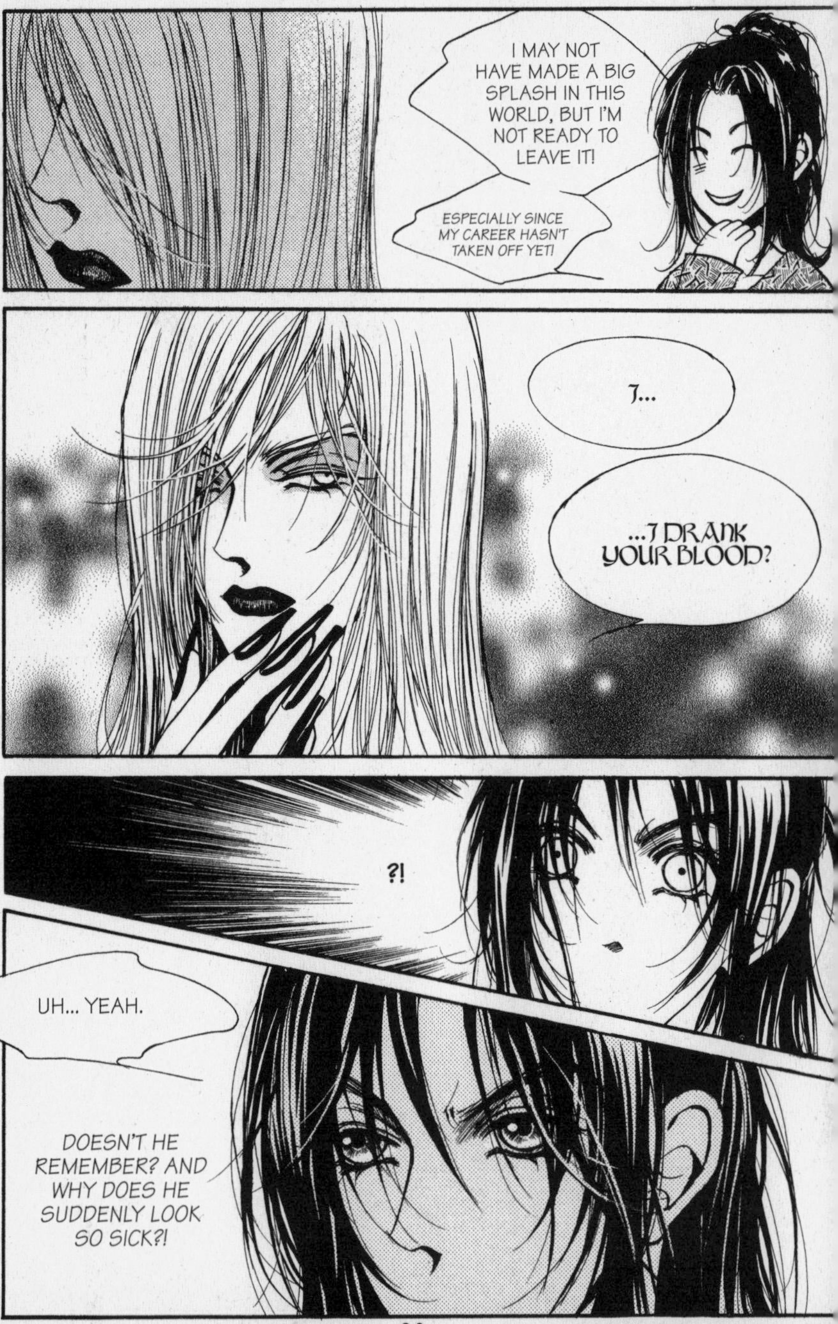
I MAY NOT HAVE MADE A BIG SPLASH IN THIS WORLD, BUT I'M NOT READY TO LEAVE IT!
ESPECIALLY SINCE MY CAREER HASN'T TAKEN OFF YET!
I...
...I DRANK YOUR BLOOD?
?!
UH... YEAH.
DOESN'T HE REMEMBER? AND WHY DOES HE SUDDENLY LOOK SO SICK?!

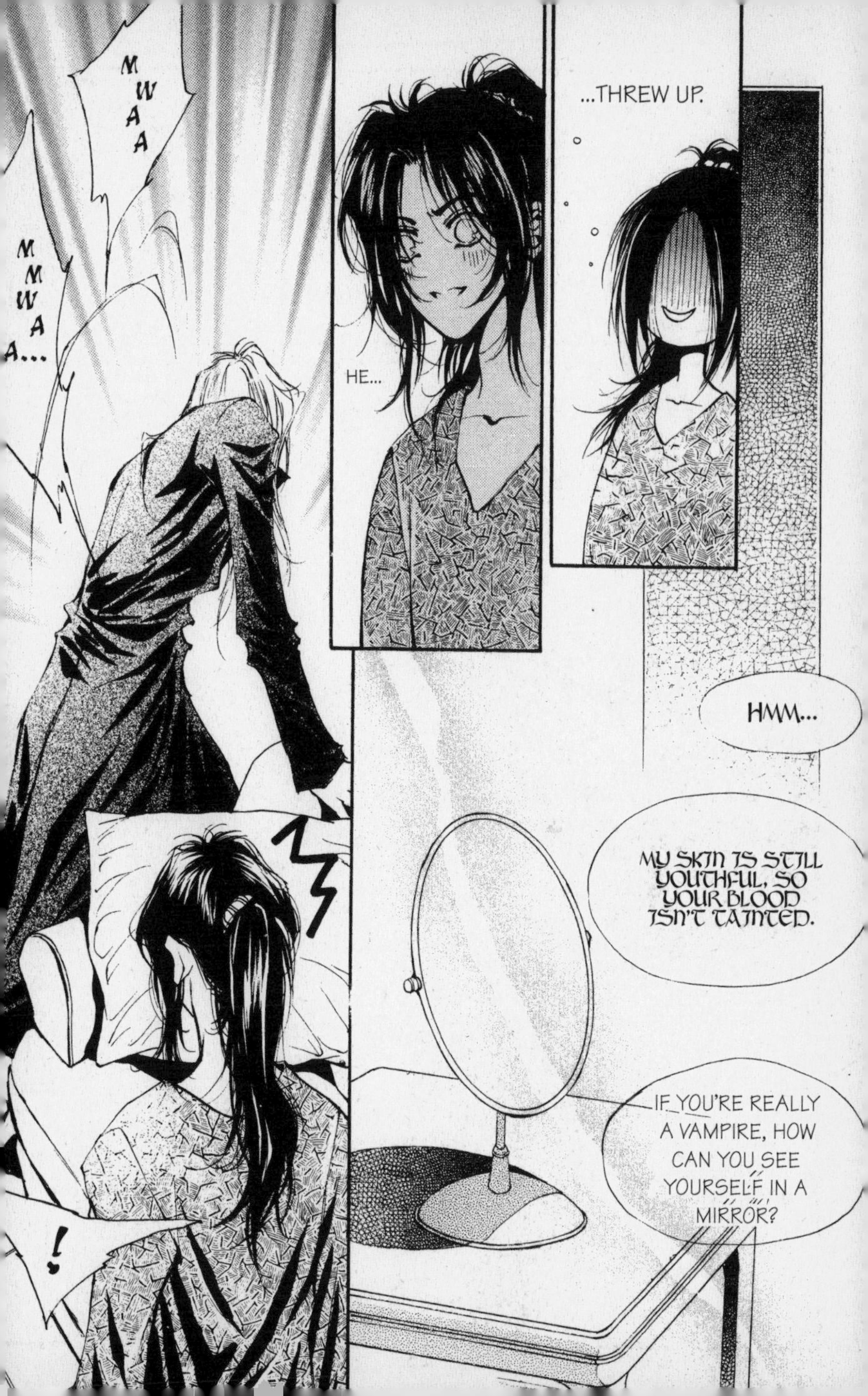
MWAA
MMWAA...
!
HE...
...THREW UP.
HMM...
MY SKIN IS STILL YOUTHFUL, SO YOUR BLOOD ISN'T TAINTED.
IF YOU'RE REALLY A VAMPIRE, HOW CAN YOU SEE YOURSELF IN A MIRROR?

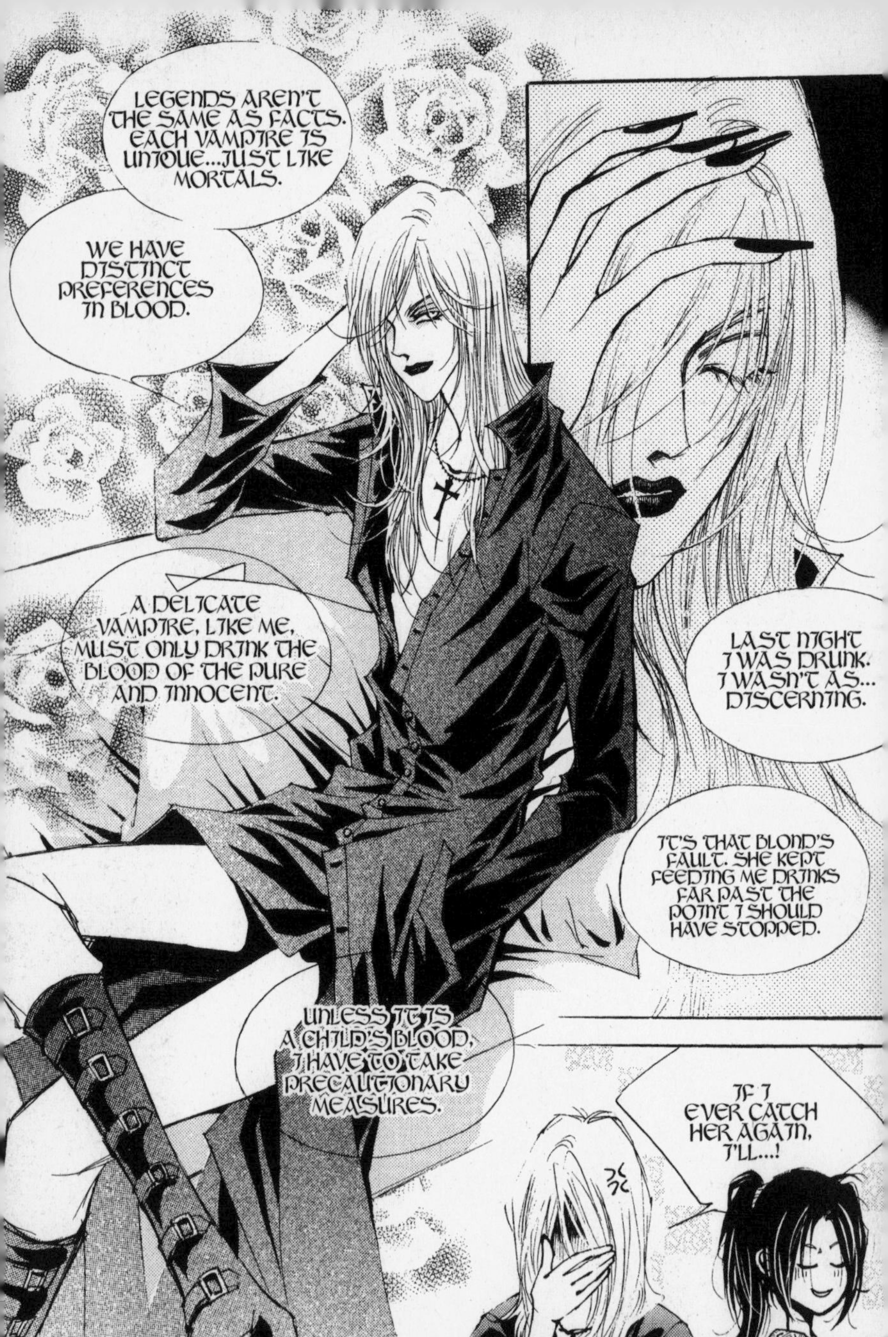
LEGENDS AREN'T THE SAME AS FACTS. EACH VAMPIRE IS UNIQUE...JUST LIKE MORTALS.
WE HAVE DISTINCT PREFERENCES IN BLOOD.
A DELICATE VAMPIRE, LIKE ME, MUST ONLY DRINK THE BLOOD OF THE PURE AND INNOCENT.
UNLESS IT IS A CHILD'S BLOOD, I HAVE TO TAKE PRECAUTIONARY MEASURES.
LAST NIGHT I WAS DRUNK. I WASN'T AS... DISCERNING.
IT'S THAT BLOND'S FAULT. SHE KEPT FEEDING ME DRINKS FAR PAST THE POINT I SHOULD HAVE STOPPED.
IF I EVER CATCH HER AGAIN, I'LL...!
MELISSA

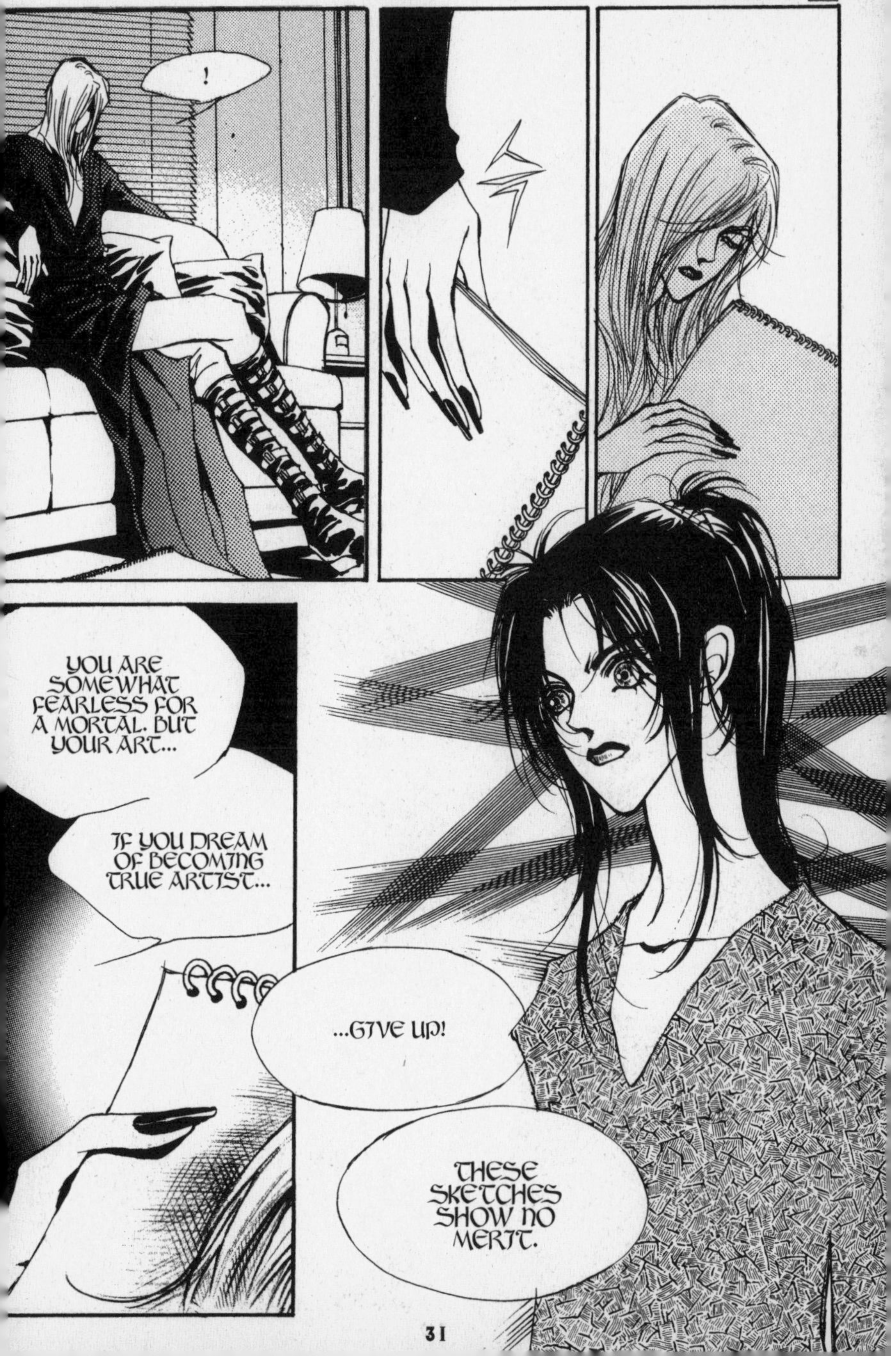
!
YOU ARE SOMEWHAT FEARLESS FOR A MORTAL. BUT YOUR ART...
IF YOU DREAM OF BECOMING TRUE ARTIST...
...GIVE UP!
THESE SKETCHES SHOW NO MERIT.

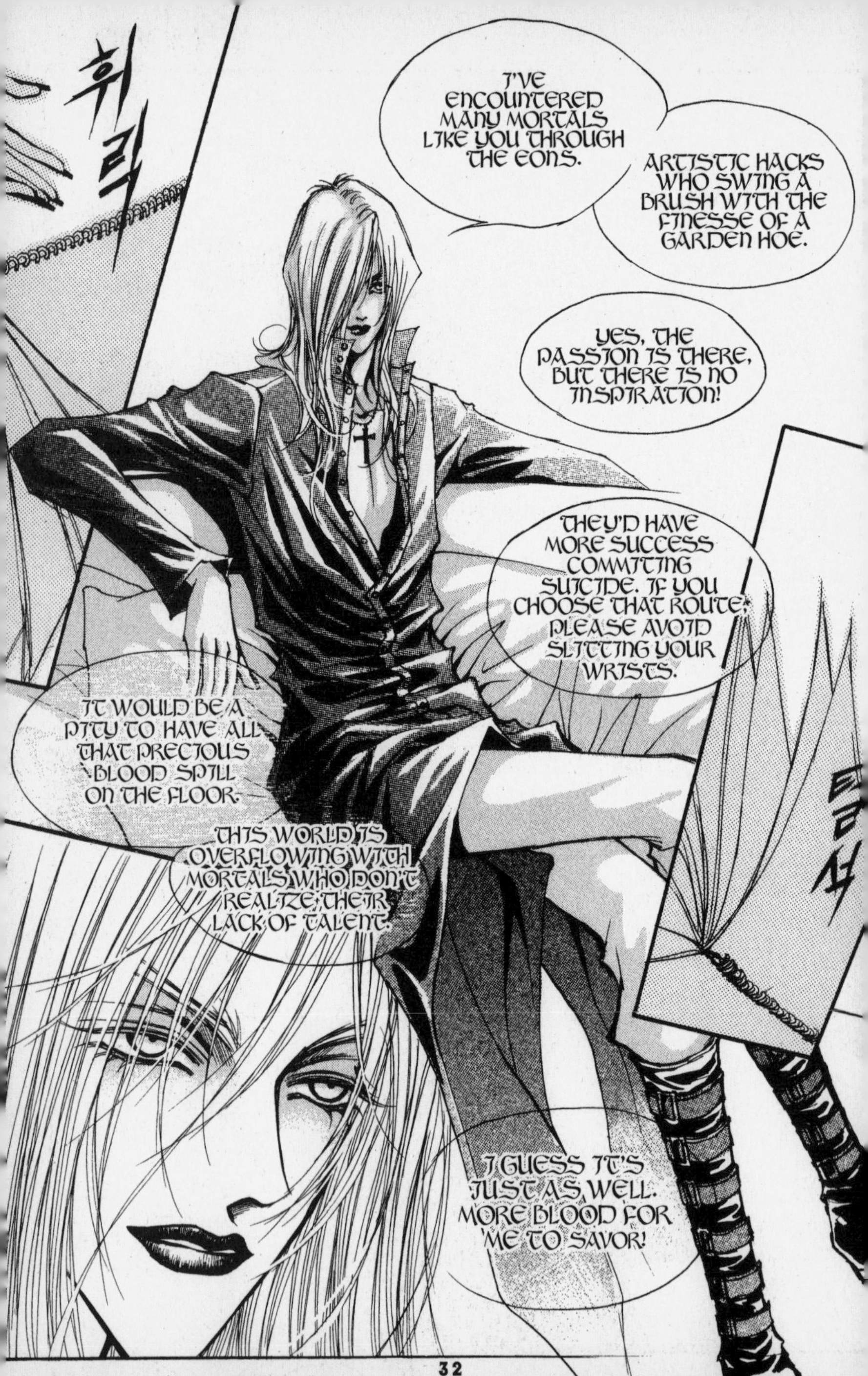
휘릭
I'VE ENCOUNTERED MANY MORTALS LIKE YOU THROUGH THE EONS.
ARTISTIC HACKS WHO SWING A BRUSH WITH THE FINESSE OF A GARDEN HOE.
YES, THE PASSION IS THERE, BUT THERE IS NO INSPIRATION!
THEY'D HAVE MORE SUCCESS COMMITTING SUICIDE. IF YOU CHOOSE THAT ROUTE, PLEASE AVOID SLITTING YOUR WRISTS.
IT WOULD BE A PITY TO HAVE ALL THAT PRECIOUS BLOOD SPILL ON THE FLOOR.
THIS WORLD IS OVERFLOWING WITH MORTALS WHO DON'T REALIZE THEIR LACK OF TALENT.
I GUESS IT'S JUST AS WELL. MORE BLOOD FOR ME TO SAVOR!

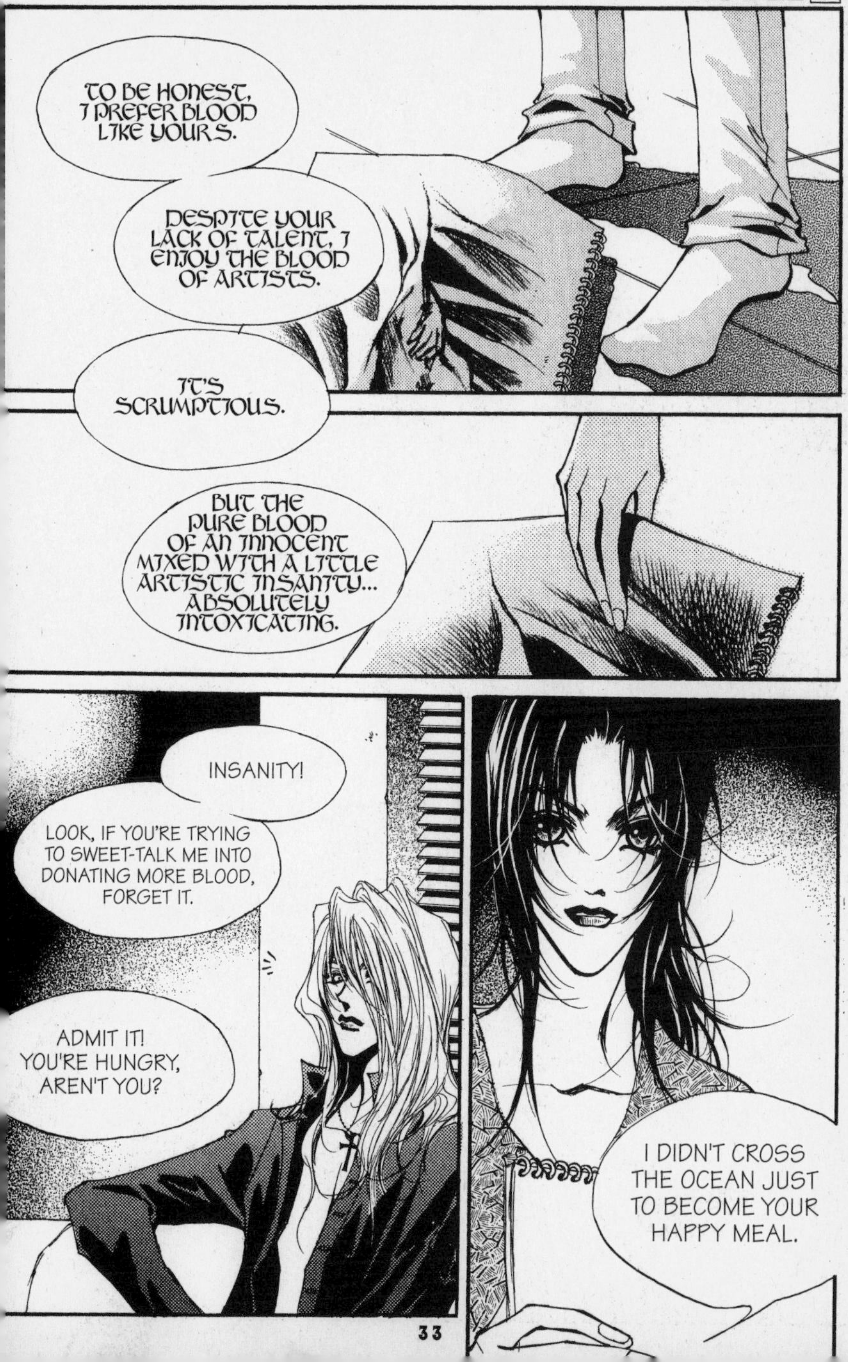
TO BE HONEST, I PREFER BLOOD LIKE YOURS.
DESPITE YOUR LACK OF TALENT, I ENJOY THE BLOOD OF ARTISTS.
IT'S SCRUMPTIOUS.
BUT THE PURE BLOOD OF AN INNOCENT MIXED WITH A LITTLE ARTISTIC INSANITY... ABSOLUTELY INTOXICATING.
INSANITY!
LOOK, IF YOU'RE TRYING TO SWEET-TALK ME INTO DONATING MORE BLOOD, FORGET IT.
ADMIT IT! YOU'RE HUNGRY, AREN'T YOU?
I DIDN'T CROSS THE OCEAN JUST TO BECOME YOUR HAPPY MEAL.

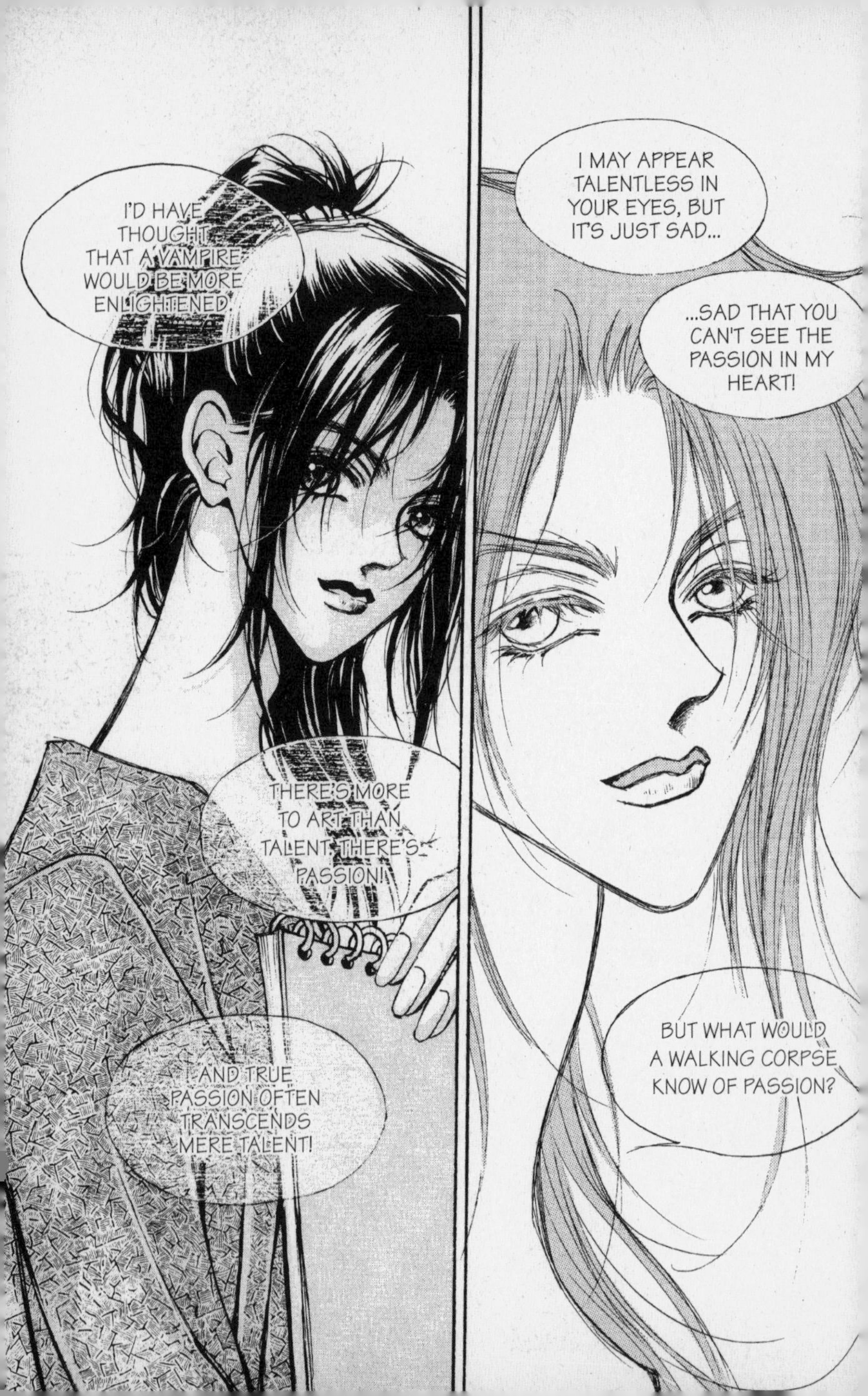
I'D HAVE THOUGHT THAT A VAMPIRE WOULD BE MORE ENLIGHTENED.
THERE'S MORE TO ART THAN TALENT. THERE'S PASSION!
...AND TRUE PASSION OFTEN TRANSCENDS MERE TALENT!
I MAY APPEAR TALENTLESS IN YOUR EYES, BUT IT'S JUST SAD...
...SAD THAT YOU CAN'T SEE THE PASSION IN MY HEART!
BUT WHAT WOULD A WALKING CORPSE KNOW OF PASSION?

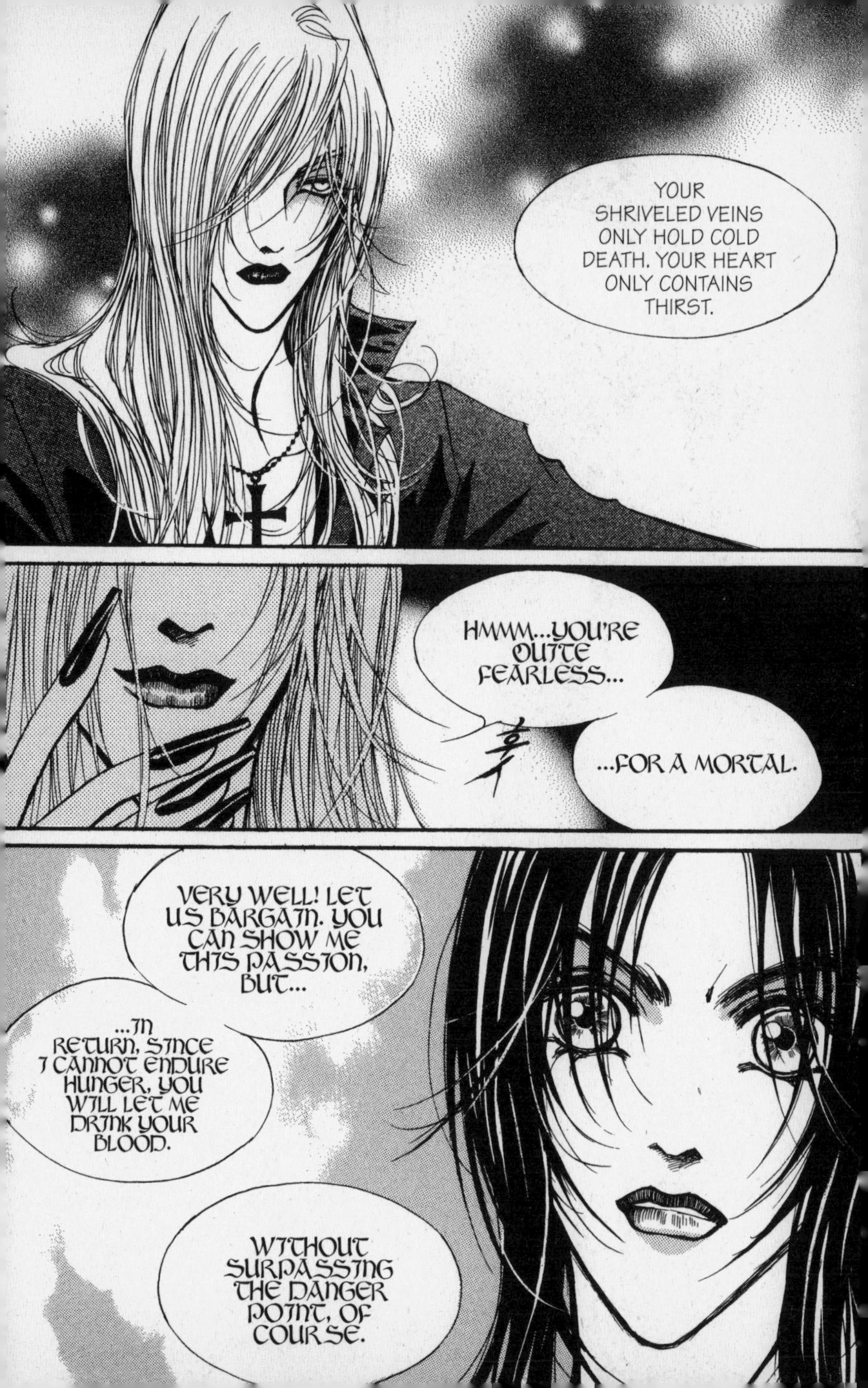
YOUR SHRIVELED VEINS ONLY HOLD COLD DEATH. YOUR HEART ONLY CONTAINS THIRST.
HMMM...YOU'RE QUITE FEARLESS...
...FOR A MORTAL.
VERY WELL! LET US BARGAIN. YOU CAN SHOW ME THIS PASSION, BUT...
...IN RETURN, SINCE I CANNOT ENDURE HUNGER, YOU WILL LET ME DRINK YOUR BLOOD.
WITHOUT SURPASSING THE DANGER POINT, OF COURSE.

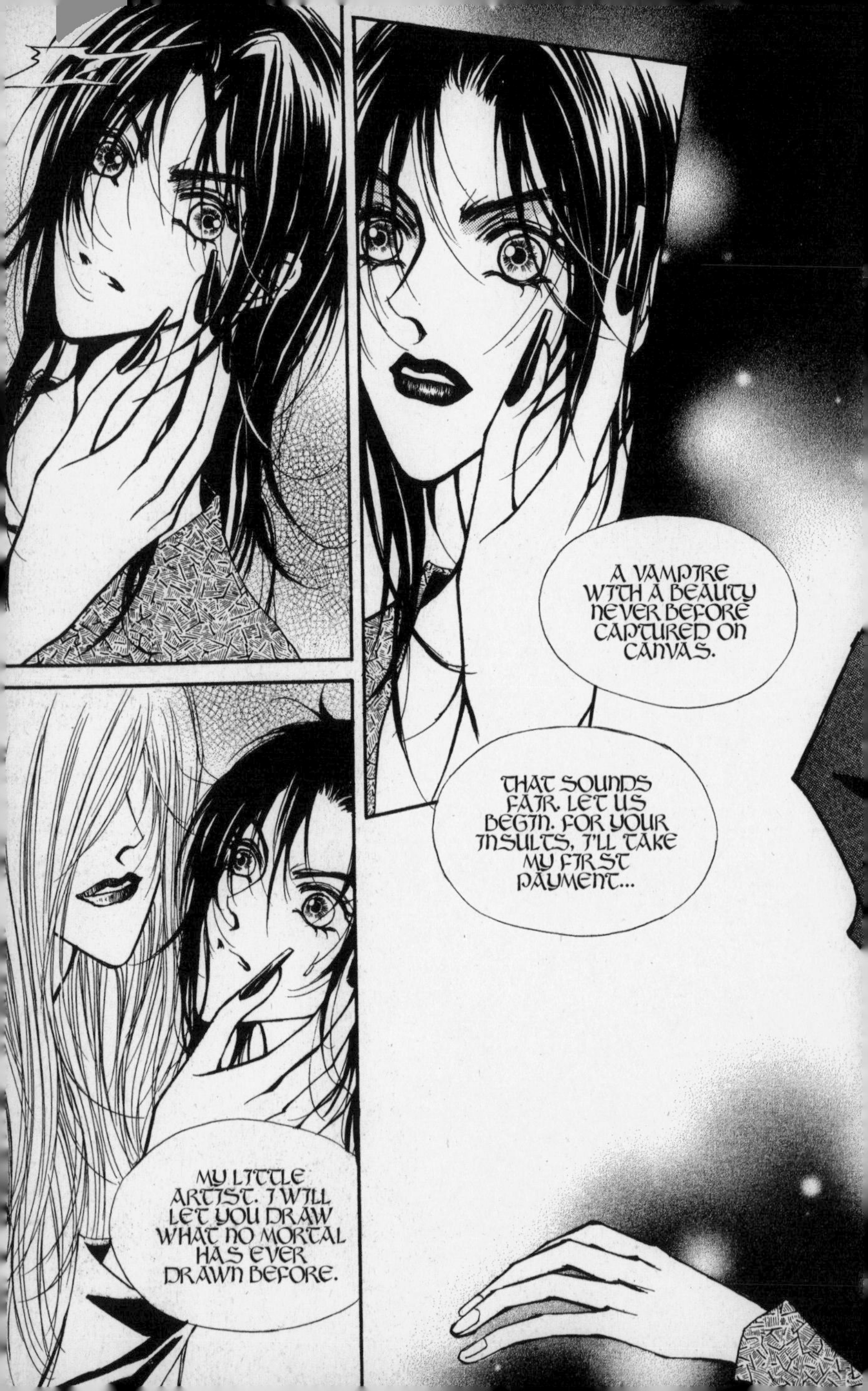
MY LITTLE ARTIST. I WILL LET YOU DRAW WHAT NO MORTAL HAS EVER DRAWN BEFORE.
A VAMPIRE WITH A BEAUTY NEVER BEFORE CAPTURED ON CANVAS.
THAT SOUNDS FAIR. LET US BEGIN. FOR YOUR INSULTS, I'LL TAKE MY FIRST PAYMENT...

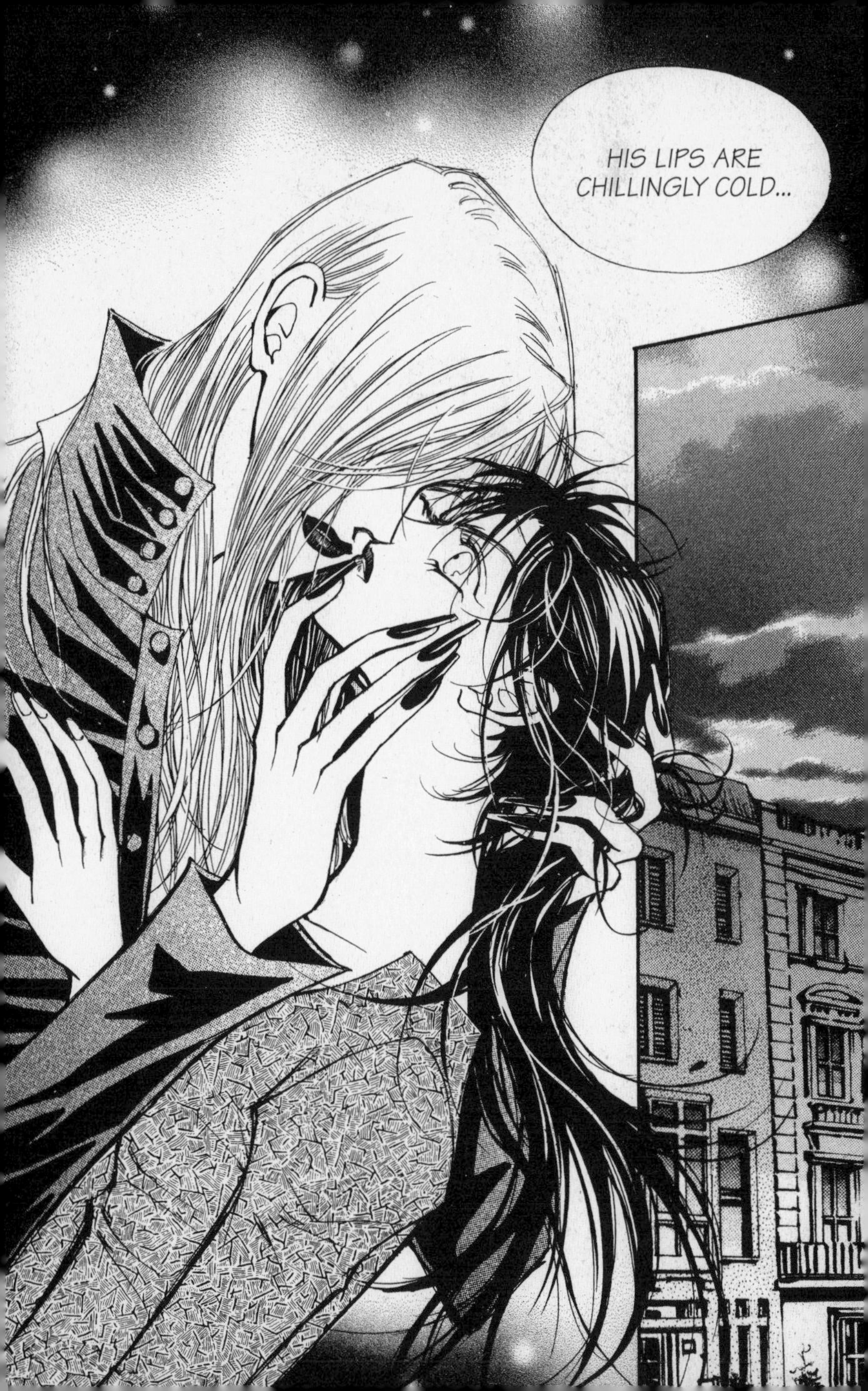
HIS LIPS ARE CHILLINGLY COLD...

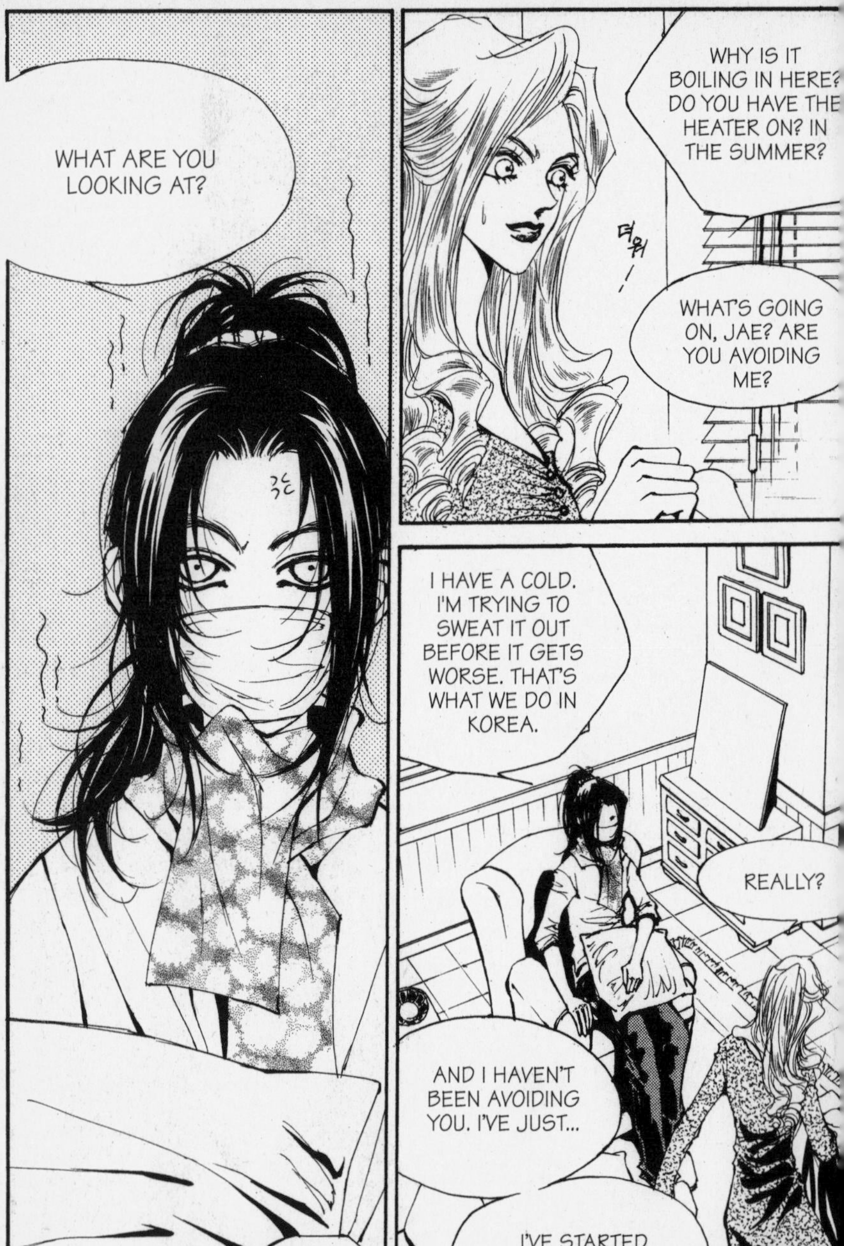
WHAT ARE YOU LOOKING AT?
WHY IS IT BOILING IN HERE? DO YOU HAVE THE HEATER ON? IN THE SUMMER?
더워
WHAT'S GOING ON, JAE? ARE YOU AVOIDING ME?
I HAVE A COLD. I'M TRYING TO SWEAT IT OUT BEFORE IT GETS WORSE. THAT'S WHAT WE DO IN KOREA.
REALLY?
AND I HAVEN'T BEEN AVOIDING YOU. I'VE JUST...
I'VE STARTED DRAWING AGAIN.

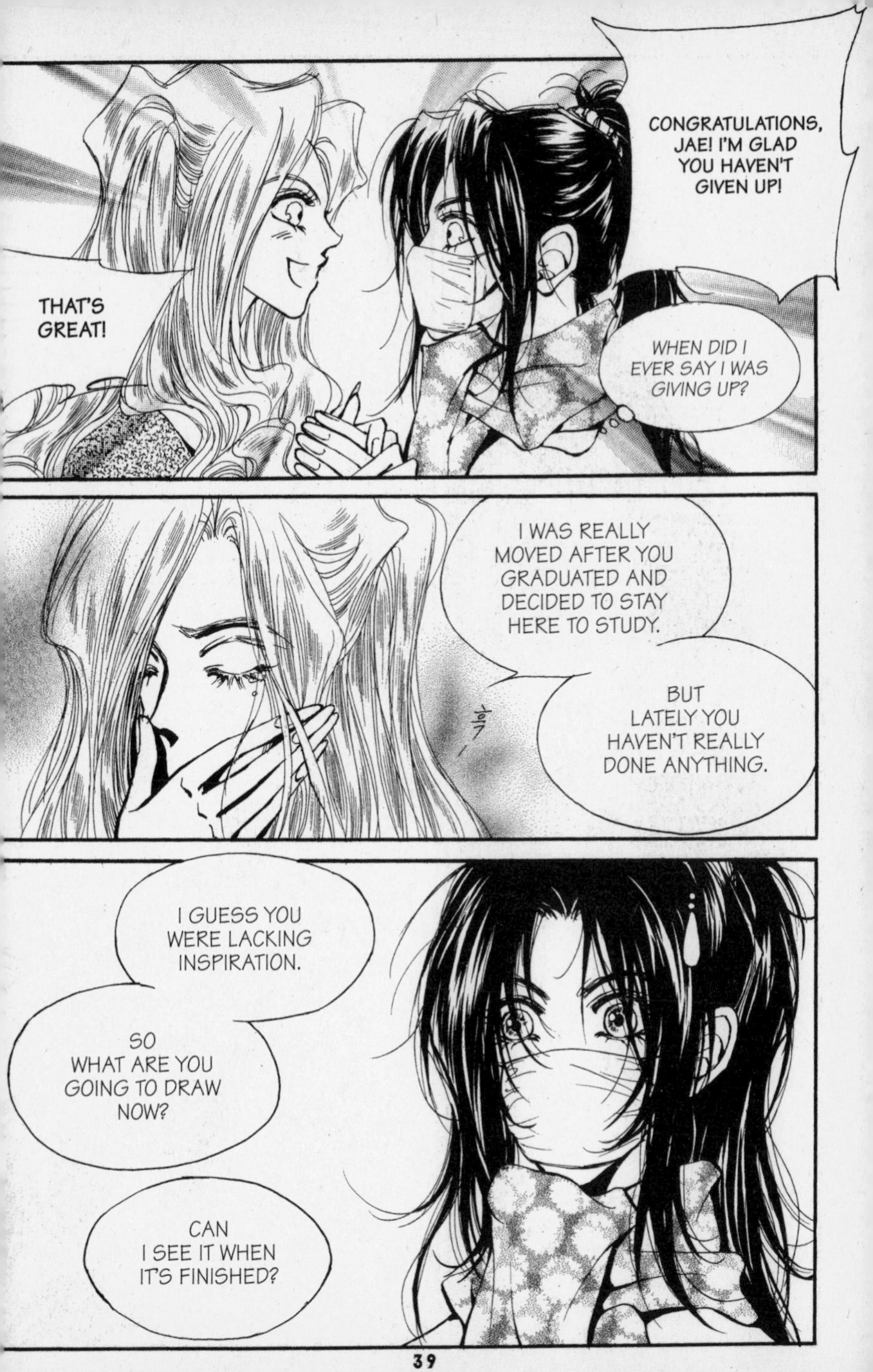

CONGRATULATIONS, JAE! I'M GLAD YOU HAVEN'T GIVEN UP!
THAT'S GREAT!
WHEN DID I EVER SAY I WAS GIVING UP?
I WAS REALLY MOVED AFTER YOU GRADUATED AND DECIDED TO STAY HERE TO STUDY.
BUT LATELY YOU HAVEN'T REALLY DONE ANYTHING.
I GUESS YOU WERE LACKING INSPIRATION.
SO WHAT ARE YOU GOING TO DRAW NOW?
CAN I SEE IT WHEN IT'S FINISHED?

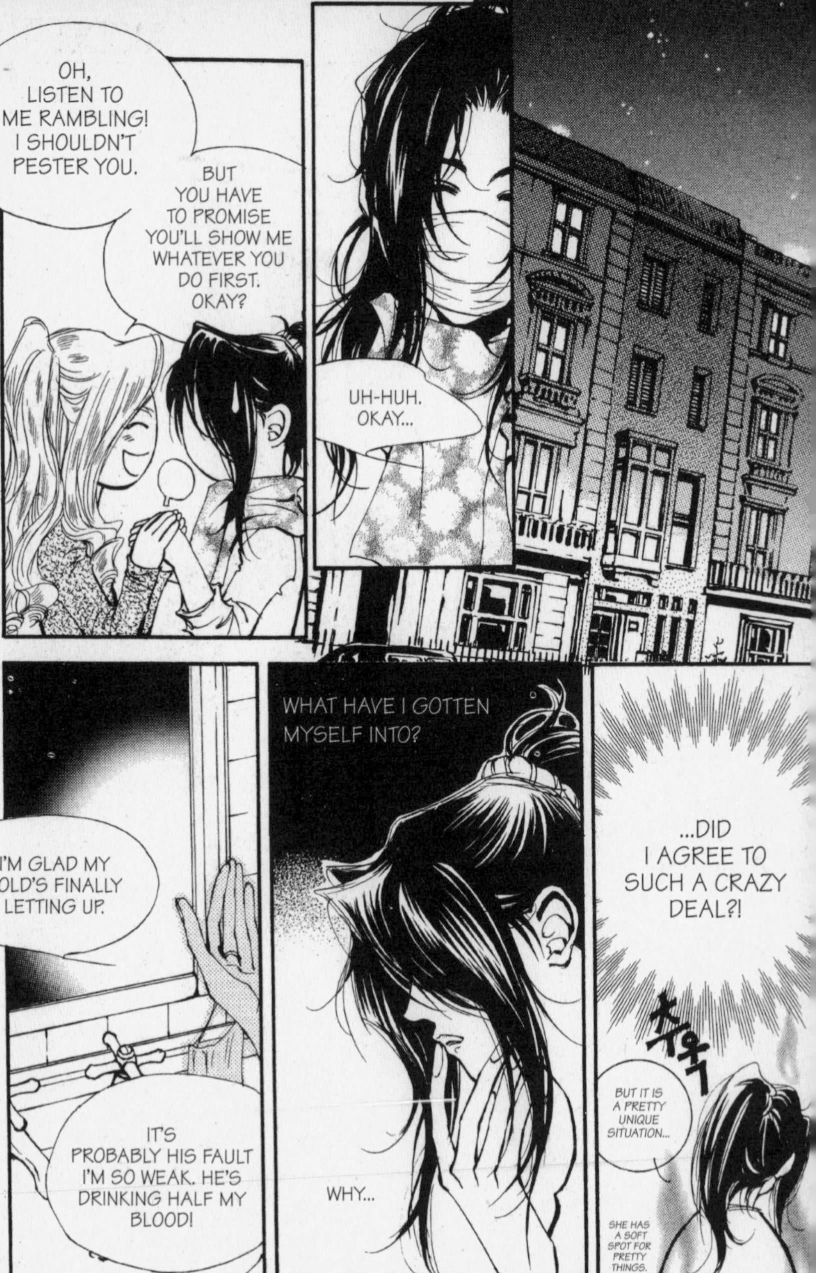
OH, LISTEN TO ME RAMBLING! I SHOULDN'T PESTER YOU.
BUT YOU HAVE TO PROMISE YOU'LL SHOW ME WHATEVER YOU DO FIRST. OKAY?
UH-HUH. OKAY...
I'M GLAD MY COLD'S FINALLY LETTING UP.
IT'S PROBABLY HIS FAULT I'M SO WEAK. HE'S DRINKING HALF MY BLOOD!
WHAT HAVE I GOTTEN MYSELF INTO?
WHY...
...DID I AGREE TO SUCH A CRAZY DEAL?!
BUT IT IS A PRETTY UNIQUE SITUATION...
SHE HAS A SOFT SPOT FOR PRETTY THINGS.

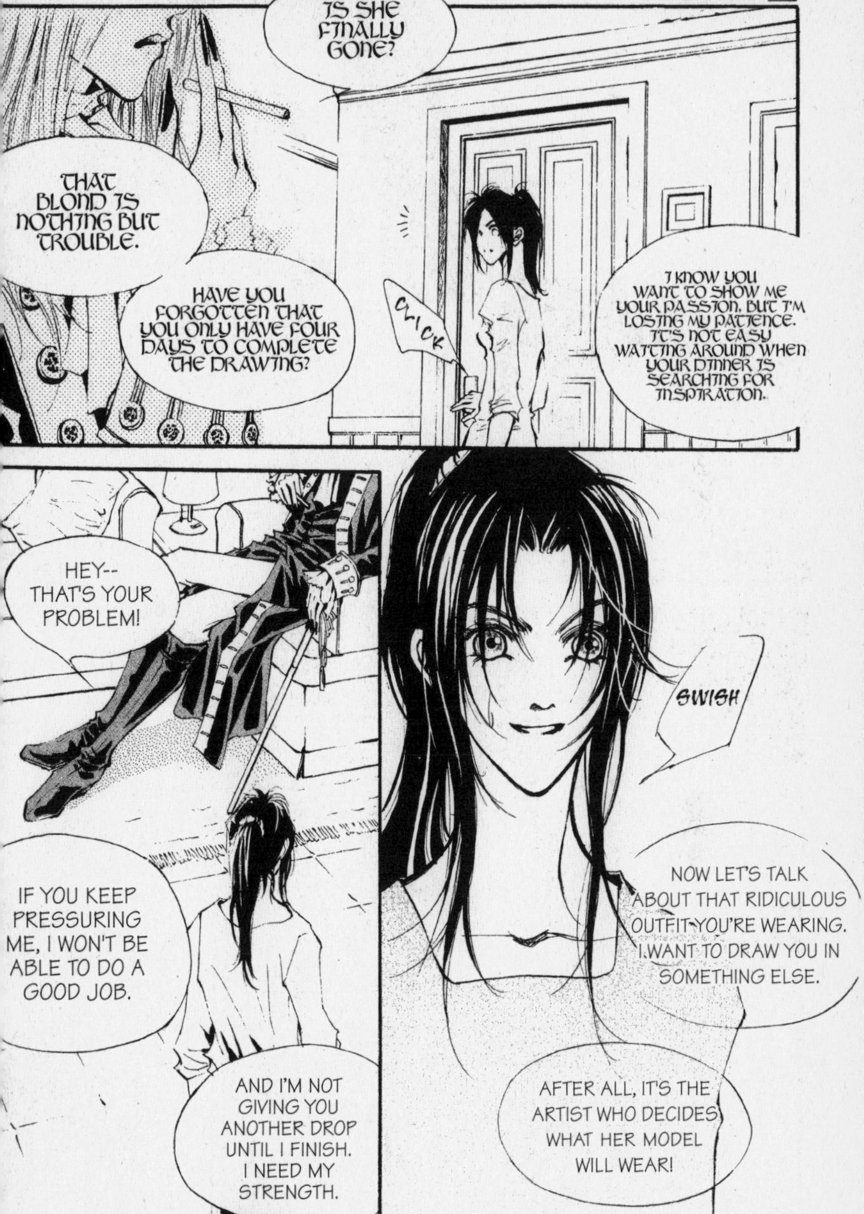
IS SHE FINALLY GONE?
THAT BLOND IS NOTHING BUT TROUBLE.
HAVE YOU FORGOTTEN THAT YOU ONLY HAVE FOUR DAYS TO COMPLETE THE DRAWING?
CLICK
I KNOW YOU WANT TO SHOW ME YOUR PASSION, BUT I'M LOSING MY PATIENCE. IT'S NOT EASY WAITING AROUND WHEN YOUR DINNER IS SEARCHING FOR INSPIRATION.
HEY-- THAT'S YOUR PROBLEM!
IF YOU KEEP PRESSURING ME, I WON'T BE ABLE TO DO A GOOD JOB.
AND I'M NOT GIVING YOU ANOTHER DROP UNTIL I FINISH. I NEED MY STRENGTH.
SWISH
NOW LET'S TALK ABOUT THAT RIDICULOUS OUTFIT YOU'RE WEARING. I WANT TO DRAW YOU IN SOMETHING ELSE.
AFTER ALL, IT'S THE ARTIST WHO DECIDES WHAT HER MODEL WILL WEAR!

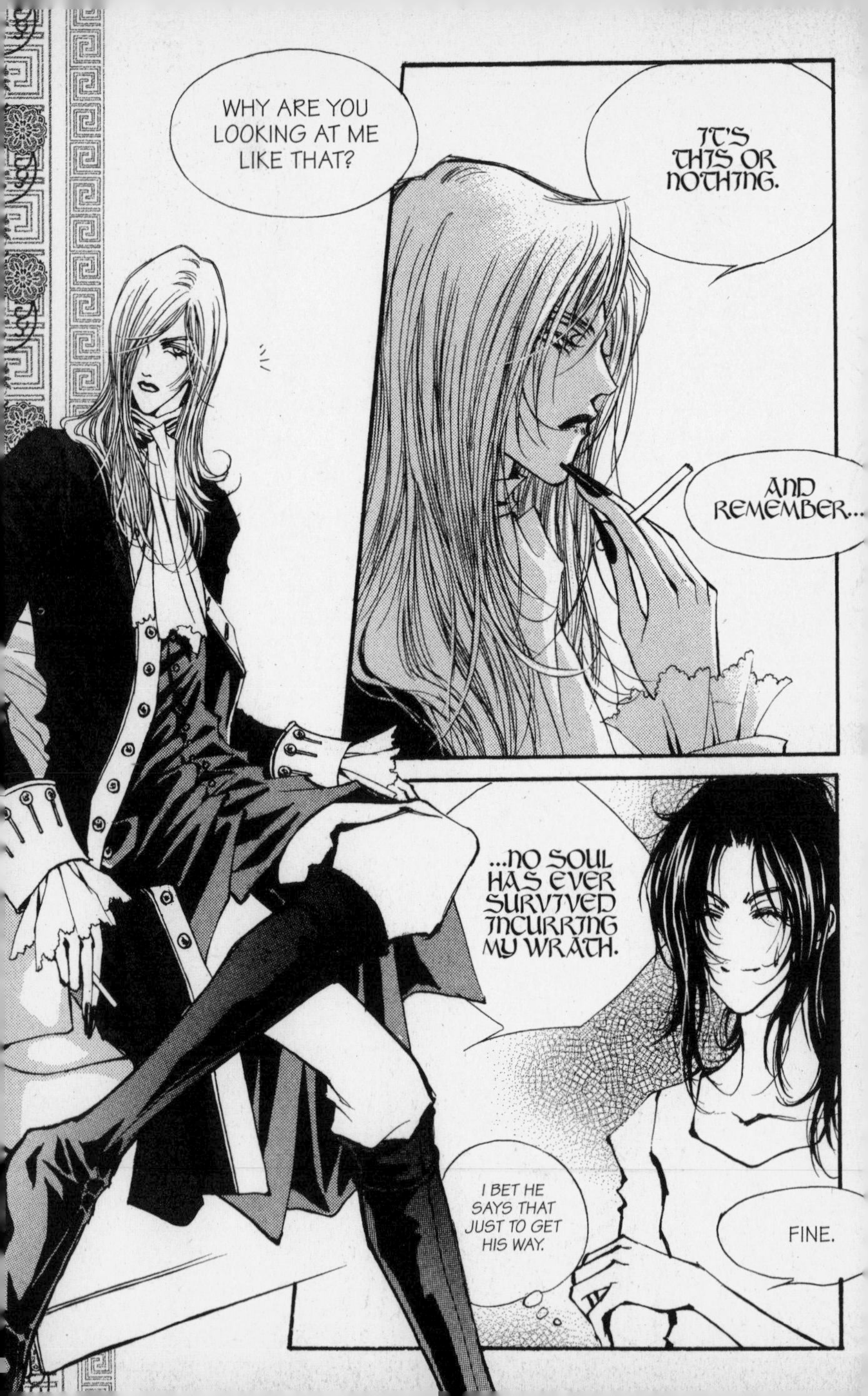
WHY ARE YOU LOOKING AT ME LIKE THAT?
IT'S THIS OR NOTHING.
AND REMEMBER...
...NO SOUL HAS EVER SURVIVED INCURRING MY WRATH.
I BET HE SAYS THAT JUST TO GET HIS WAY.
FINE.

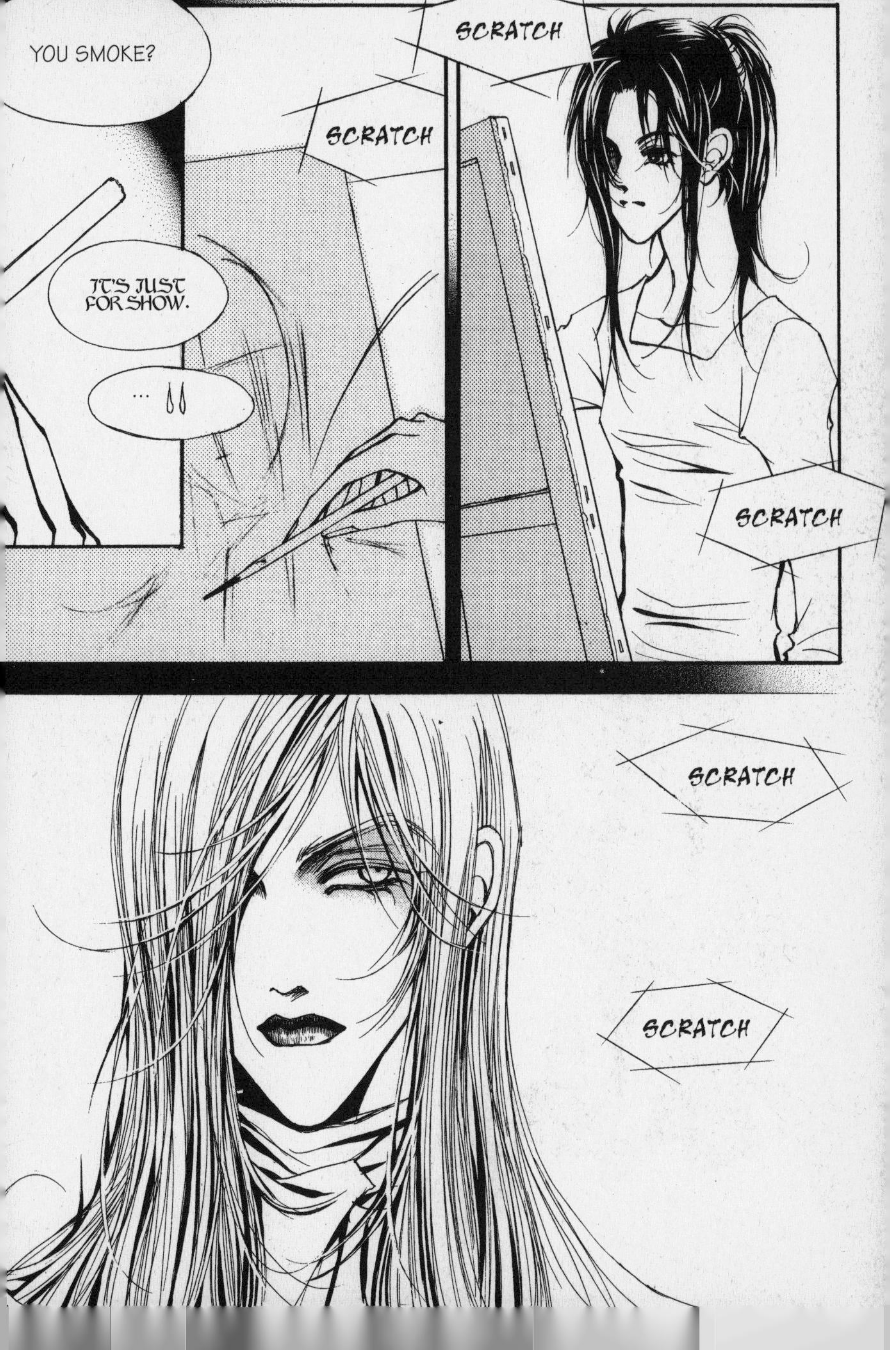
YOU SMOKE?
SCRATCH
SCRATCH
IT'S JUST FOR SHOW.
...
SCRATCH
SCRATCH
SCRATCH

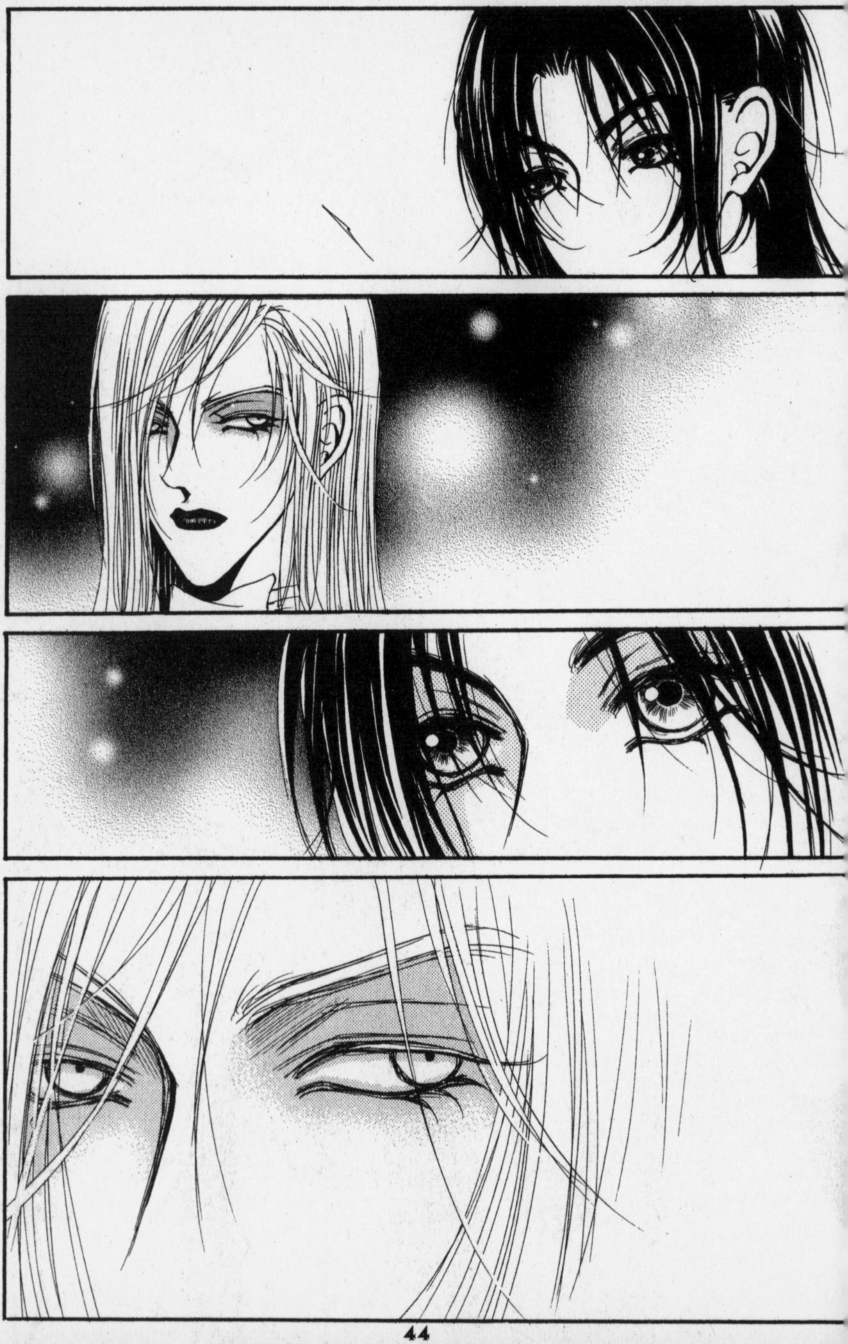

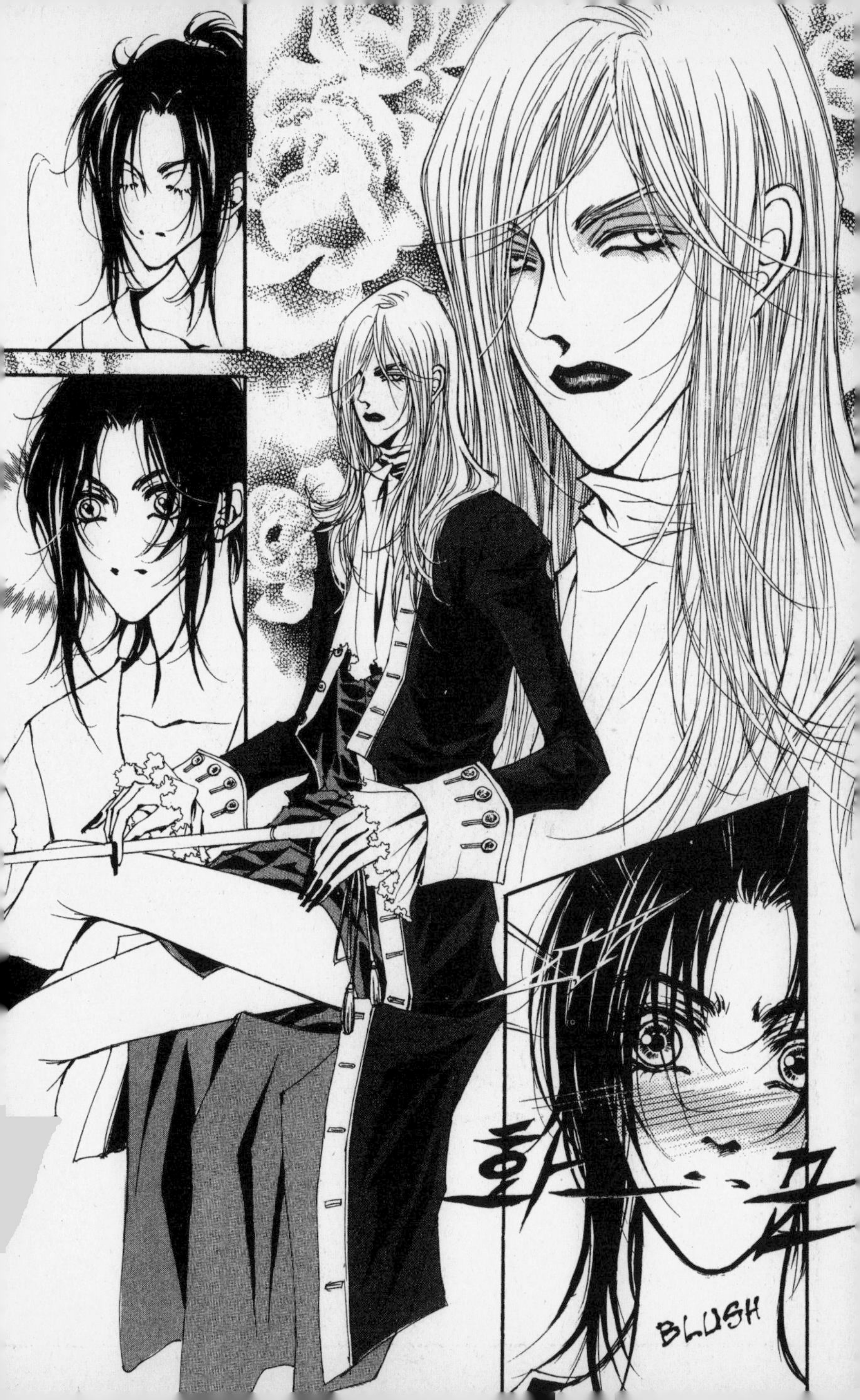
BLUSH

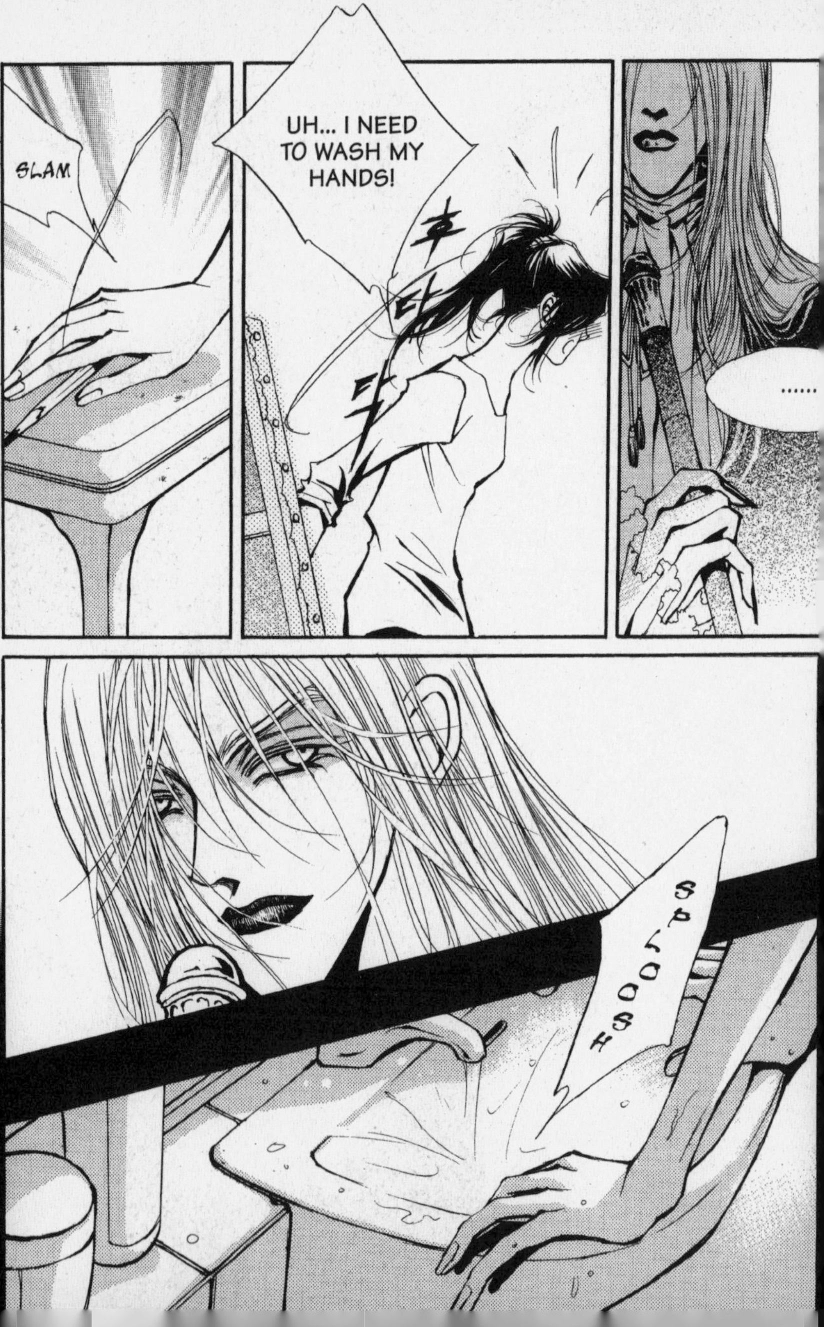
SLAM
UH... I NEED TO WASH MY HANDS!
......
SPLOOSH

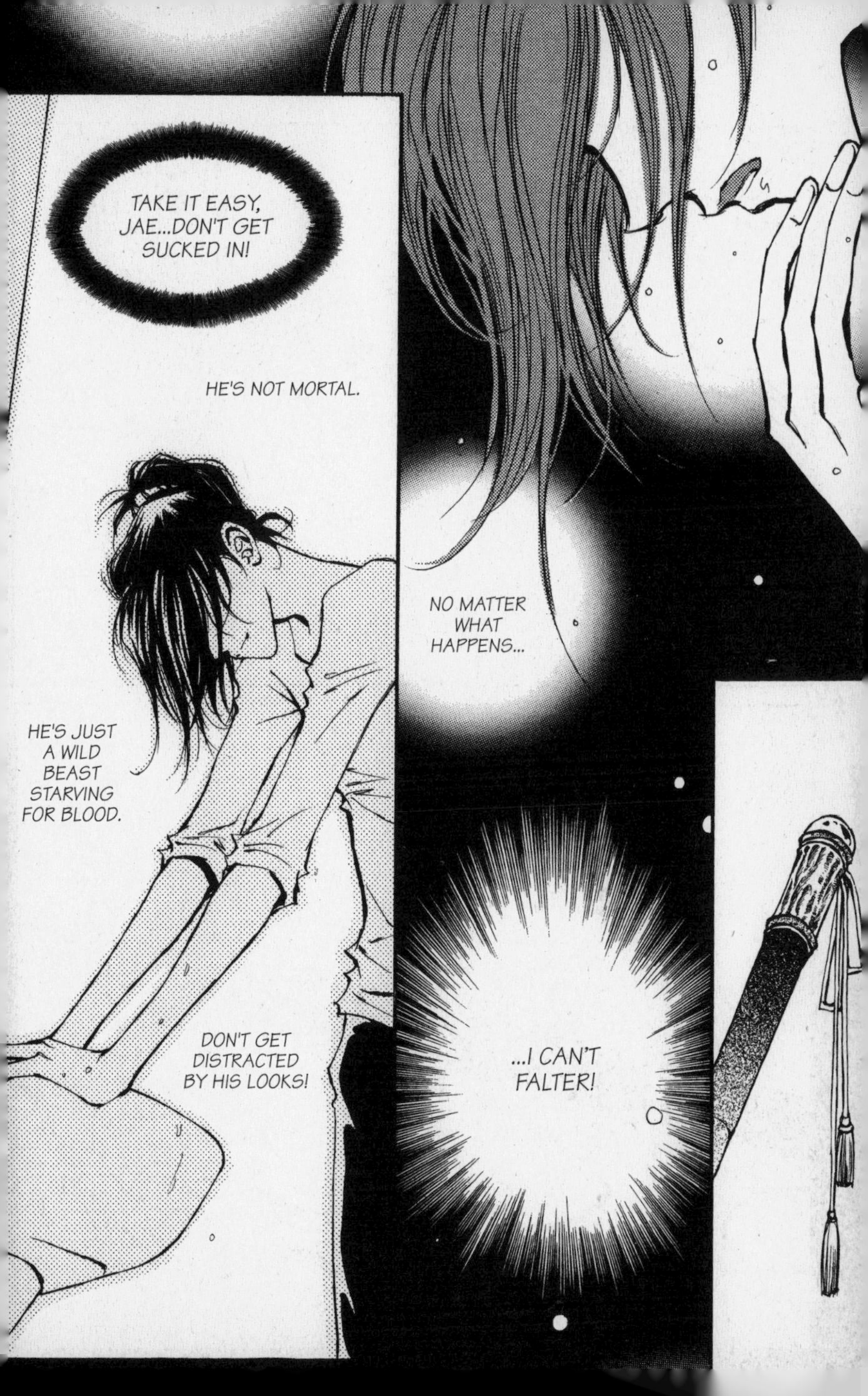
TAKE IT EASY, JAE...DON'T GET SUCKED IN!
HE'S NOT MORTAL.
HE'S JUST A WILD BEAST STARVING FOR BLOOD.
DON'T GET DISTRACTED BY HIS LOOKS!
NO MATTER WHAT HAPPENS...
...I CAN'T FALTER!

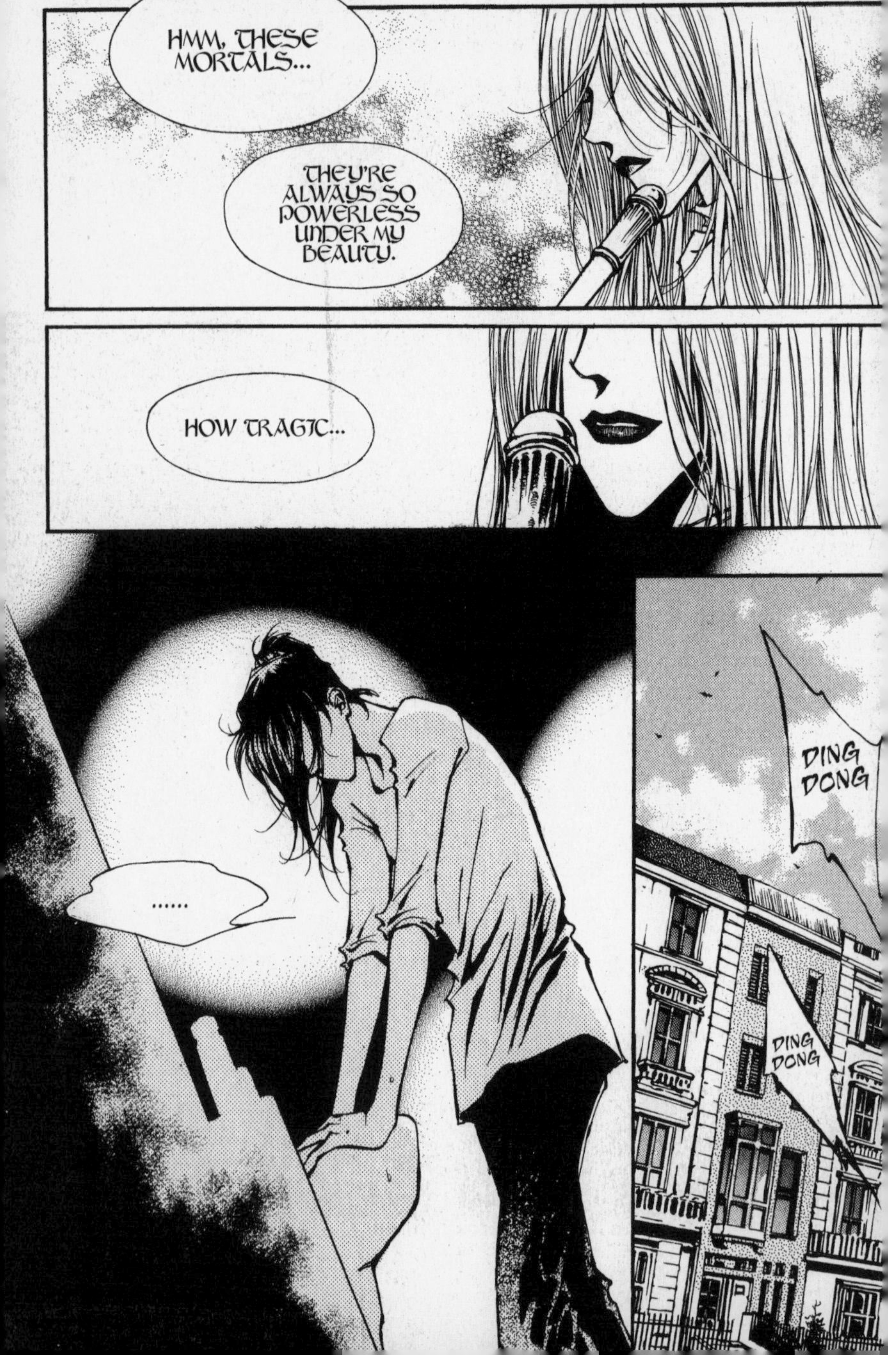
HMM, THESE MORTALS...
THEY'RE ALWAYS SO POWERLESS UNDER MY BEAUTY.
HOW TRAGIC...
......
DING DONG
DING DONG

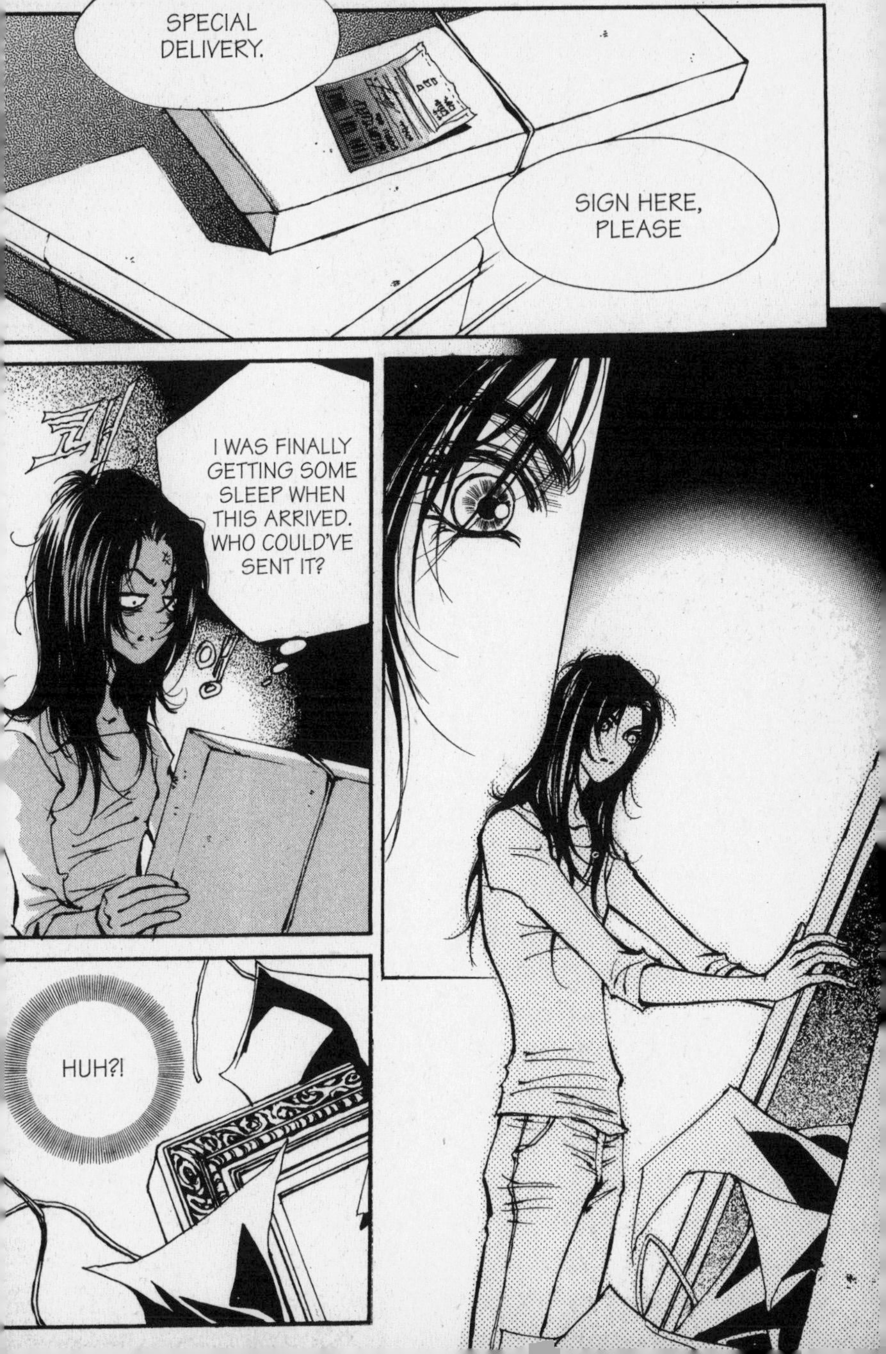
SPECIAL DELIVERY.
SIGN HERE, PLEASE
I WAS FINALLY GETTING SOME SLEEP WHEN THIS ARRIVED. WHO COULD'VE SENT IT?
HUH?!

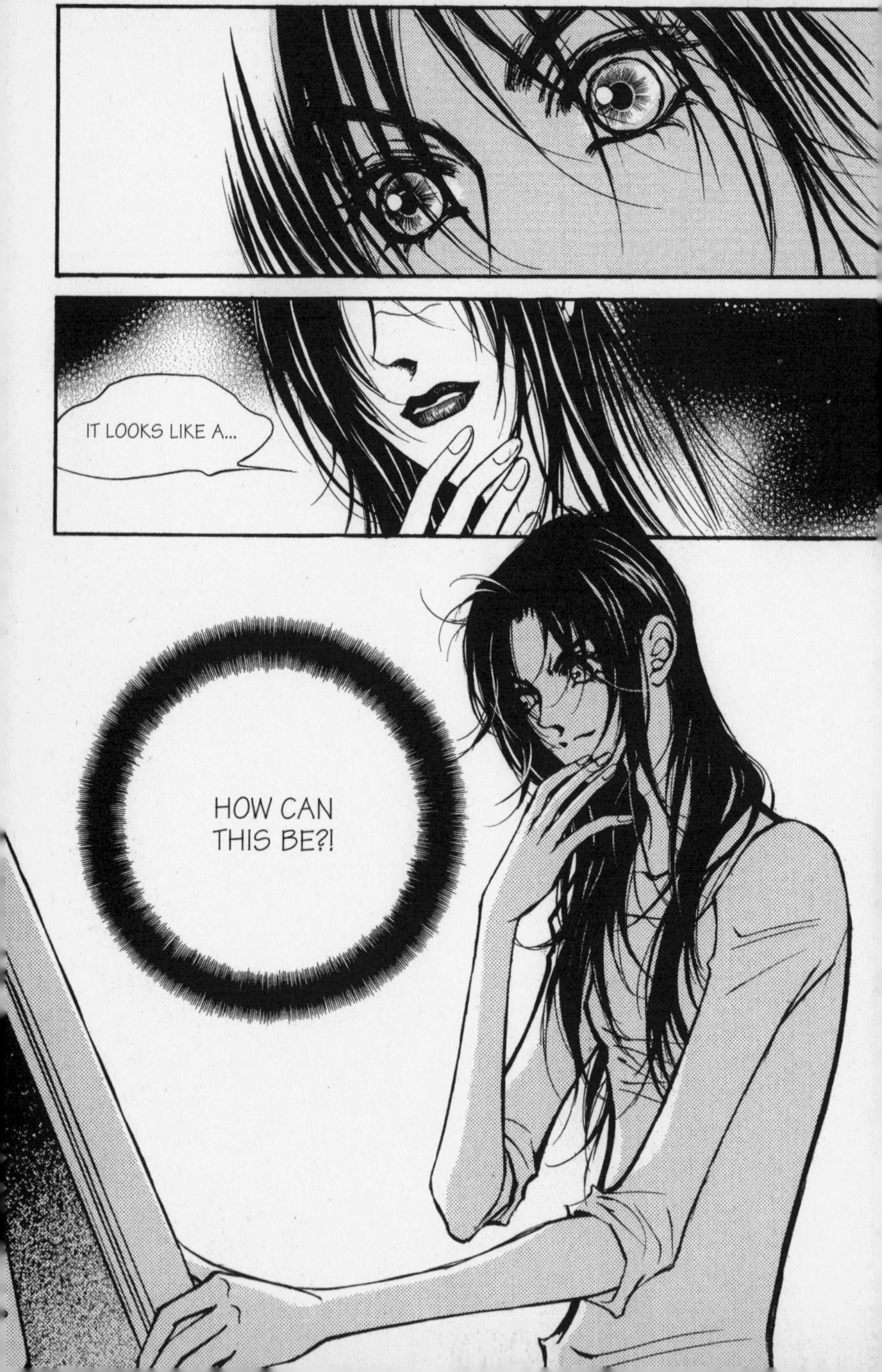
IT LOOKS LIKE A...
HOW CAN THIS BE?!

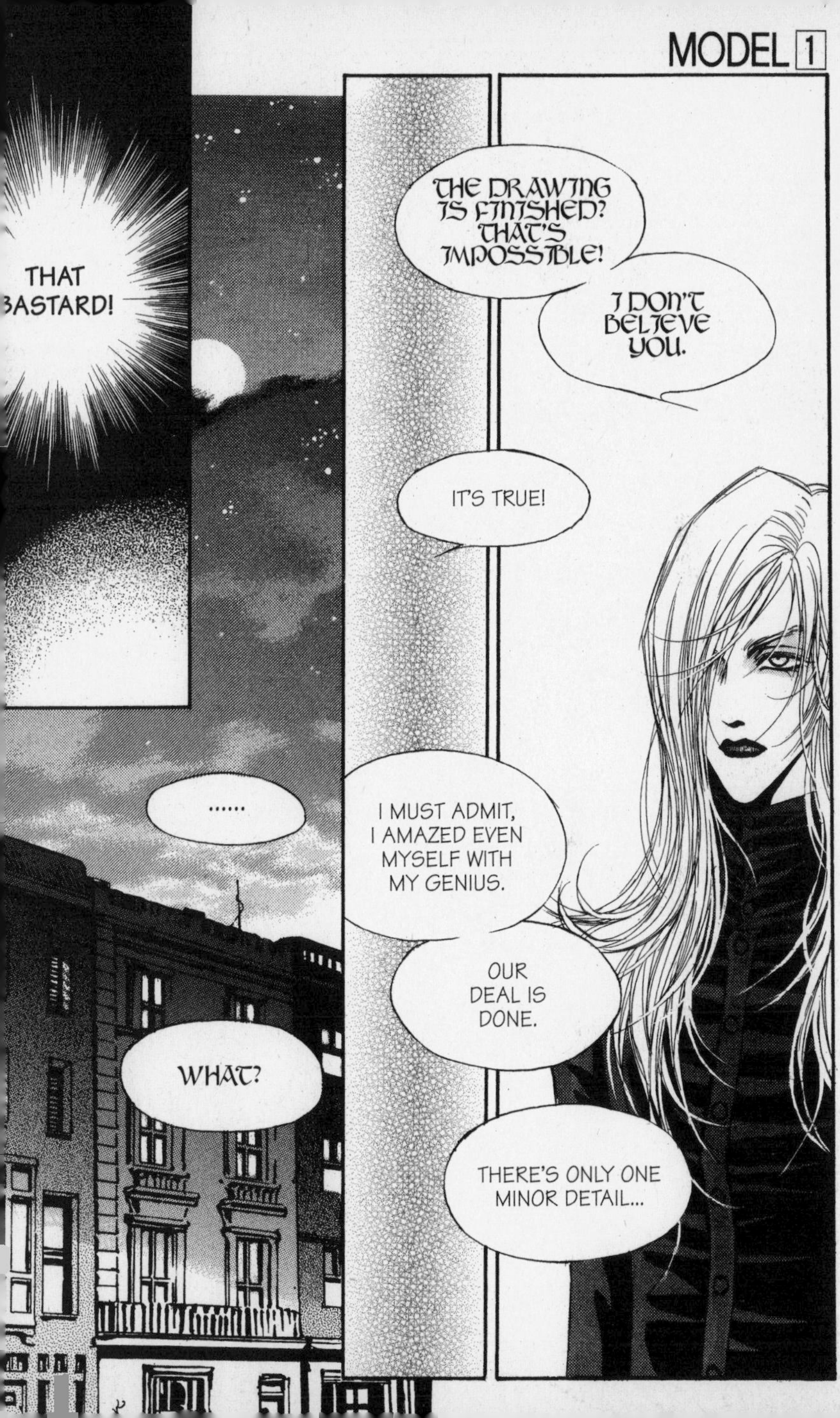
THAT BASTARD!
......
WHAT?
THE DRAWING IS FINISHED? THAT'S IMPOSSIBLE!
I DON'T BELIEVE YOU.
IT'S TRUE!
I MUST ADMIT, I AMAZED EVEN MYSELF WITH MY GENIUS.
OUR DEAL IS DONE.
THERE'S ONLY ONE MINOR DETAIL...

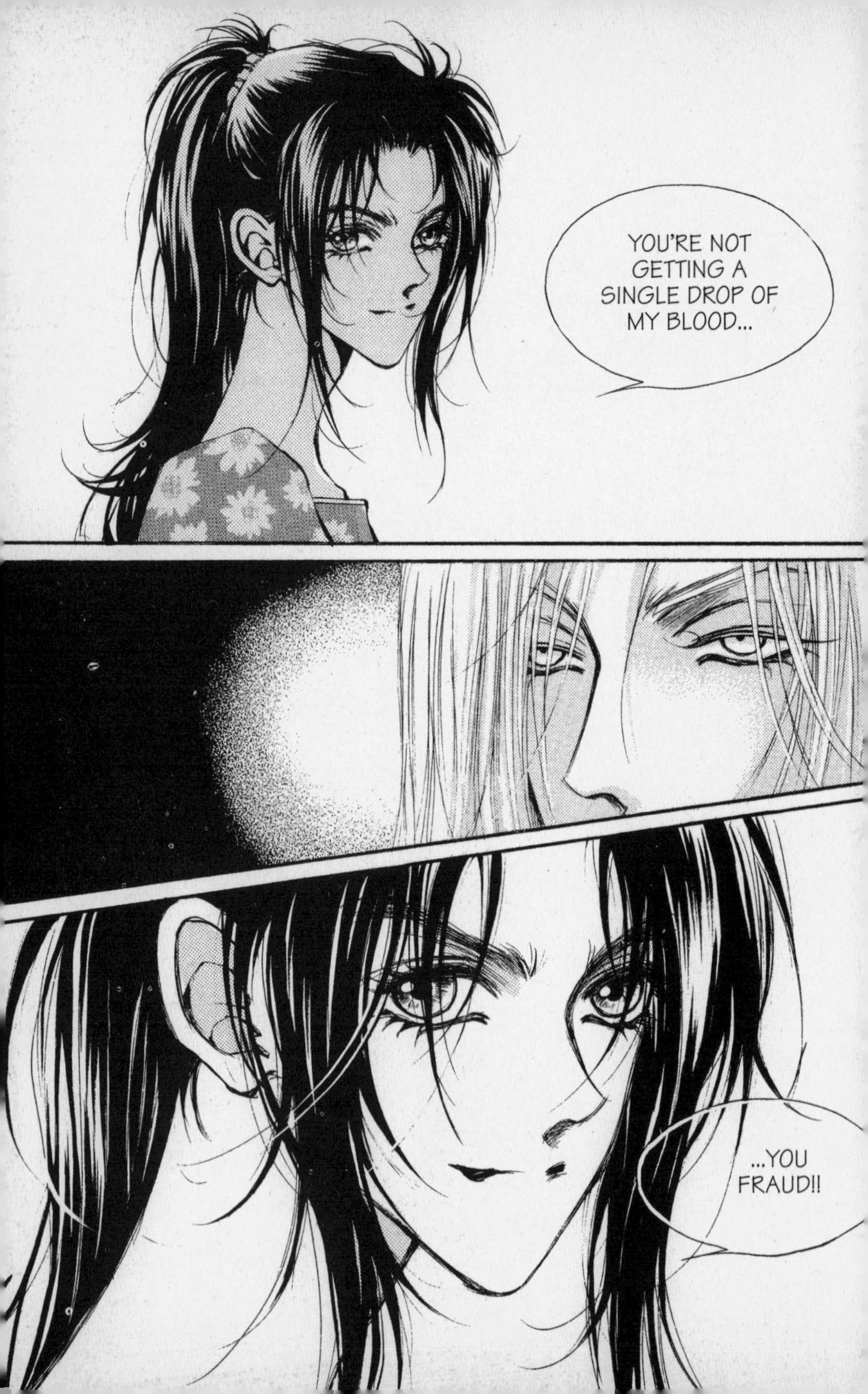
YOU'RE NOT GETTING A SINGLE DROP OF MY BLOOD...
...YOU FRAUD!!

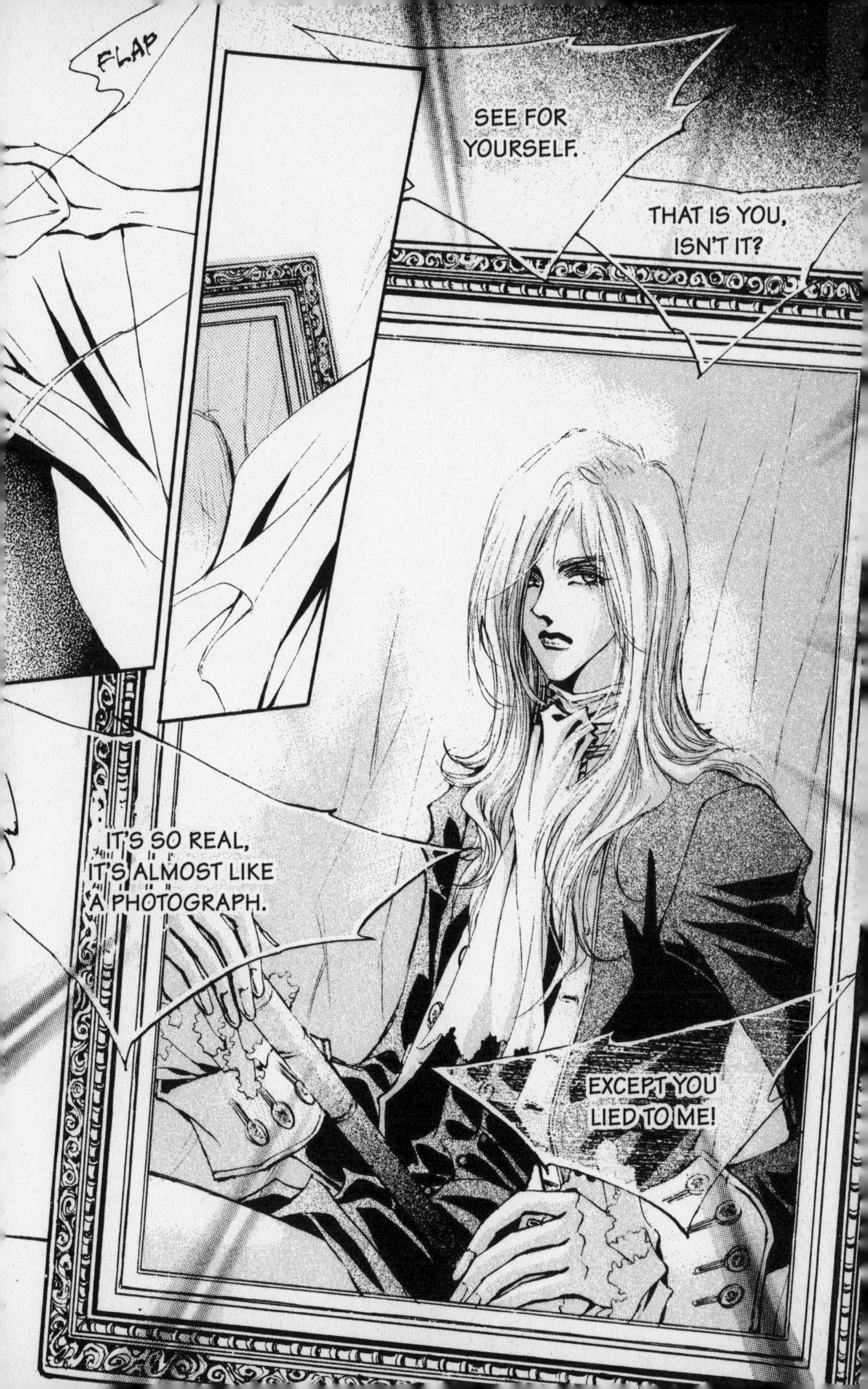
FLAP
SEE FOR YOURSELF.
THAT IS YOU, ISN'T IT?
IT'S SO REAL, IT'S ALMOST LIKE A PHOTOGRAPH.
EXCEPT YOU LIED TO ME!

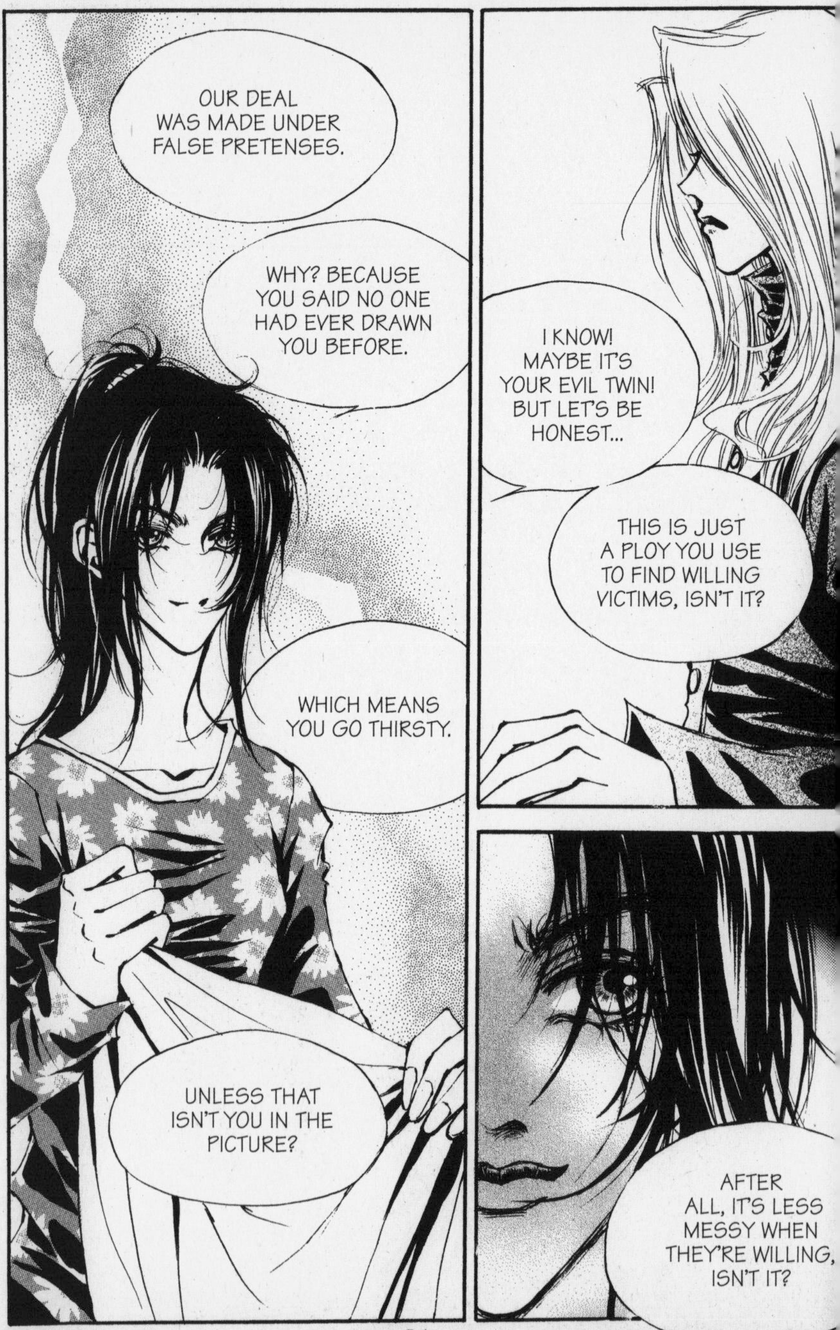
OUR DEAL WAS MADE UNDER FALSE PRETENSES.
WHY? BECAUSE YOU SAID NO ONE HAD EVER DRAWN YOU BEFORE.
WHICH MEANS YOU GO THIRSTY.
UNLESS THAT ISN'T YOU IN THE PICTURE?
I KNOW! MAYBE IT'S YOUR EVIL TWIN! BUT LET'S BE HONEST...
THIS IS JUST A PLOY YOU USE TO FIND WILLING VICTIMS, ISN'T IT?
AFTER ALL, IT'S LESS MESSY WHEN THEY'RE WILLING, ISN'T IT?

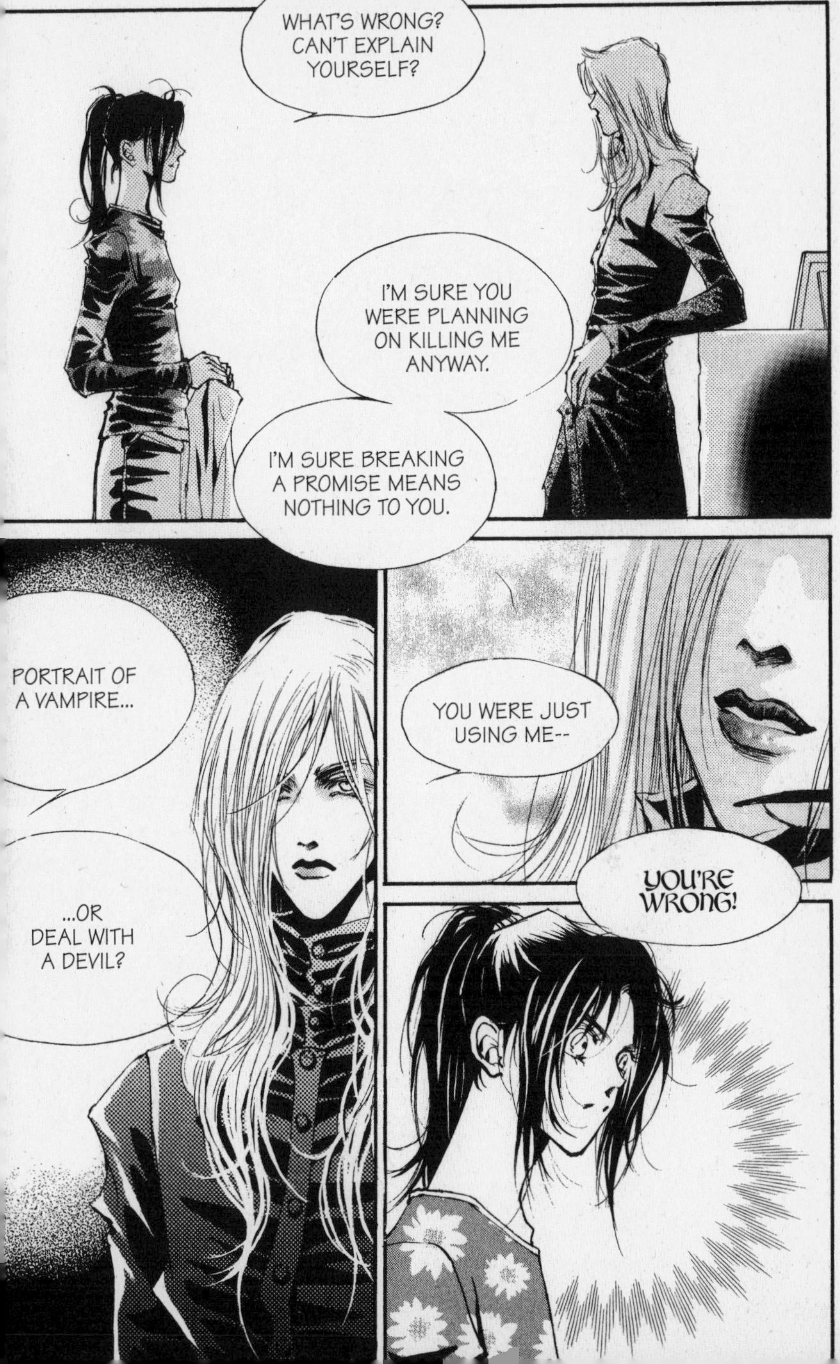
WHAT'S WRONG? CAN'T EXPLAIN YOURSELF?
I'M SURE YOU WERE PLANNING ON KILLING ME ANYWAY.
I'M SURE BREAKING A PROMISE MEANS NOTHING TO YOU.
PORTRAIT OF A VAMPIRE...
...OR DEAL WITH A DEVIL?
YOU WERE JUST USING ME--
YOU'RE WRONG!

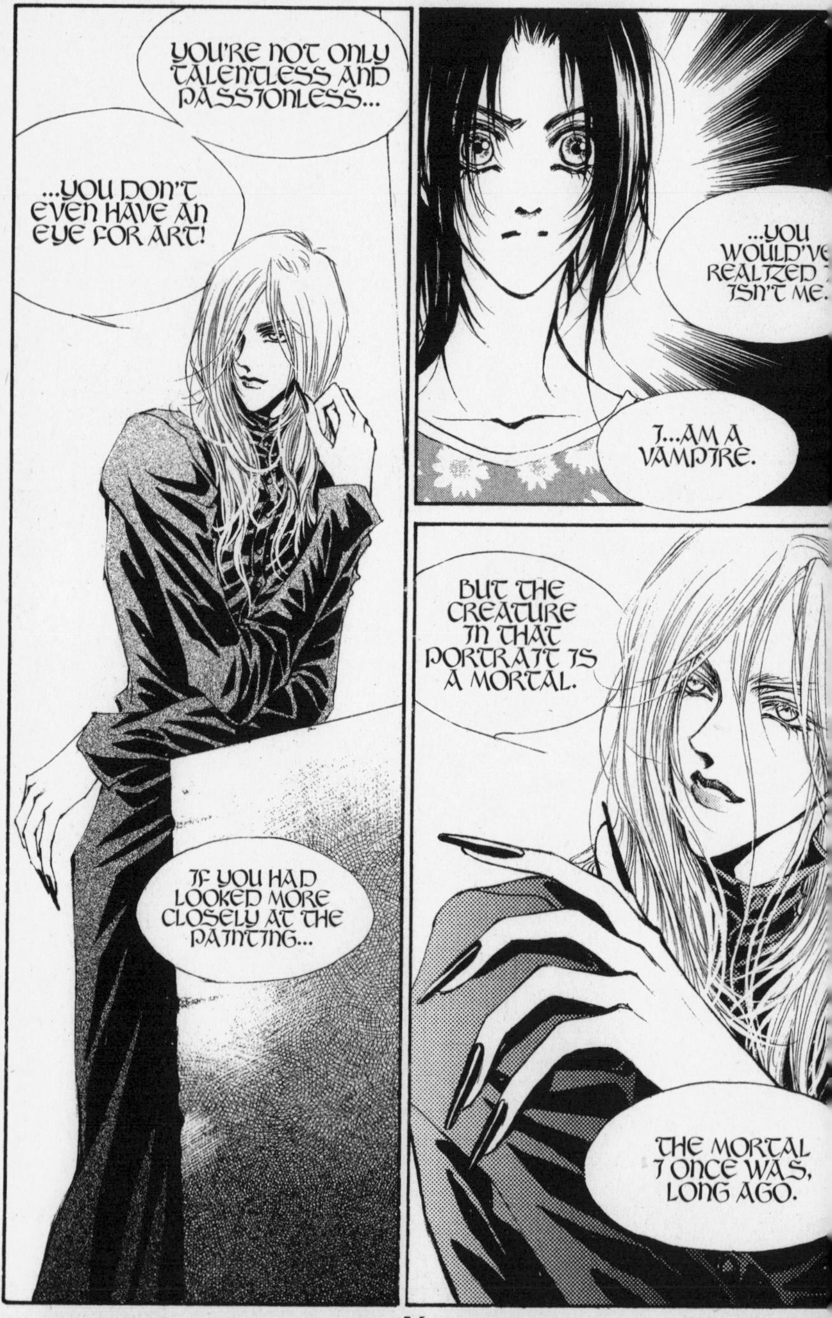
YOU'RE NOT ONLY TALENTLESS AND PASSIONLESS...
...YOU DON'T EVEN HAVE AN EYE FOR ART!
IF YOU HAD LOOKED MORE CLOSELY AT THE PAINTING...
...YOU WOULD'VE REALIZED ISN'T ME.
I...AM A VAMPIRE.
BUT THE CREATURE IN THAT PORTRAIT IS A MORTAL.
THE MORTAL I ONCE WAS, LONG AGO.

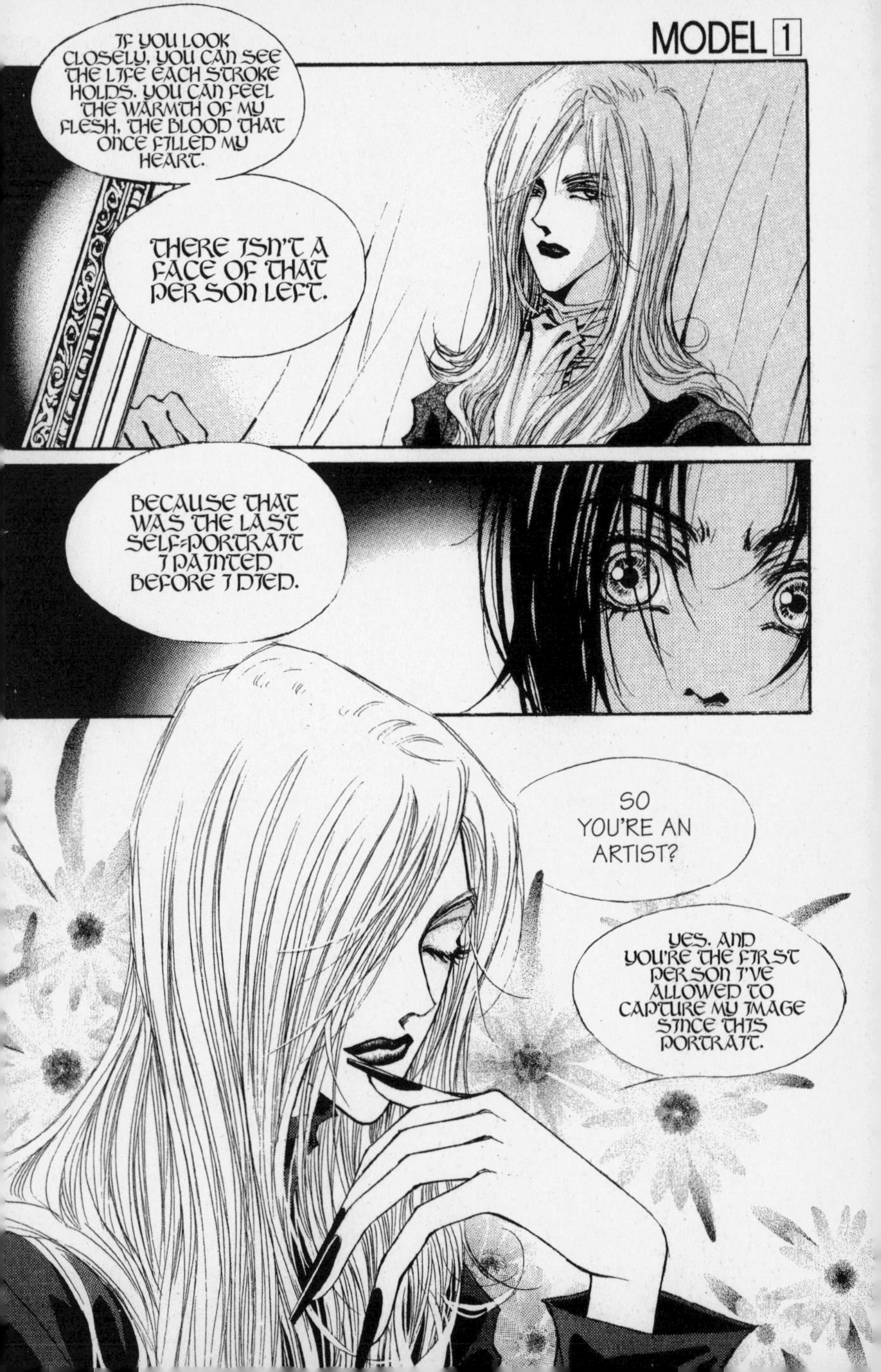
IF YOU LOOK CLOSELY, YOU CAN SEE THE LIFE EACH STROKE HOLDS. YOU CAN FEEL THE WARMTH OF MY FLESH, THE BLOOD THAT ONCE FILLED MY HEART.
THERE ISN'T A FACE OF THAT PERSON LEFT.
BECAUSE THAT WAS THE LAST SELF-PORTRAIT I PAINTED BEFORE I DIED.
SO YOU'RE AN ARTIST?
YES. AND YOU'RE THE FIRST PERSON I'VE ALLOWED TO CAPTURE MY IMAGE SINCE THIS PORTRAIT.

YOU UNDERSTAND MY NARCISSISM, DON'T YOU?
I DIDN'T WANT TO LOSE MY BEAUTY.
THAT ETERNAL FEAR OF ALL MORTALS!
THAT'S WHY I CHOSE TO BECOME A VAMPIRE.
BUT THE COST OF MAINTAINING MY BEAUTY IS AN UNQUENCHABLE THIRST FOR BLOOD!
ONLY BY STEALING THE YOUTH OF OTHERS...

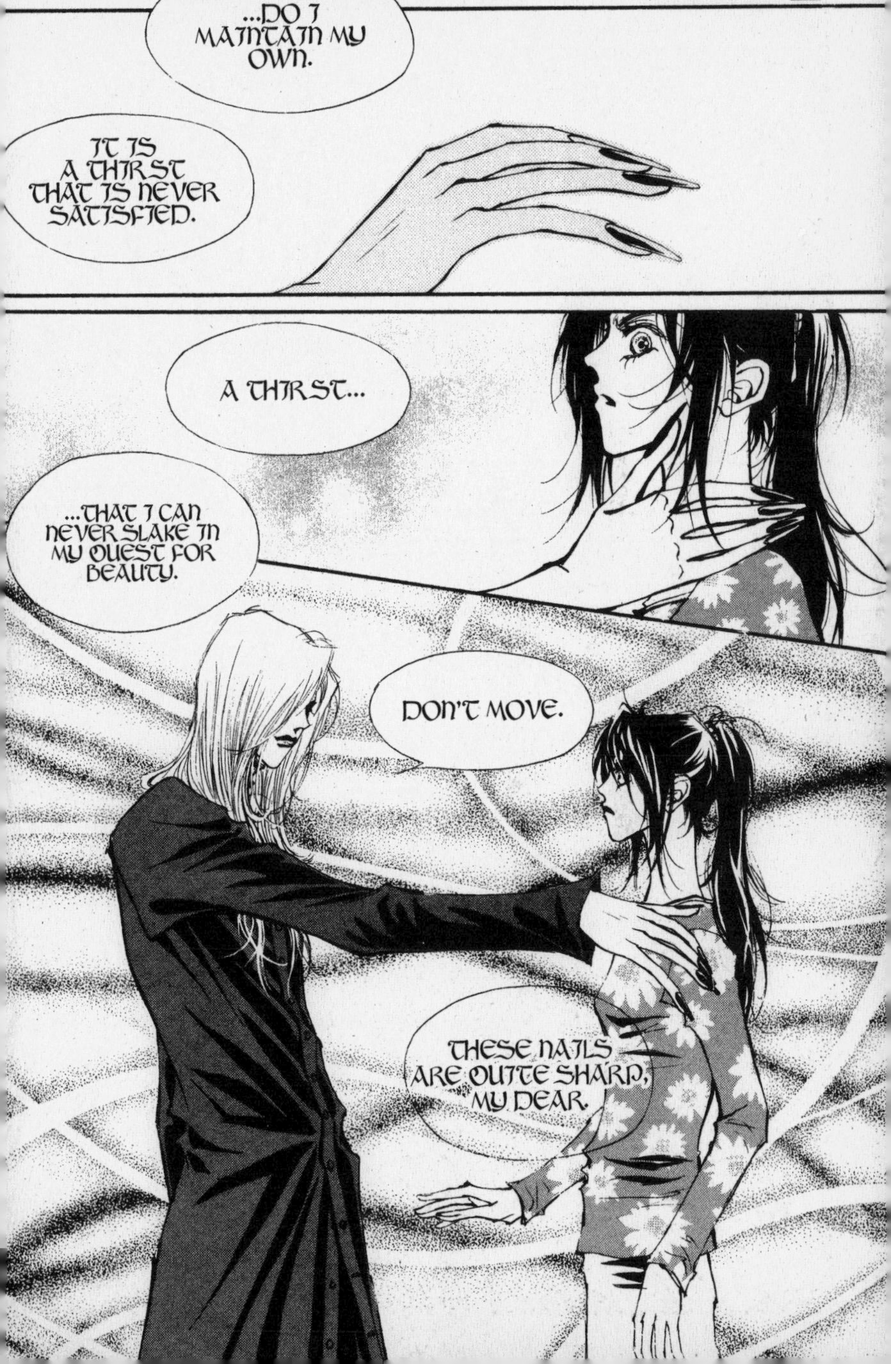
...DO I MAINTAIN MY OWN.
IT IS A THIRST THAT IS NEVER SATISFIED.
A THIRST...
...THAT I CAN NEVER SLAKE IN MY QUEST FOR BEAUTY.
DON'T MOVE.
THESE NAILS ARE QUITE SHARP, MY DEAR.

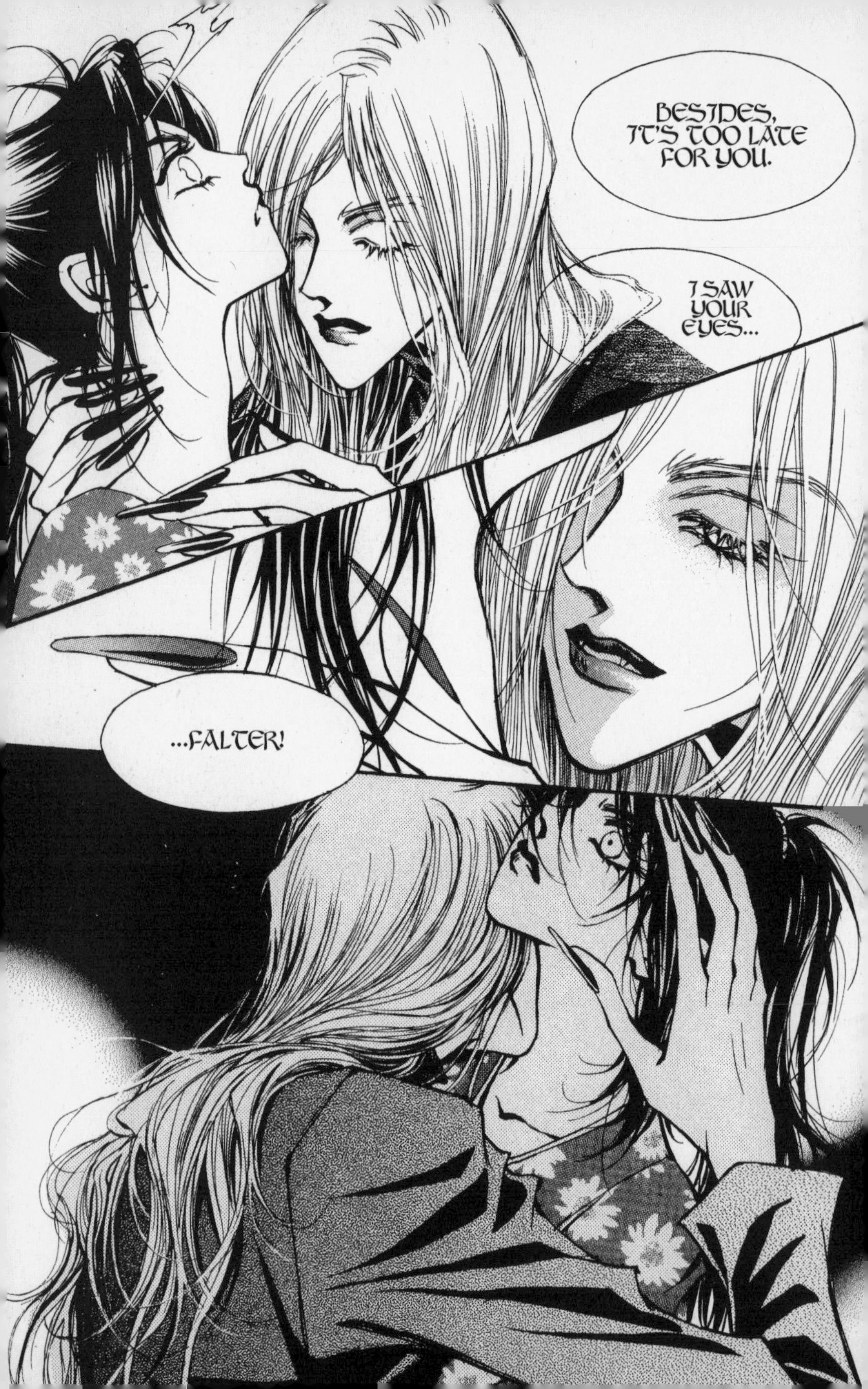
BESIDES, IT'S TOO LATE FOR YOU.
I SAW YOUR EYES...
...FALTER!

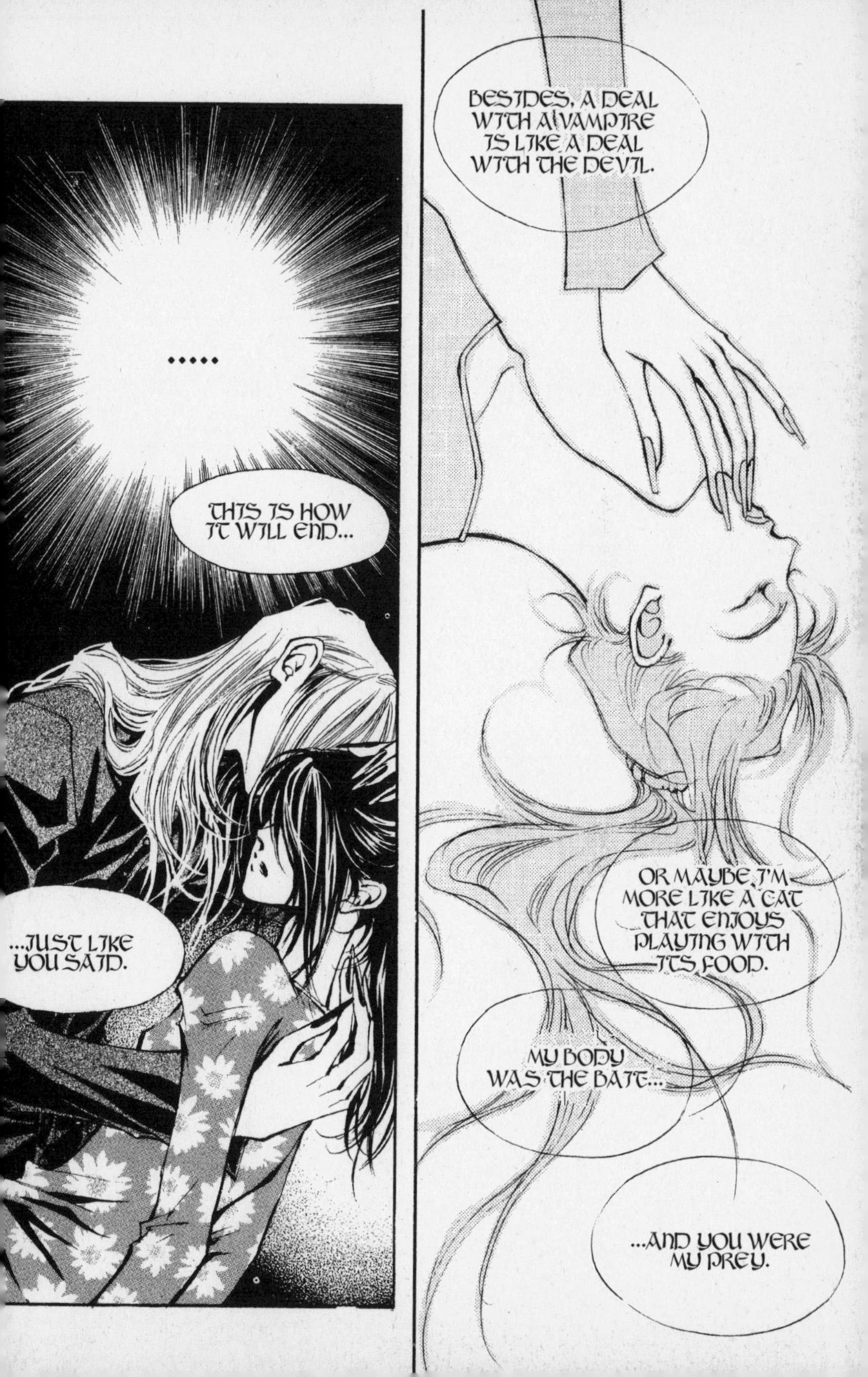
.....
THIS IS HOW IT WILL END...
...JUST LIKE YOU SAID.
BESIDES, A DEAL WITH A VAMPIRE IS LIKE A DEAL WITH THE DEVIL.
OR MAYBE I'M MORE LIKE A CAT THAT ENJOYS PLAYING WITH ITS FOOD.
MY BODY WAS THE BAIT...
...AND YOU WERE MY PREY.

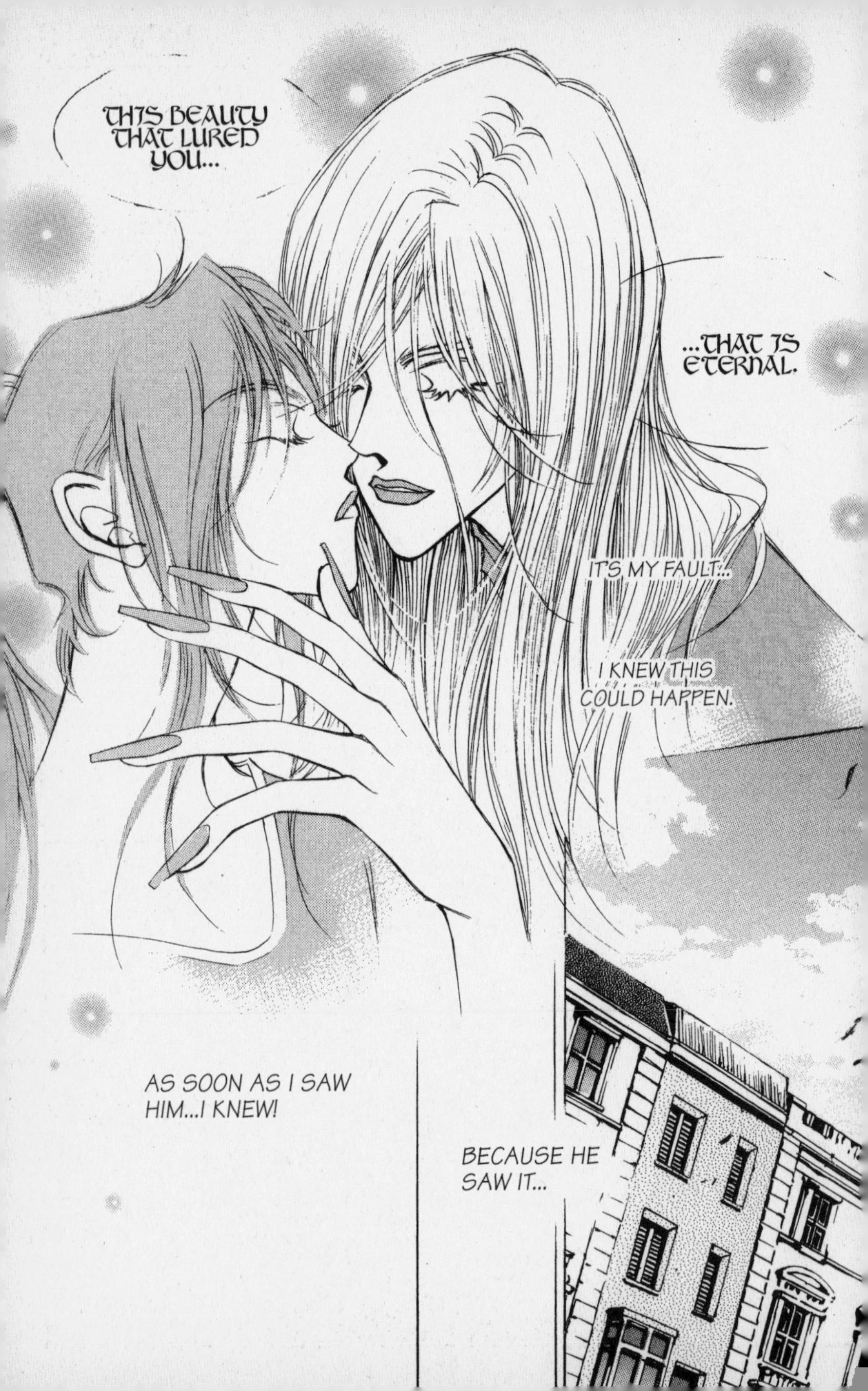
THIS BEAUTY THAT LURED YOU...
...THAT IS ETERNAL.
IT'S MY FAULT...
I KNEW THIS COULD HAPPEN.
AS SOON AS I SAW HIM...I KNEW!
BECAUSE HE SAW IT...

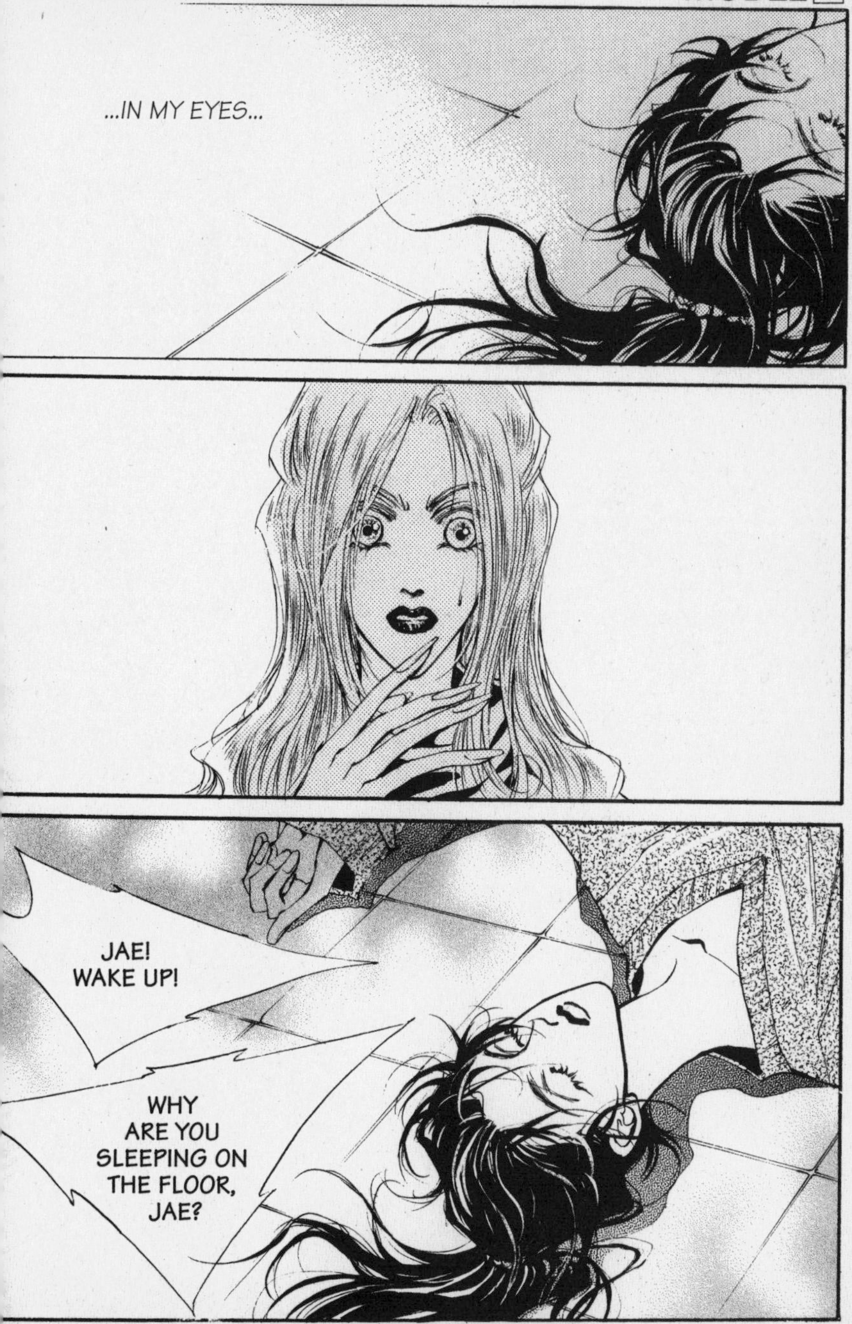
...IN MY EYES...
JAE! WAKE UP!
WHY ARE YOU SLEEPING ON THE FLOOR, JAE?

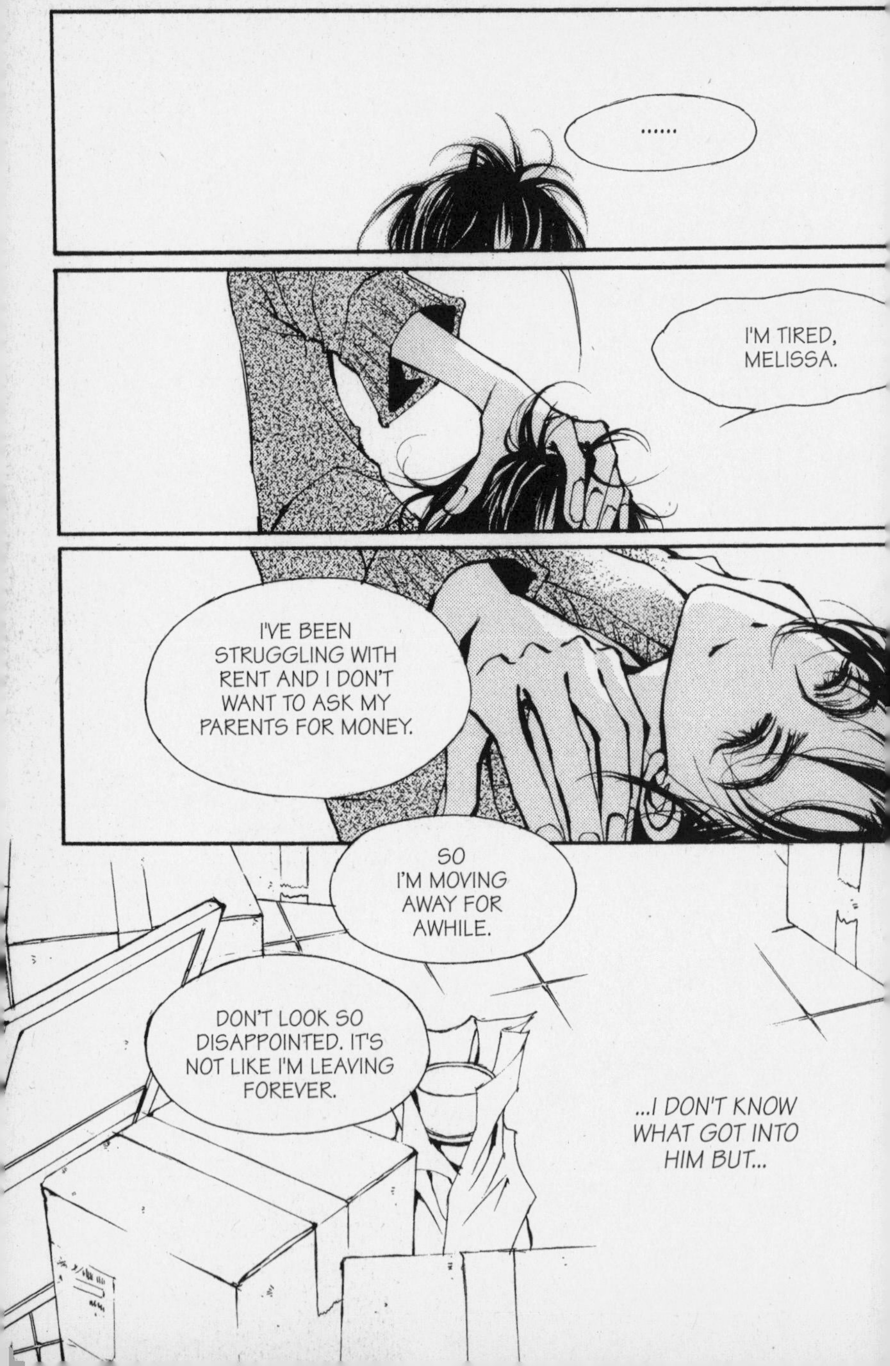
......
I'M TIRED, MELISSA.
I'VE BEEN STRUGGLING WITH RENT AND I DON'T WANT TO ASK MY PARENTS FOR MONEY.
SO I'M MOVING AWAY FOR AWHILE.
DON'T LOOK SO DISAPPOINTED. IT'S NOT LIKE I'M LEAVING FOREVER.
...I DON'T KNOW WHAT GOT INTO HIM BUT...

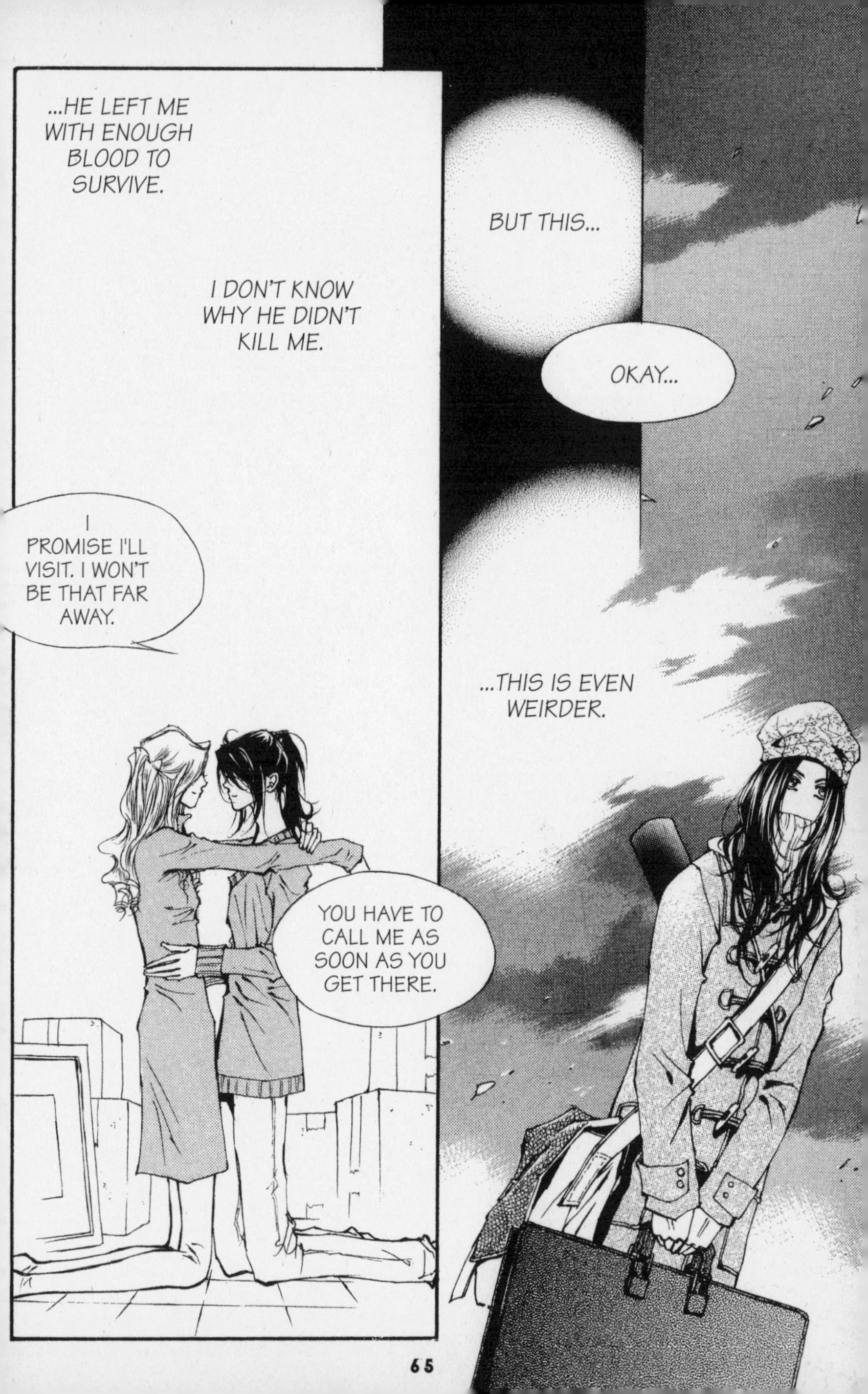
...HE LEFT ME WITH ENOUGH BLOOD TO SURVIVE.
I DON'T KNOW WHY HE DIDN'T KILL ME.
I PROMISE I'LL VISIT. I WON'T BE THAT FAR AWAY.
YOU HAVE TO CALL ME AS SOON AS YOU GET THERE.
BUT THIS...
OKAY...
...THIS IS EVEN WEIRDER.

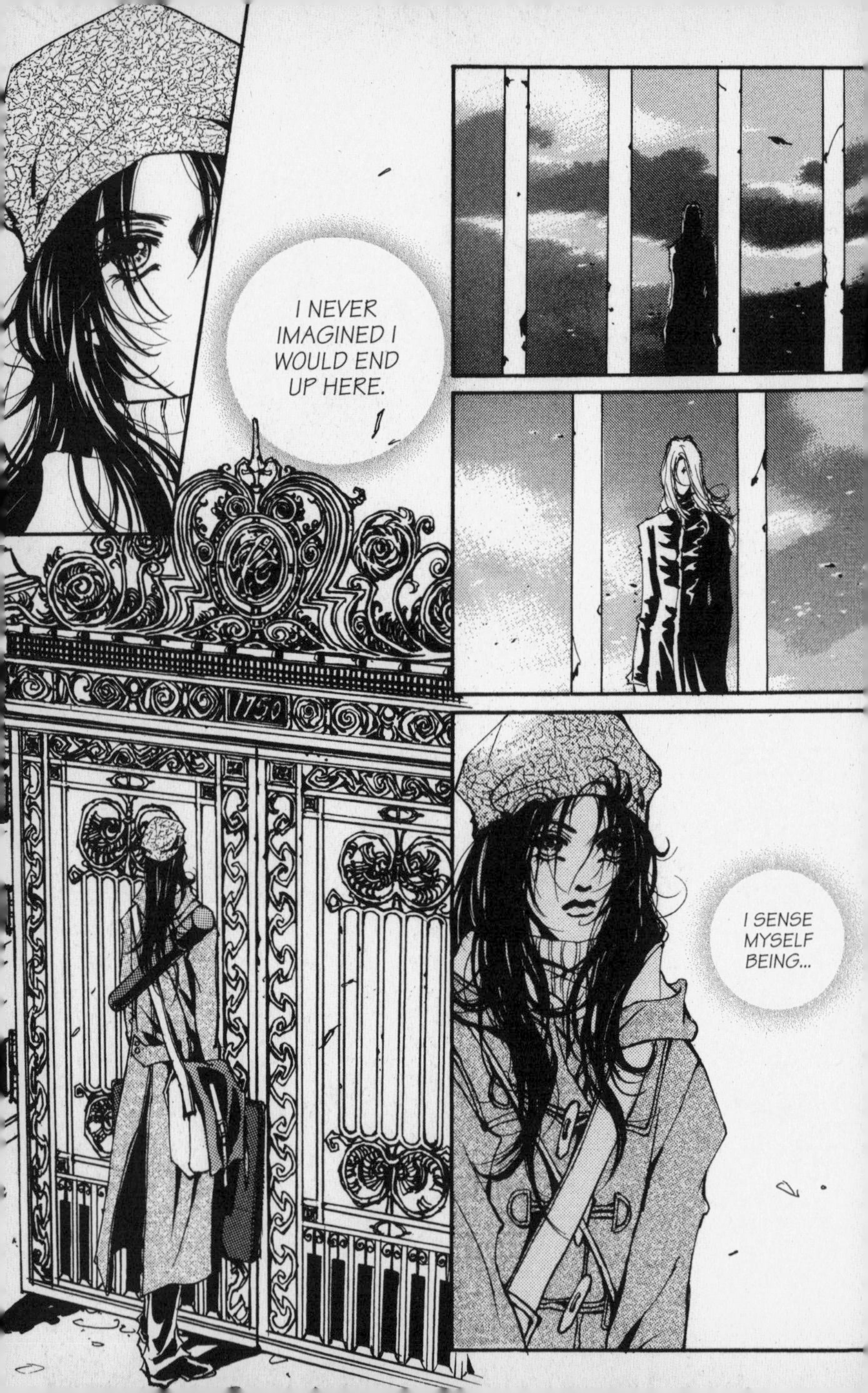
I NEVER IMAGINED I WOULD END UP HERE.
1750
I SENSE MYSELF BEING...

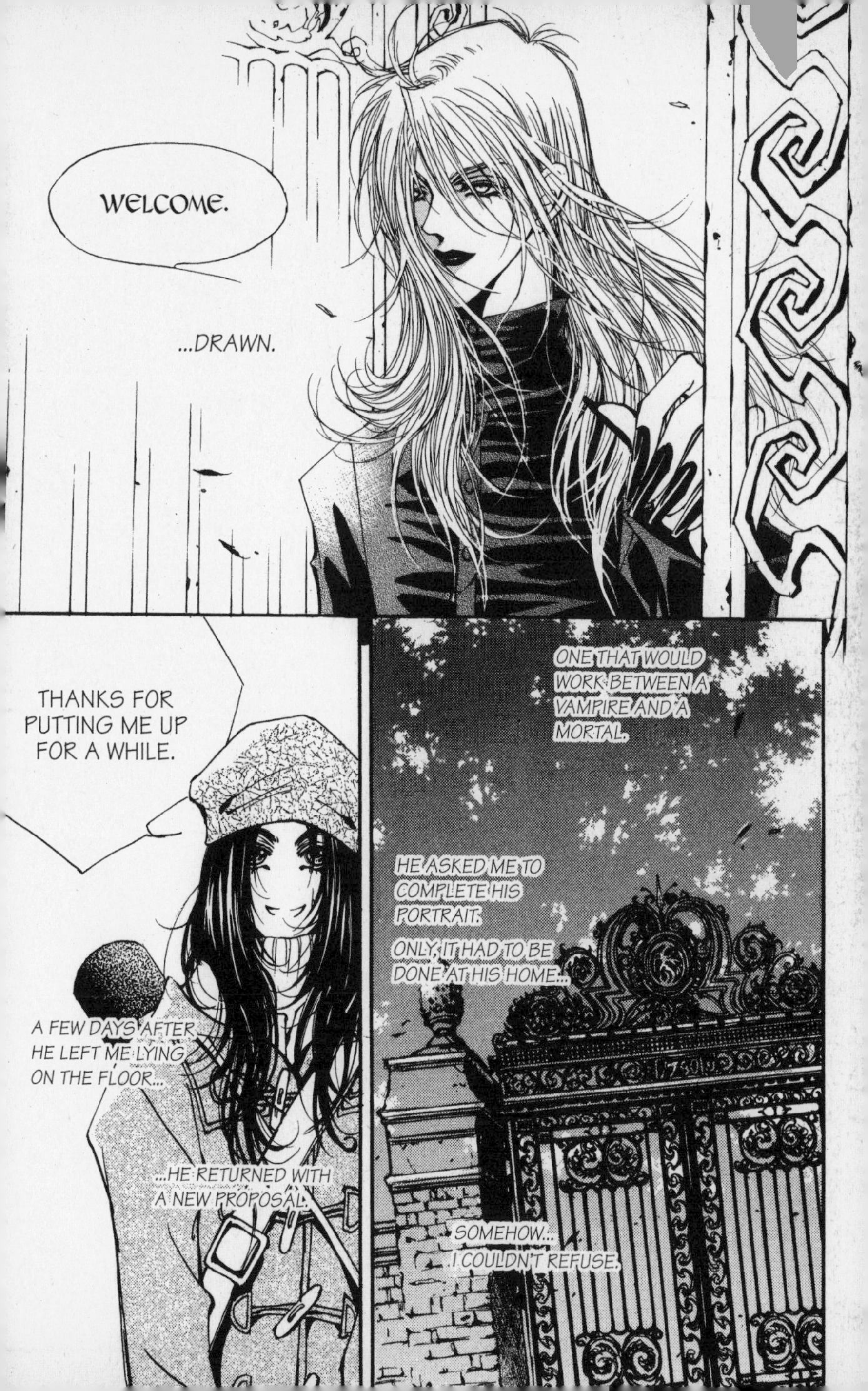
WELCOME.
...DRAWN.
THANKS FOR PUTTING ME UP FOR A WHILE.
A FEW DAYS AFTER HE LEFT ME LYING ON THE FLOOR...
...HE RETURNED WITH A NEW PROPOSAL.
ONE THAT WOULD WORK BETWEEN A VAMPIRE AND A MORTAL.
HE ASKED ME TO COMPLETE HIS PORTRAIT.
ONLY, IT HAD TO BE DONE AT HIS HOME...
SOMEHOW... I COULDN'T REFUSE.

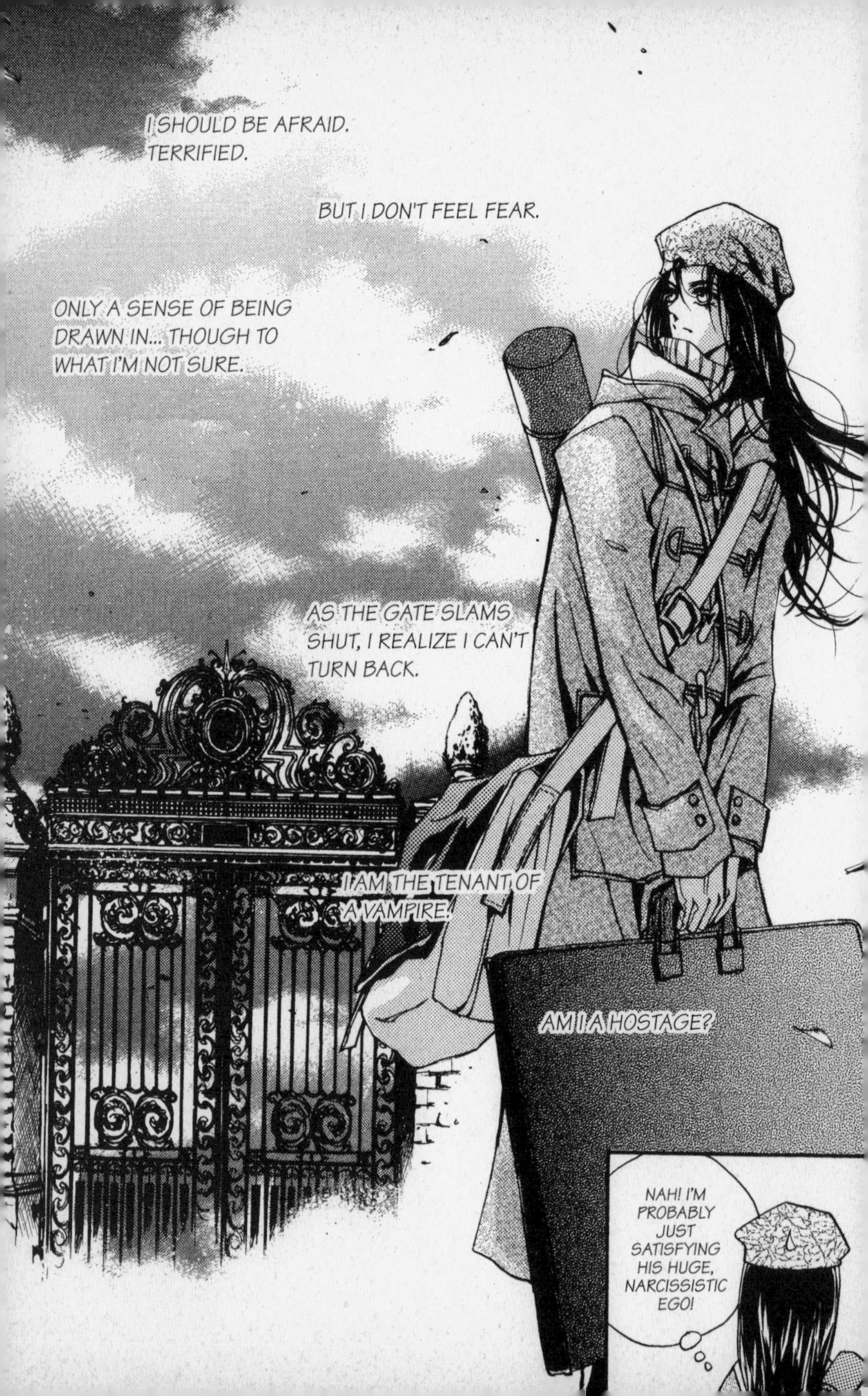
I SHOULD BE AFRAID. TERRIFIED.
BUT I DON'T FEEL FEAR.
ONLY A SENSE OF BEING DRAWN IN... THOUGH TO WHAT I'M NOT SURE.
AS THE GATE SLAMS SHUT, I REALIZE I CAN'T TURN BACK.
I AM THE TENANT OF A VAMPIRE.
AM I A HOSTAGE?
NAH! I'M PROBABLY JUST SATISFYING HIS HUGE, NARCISSISTIC EGO!

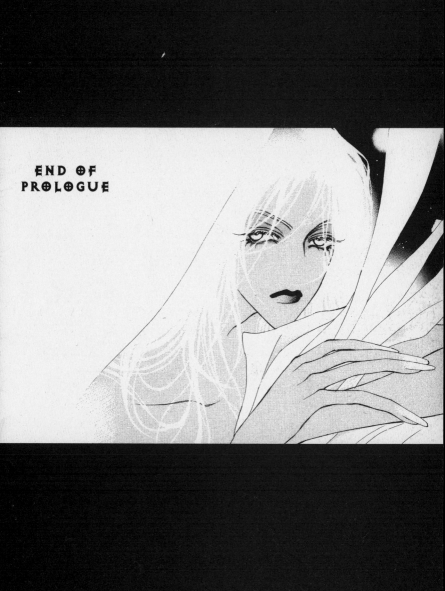

END OF
PROLOGUE

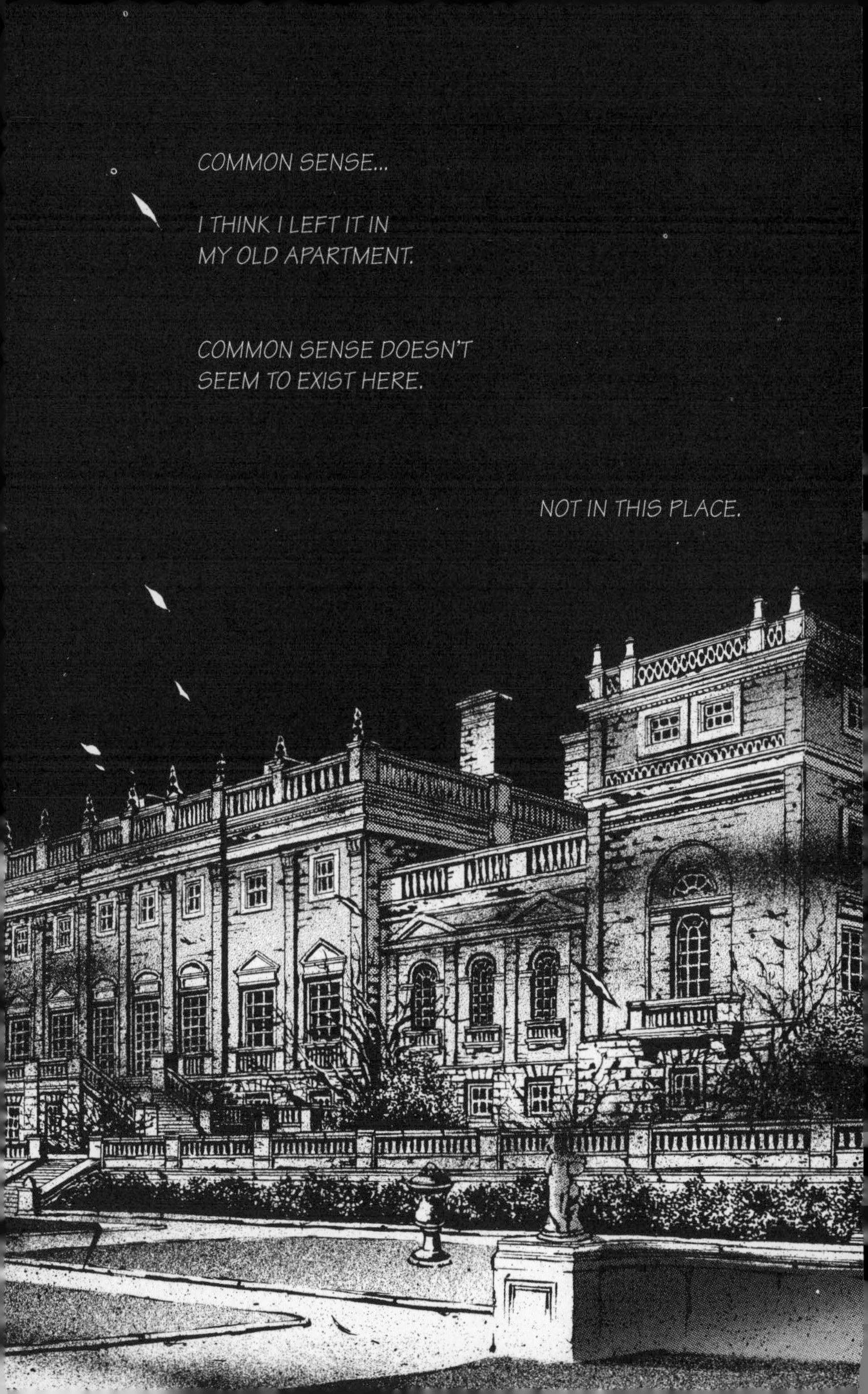
COMMON SENSE...
I THINK I LEFT IT IN MY OLD APARTMENT.
COMMON SENSE DOESN'T SEEM TO EXIST HERE.
NOT IN THIS PLACE.

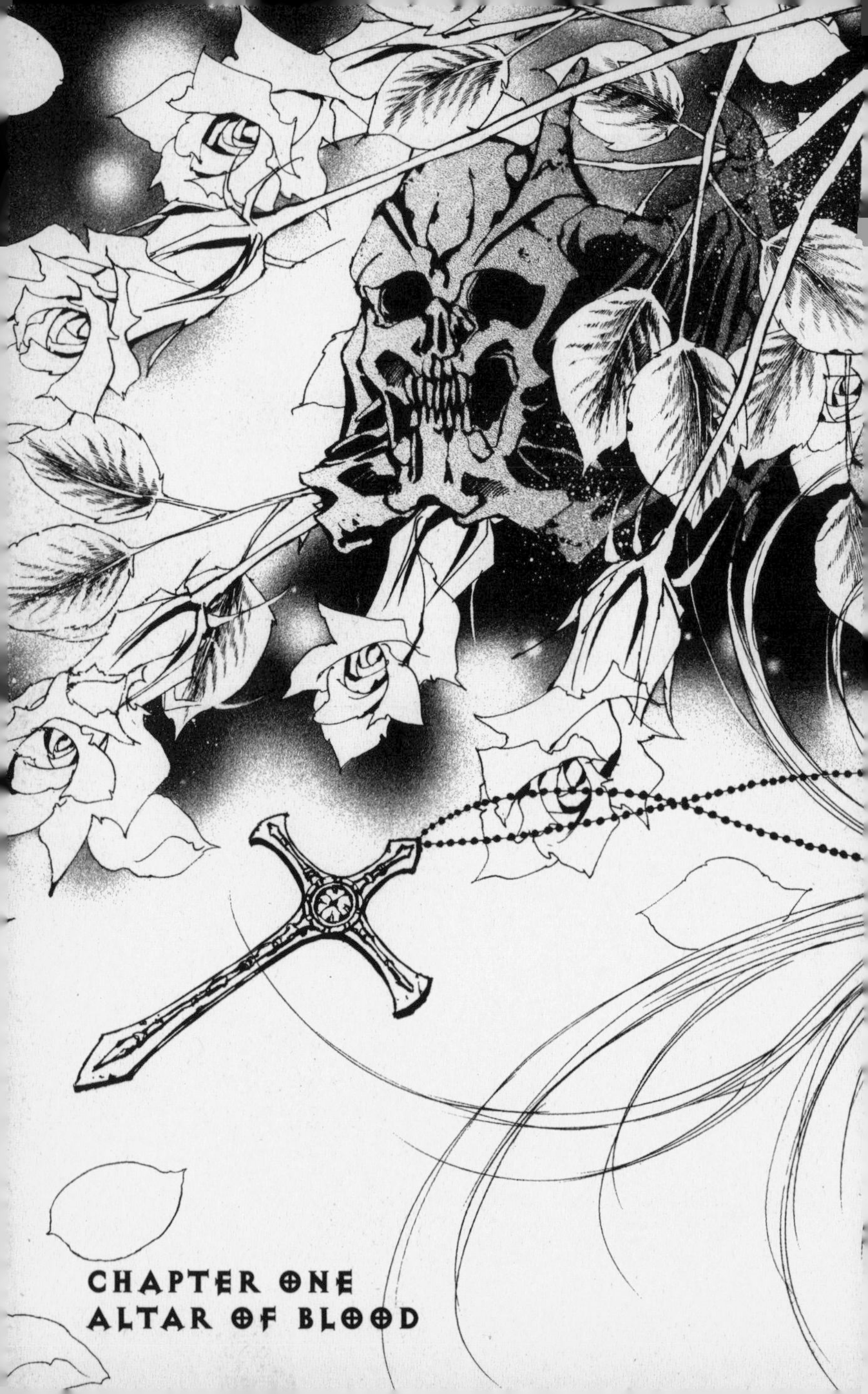

# CHAPTER ONE
# ALTAR OF BLOOD

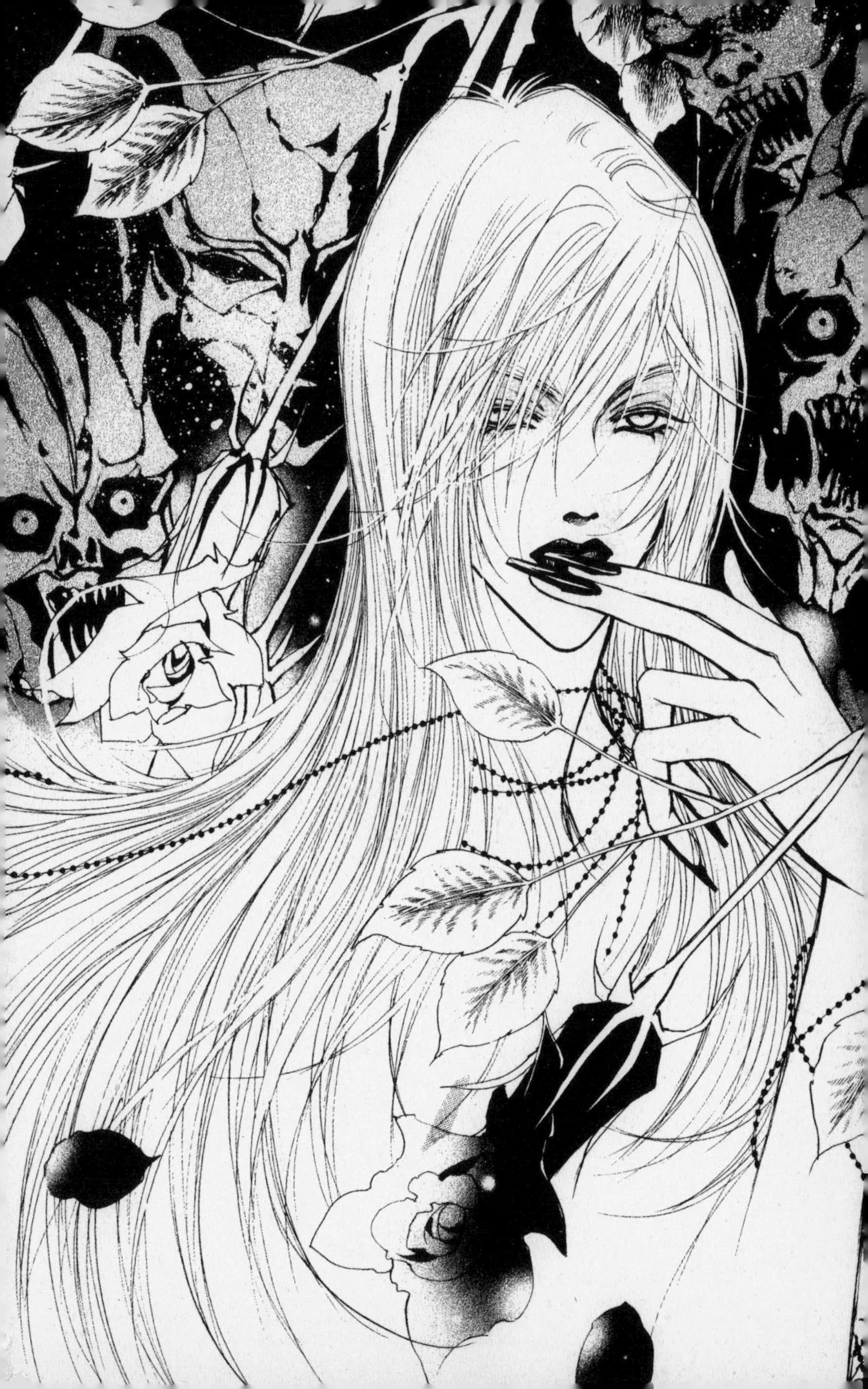

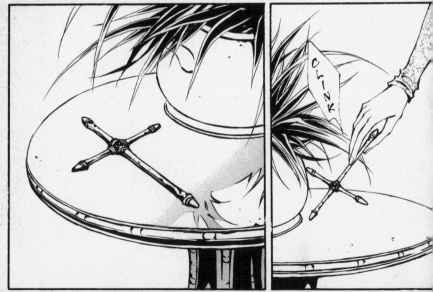

CLINK

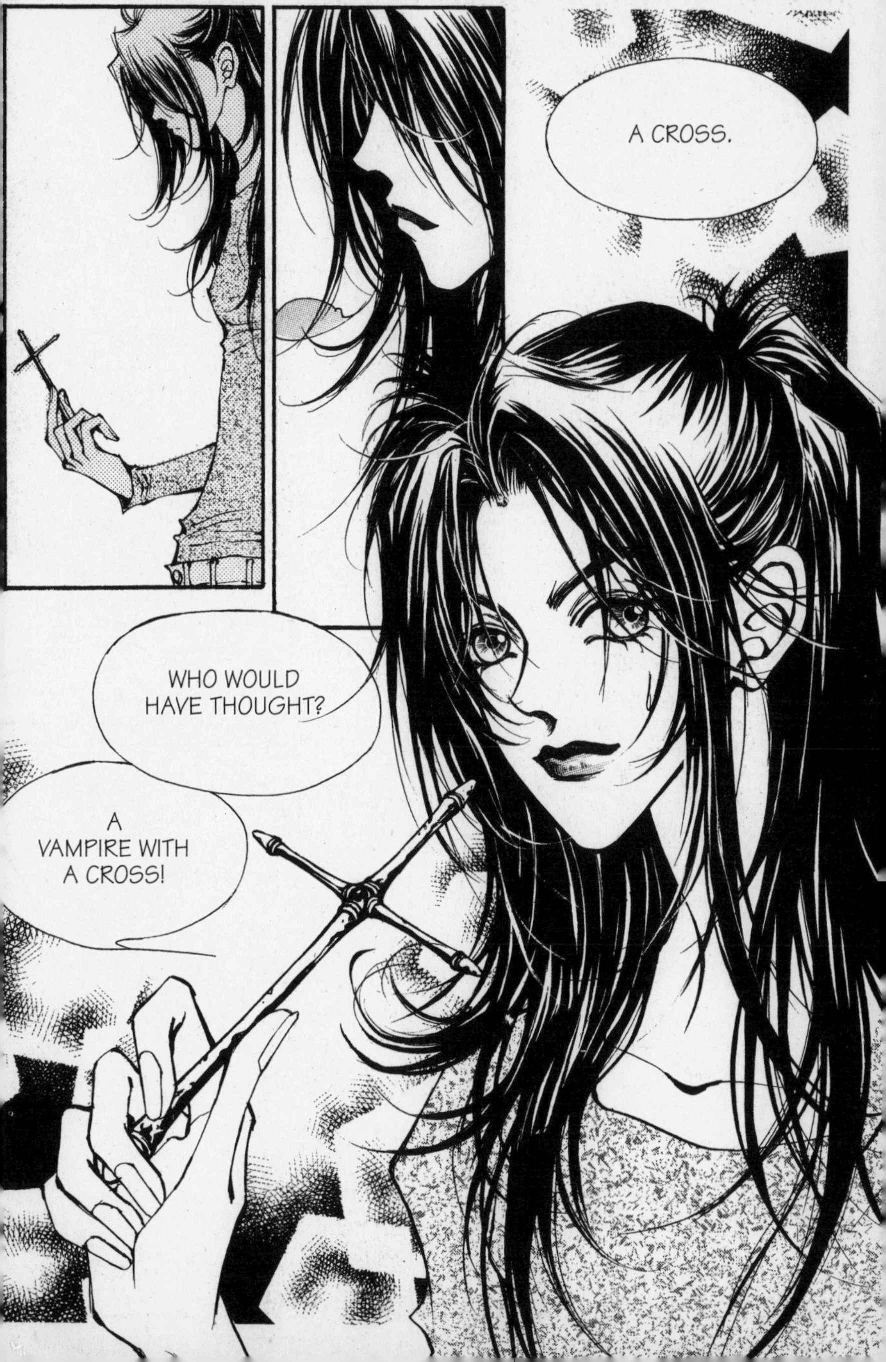
A CROSS.
WHO WOULD HAVE THOUGHT?
A VAMPIRE WITH A CROSS!

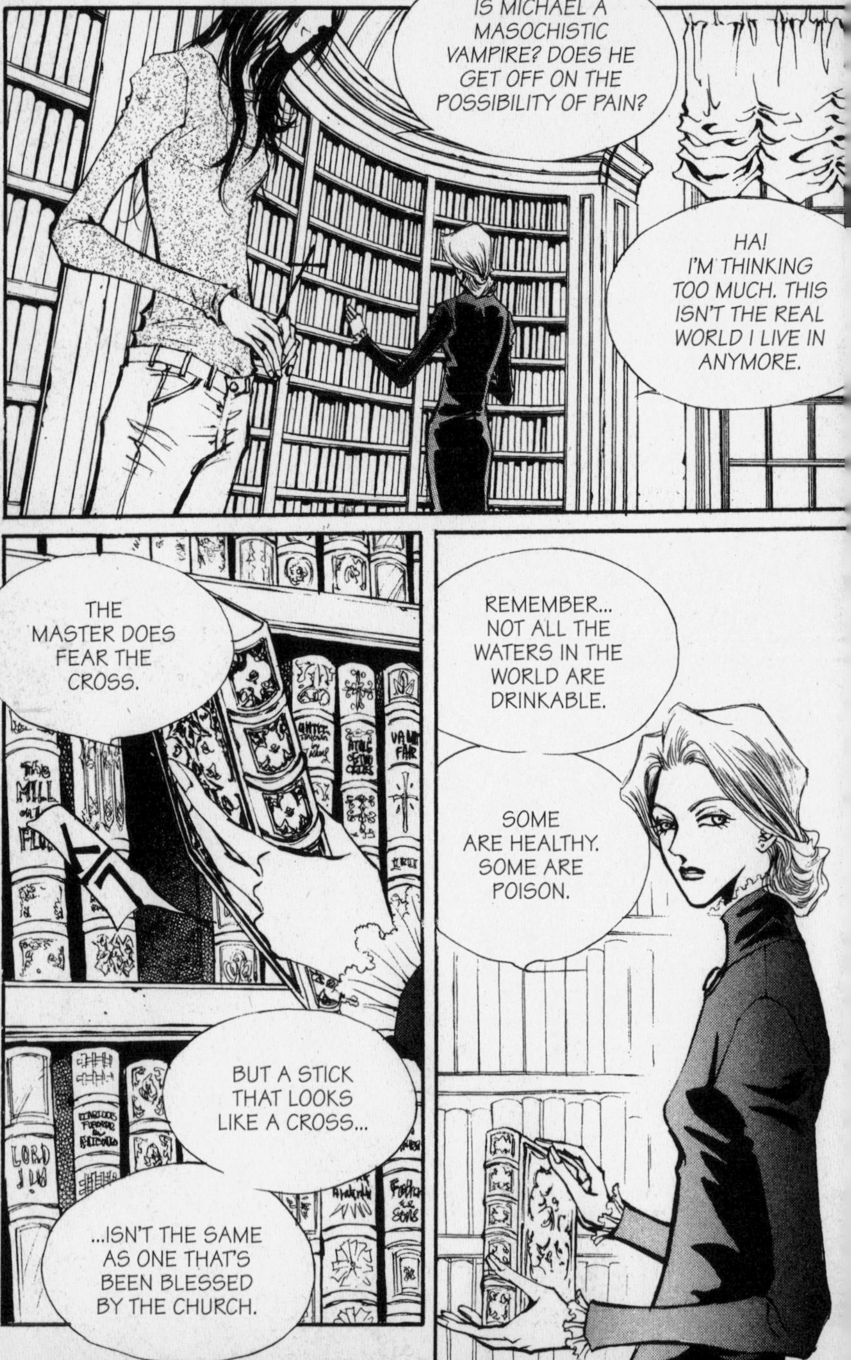
IS MICHAEL A MASOCHISTIC VAMPIRE? DOES HE GET OFF ON THE POSSIBILITY OF PAIN?
HA! I'M THINKING TOO MUCH. THIS ISN'T THE REAL WORLD I LIVE IN ANYMORE.
THE MASTER DOES FEAR THE CROSS.
BUT A STICK THAT LOOKS LIKE A CROSS...
...ISN'T THE SAME AS ONE THAT'S BEEN BLESSED BY THE CHURCH.
REMEMBER... NOT ALL THE WATERS IN THE WORLD ARE DRINKABLE.
SOME ARE HEALTHY. SOME ARE POISON.

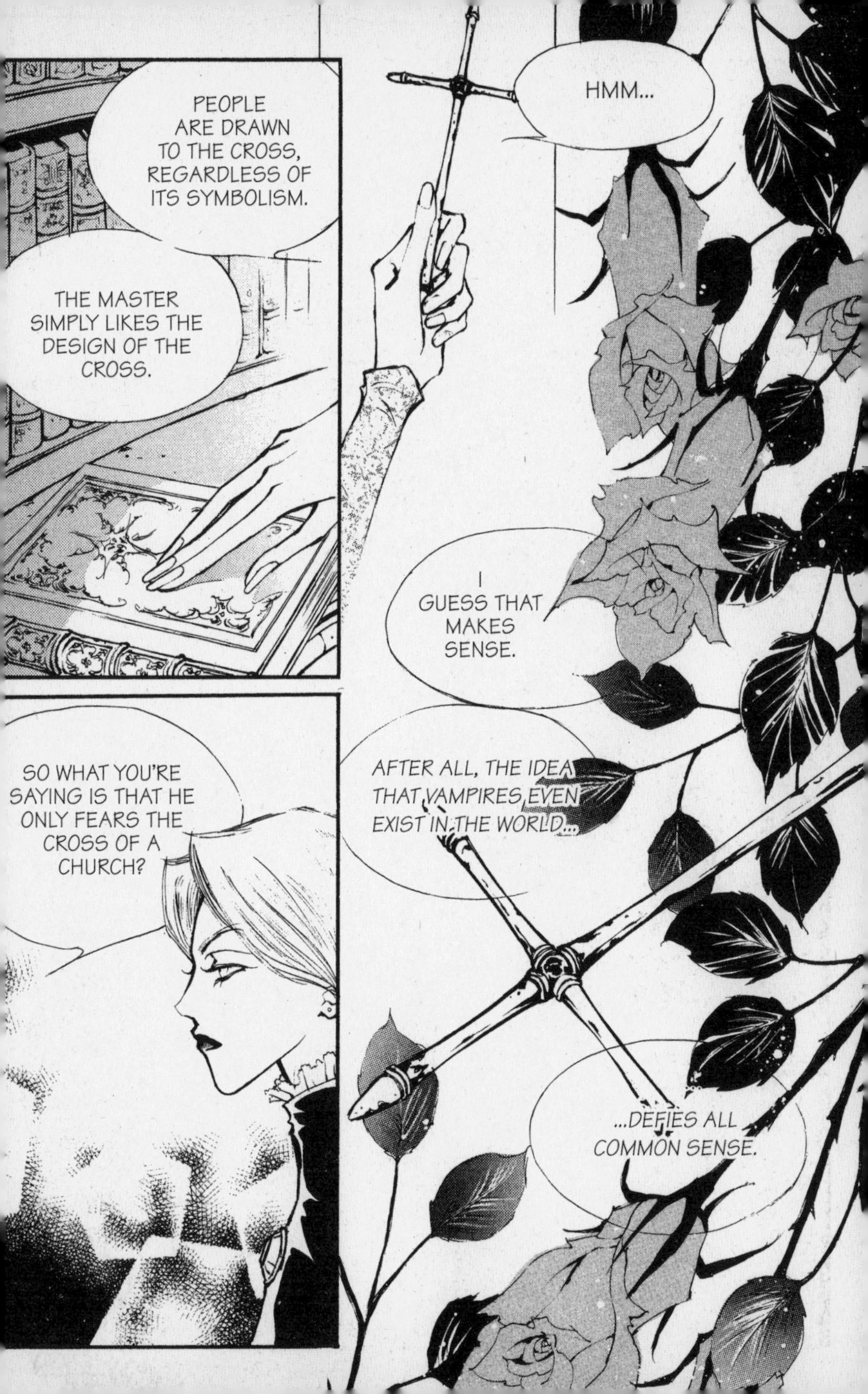
PEOPLE ARE DRAWN TO THE CROSS, REGARDLESS OF ITS SYMBOLISM.
THE MASTER SIMPLY LIKES THE DESIGN OF THE CROSS.
HMM...
I GUESS THAT MAKES SENSE.
SO WHAT YOU'RE SAYING IS THAT HE ONLY FEARS THE CROSS OF A CHURCH?
AFTER ALL, THE IDEA THAT VAMPIRES EVEN EXIST IN THE WORLD...
...DEFIES ALL COMMON SENSE.

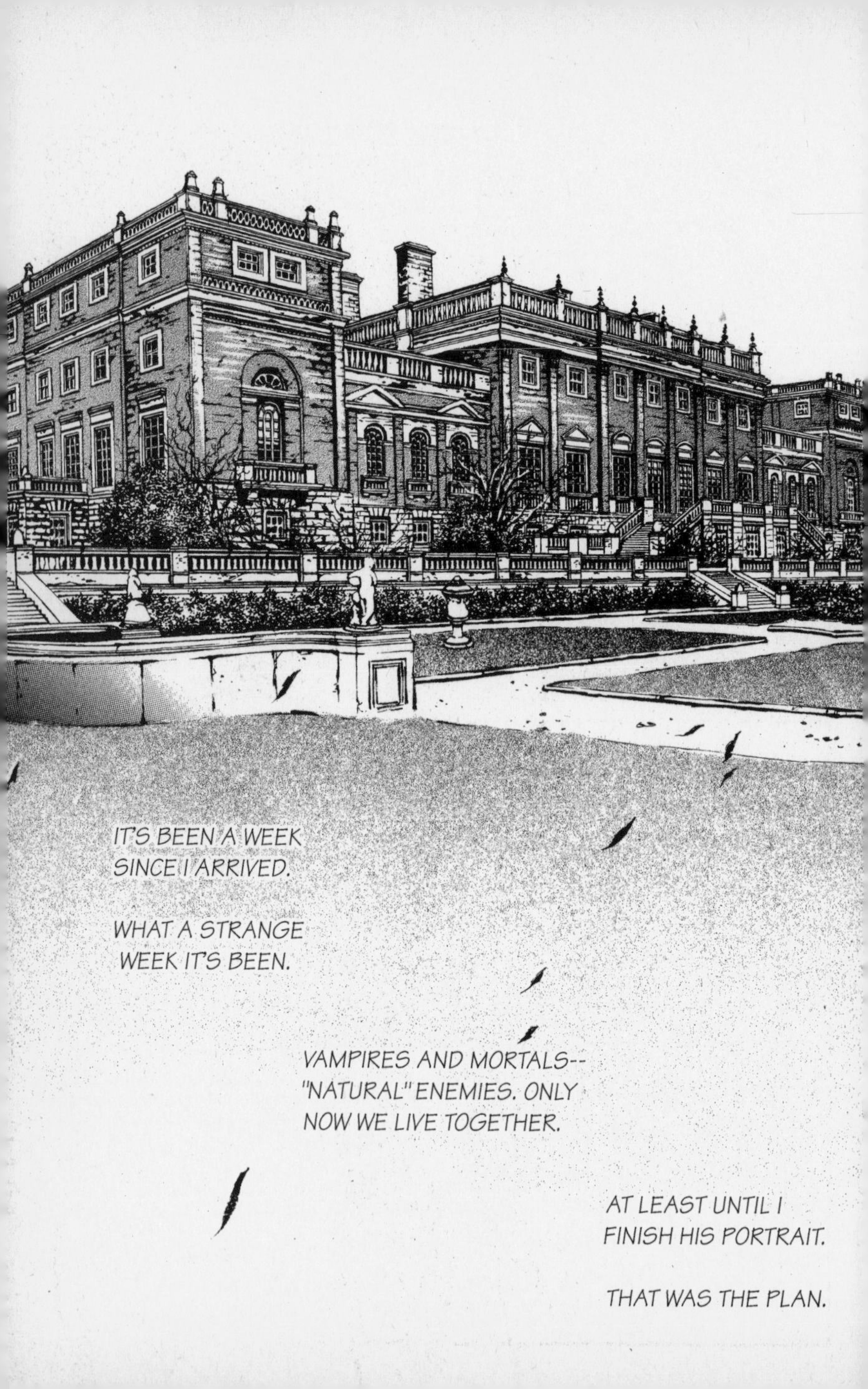
IT'S BEEN A WEEK SINCE I ARRIVED.
WHAT A STRANGE WEEK IT'S BEEN.
VAMPIRES AND MORTALS-- "NATURAL" ENEMIES. ONLY NOW WE LIVE TOGETHER.
AT LEAST UNTIL I FINISH HIS PORTRAIT.
THAT WAS THE PLAN.

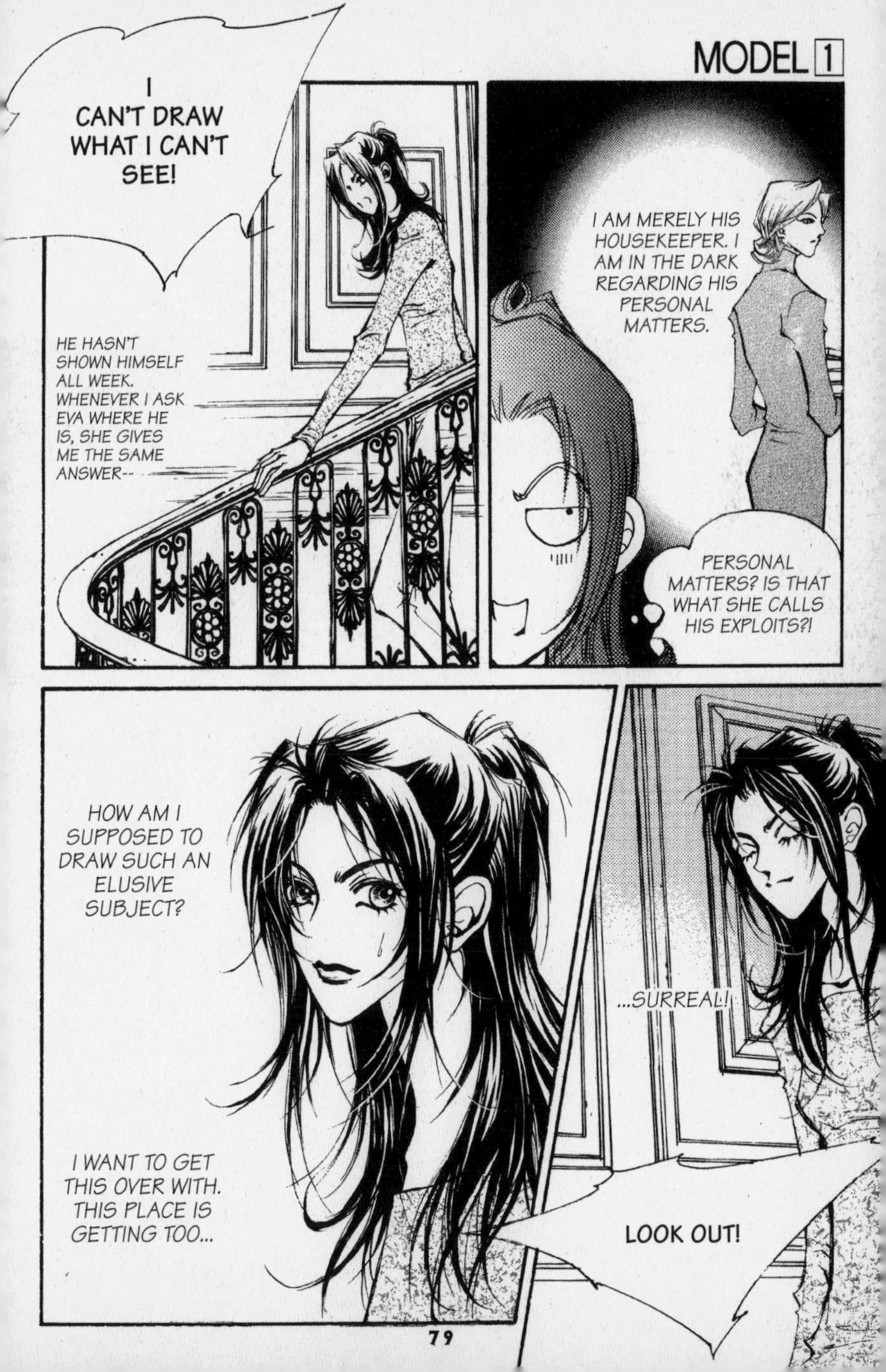
I CAN'T DRAW WHAT I CAN'T SEE!
HE HASN'T SHOWN HIMSELF ALL WEEK. WHENEVER I ASK EVA WHERE HE IS, SHE GIVES ME THE SAME ANSWER--
I AM MERELY HIS HOUSEKEEPER. I AM IN THE DARK REGARDING HIS PERSONAL MATTERS.
PERSONAL MATTERS? IS THAT WHAT SHE CALLS HIS EXPLOITS?!
HOW AM I SUPPOSED TO DRAW SUCH AN ELUSIVE SUBJECT?
I WANT TO GET THIS OVER WITH. THIS PLACE IS GETTING TOO...
...SURREAL!
LOOK OUT!

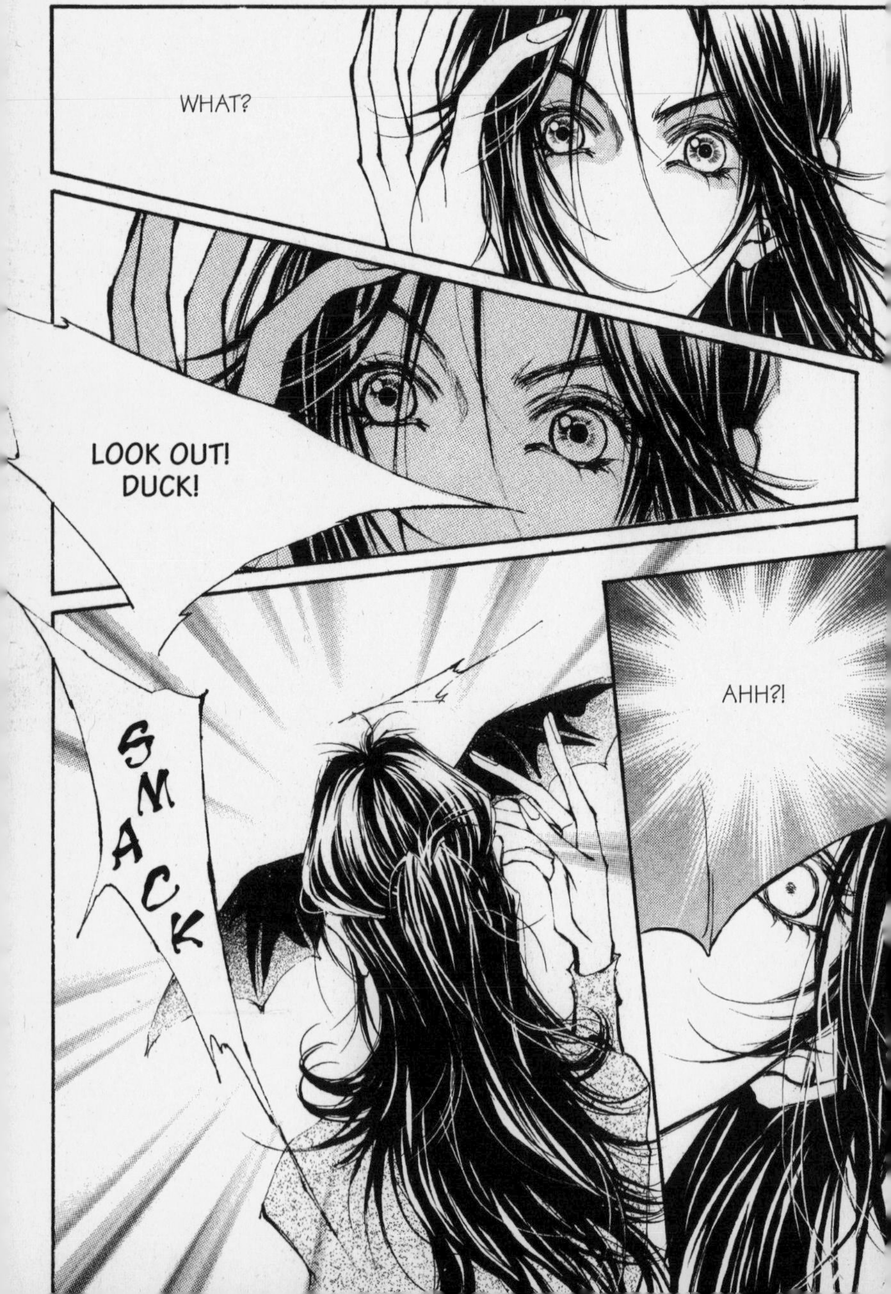
WHAT?
LOOK OUT! DUCK!
SMACK
AHH?!

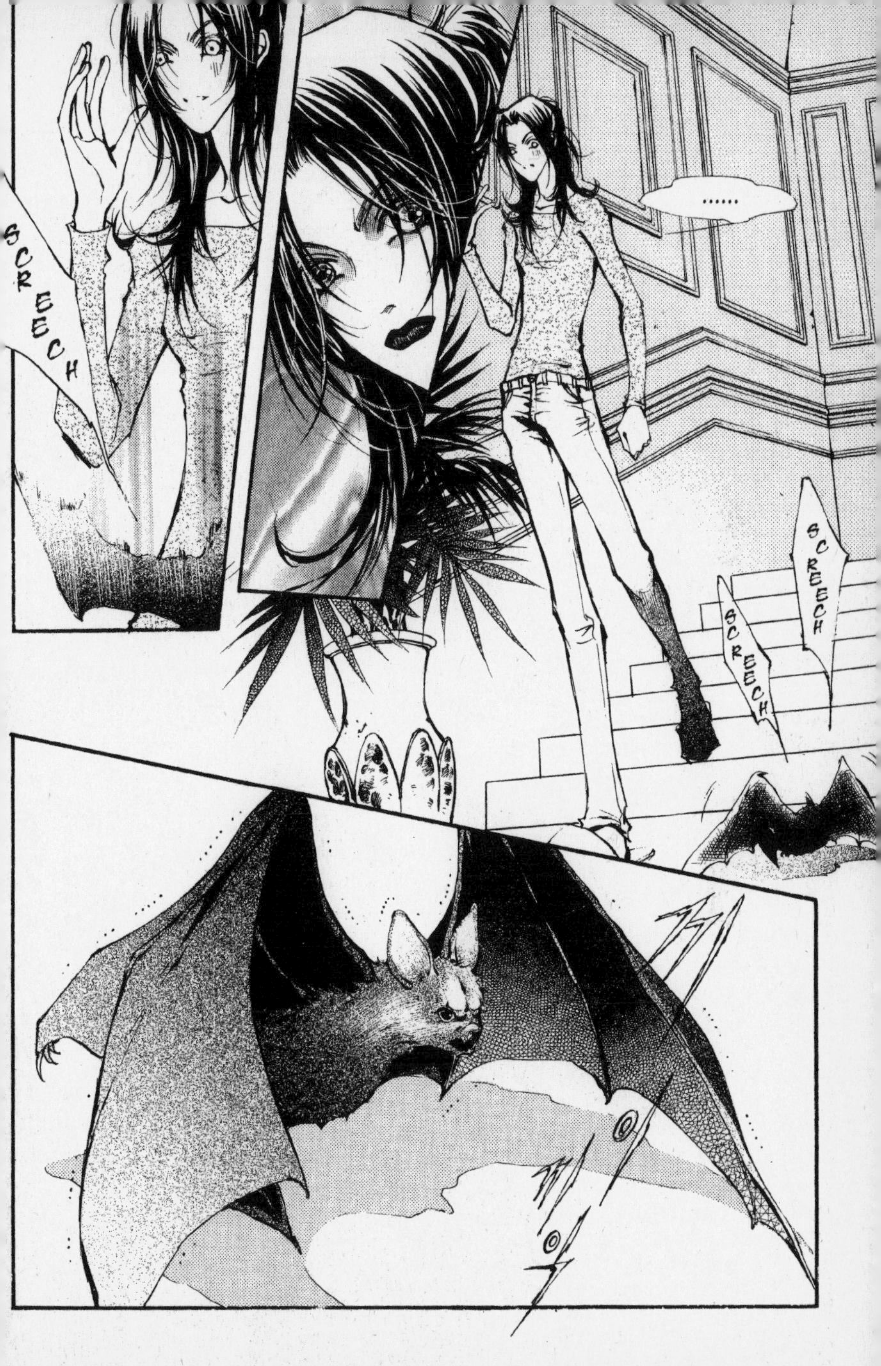
SCREECH
.......
SCREECH
SCREECH

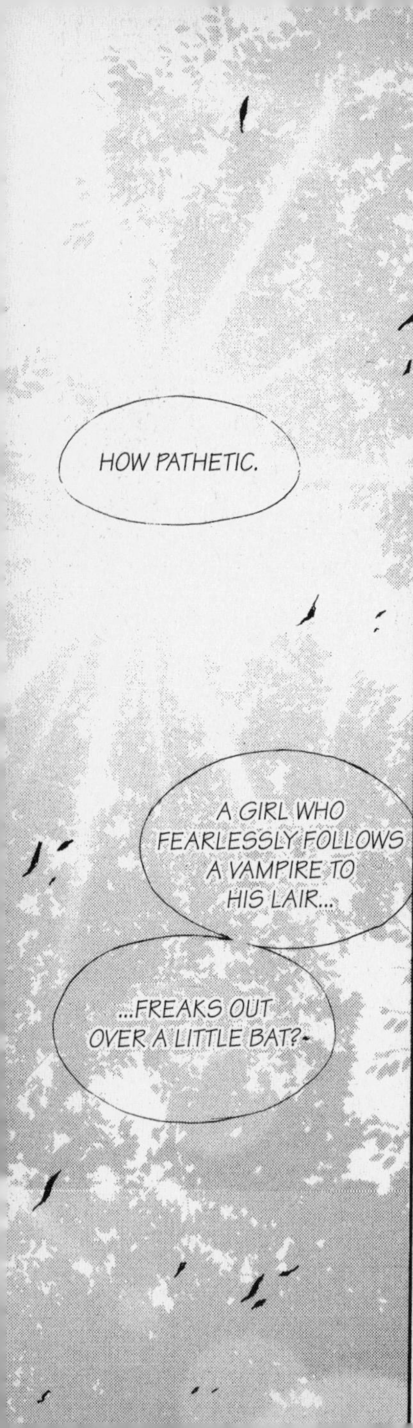
HOW PATHETIC.
A GIRL WHO FEARLESSLY FOLLOWS A VAMPIRE TO HIS LAIR...
...FREAKS OUT OVER A LITTLE BAT?

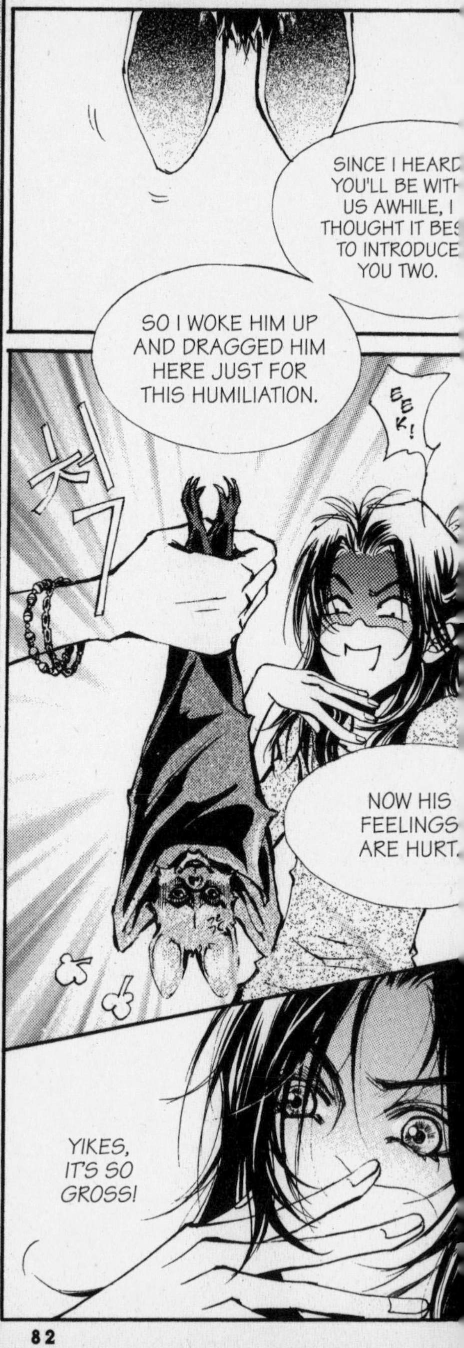
SINCE I HEARD YOU'LL BE WITH US AWHILE, I THOUGHT IT BEST TO INTRODUCE YOU TWO.
SO I WOKE HIM UP AND DRAGGED HIM HERE JUST FOR THIS HUMILIATION.
EEK!
NOW HIS FEELINGS ARE HURT.
YIKES, IT'S SO GROSS!

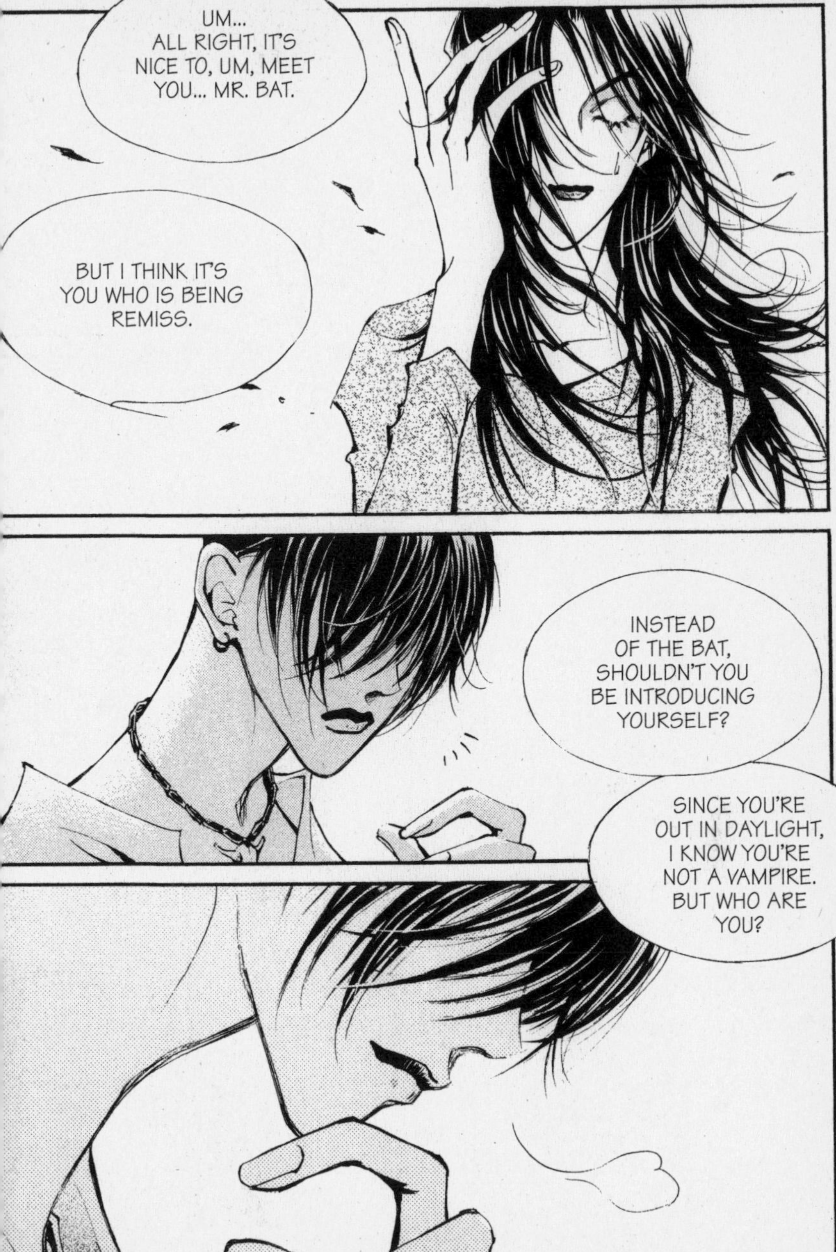
UM... ALL RIGHT, IT'S NICE TO, UM, MEET YOU... MR. BAT.
BUT I THINK IT'S YOU WHO IS BEING REMISS.
INSTEAD OF THE BAT, SHOULDN'T YOU BE INTRODUCING YOURSELF?
SINCE YOU'RE OUT IN DAYLIGHT, I KNOW YOU'RE NOT A VAMPIRE. BUT WHO ARE YOU?

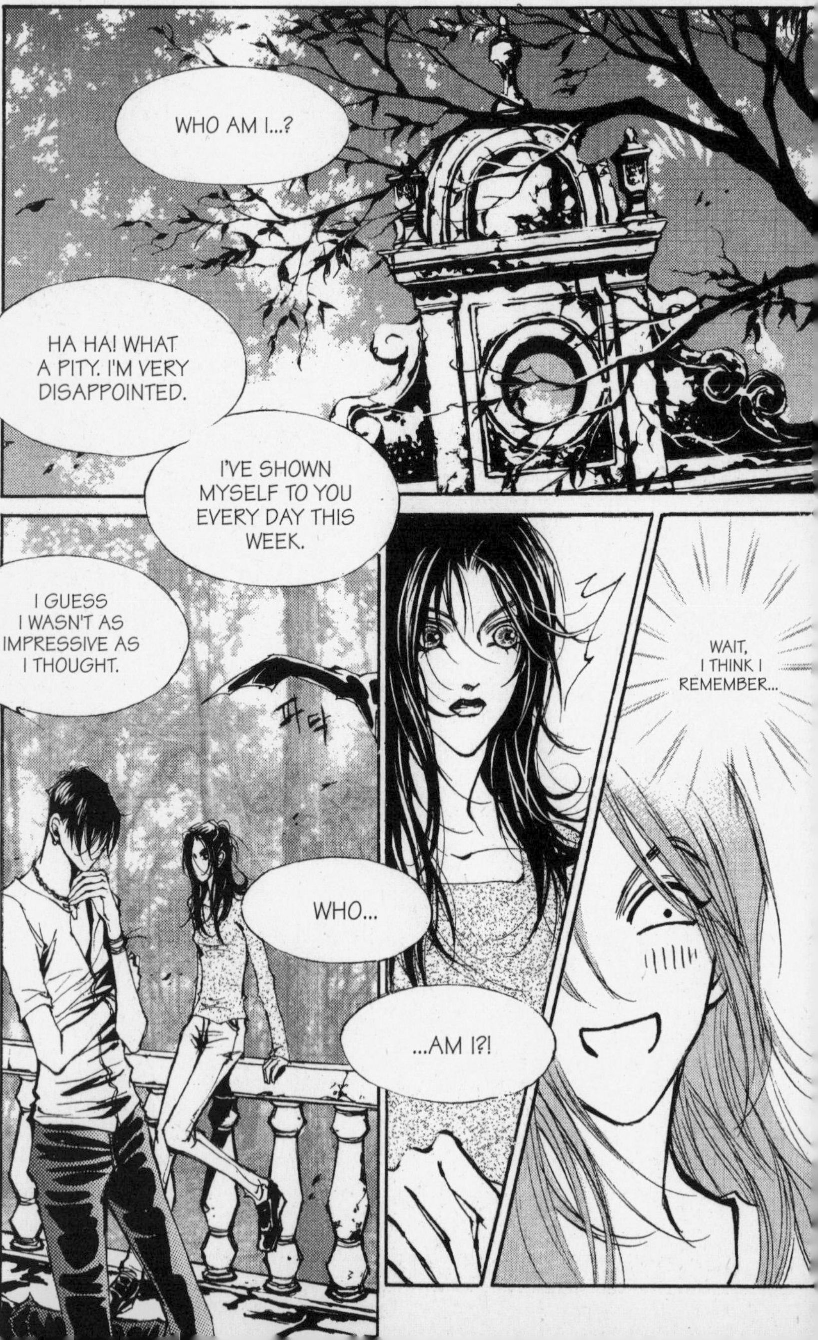
WHO AM I...?
HA HA! WHAT A PITY. I'M VERY DISAPPOINTED.
I'VE SHOWN MYSELF TO YOU EVERY DAY THIS WEEK.
I GUESS I WASN'T AS IMPRESSIVE AS I THOUGHT.
WHO...
...AM I?!
WAIT, I THINK I REMEMBER...

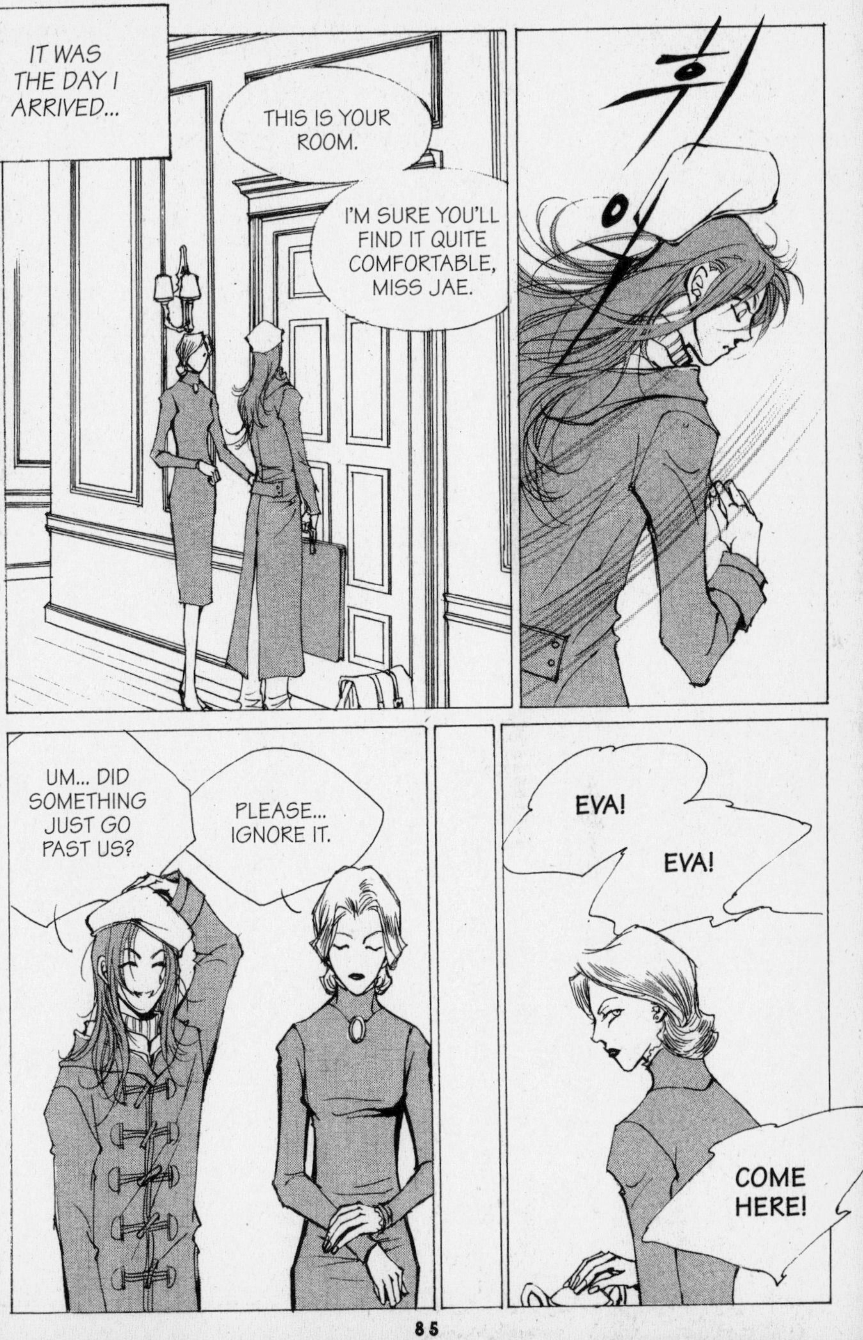
IT WAS THE DAY I ARRIVED...
THIS IS YOUR ROOM.
I'M SURE YOU'LL FIND IT QUITE COMFORTABLE, MISS JAE.
UM... DID SOMETHING JUST GO PAST US?
PLEASE... IGNORE IT.
EVA!
EVA!
COME HERE!

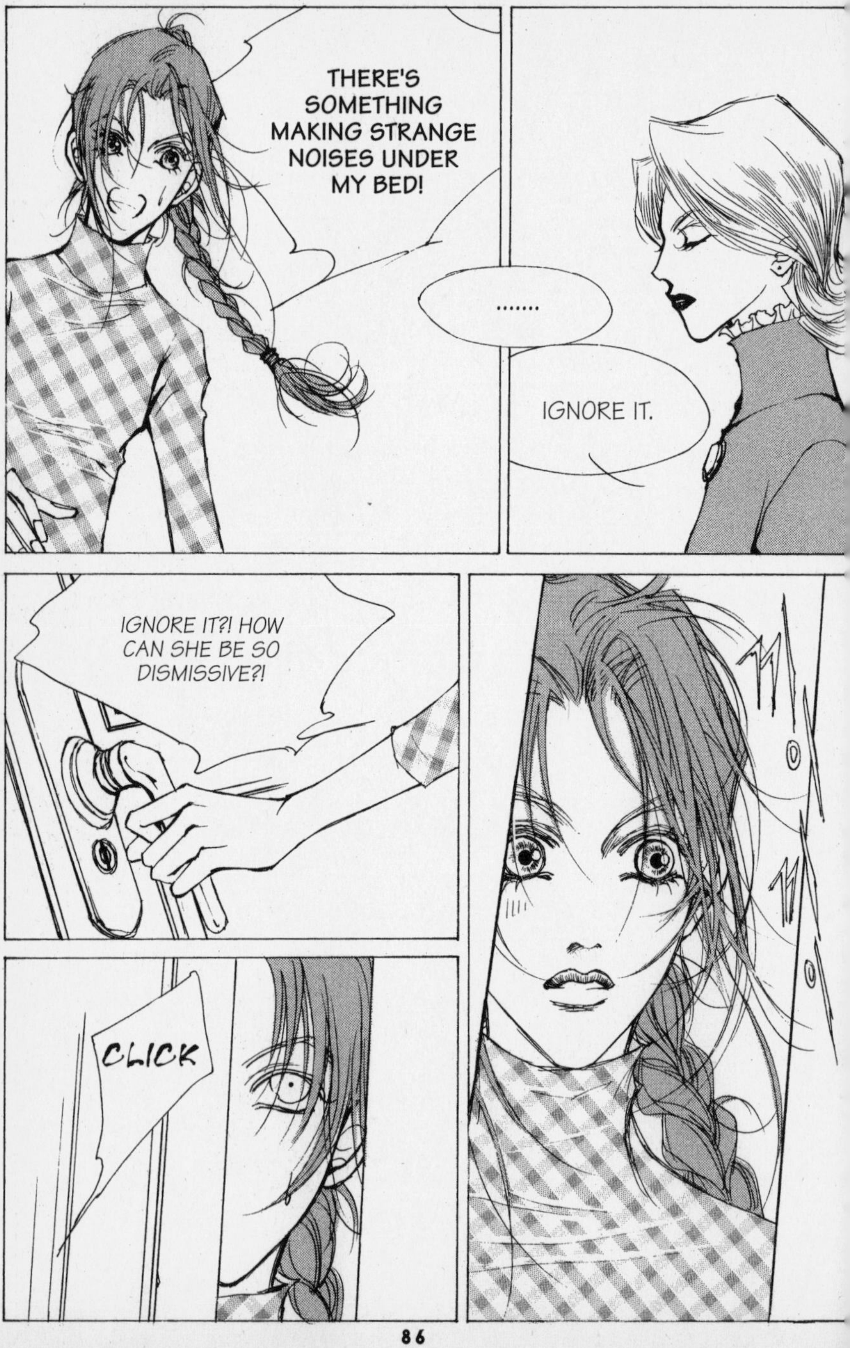
THERE'S SOMETHING MAKING STRANGE NOISES UNDER MY BED!
.......
IGNORE IT.
IGNORE IT?! HOW CAN SHE BE SO DISMISSIVE?!
CLICK

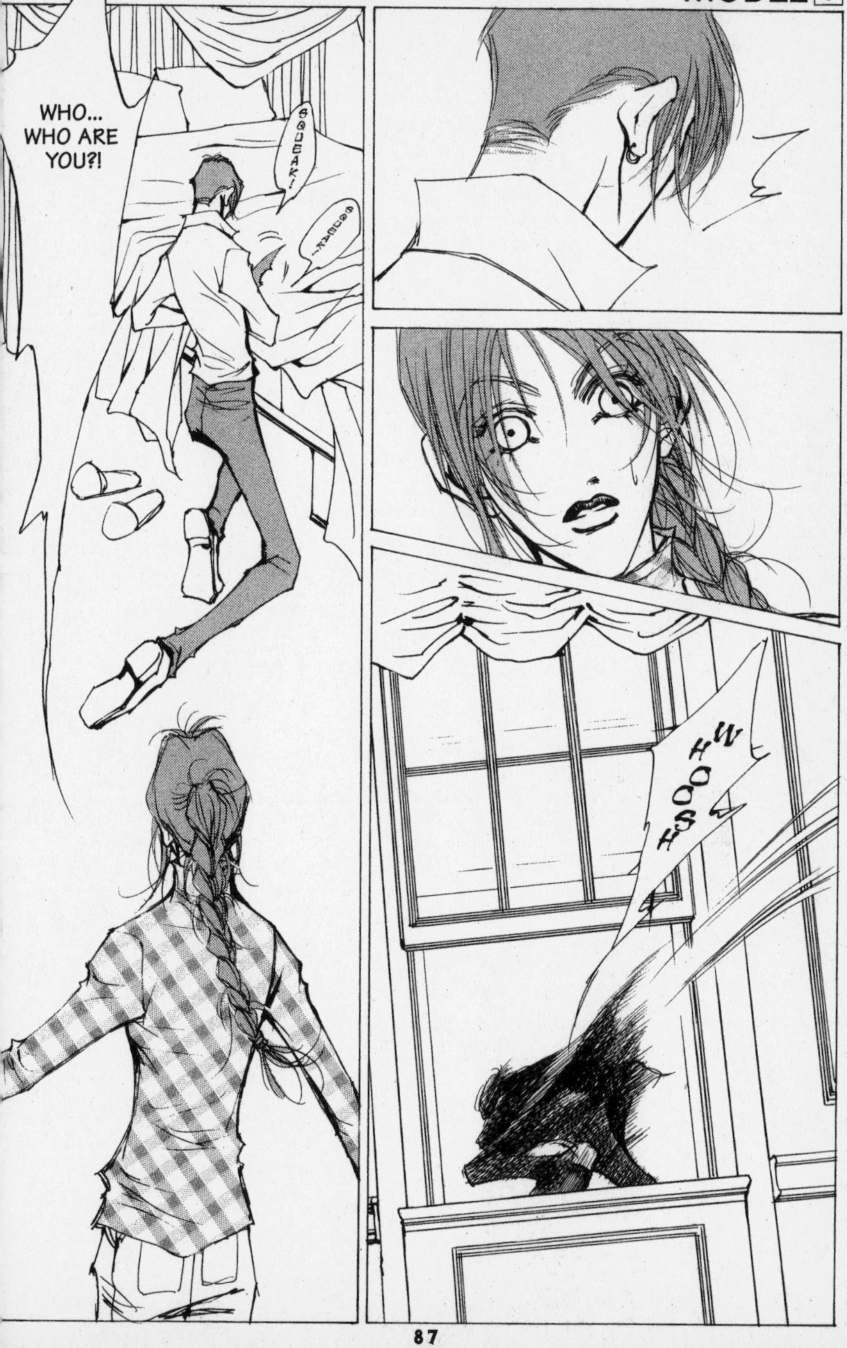
WHO... WHO ARE YOU?!
SQUEAK!
SQUEAK!
WHOOSH

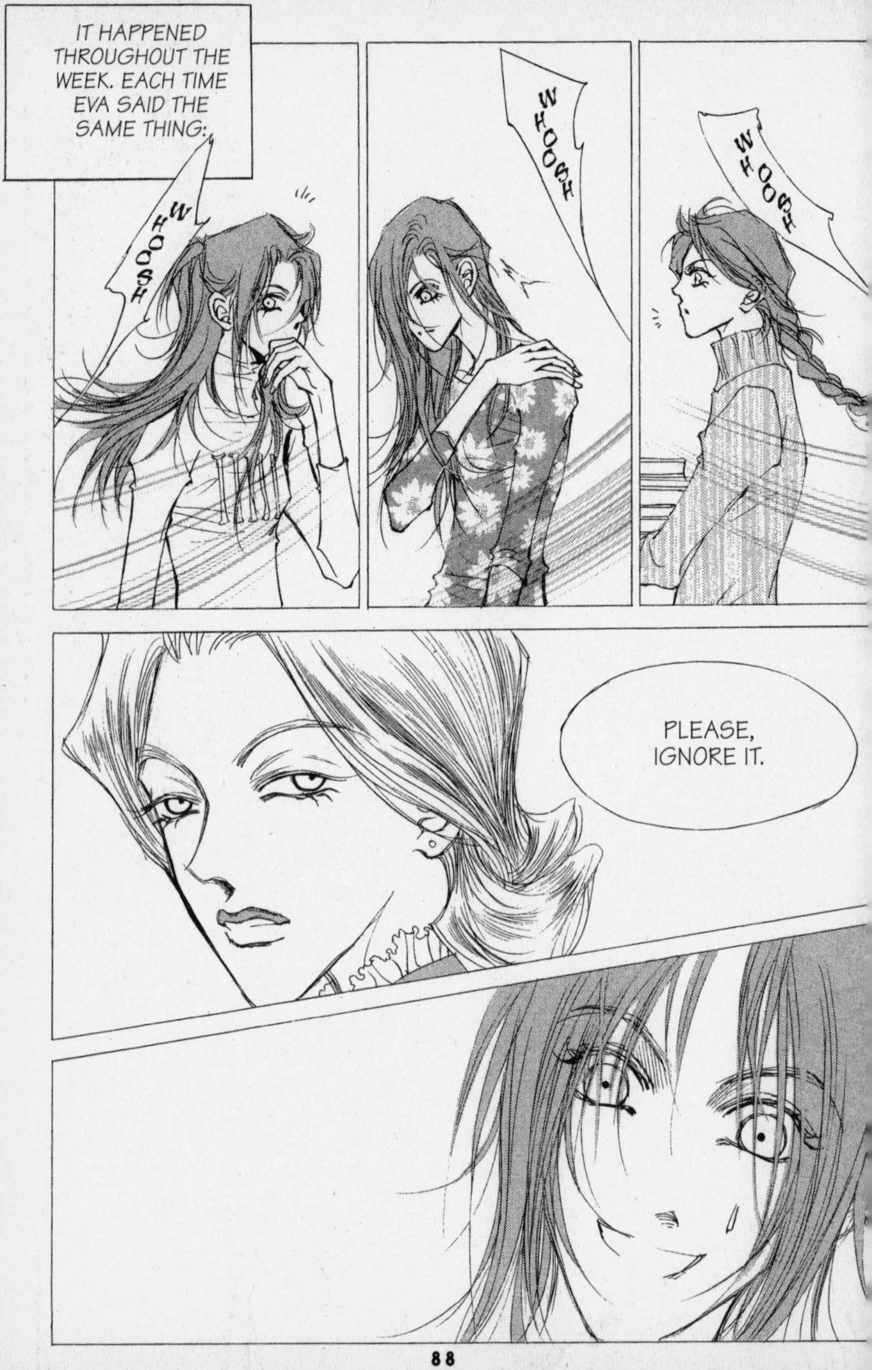
IT HAPPENED THROUGHOUT THE WEEK. EACH TIME EVA SAID THE SAME THING:
WHOOSH
WHOOSH
WHOOSH
PLEASE, IGNORE IT.

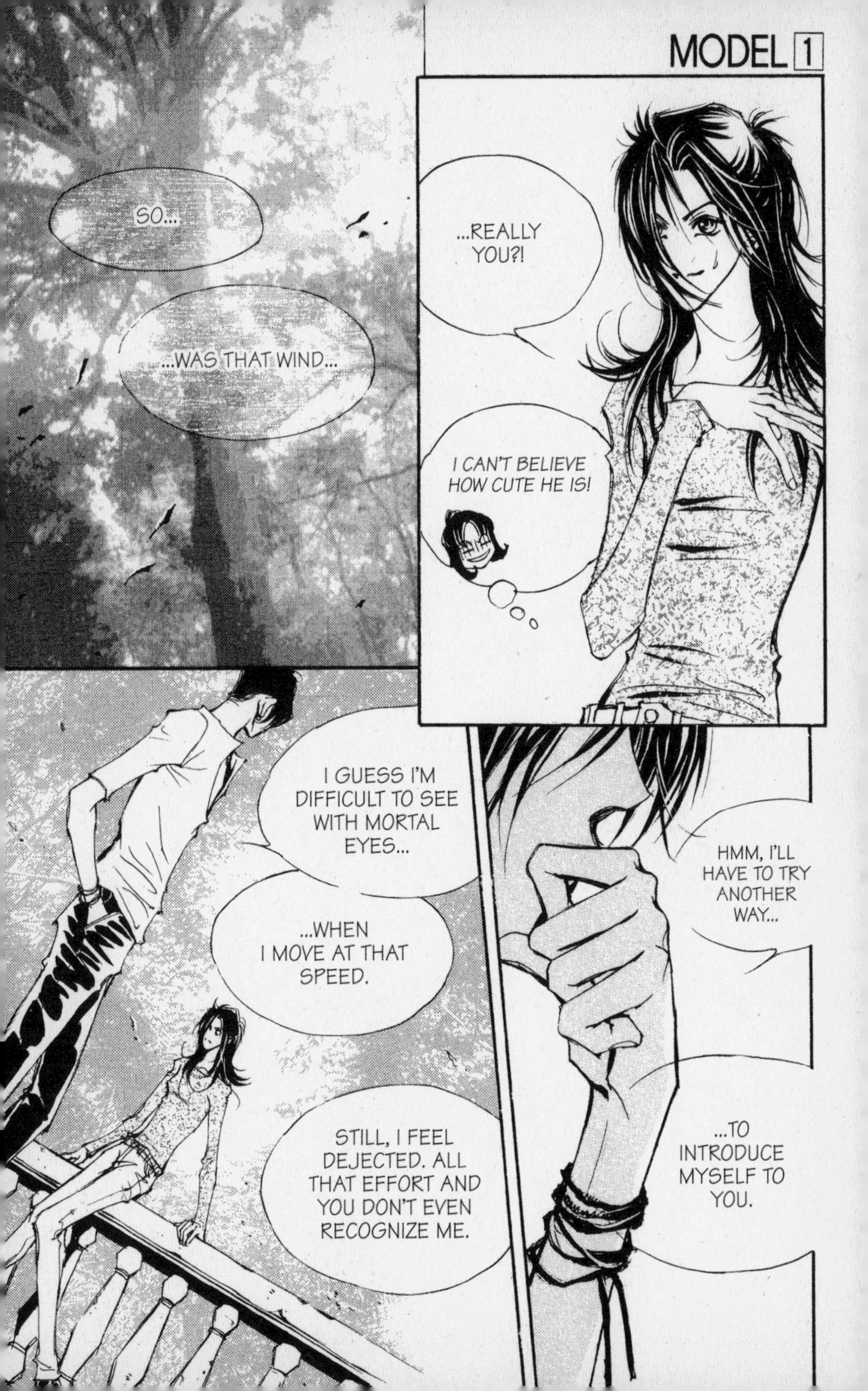
SO...
...WAS THAT WIND...
...REALLY YOU?!
I CAN'T BELIEVE HOW CUTE HE IS!
I GUESS I'M DIFFICULT TO SEE WITH MORTAL EYES...
...WHEN I MOVE AT THAT SPEED.
STILL, I FEEL DEJECTED. ALL THAT EFFORT AND YOU DON'T EVEN RECOGNIZE ME.
HMM, I'LL HAVE TO TRY ANOTHER WAY...
...TO INTRODUCE MYSELF TO YOU.

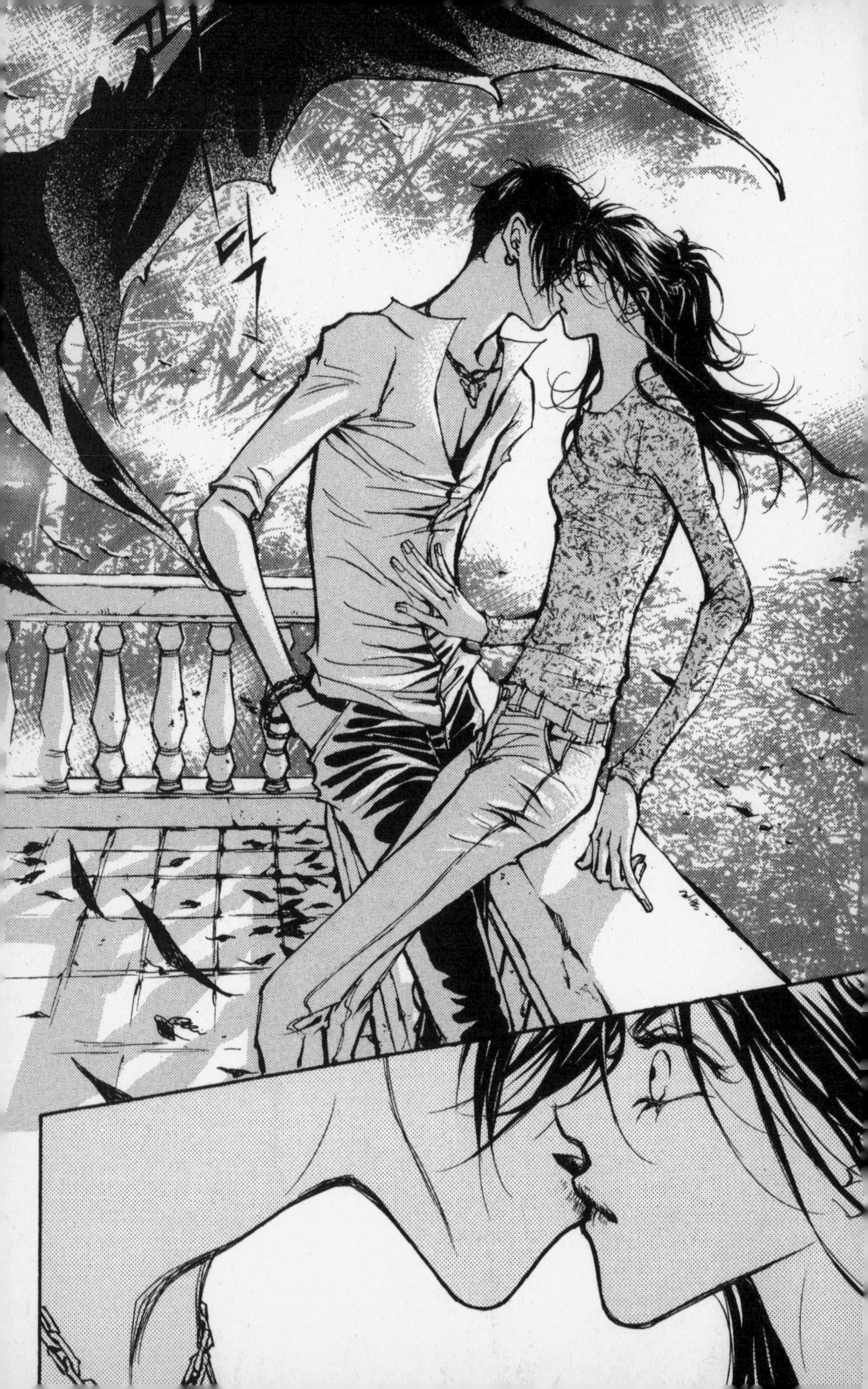

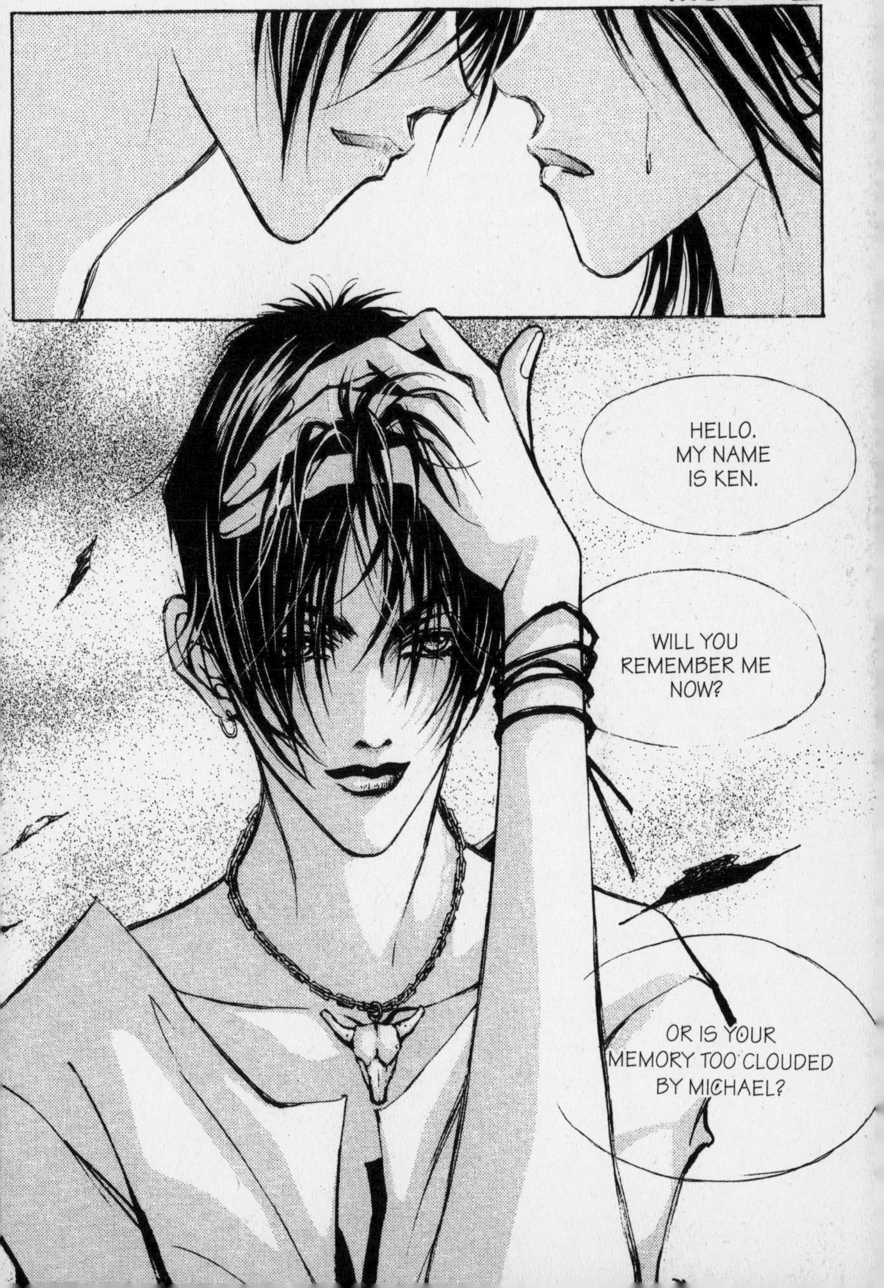
HELLO. MY NAME IS KEN.
WILL YOU REMEMBER ME NOW?
OR IS YOUR MEMORY TOO CLOUDED BY MICHAEL?

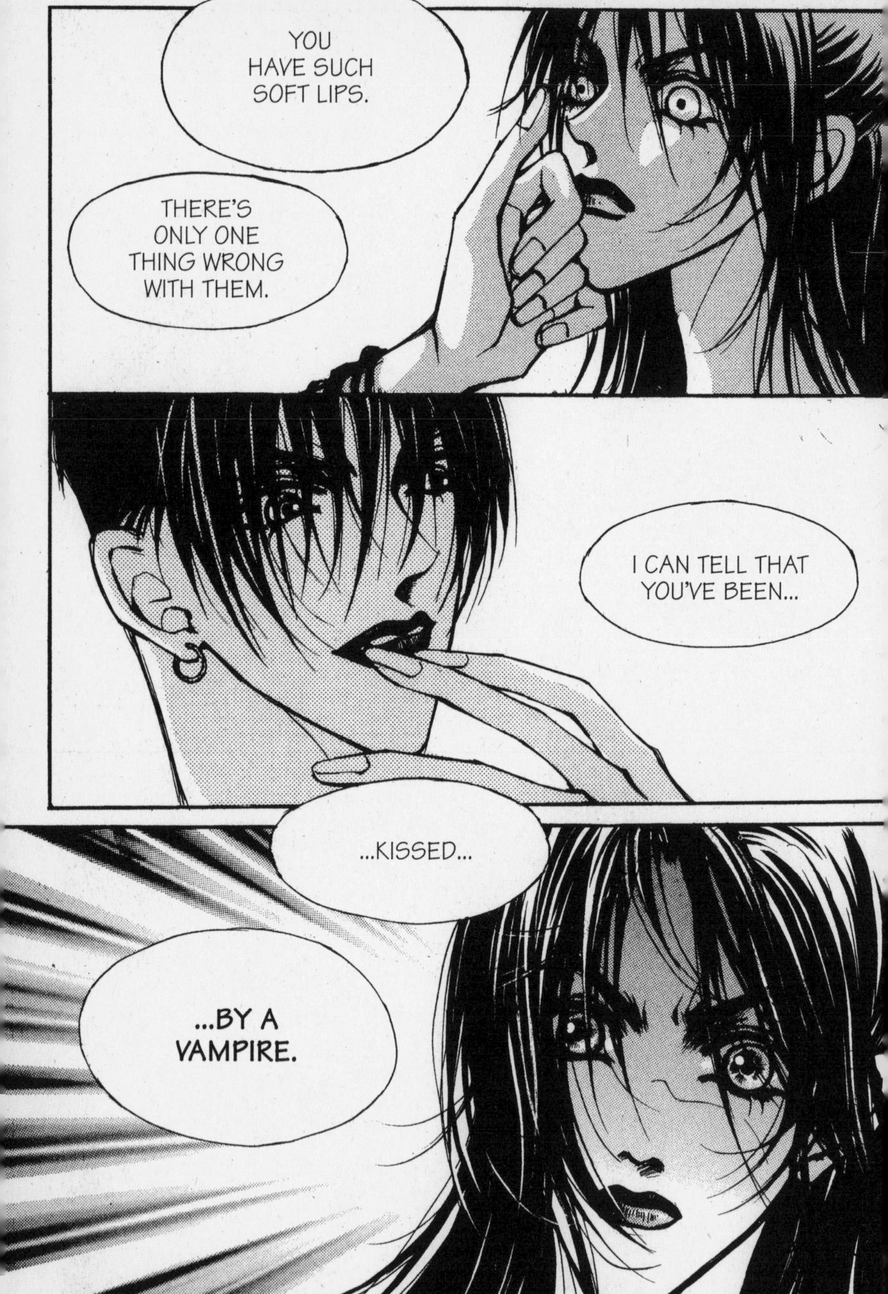
YOU HAVE SUCH SOFT LIPS.
THERE'S ONLY ONE THING WRONG WITH THEM.
I CAN TELL THAT YOU'VE BEEN...
...KISSED...
...BY A VAMPIRE.

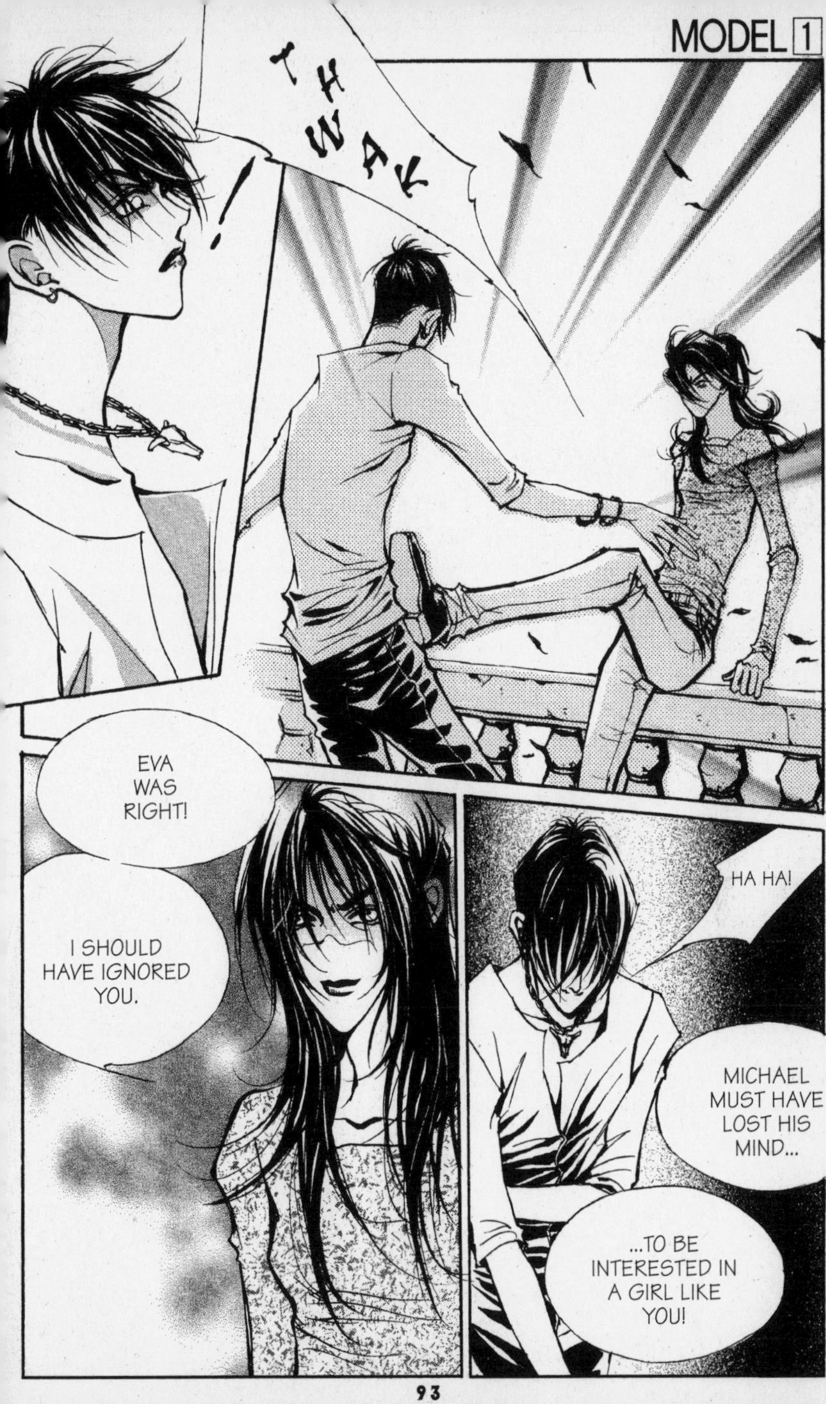
THWAK
!
EVA WAS RIGHT!
I SHOULD HAVE IGNORED YOU.
HA HA!
MICHAEL MUST HAVE LOST HIS MIND...
...TO BE INTERESTED IN A GIRL LIKE YOU!

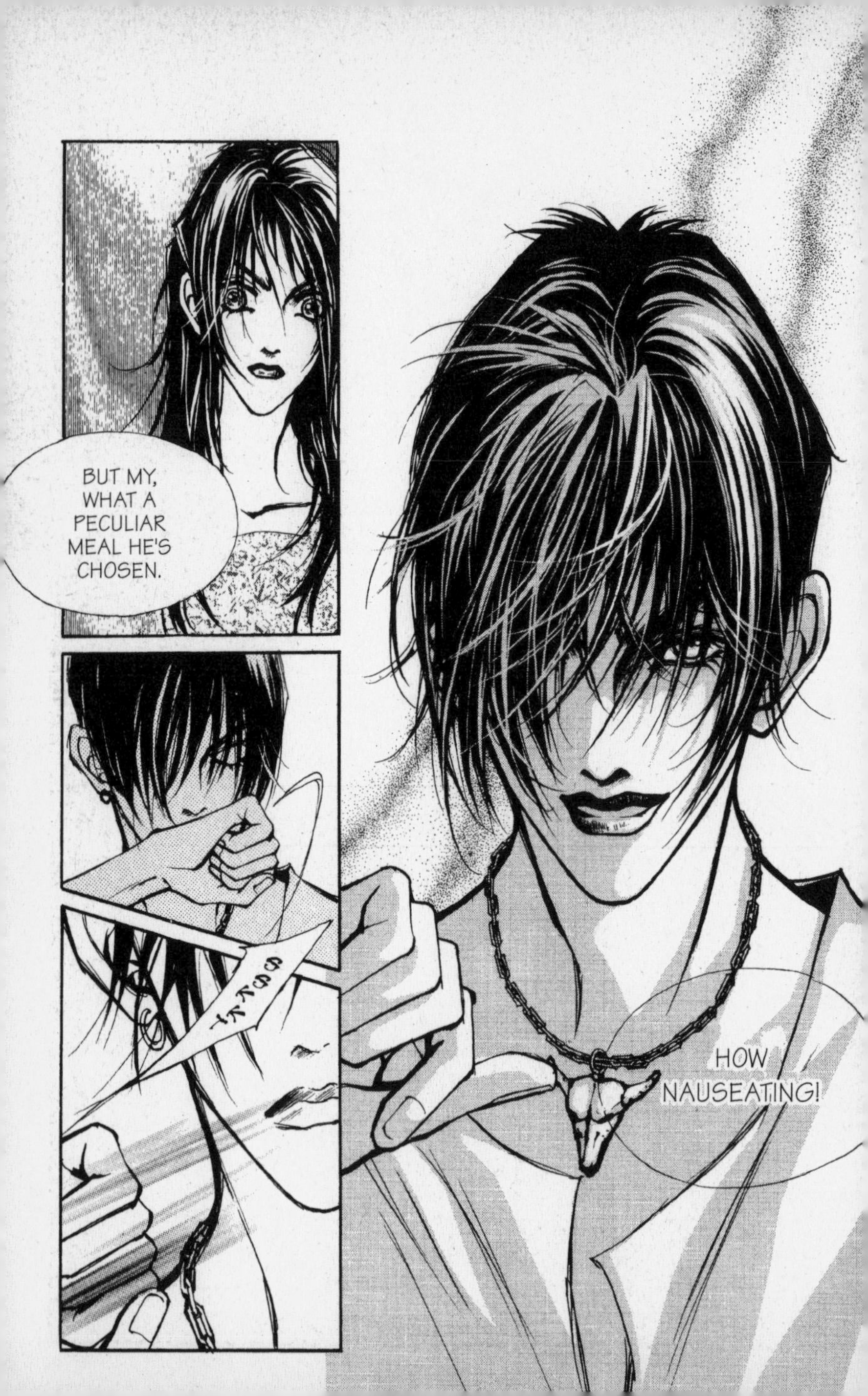
BUT MY, WHAT A PECULIAR MEAL HE'S CHOSEN.
HOW NAUSEATING!

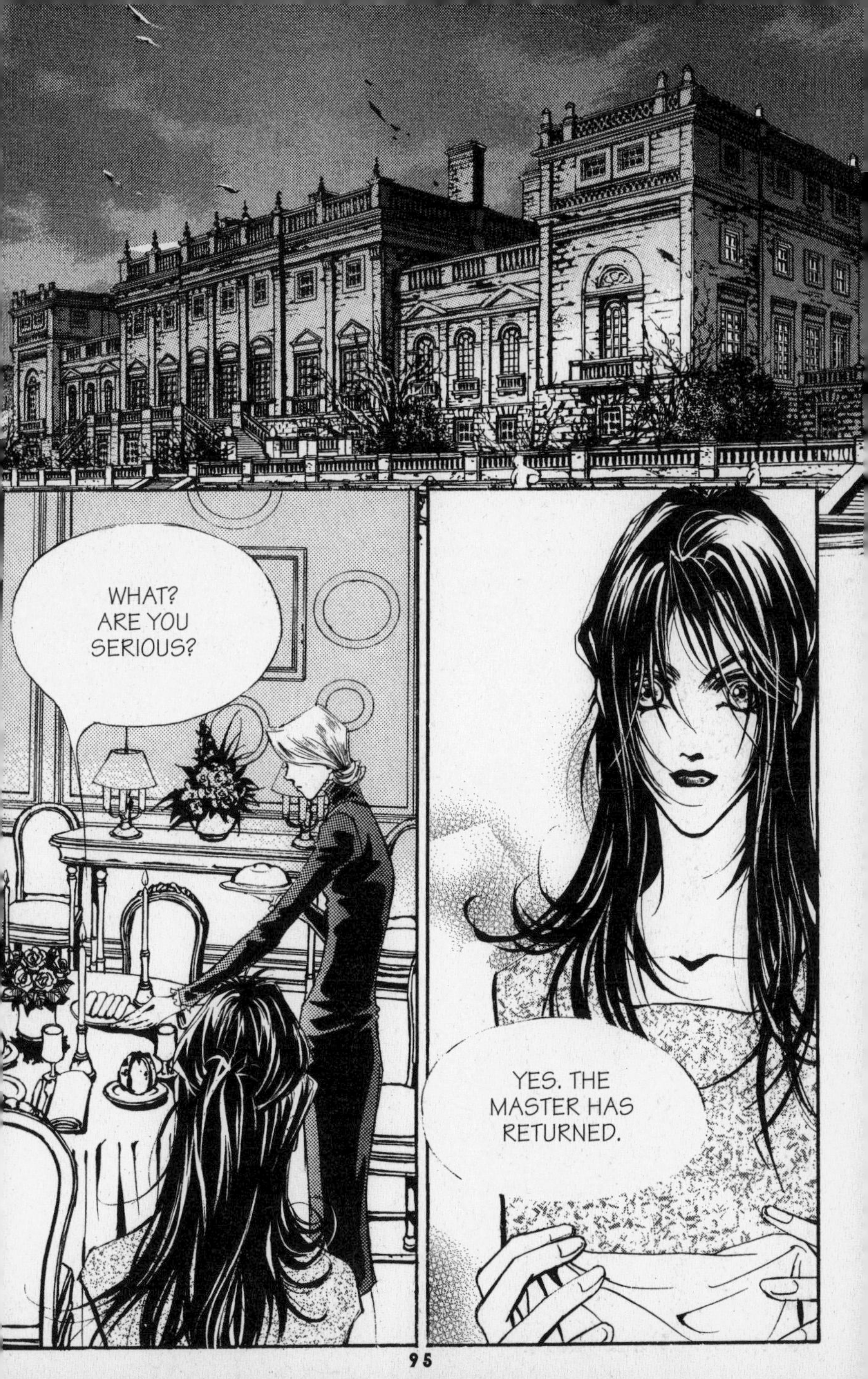
WHAT? ARE YOU SERIOUS?
YES. THE MASTER HAS RETURNED.

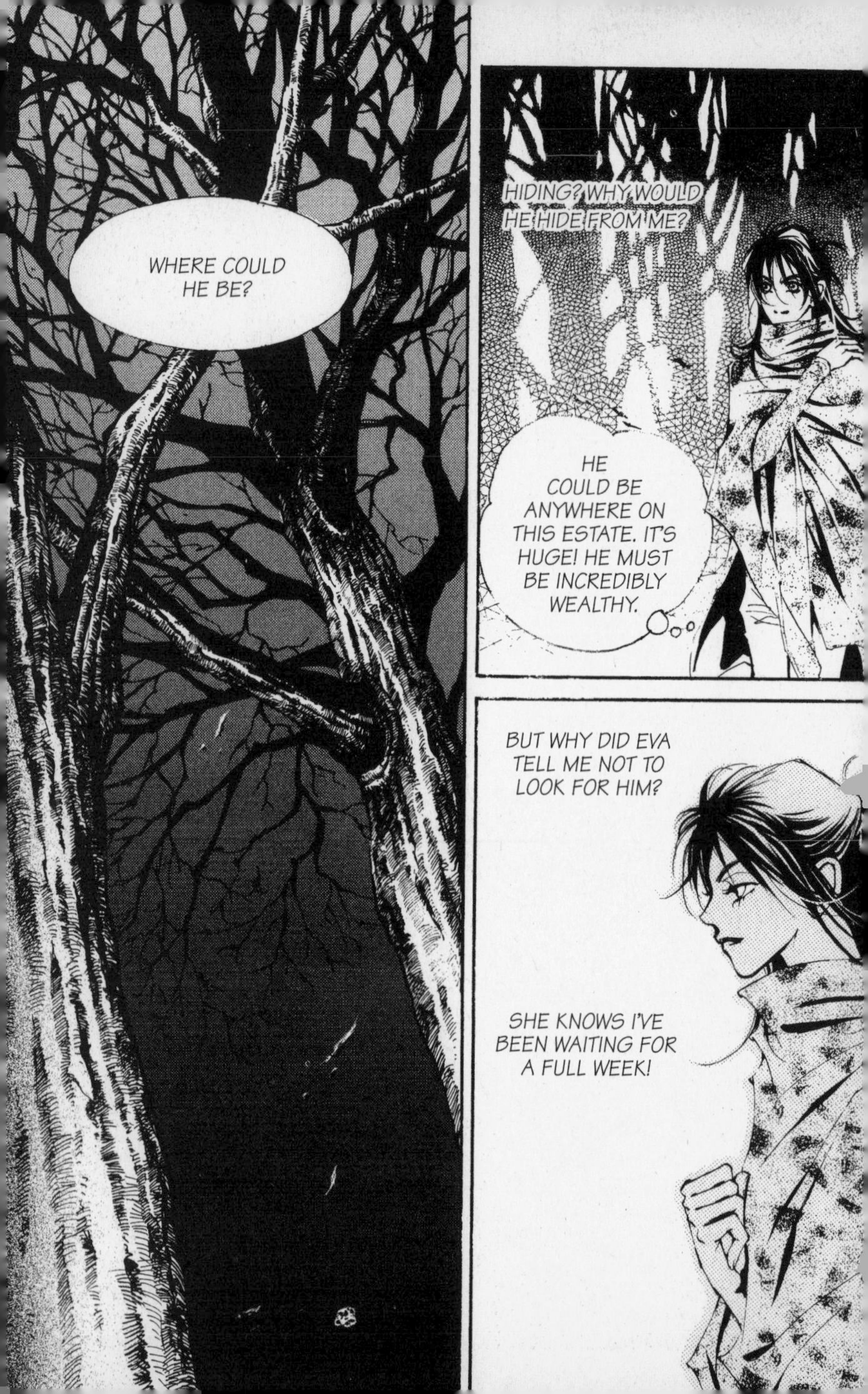
WHERE COULD HE BE?
HIDING? WHY WOULD HE HIDE FROM ME?
HE COULD BE ANYWHERE ON THIS ESTATE. IT'S HUGE! HE MUST BE INCREDIBLY WEALTHY.
BUT WHY DID EVA TELL ME NOT TO LOOK FOR HIM?
SHE KNOWS I'VE BEEN WAITING FOR A FULL WEEK!

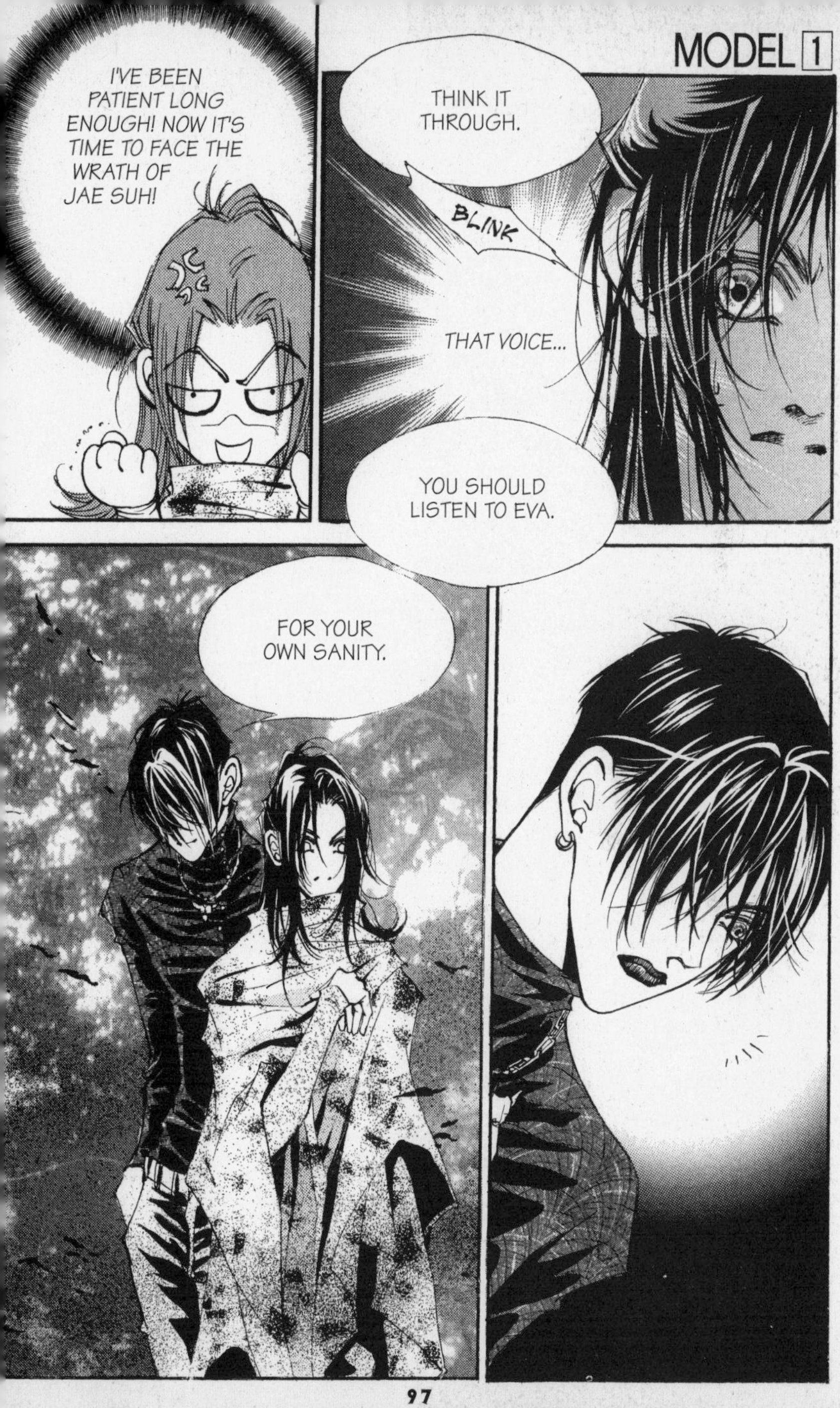
I'VE BEEN PATIENT LONG ENOUGH! NOW IT'S TIME TO FACE THE WRATH OF JAE SUH!
THINK IT THROUGH.
BLINK
THAT VOICE...
YOU SHOULD LISTEN TO EVA.
FOR YOUR OWN SANITY.

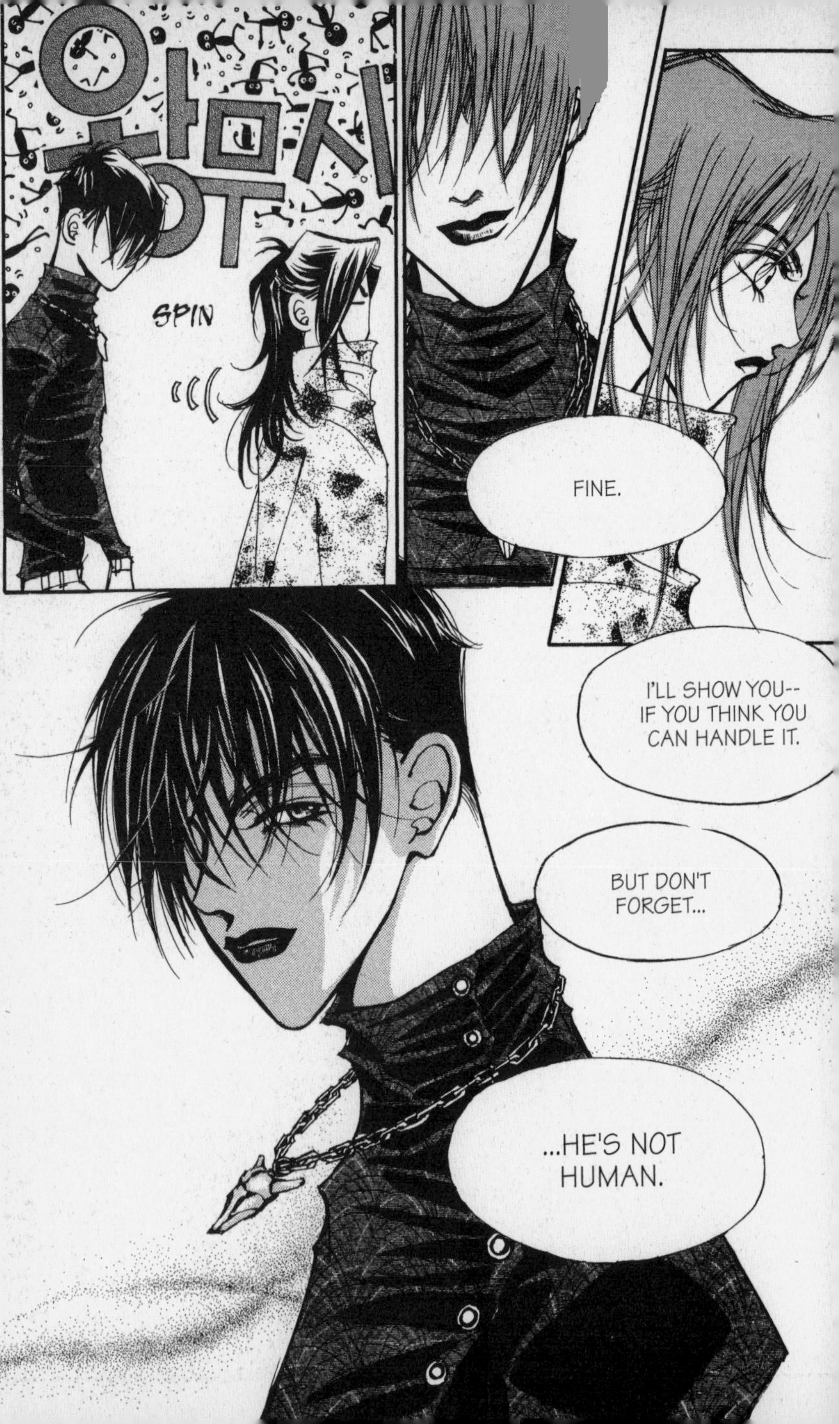
SPIN
FINE.
I'LL SHOW YOU-- IF YOU THINK YOU CAN HANDLE IT.
BUT DON'T FORGET...
...HE'S NOT HUMAN.

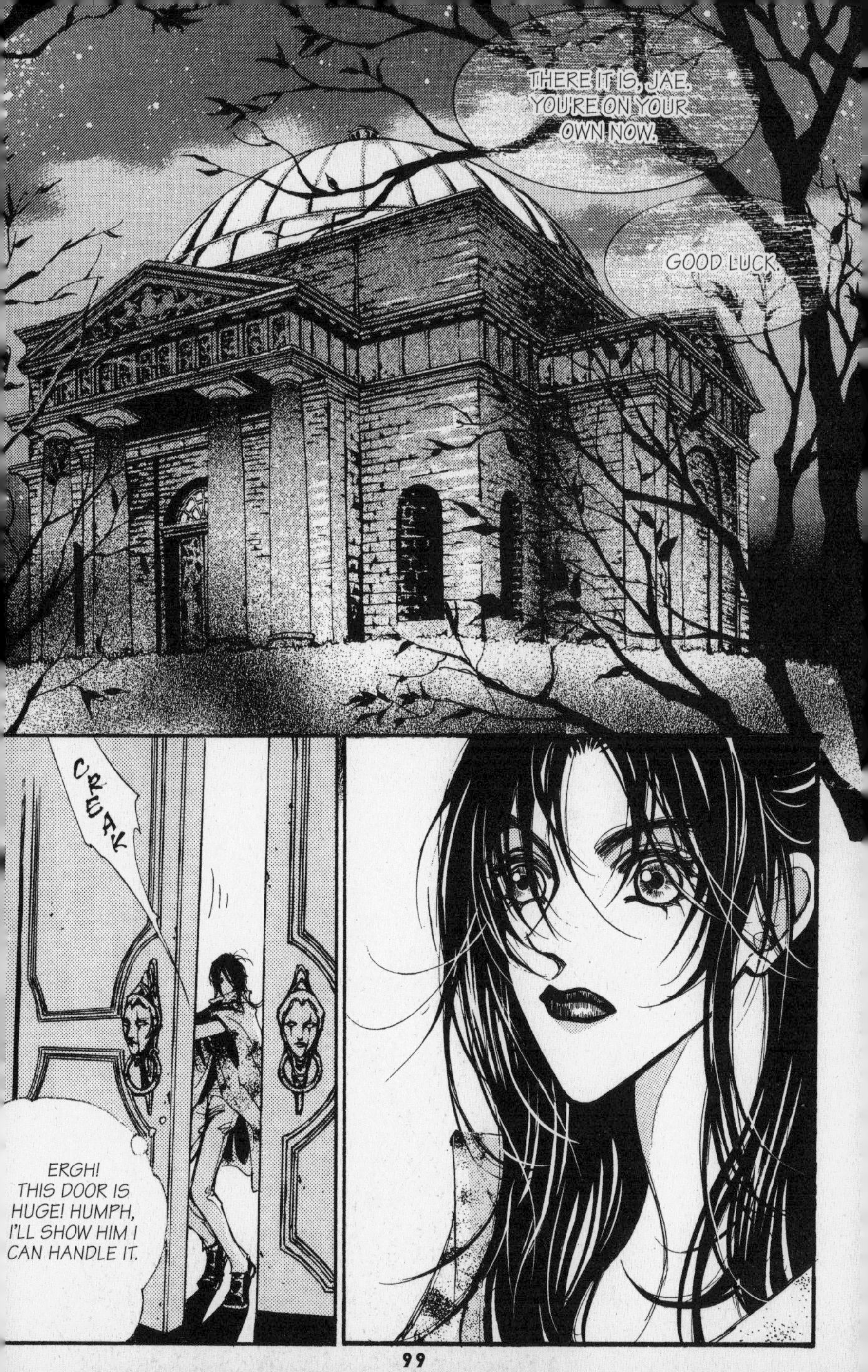
THERE IT IS, JAE. YOU'RE ON YOUR OWN NOW.
GOOD LUCK.
CREAK
ERGH! THIS DOOR IS HUGE! HUMPH, I'LL SHOW HIM I CAN HANDLE IT.

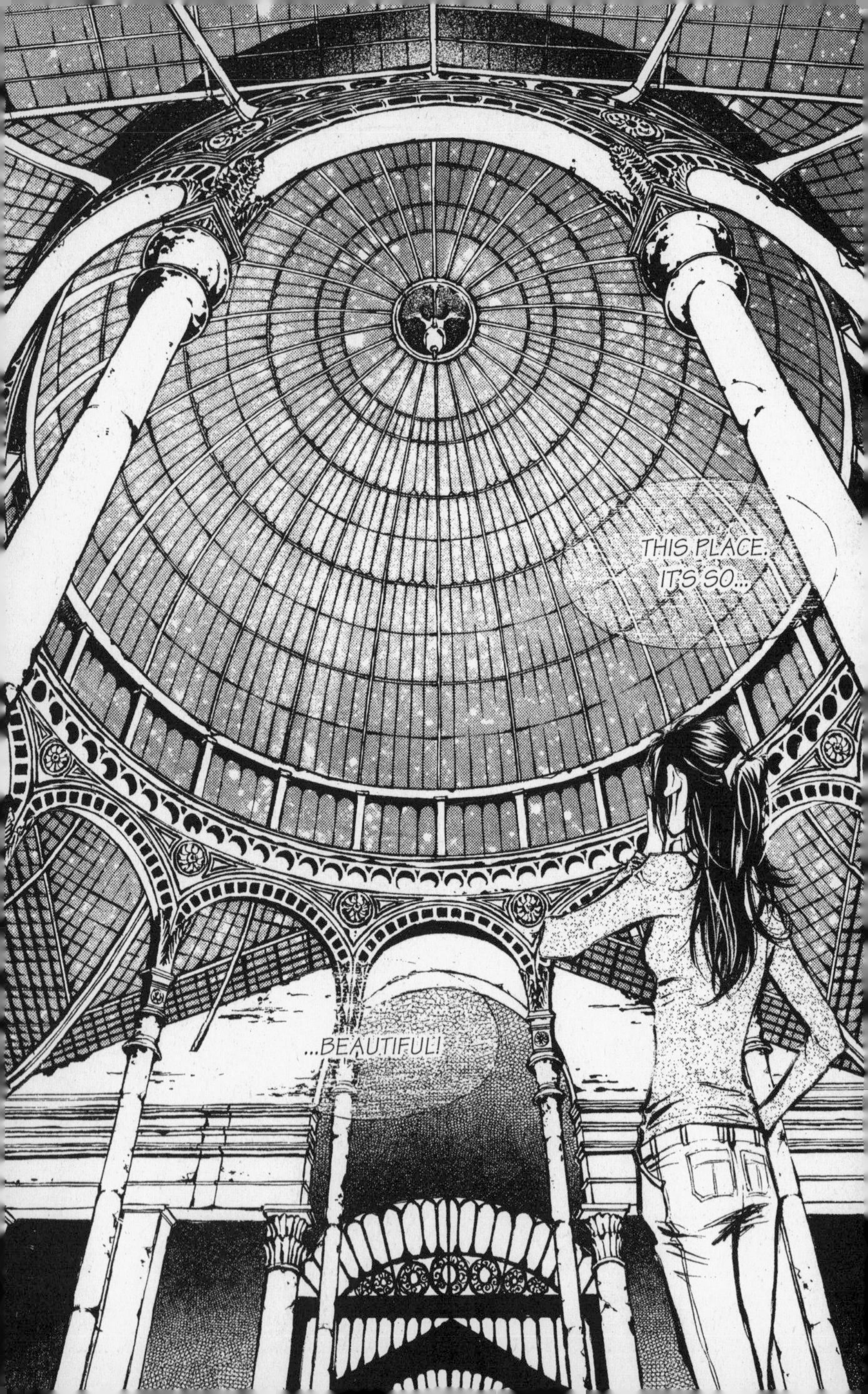
THIS PLACE. IT'S SO...
...BEAUTIFUL!

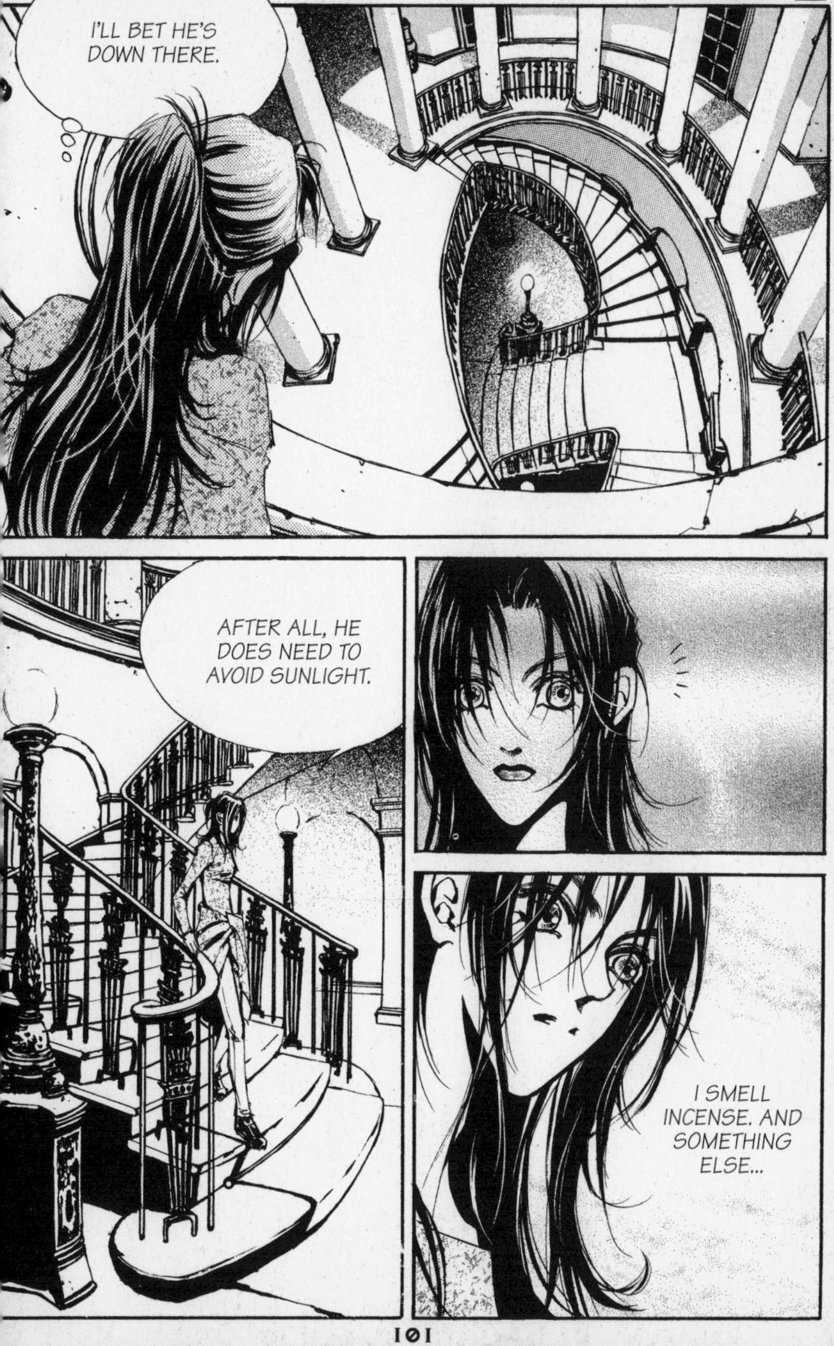
I'LL BET HE'S DOWN THERE.
AFTER ALL, HE DOES NEED TO AVOID SUNLIGHT.
I SMELL INCENSE. AND SOMETHING ELSE...

WHOA! WHAT STRANGE STATUES. THIS PLACE IS SO CLUTTERED.

AND IT SMELLS FUNKY.

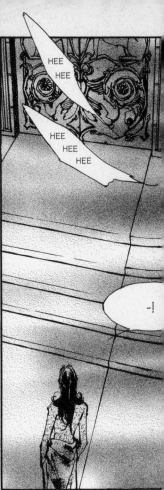

HEE HEE

HEE HEE HEE

-!

A WOMAN'S VOICE?

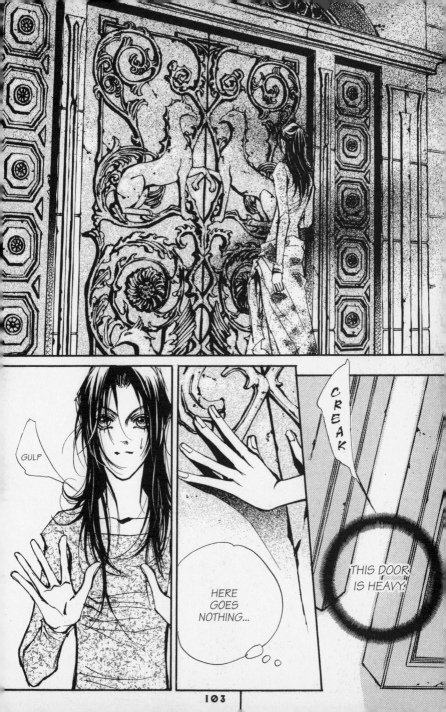

GULP

HERE GOES NOTHING...

C R E A K

THIS DOOR IS HEAVY.

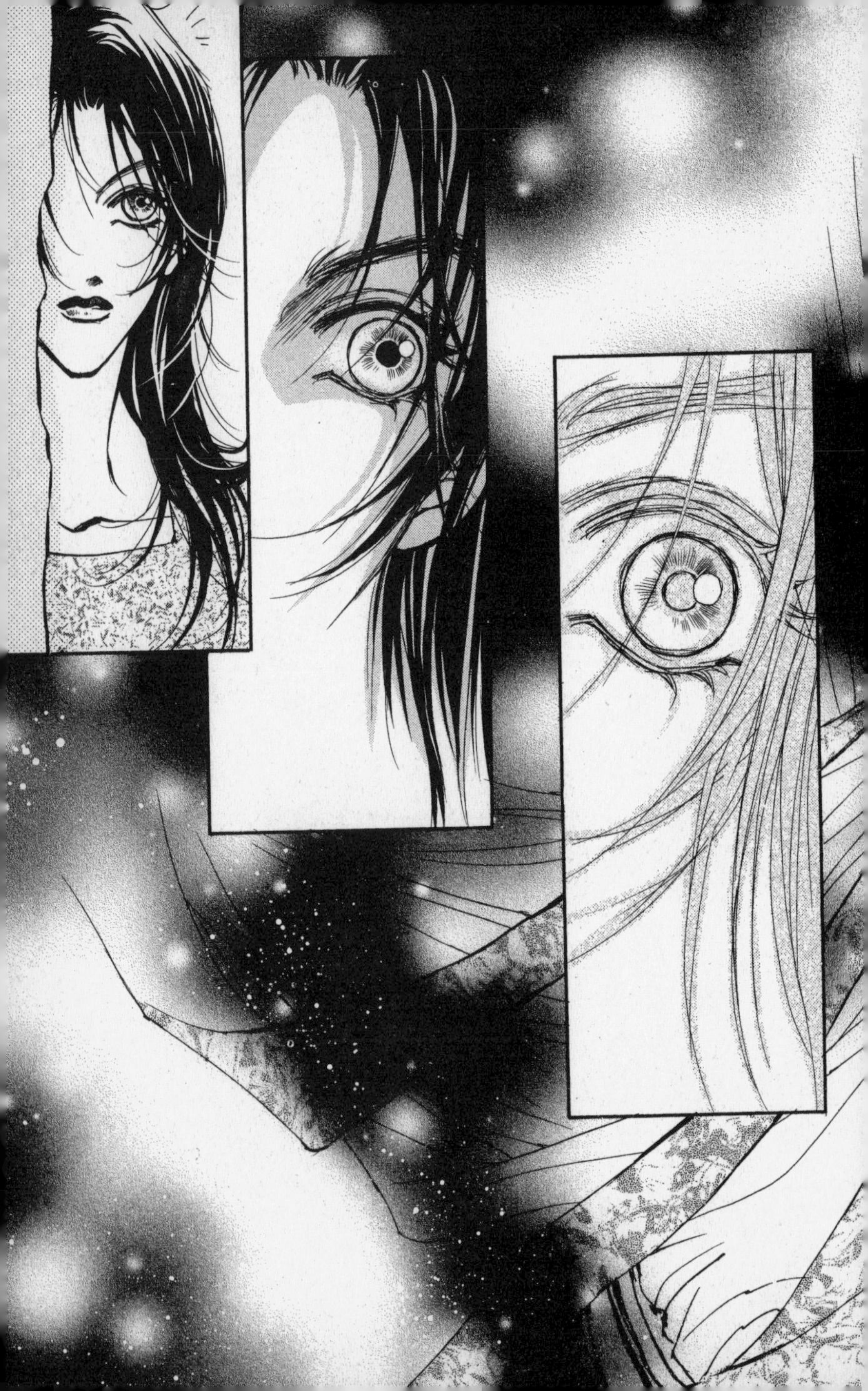

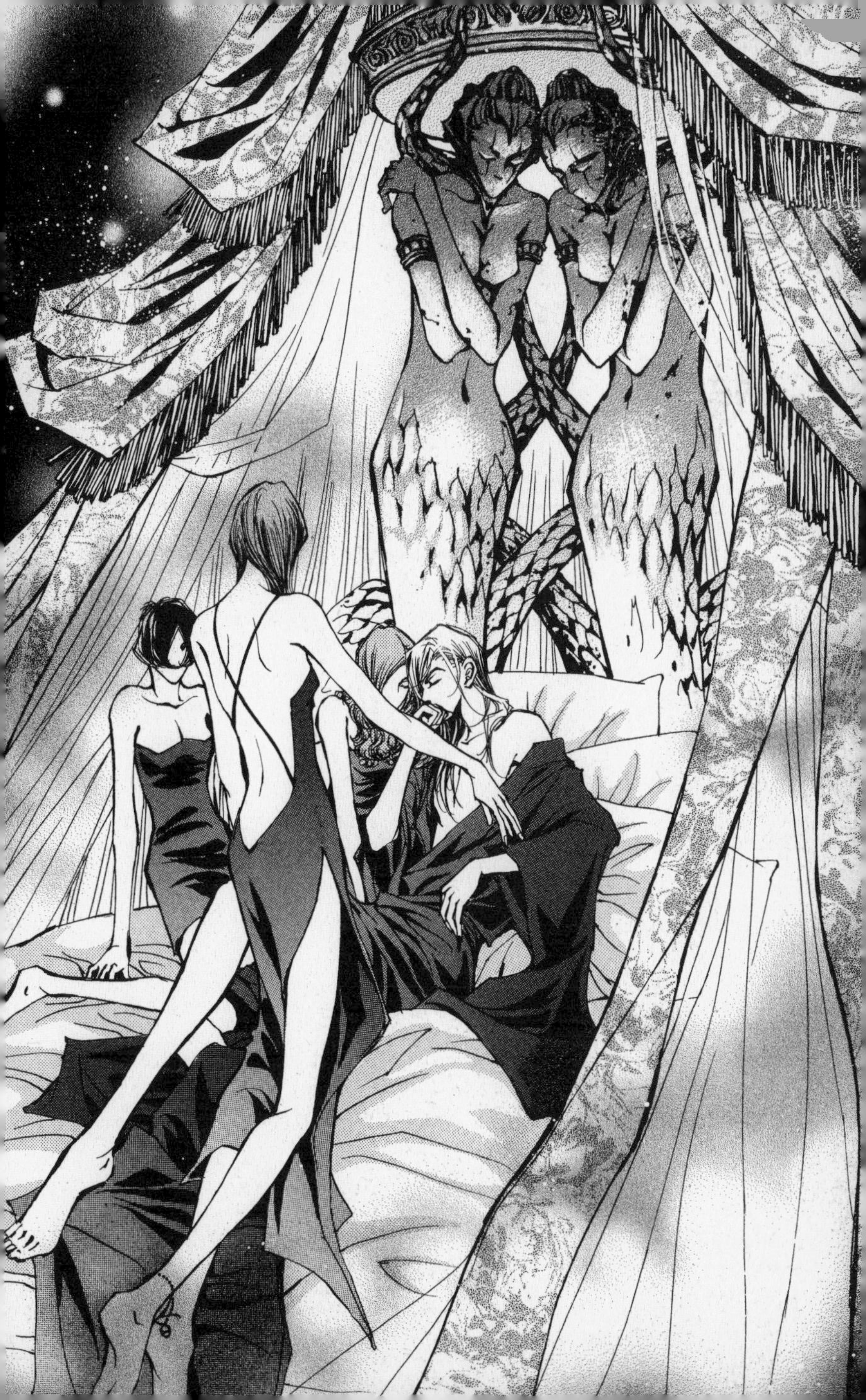

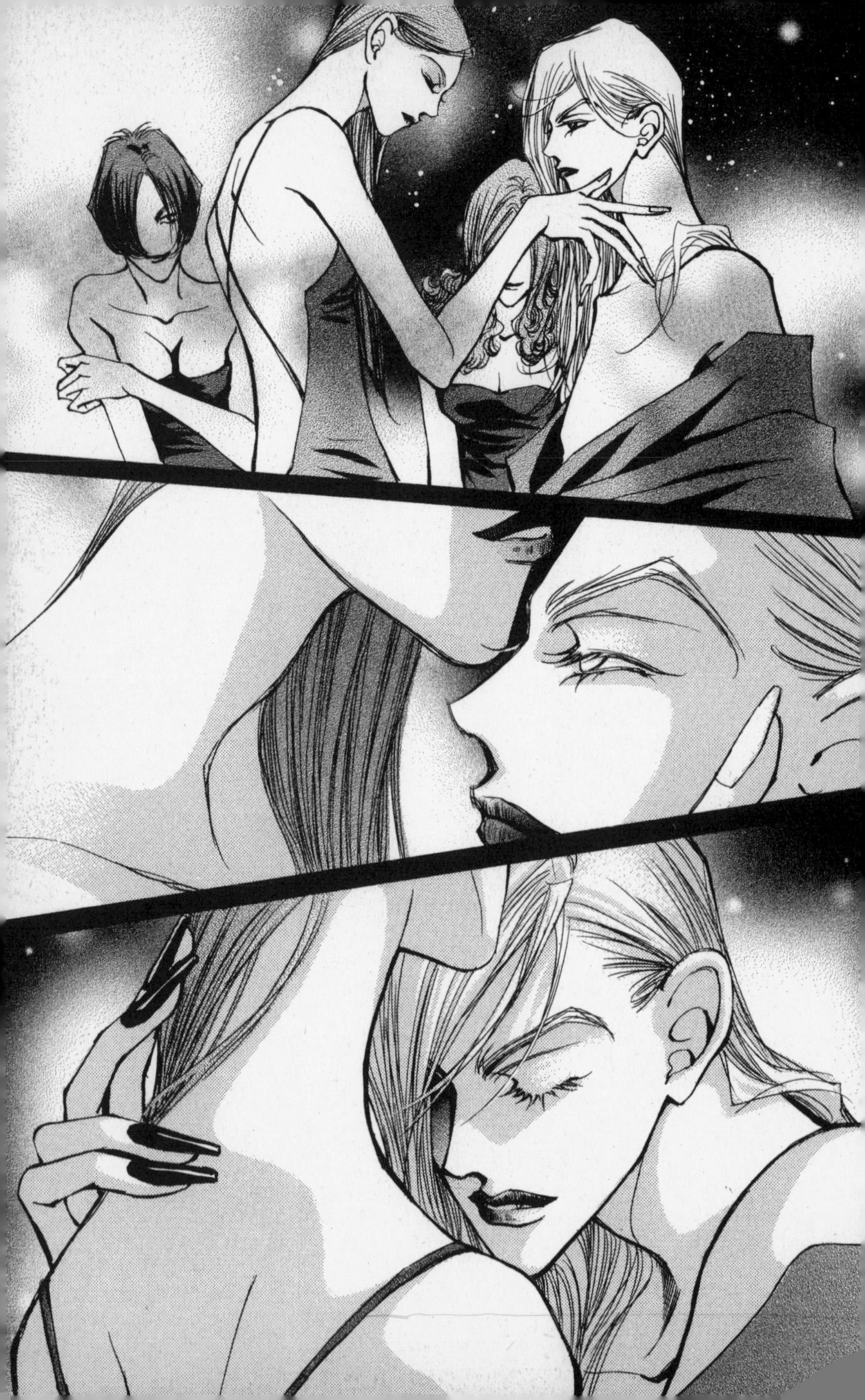

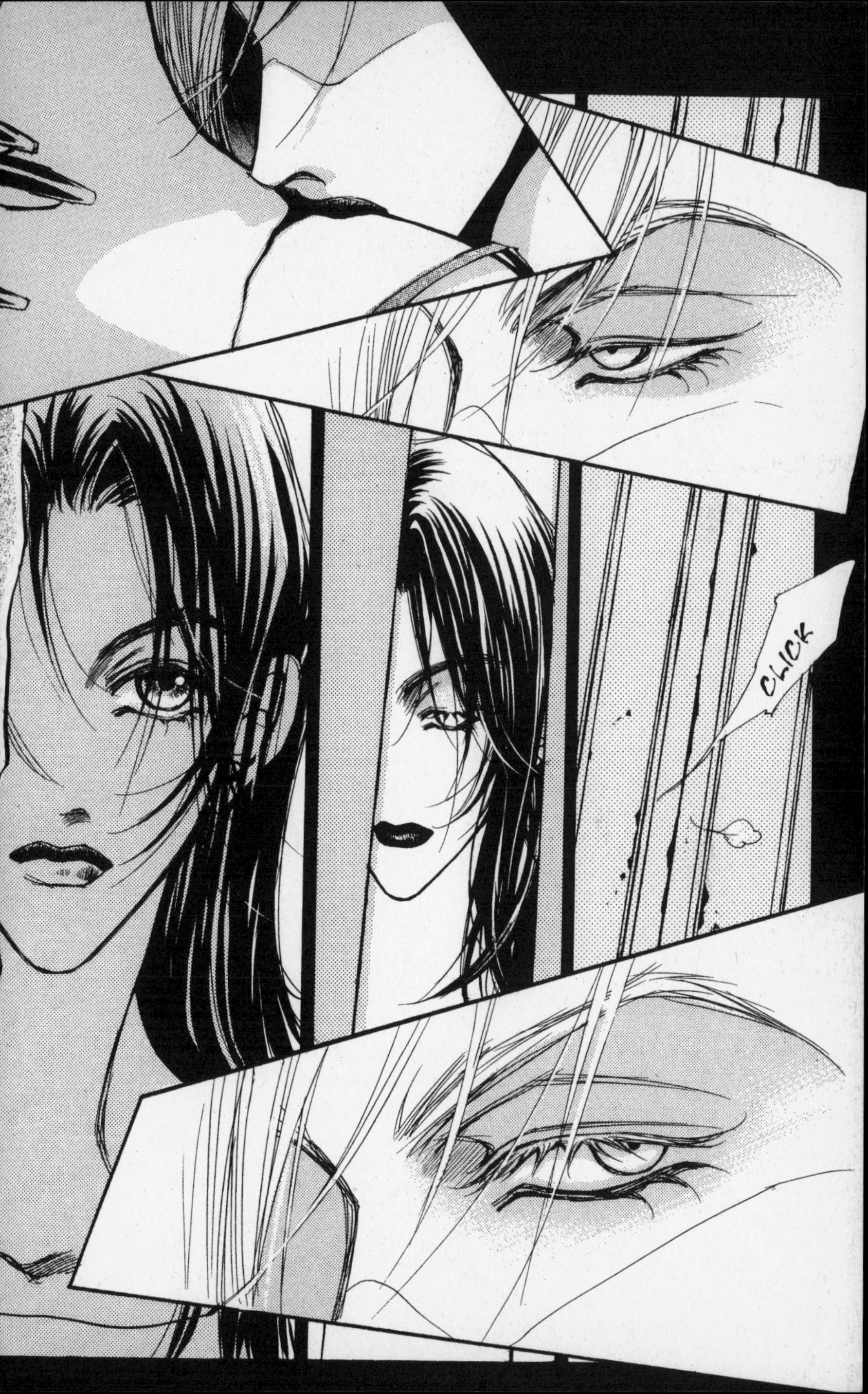
CLICK

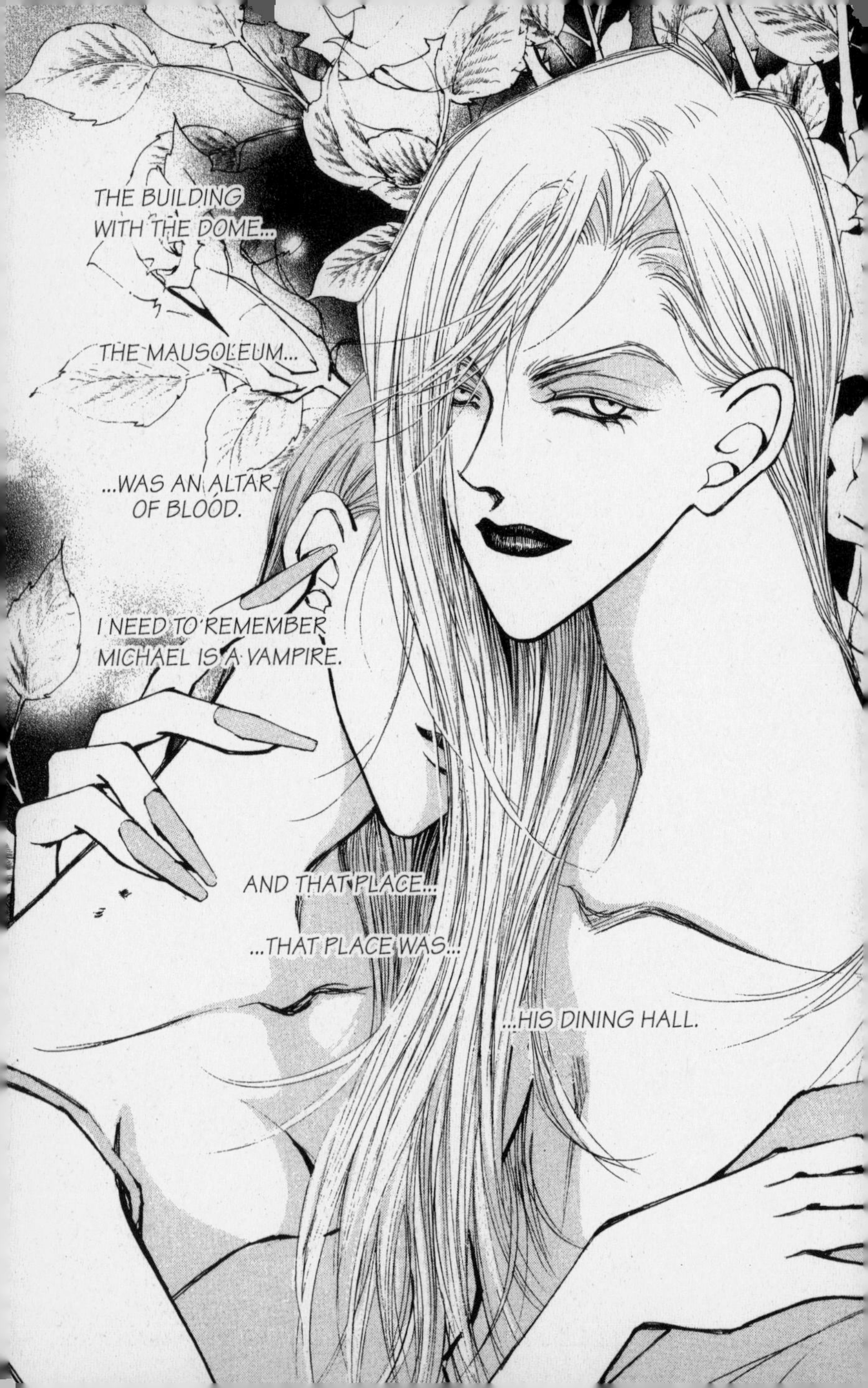
THE BUILDING WITH THE DOME...
THE MAUSOLEUM...
...WAS AN ALTAR OF BLOOD.
I NEED TO REMEMBER MICHAEL IS A VAMPIRE.
AND THAT PLACE...
...THAT PLACE WAS...
...HIS DINING HALL.

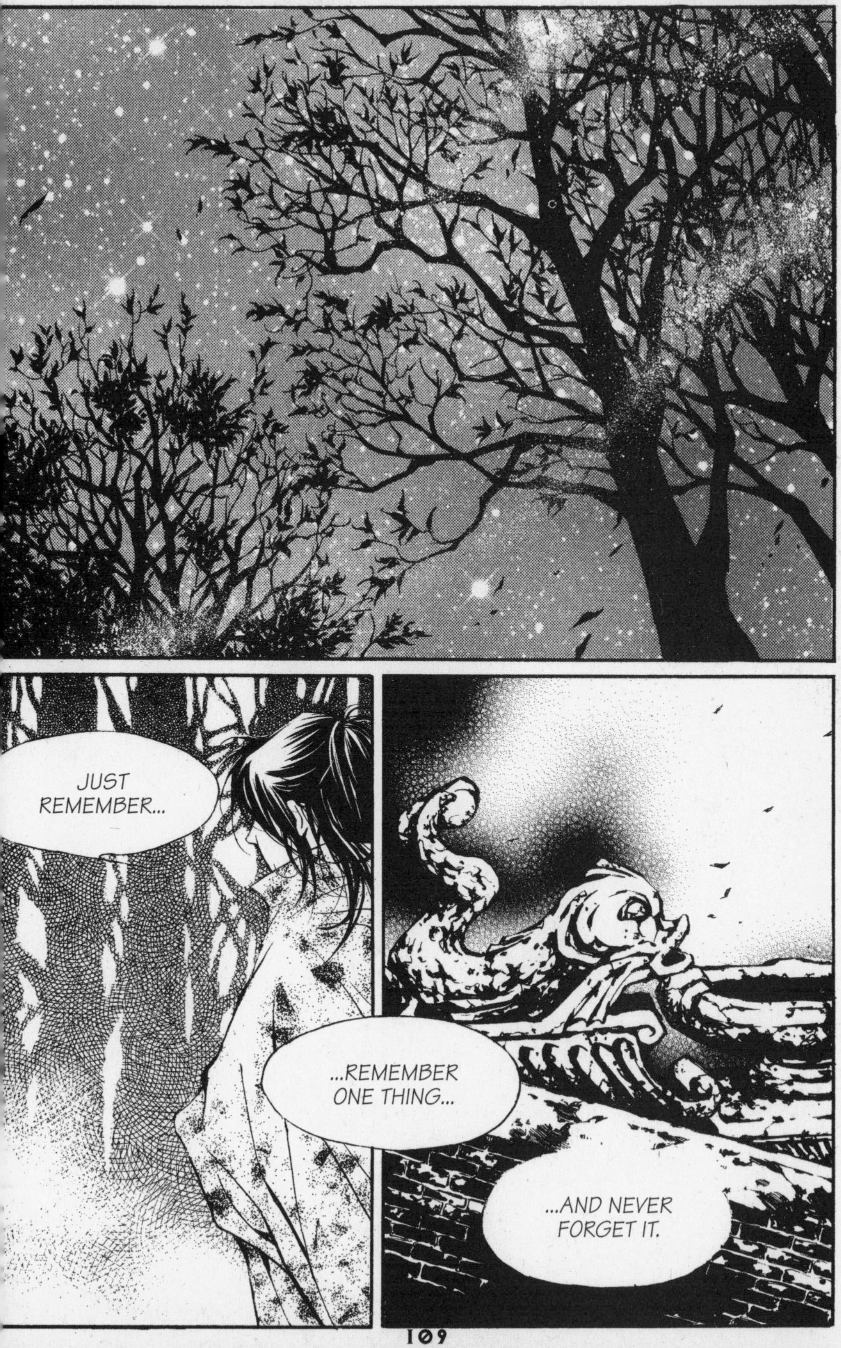
JUST REMEMBER...
...REMEMBER ONE THING...
...AND NEVER FORGET IT.

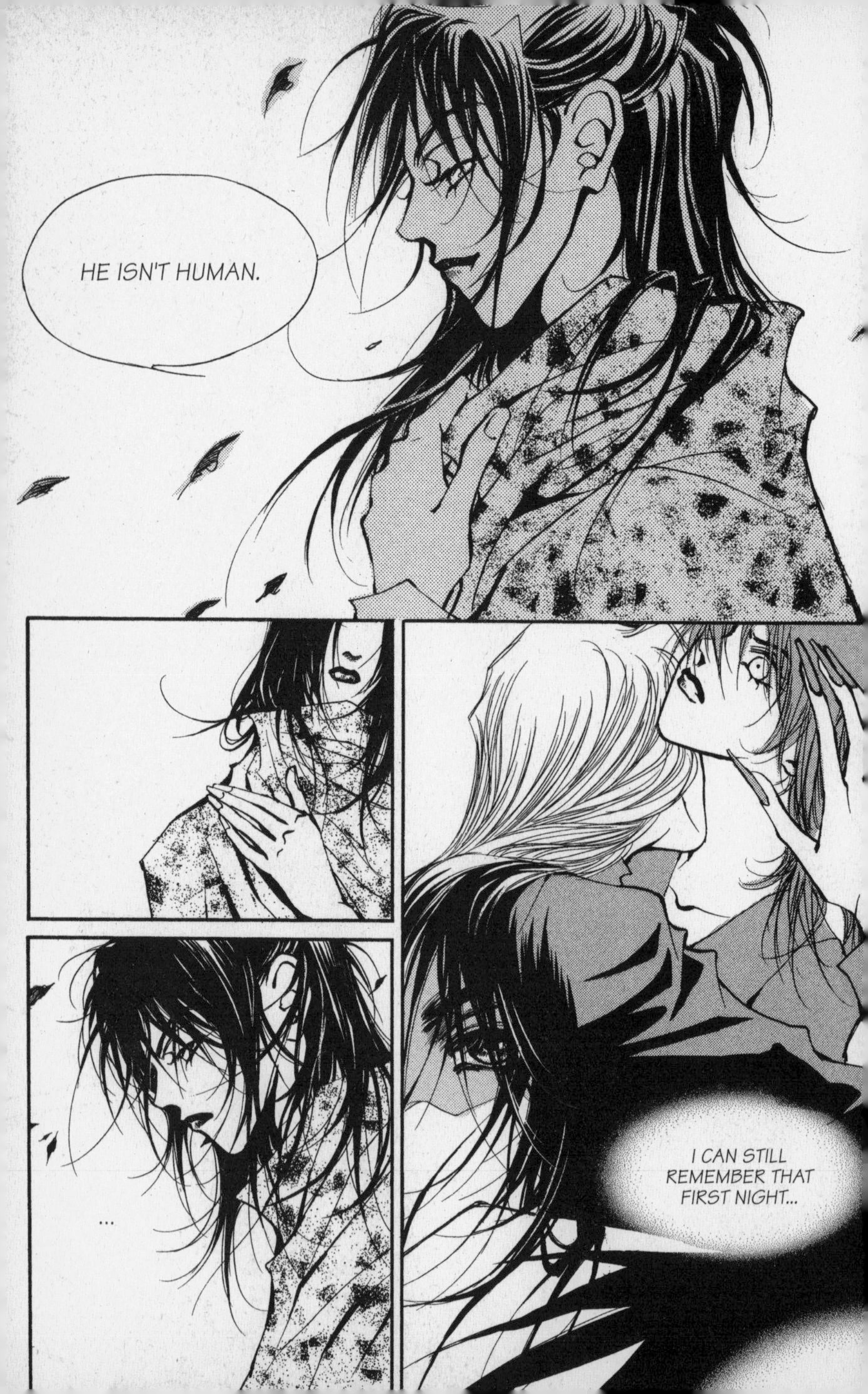
HE ISN'T HUMAN.
...
I CAN STILL REMEMBER THAT FIRST NIGHT...

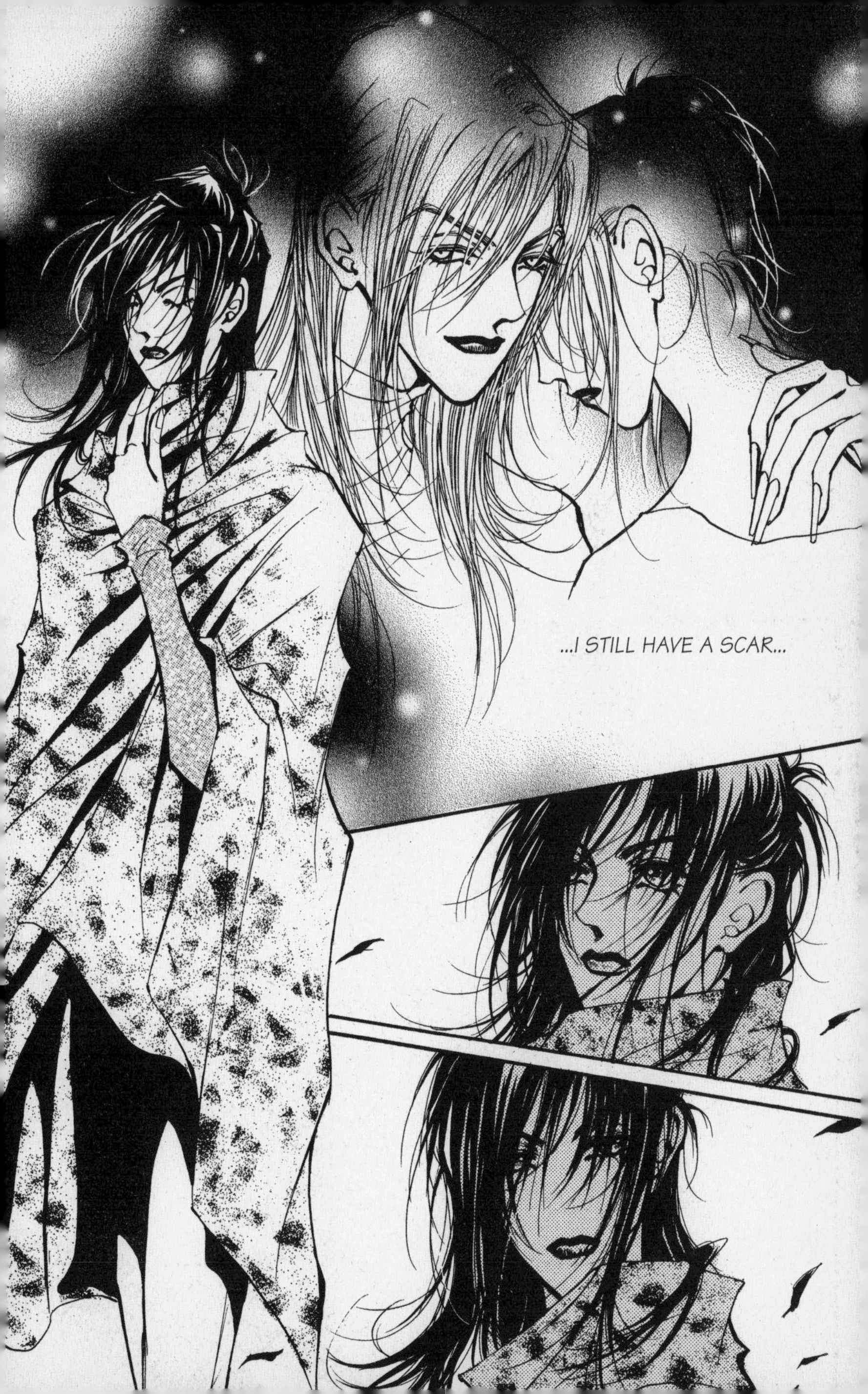
...I STILL HAVE A SCAR...

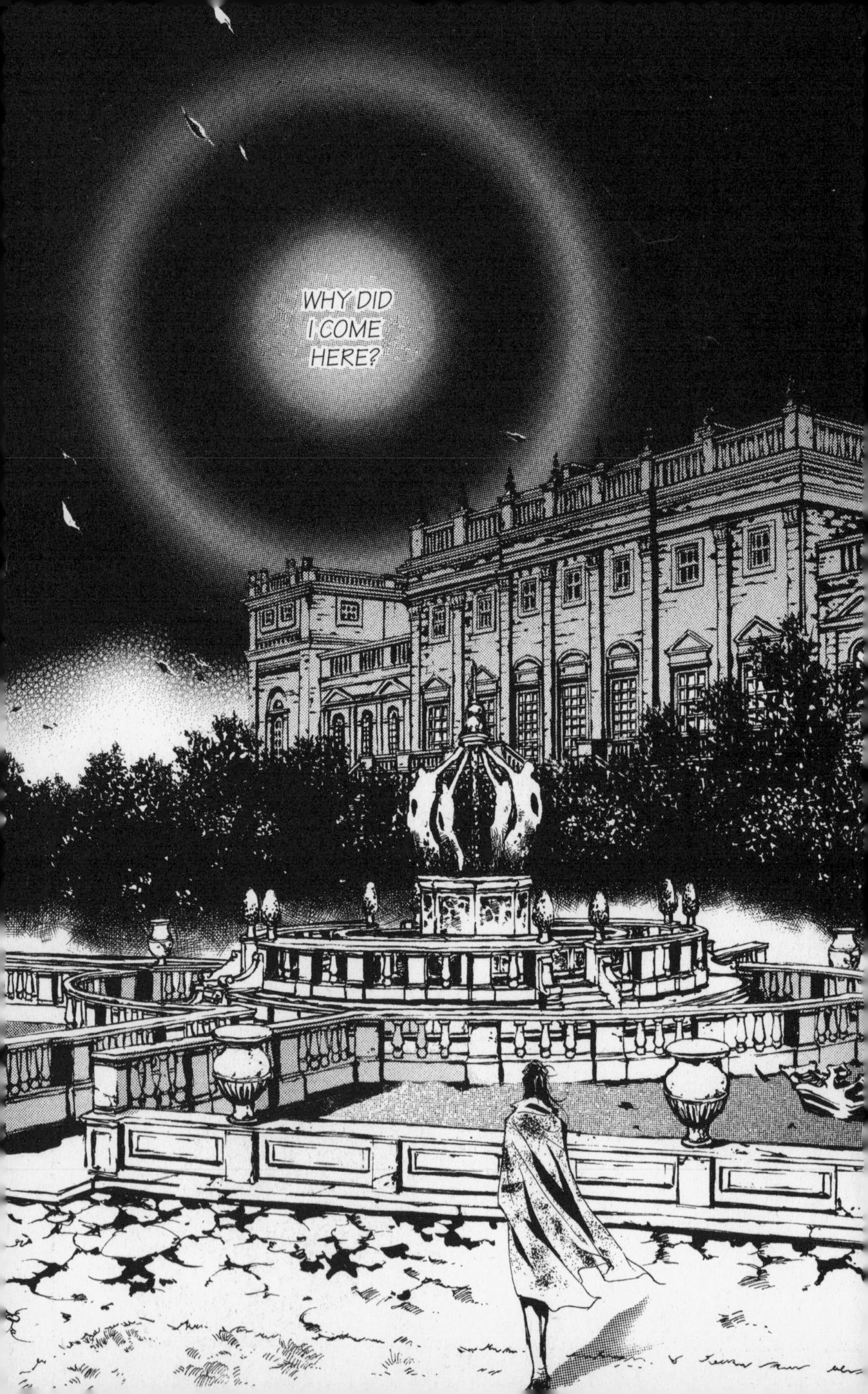
WHY DID I COME HERE?

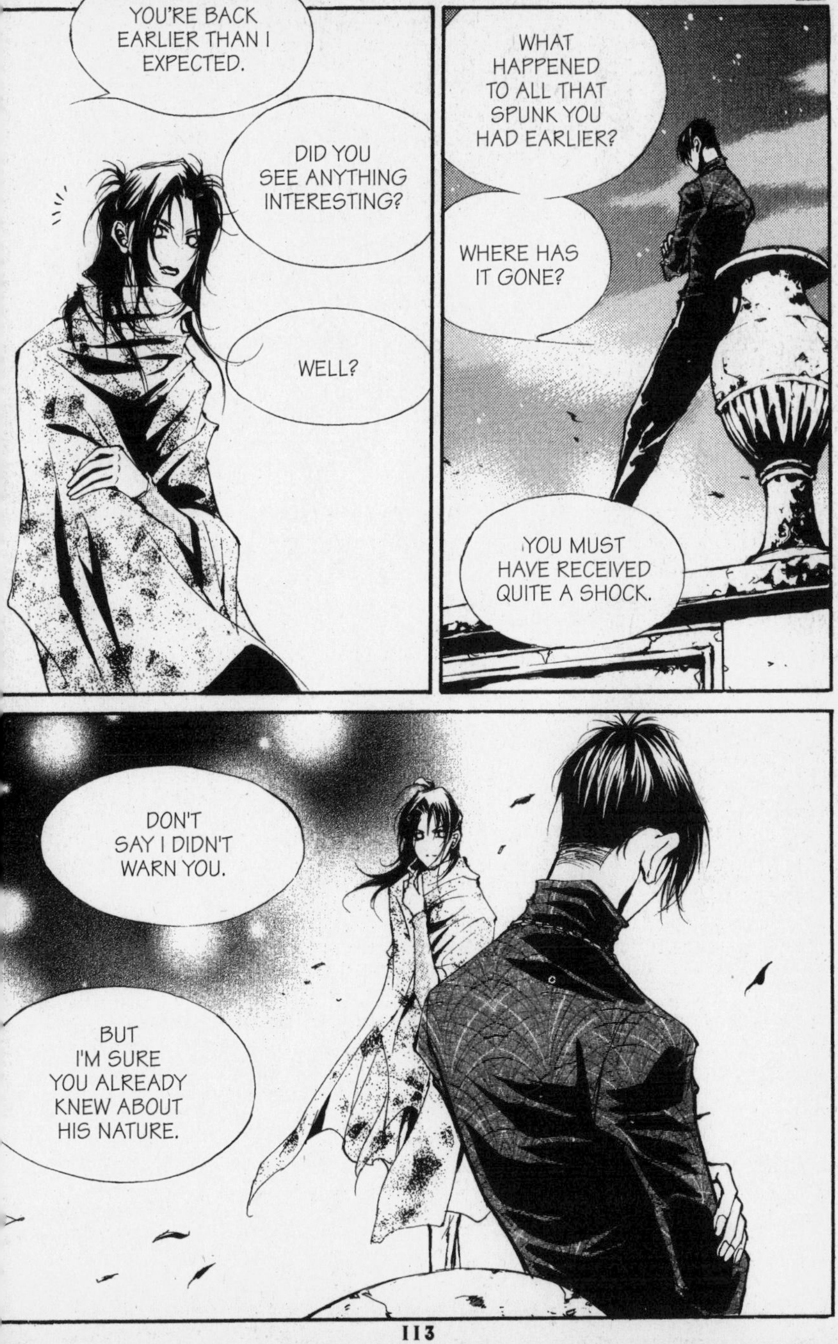
YOU'RE BACK EARLIER THAN I EXPECTED.
DID YOU SEE ANYTHING INTERESTING?
WELL?
WHAT HAPPENED TO ALL THAT SPUNK YOU HAD EARLIER?
WHERE HAS IT GONE?
YOU MUST HAVE RECEIVED QUITE A SHOCK.
DON'T SAY I DIDN'T WARN YOU.
BUT I'M SURE YOU ALREADY KNEW ABOUT HIS NATURE.

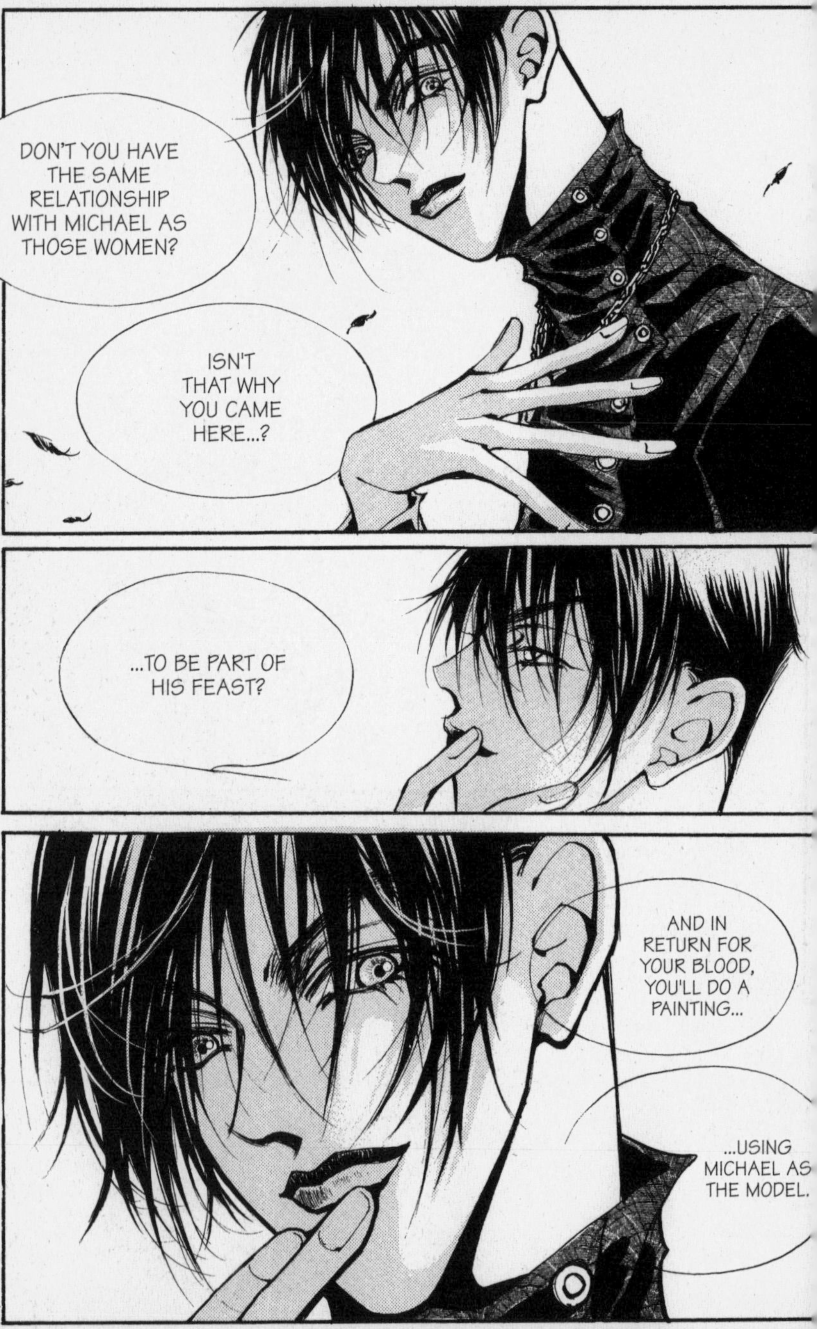
DON'T YOU HAVE THE SAME RELATIONSHIP WITH MICHAEL AS THOSE WOMEN?
ISN'T THAT WHY YOU CAME HERE...?
...TO BE PART OF HIS FEAST?
AND IN RETURN FOR YOUR BLOOD, YOU'LL DO A PAINTING...
...USING MICHAEL AS THE MODEL.

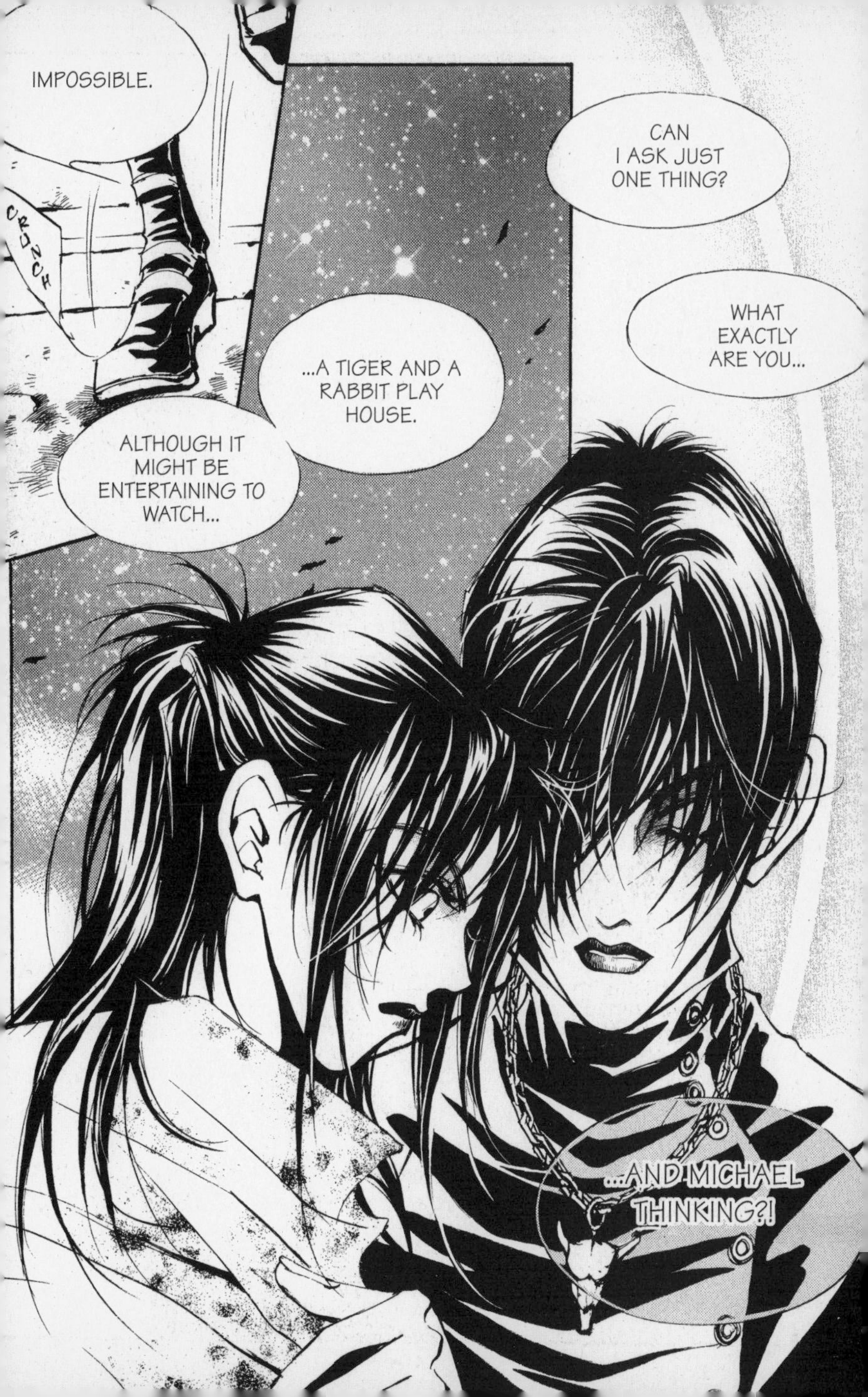
IMPOSSIBLE.
CRUNCH
ALTHOUGH IT MIGHT BE ENTERTAINING TO WATCH...
...A TIGER AND A RABBIT PLAY HOUSE.
CAN I ASK JUST ONE THING?
WHAT EXACTLY ARE YOU...
...AND MICHAEL THINKING?!

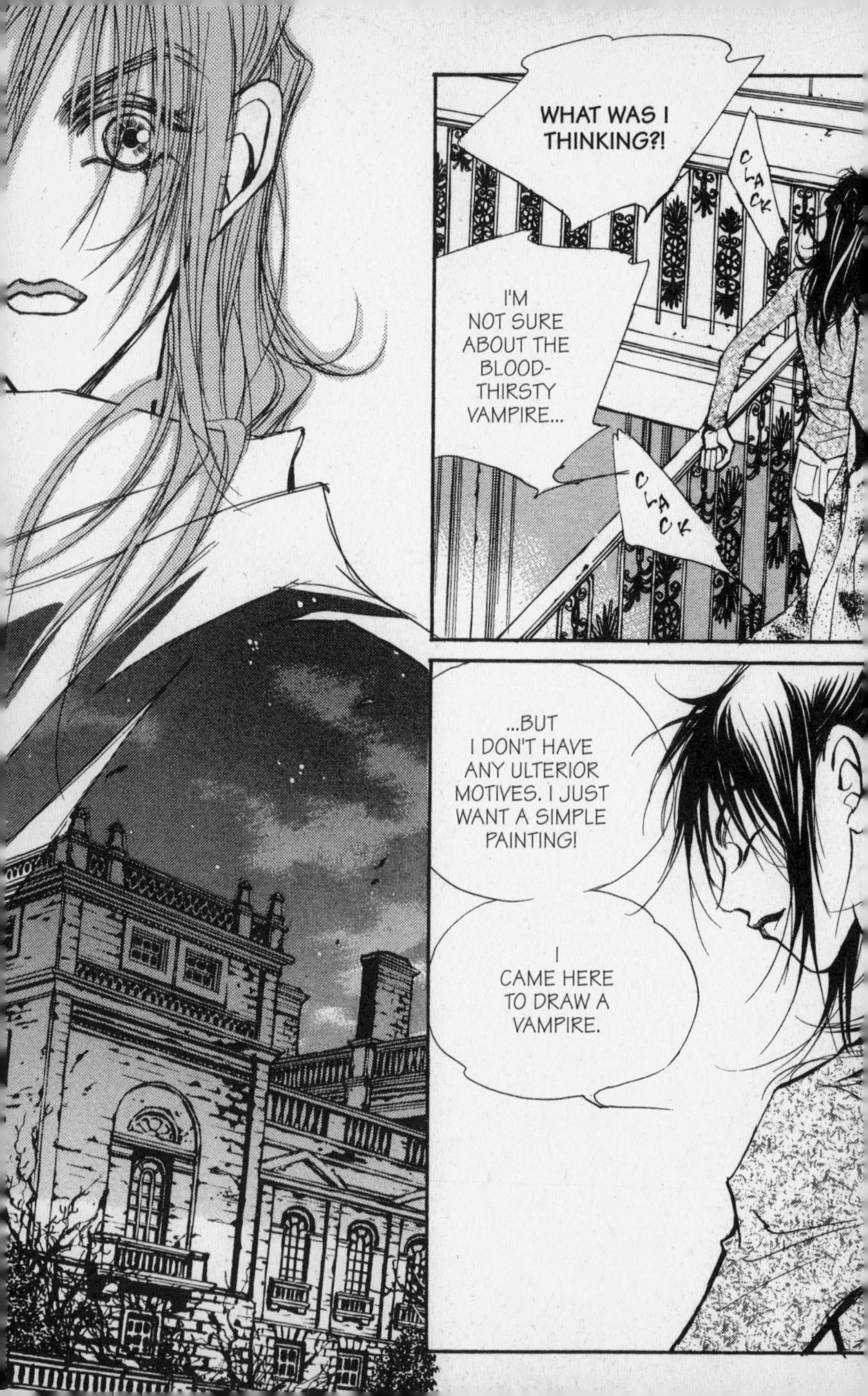
WHAT WAS I THINKING?!
CLACK
I'M NOT SURE ABOUT THE BLOOD-THIRSTY VAMPIRE...
CLACK
...BUT I DON'T HAVE ANY ULTERIOR MOTIVES. I JUST WANT A SIMPLE PAINTING!
I CAME HERE TO DRAW A VAMPIRE.

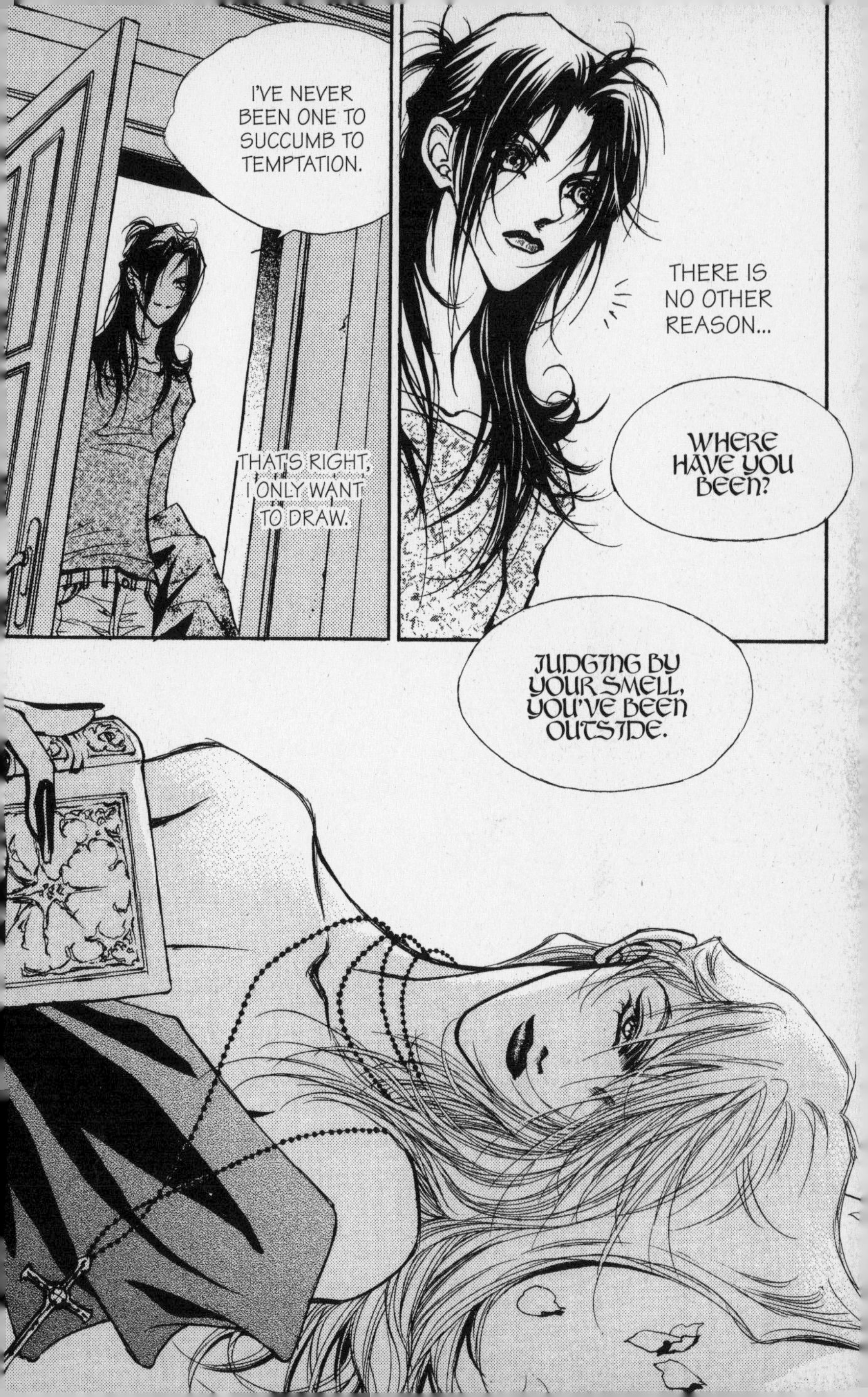
I'VE NEVER BEEN ONE TO SUCCUMB TO TEMPTATION.
THAT'S RIGHT, I ONLY WANT TO DRAW.
THERE IS NO OTHER REASON...
WHERE HAVE YOU BEEN?
JUDGING BY YOUR SMELL, YOU'VE BEEN OUTSIDE.

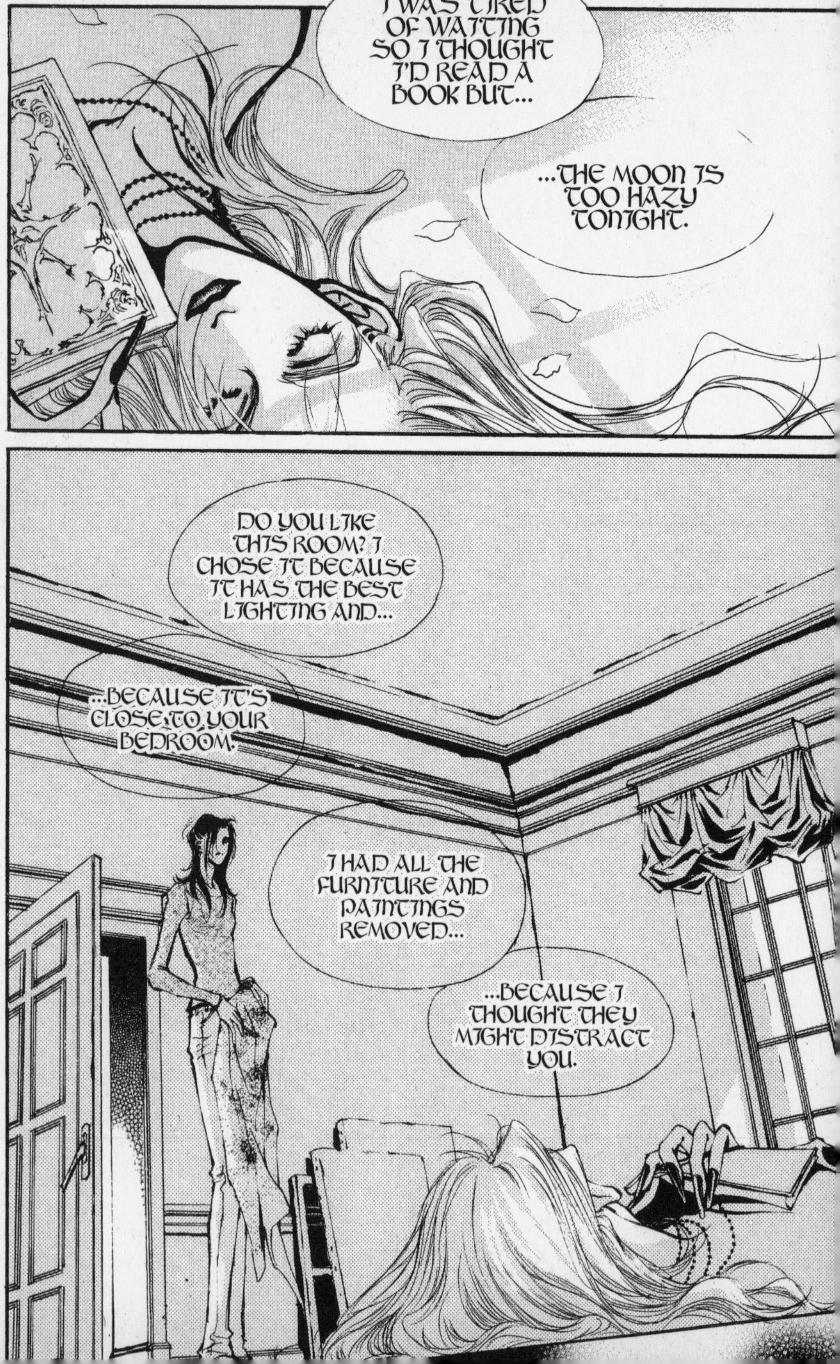
I WAS TIRED OF WAITING SO I THOUGHT I'D READ A BOOK BUT...
...THE MOON IS TOO HAZY TONIGHT.
DO YOU LIKE THIS ROOM? I CHOSE IT BECAUSE IT HAS THE BEST LIGHTING AND...
...BECAUSE IT'S CLOSE TO YOUR BEDROOM.
I HAD ALL THE FURNITURE AND PAINTINGS REMOVED...
...BECAUSE I THOUGHT THEY MIGHT DISTRACT YOU.

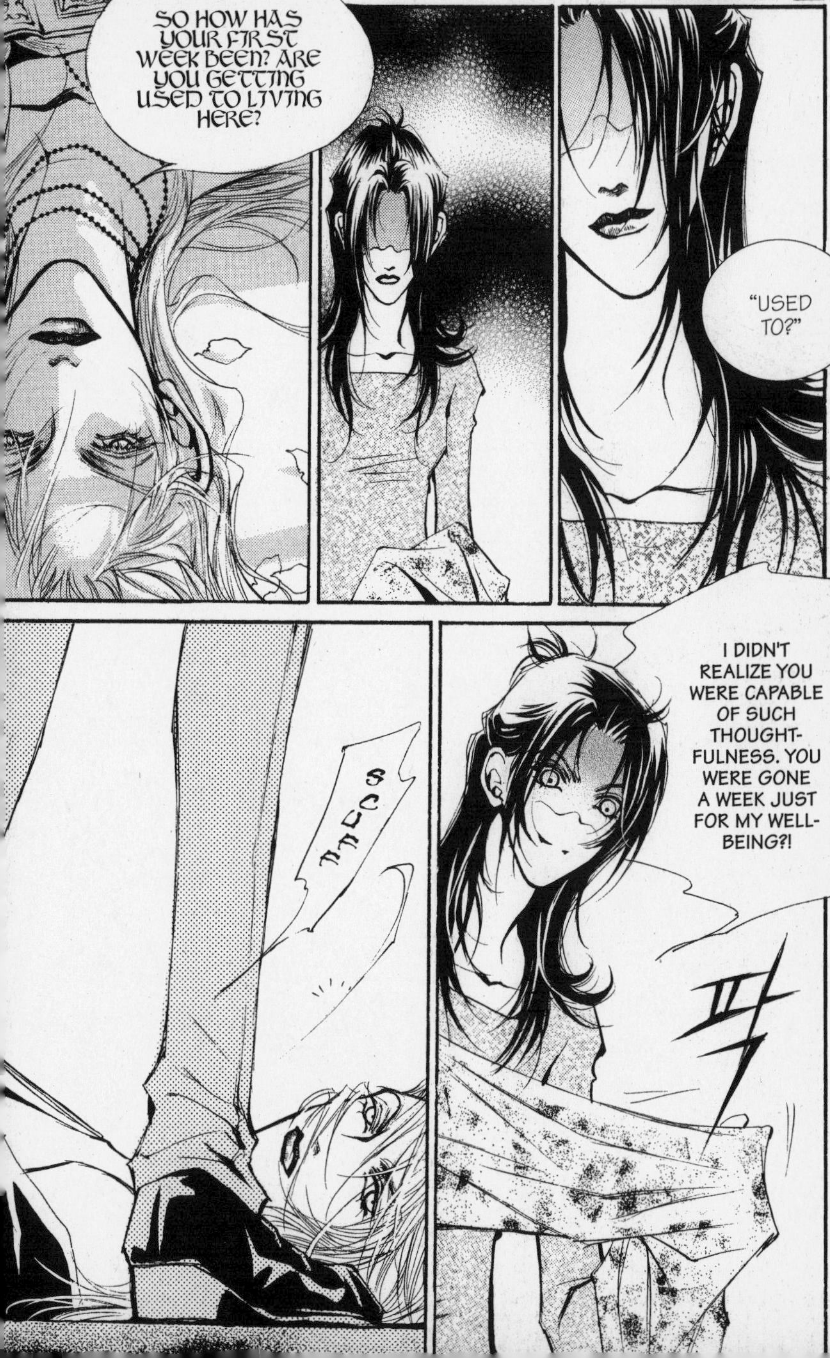
SO HOW HAS YOUR FIRST WEEK BEEN? ARE YOU GETTING USED TO LIVING HERE?
"USED TO?"
SCUFF
I DIDN'T REALIZE YOU WERE CAPABLE OF SUCH THOUGHT-FULNESS. YOU WERE GONE A WEEK JUST FOR MY WELL-BEING?!

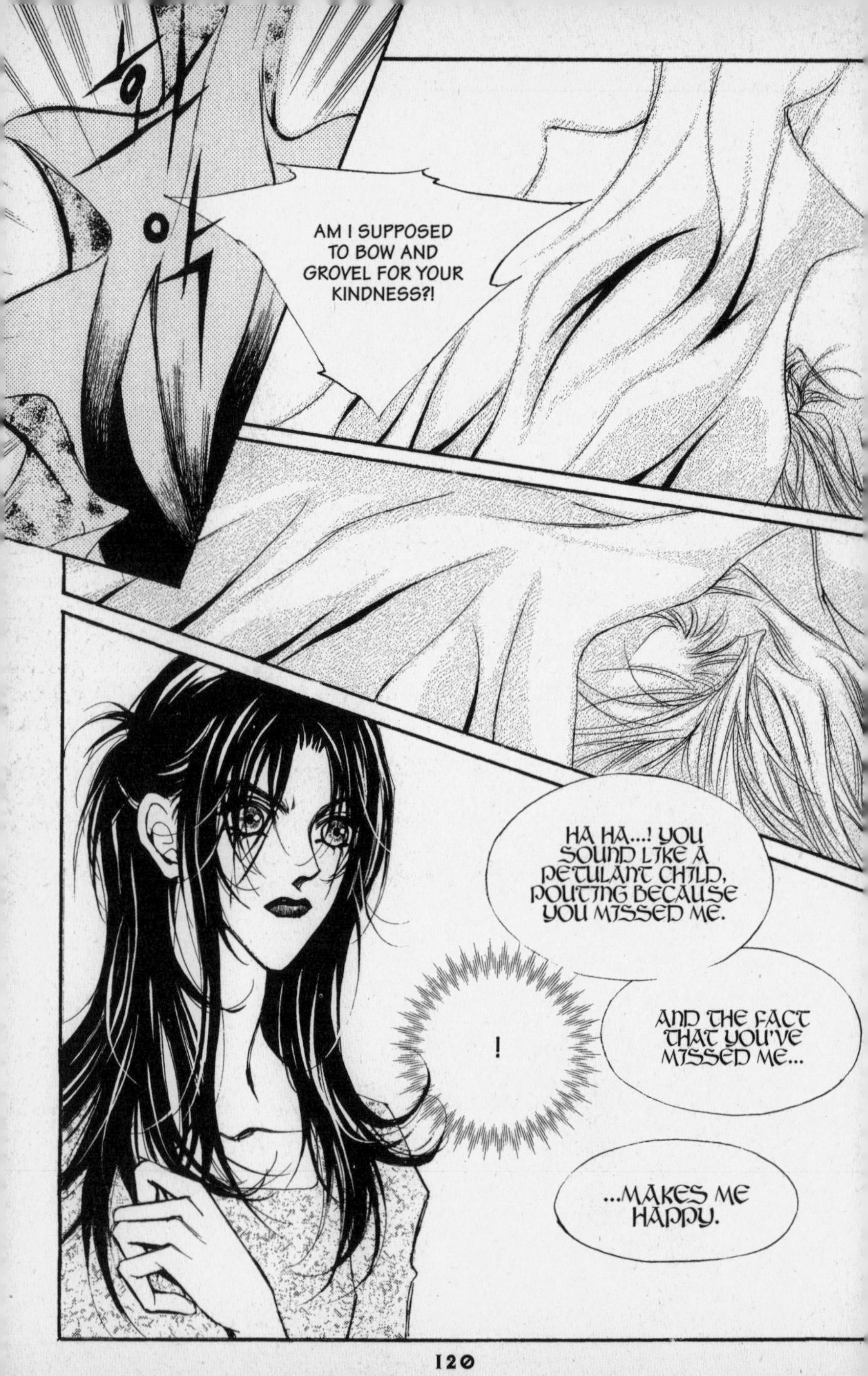
AM I SUPPOSED TO BOW AND GROVEL FOR YOUR KINDNESS?!
HA HA...! YOU SOUND LIKE A PETULANT CHILD, POUTING BECAUSE YOU MISSED ME.
!
AND THE FACT THAT YOU'VE MISSED ME...
...MAKES ME HAPPY.

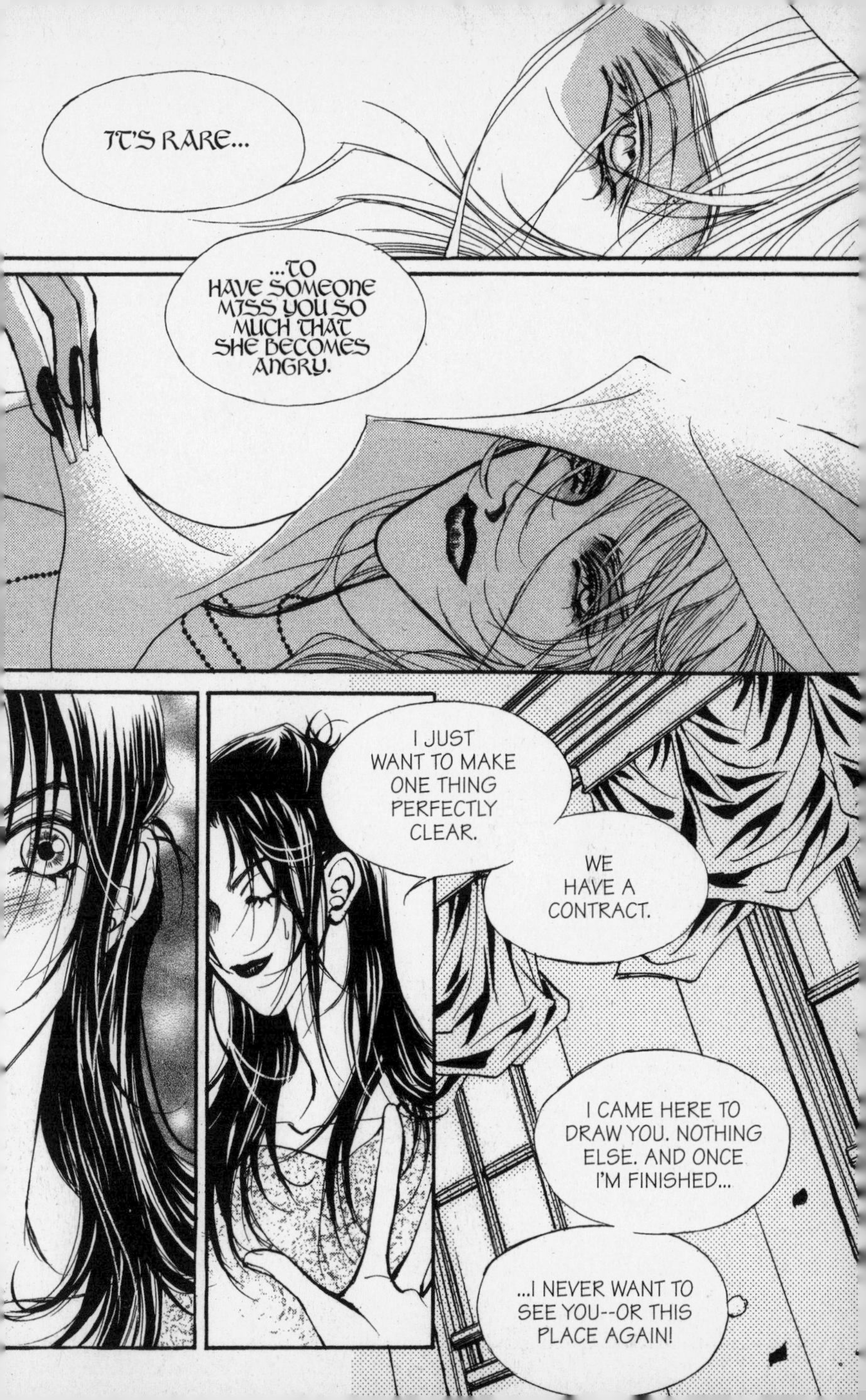
IT'S RARE...
...TO HAVE SOMEONE MISS YOU SO MUCH THAT SHE BECOMES ANGRY.
I JUST WANT TO MAKE ONE THING PERFECTLY CLEAR.
WE HAVE A CONTRACT.
I CAME HERE TO DRAW YOU. NOTHING ELSE. AND ONCE I'M FINISHED...
...I NEVER WANT TO SEE YOU--OR THIS PLACE AGAIN!

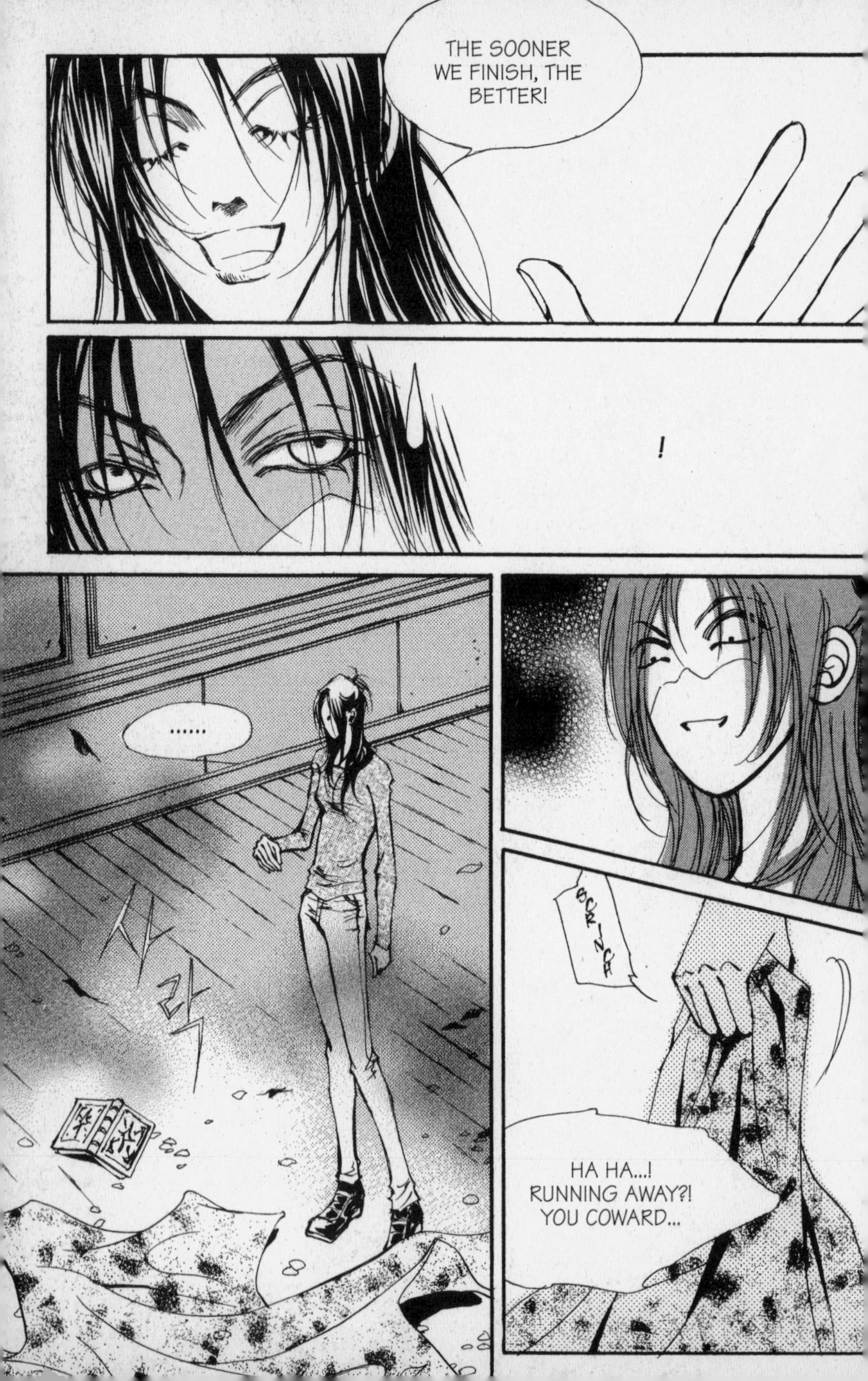
THE SOONER WE FINISH, THE BETTER!
!
......
SCRINCH
HA HA...! RUNNING AWAY?! YOU COWARD...

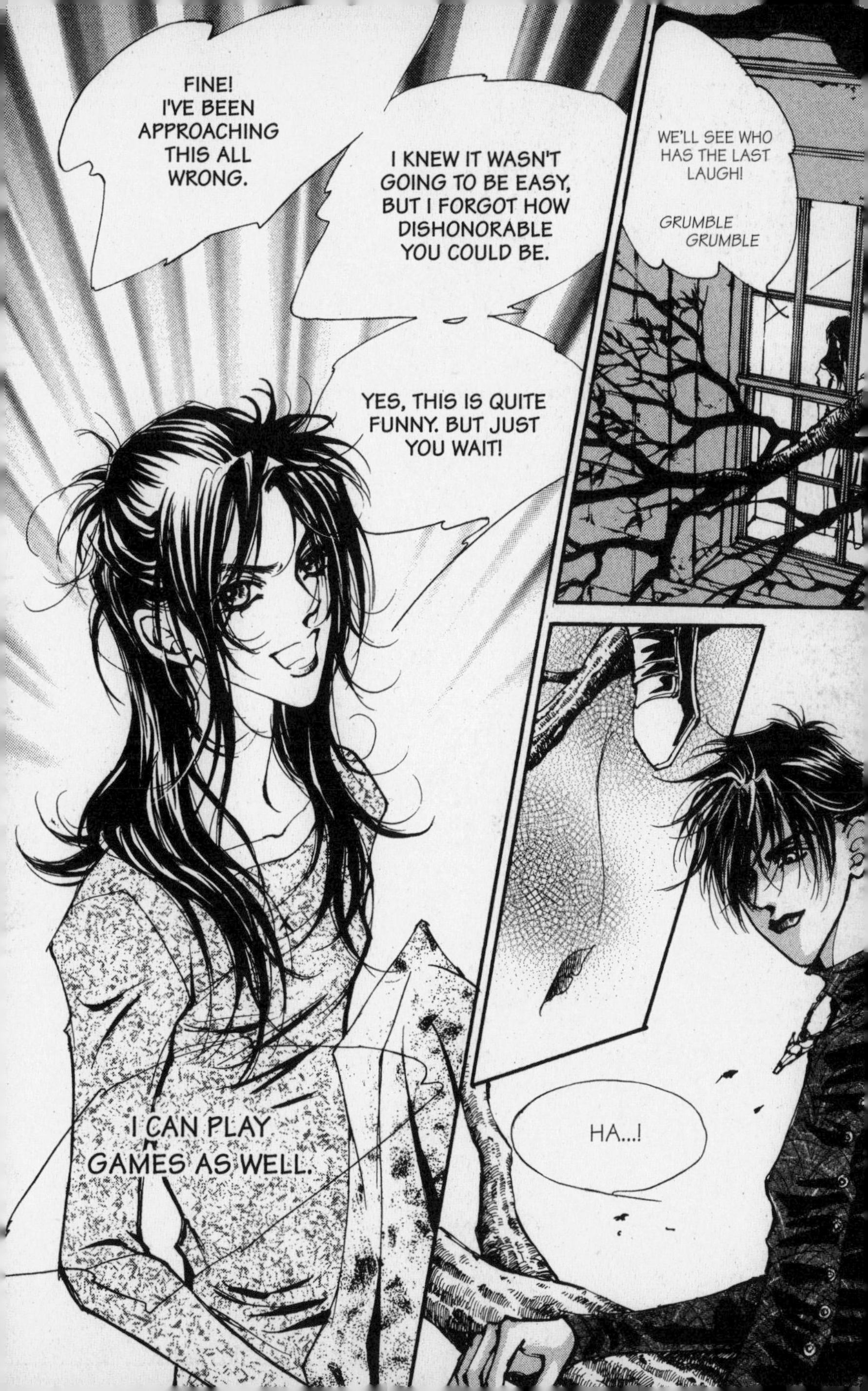
WE'LL SEE WHO HAS THE LAST LAUGH!
GRUMBLE GRUMBLE
HA...!
FINE! I'VE BEEN APPROACHING THIS ALL WRONG.
I KNEW IT WASN'T GOING TO BE EASY, BUT I FORGOT HOW DISHONORABLE YOU COULD BE.
YES, THIS IS QUITE FUNNY. BUT JUST YOU WAIT!
I CAN PLAY GAMES AS WELL.

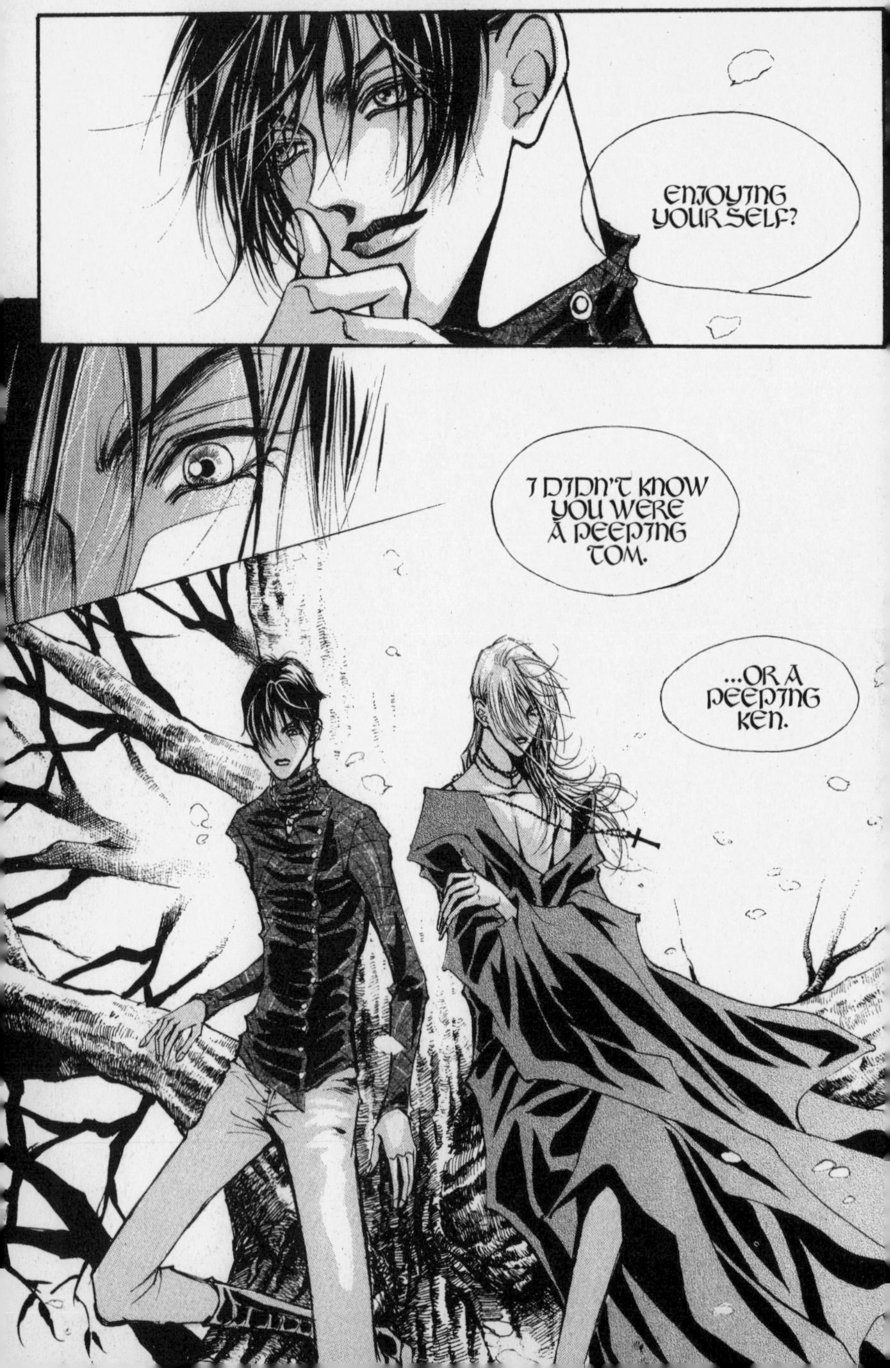
ENJOYING YOURSELF?
I DIDN'T KNOW YOU WERE A PEEPING TOM.
...OR A PEEPING KEN.

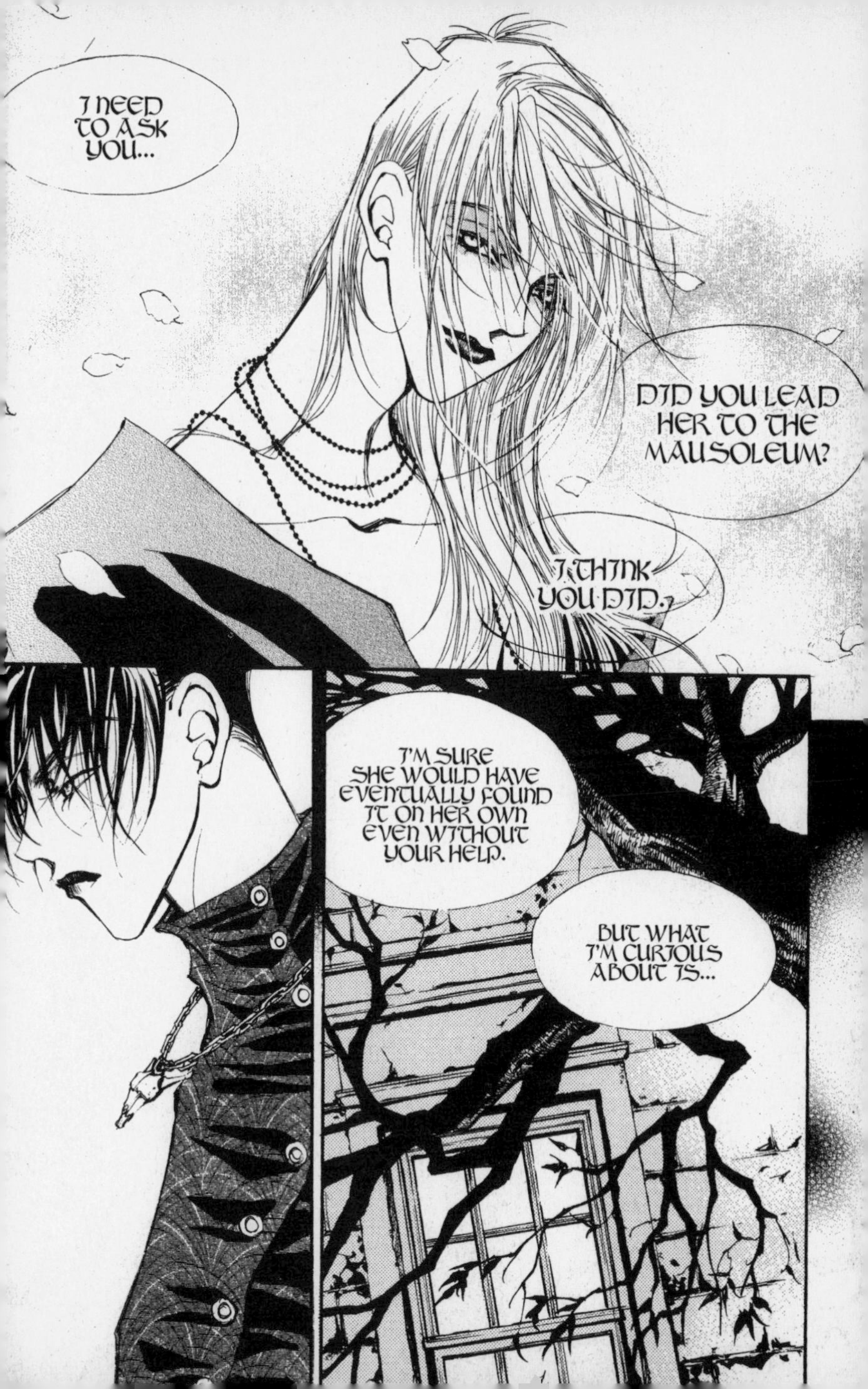
I NEED TO ASK YOU...
DID YOU LEAD HER TO THE MAUSOLEUM?
I THINK YOU DID.
I'M SURE SHE WOULD HAVE EVENTUALLY FOUND IT ON HER OWN EVEN WITHOUT YOUR HELP.
BUT WHAT I'M CURIOUS ABOUT IS...

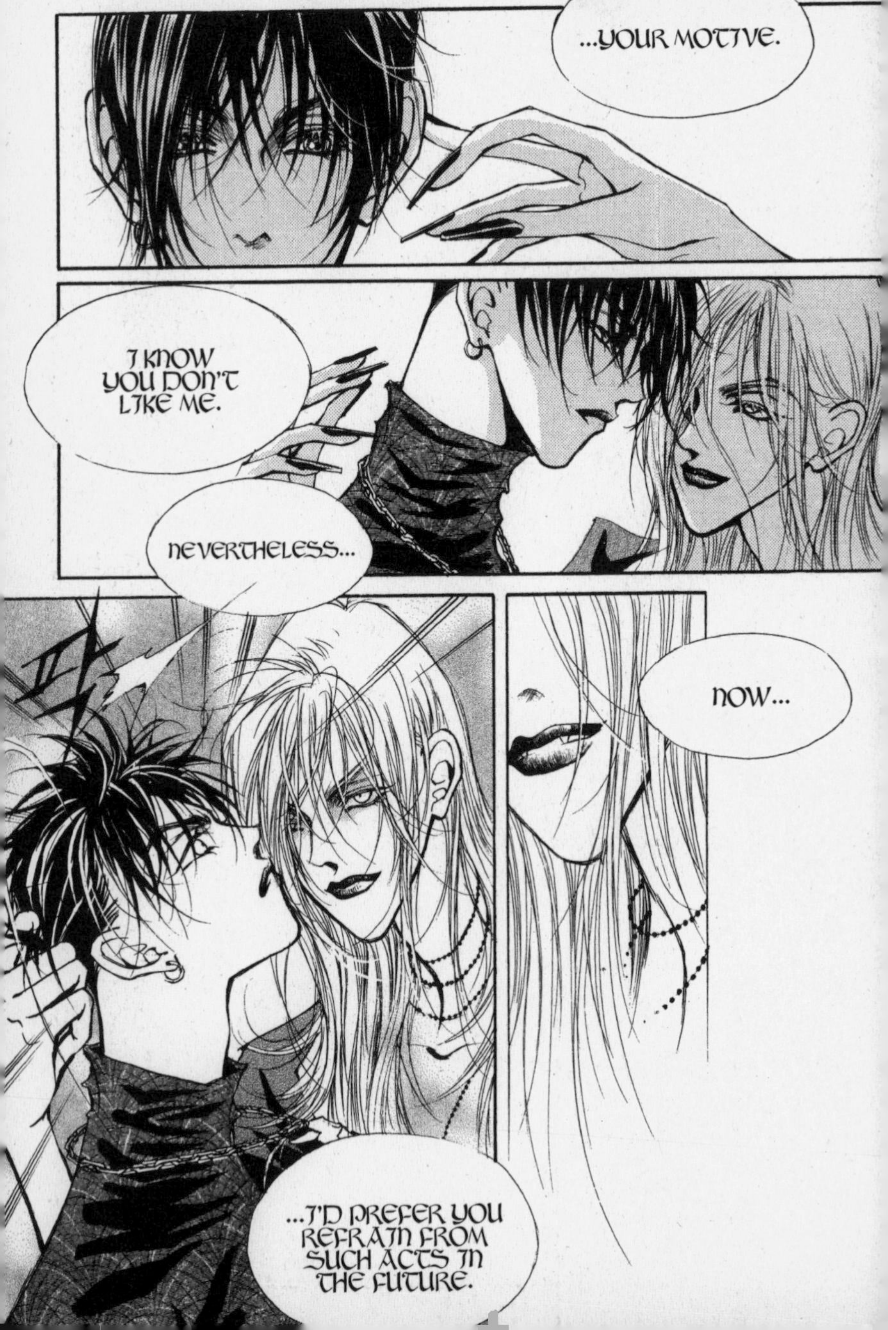
...YOUR MOTIVE.
I KNOW YOU DON'T LIKE ME.
NEVERTHELESS...
NOW...
...I'D PREFER YOU REFRAIN FROM SUCH ACTS IN THE FUTURE.

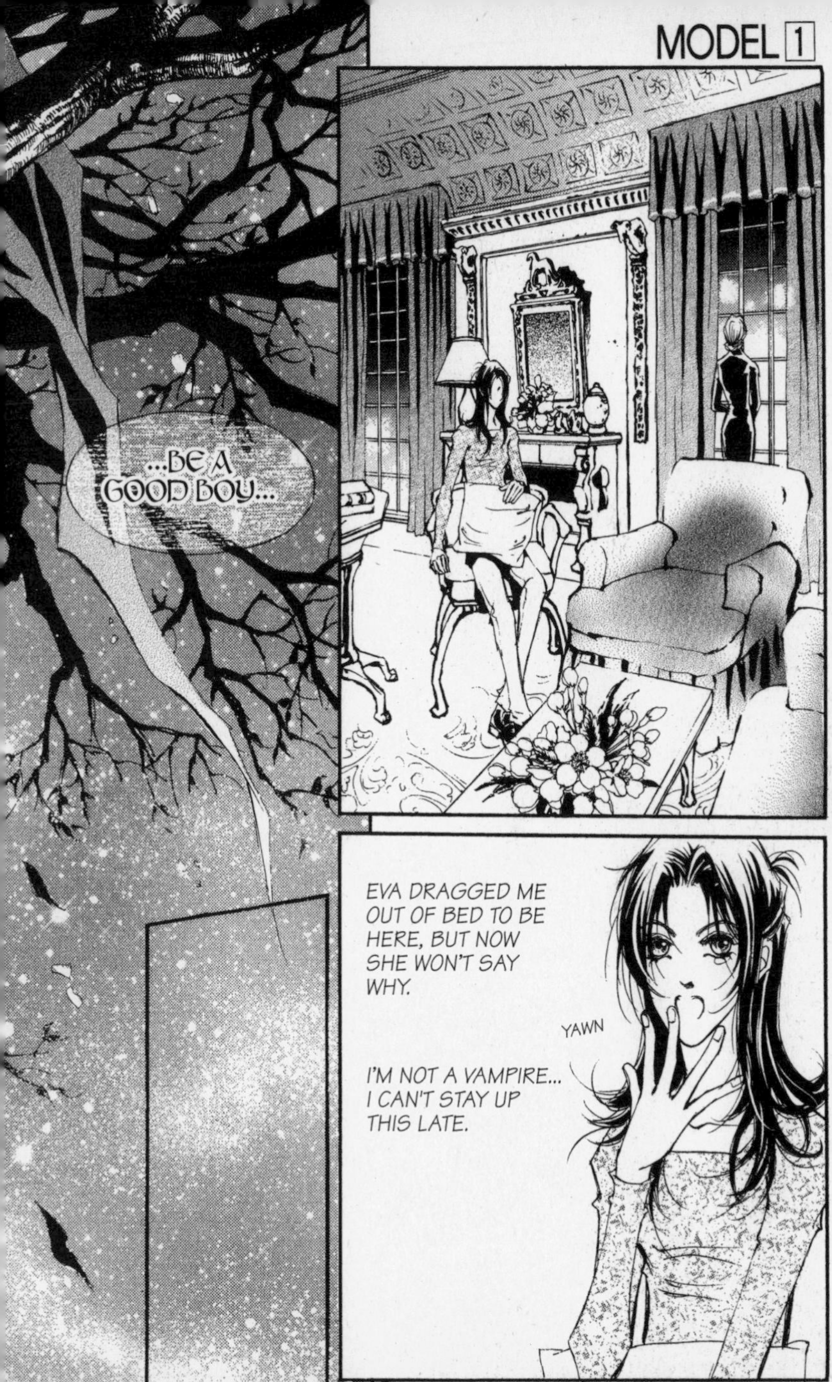
...BE A GOOD BOY...
EVA DRAGGED ME OUT OF BED TO BE HERE, BUT NOW SHE WON'T SAY WHY.
YAWN
I'M NOT A VAMPIRE... I CAN'T STAY UP THIS LATE.

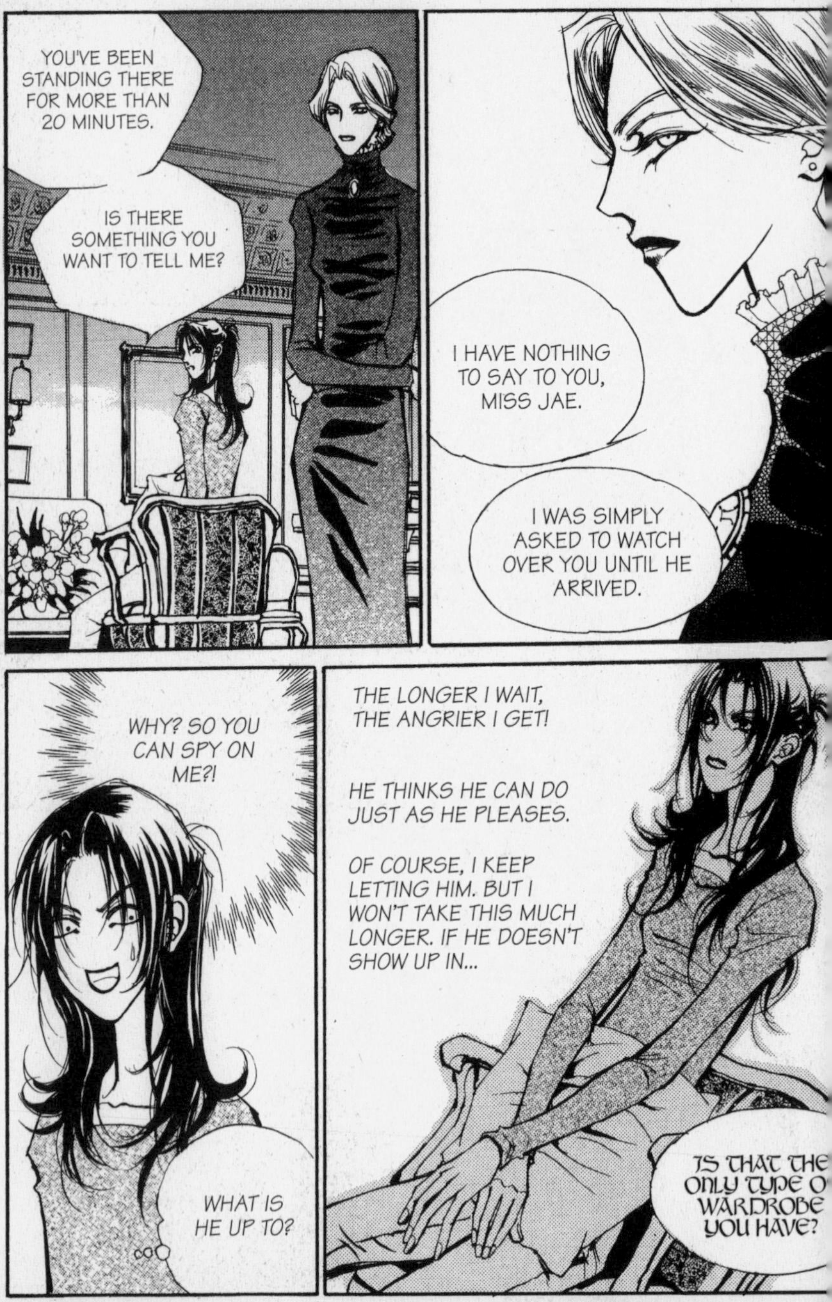
YOU'VE BEEN STANDING THERE FOR MORE THAN 20 MINUTES.
IS THERE SOMETHING YOU WANT TO TELL ME?
I HAVE NOTHING TO SAY TO YOU, MISS JAE.
I WAS SIMPLY ASKED TO WATCH OVER YOU UNTIL HE ARRIVED.
WHY? SO YOU CAN SPY ON ME?!
WHAT IS HE UP TO?
THE LONGER I WAIT, THE ANGRIER I GET!
HE THINKS HE CAN DO JUST AS HE PLEASES.
OF COURSE, I KEEP LETTING HIM. BUT I WON'T TAKE THIS MUCH LONGER. IF HE DOESN'T SHOW UP IN...
IS THAT THE ONLY TYPE O WARDROBE YOU HAVE?

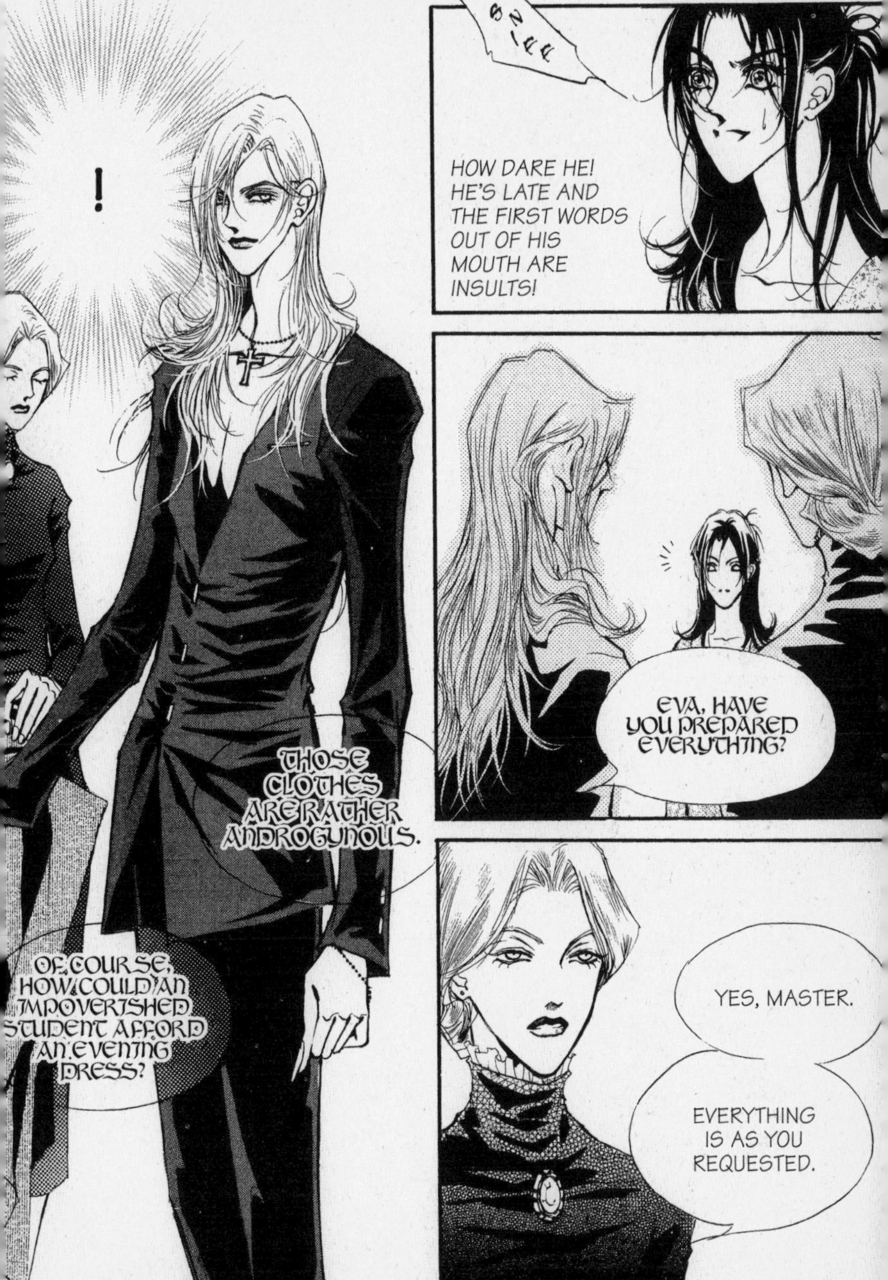
!
THOSE CLOTHES ARE RATHER ANDROGYNOUS.
OF COURSE, HOW COULD AN IMPOVERISHED STUDENT AFFORD AN EVENING DRESS?
SNIFF
HOW DARE HE! HE'S LATE AND THE FIRST WORDS OUT OF HIS MOUTH ARE INSULTS!
EVA, HAVE YOU PREPARED EVERYTHING?
YES, MASTER.
EVERYTHING IS AS YOU REQUESTED.

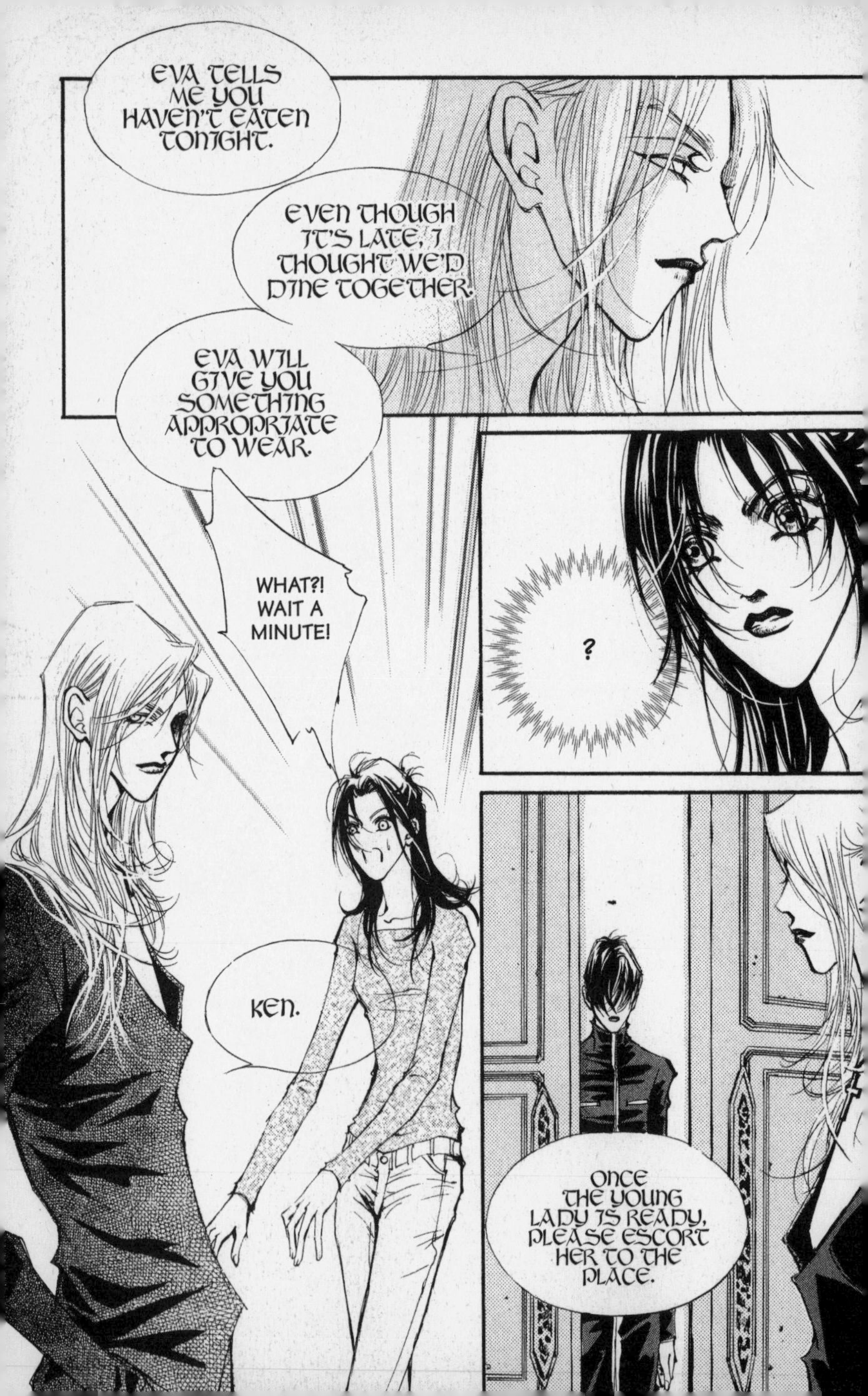
EVA TELLS ME YOU HAVEN'T EATEN TONIGHT.
EVEN THOUGH IT'S LATE, I THOUGHT WE'D DINE TOGETHER.
EVA WILL GIVE YOU SOMETHING APPROPRIATE TO WEAR.
WHAT?! WAIT A MINUTE!
?
KEN.
ONCE THE YOUNG LADY IS READY, PLEASE ESCORT HER TO THE PLACE.

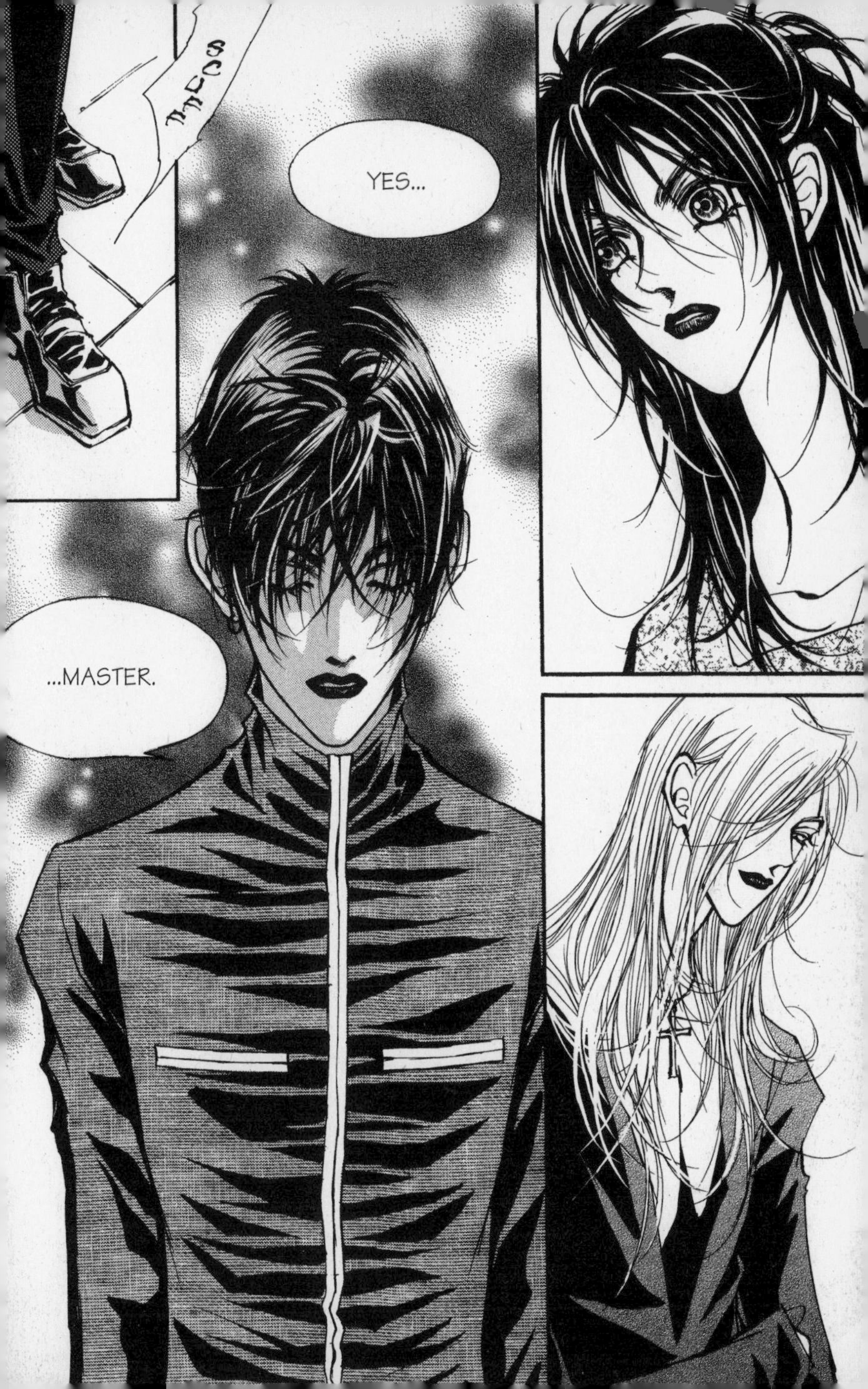
YES...
...MASTER.

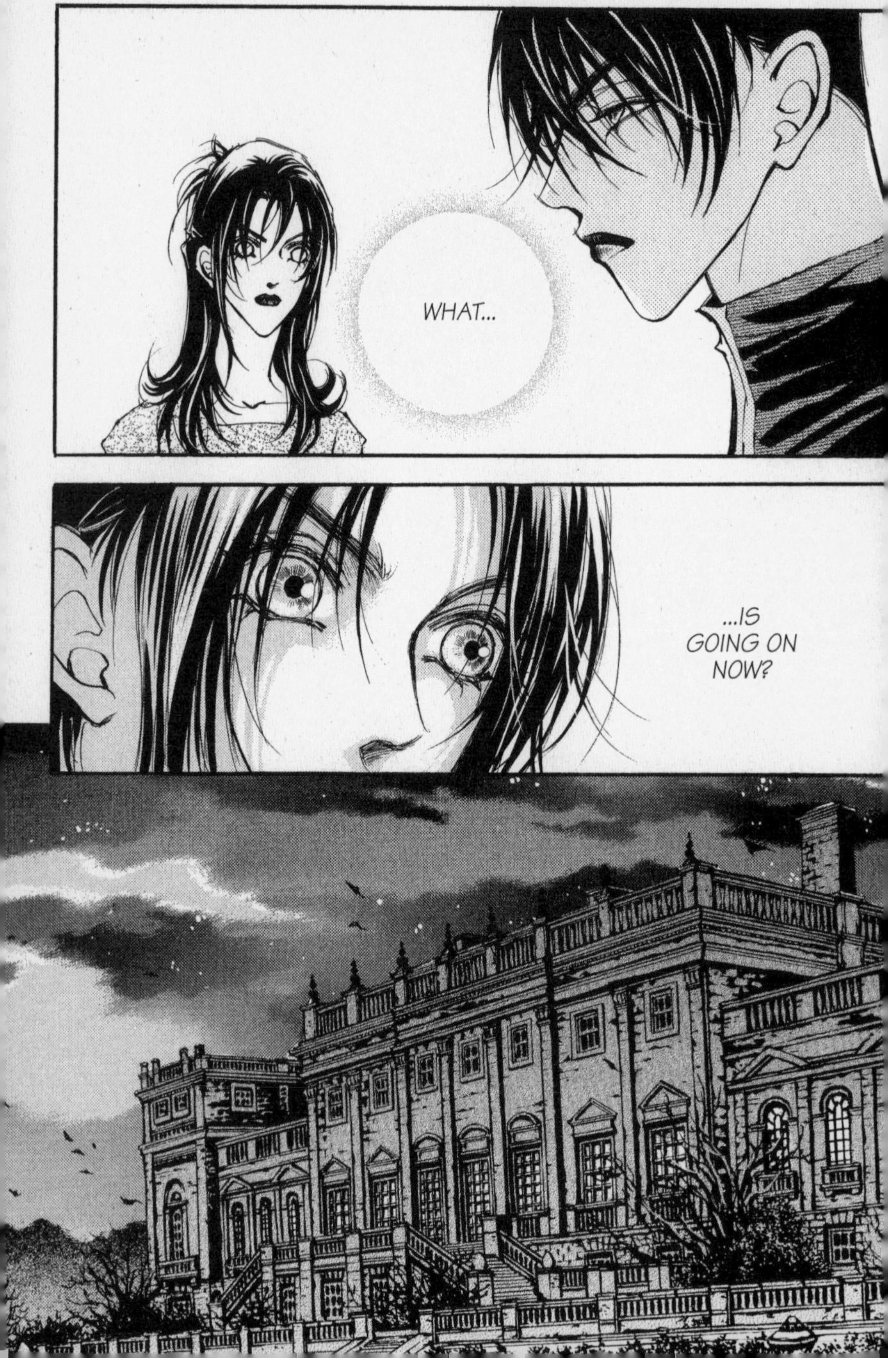
WHAT...
...IS GOING ON NOW?

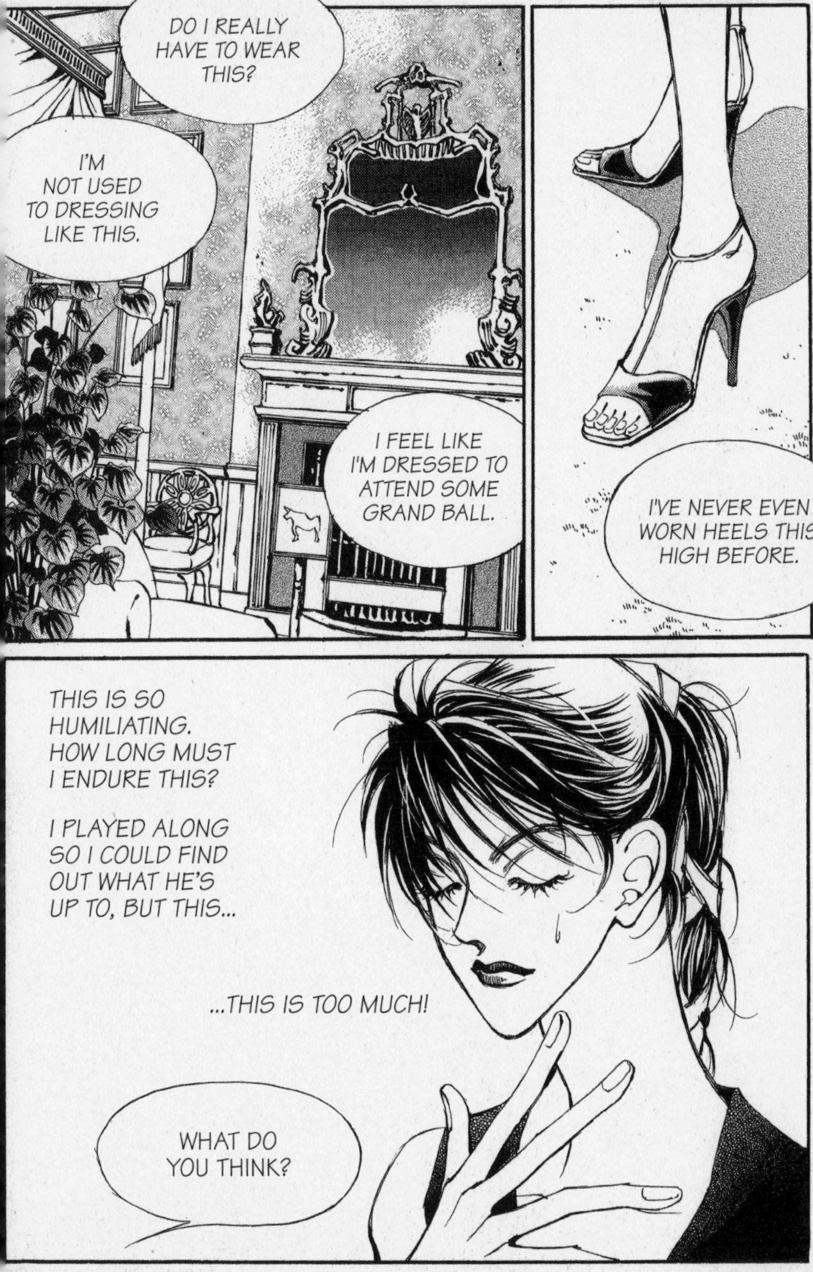
DO I REALLY HAVE TO WEAR THIS?
I'M NOT USED TO DRESSING LIKE THIS.
I FEEL LIKE I'M DRESSED TO ATTEND SOME GRAND BALL.
I'VE NEVER EVEN WORN HEELS THIS HIGH BEFORE.
THIS IS SO HUMILIATING. HOW LONG MUST I ENDURE THIS?
I PLAYED ALONG SO I COULD FIND OUT WHAT HE'S UP TO, BUT THIS...
...THIS IS TOO MUCH!
WHAT DO YOU THINK?

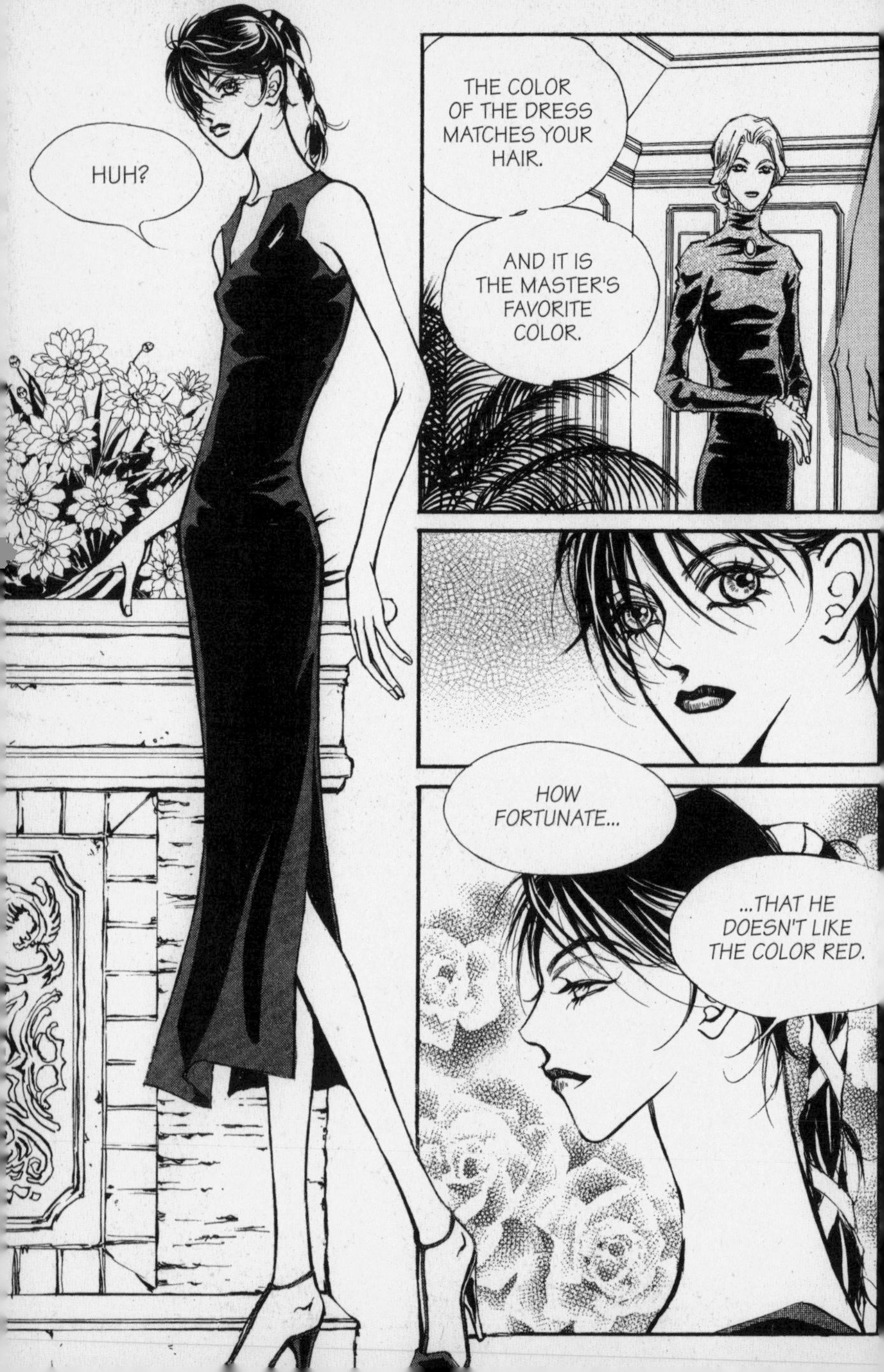
HUH?
THE COLOR OF THE DRESS MATCHES YOUR HAIR.
AND IT IS THE MASTER'S FAVORITE COLOR.
HOW FORTUNATE...
...THAT HE DOESN'T LIKE THE COLOR RED.

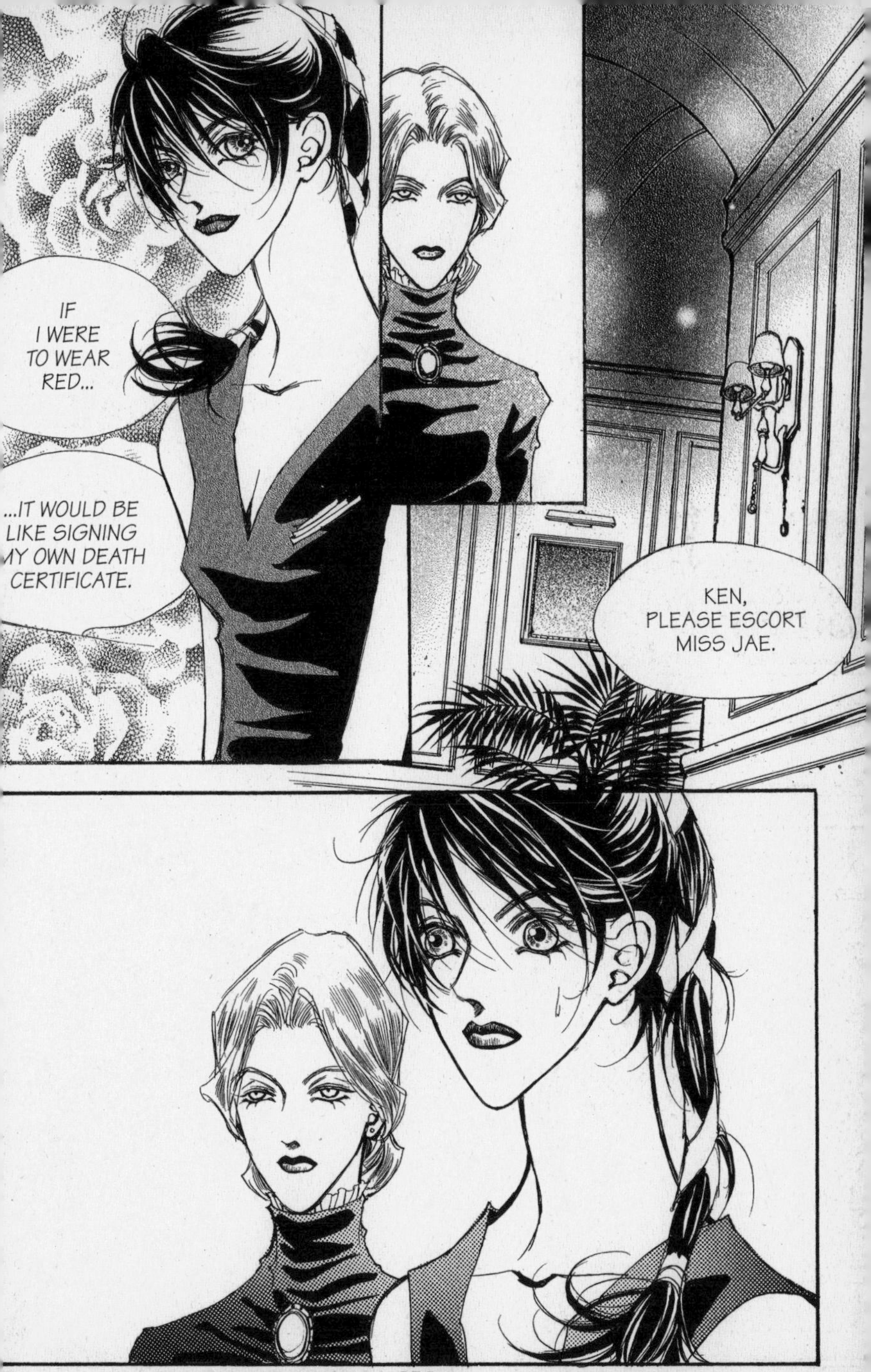
IF I WERE TO WEAR RED...
...IT WOULD BE LIKE SIGNING MY OWN DEATH CERTIFICATE.
KEN, PLEASE ESCORT MISS JAE.

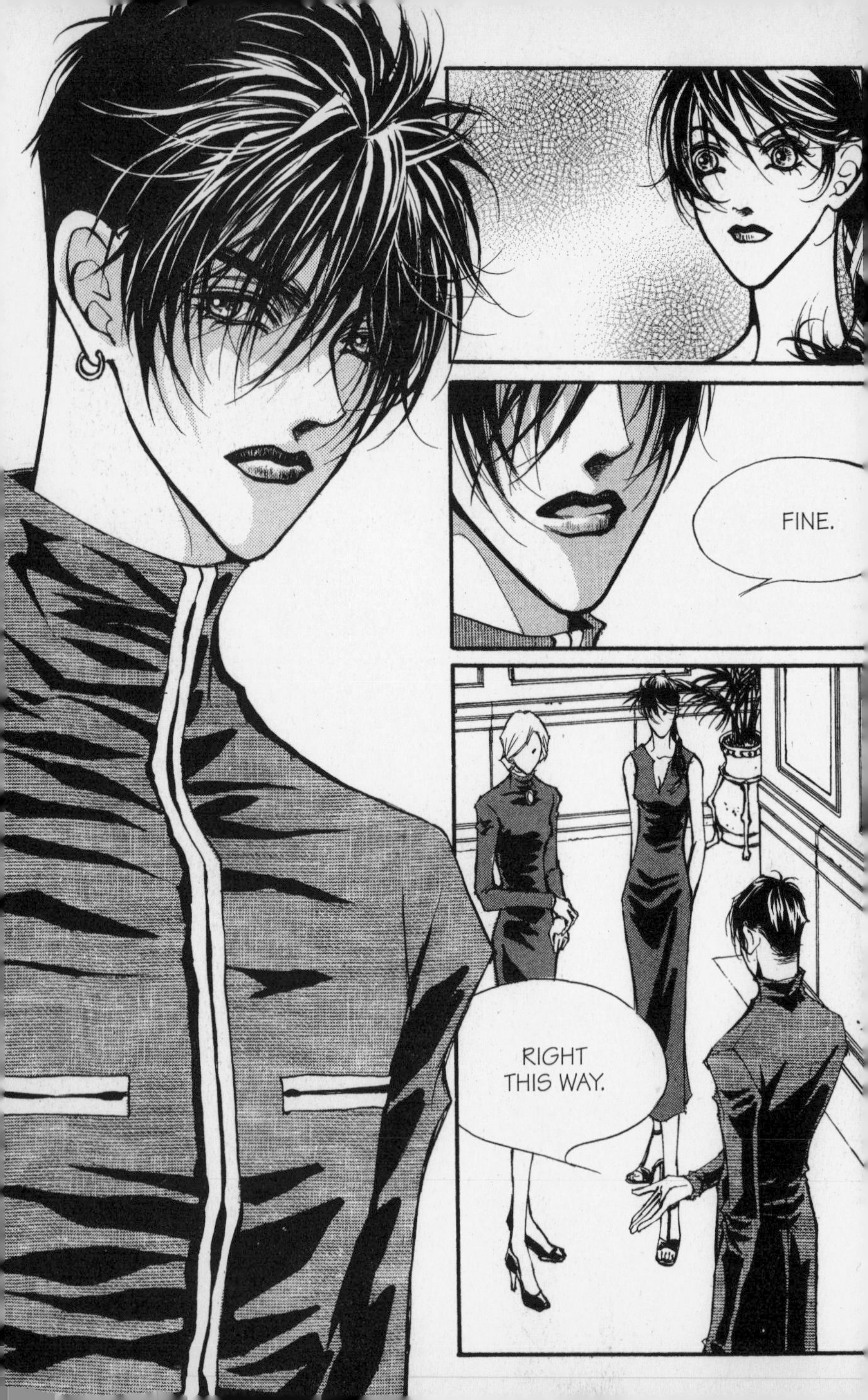
FINE.
RIGHT THIS WAY.

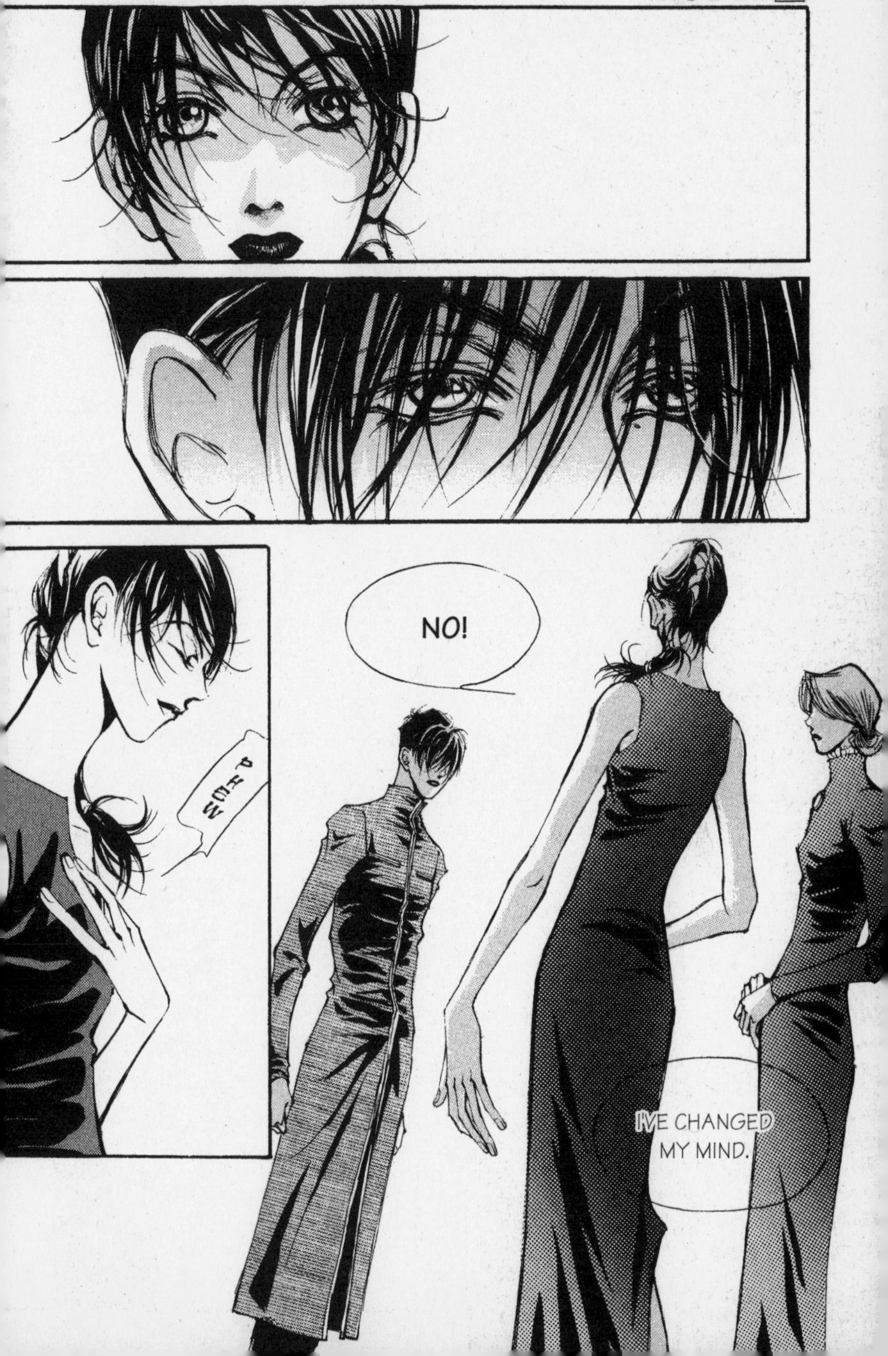
AHEM
NO!
I'VE CHANGED MY MIND.

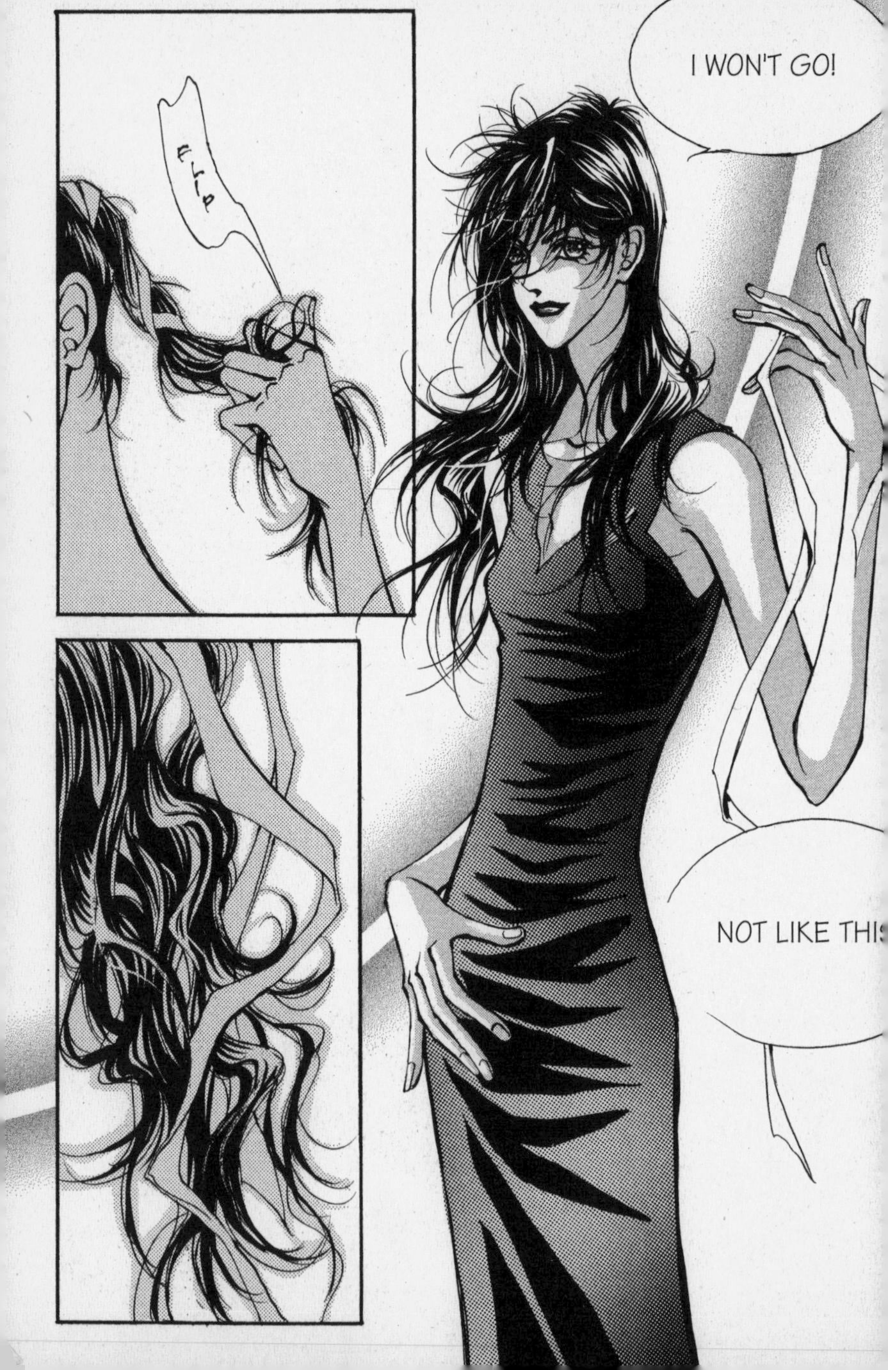
FLIP
I WON'T GO!
NOT LIKE THIS

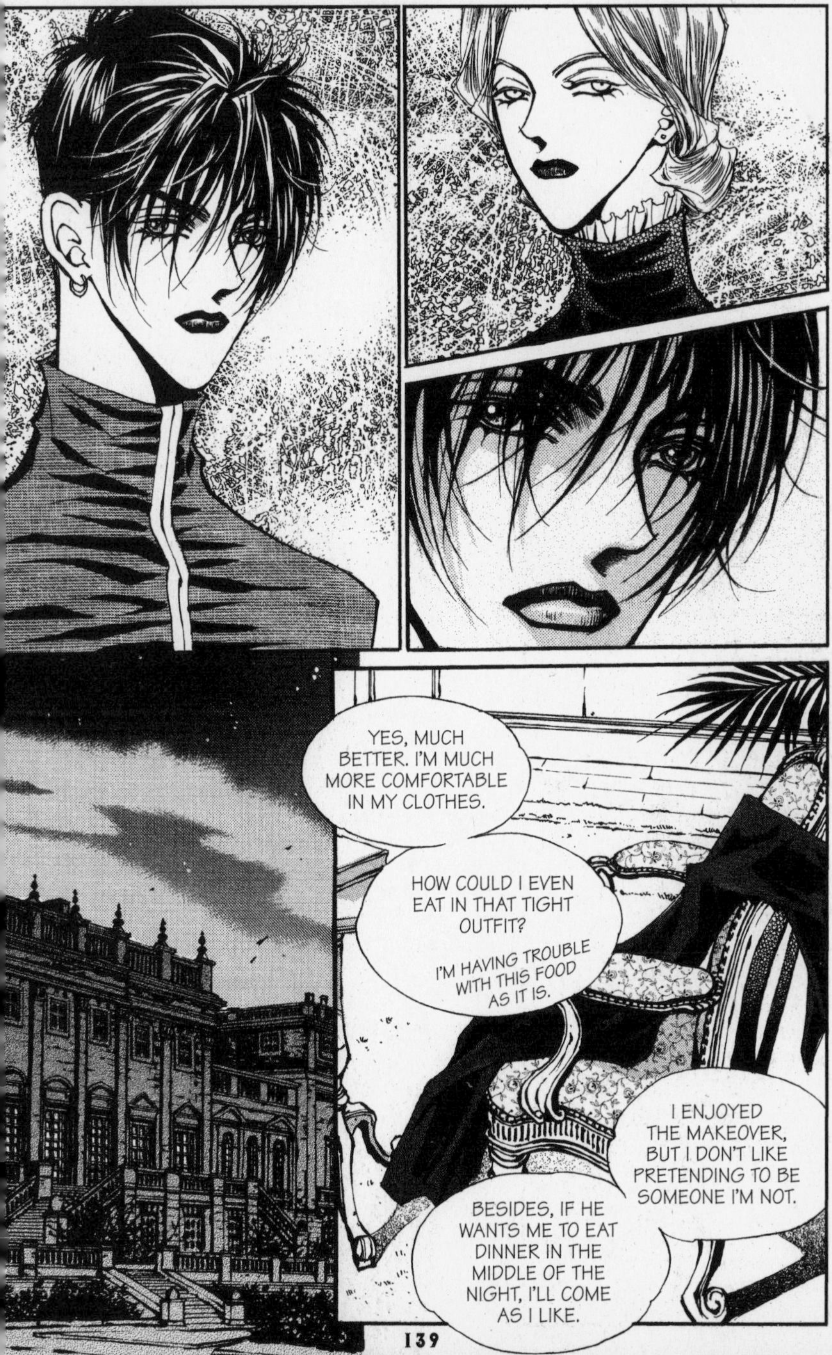
YES, MUCH BETTER. I'M MUCH MORE COMFORTABLE IN MY CLOTHES.
HOW COULD I EVEN EAT IN THAT TIGHT OUTFIT?
I'M HAVING TROUBLE WITH THIS FOOD AS IT IS.
I ENJOYED THE MAKEOVER, BUT I DON'T LIKE PRETENDING TO BE SOMEONE I'M NOT.
BESIDES, IF HE WANTS ME TO EAT DINNER IN THE MIDDLE OF THE NIGHT, I'LL COME AS I LIKE.

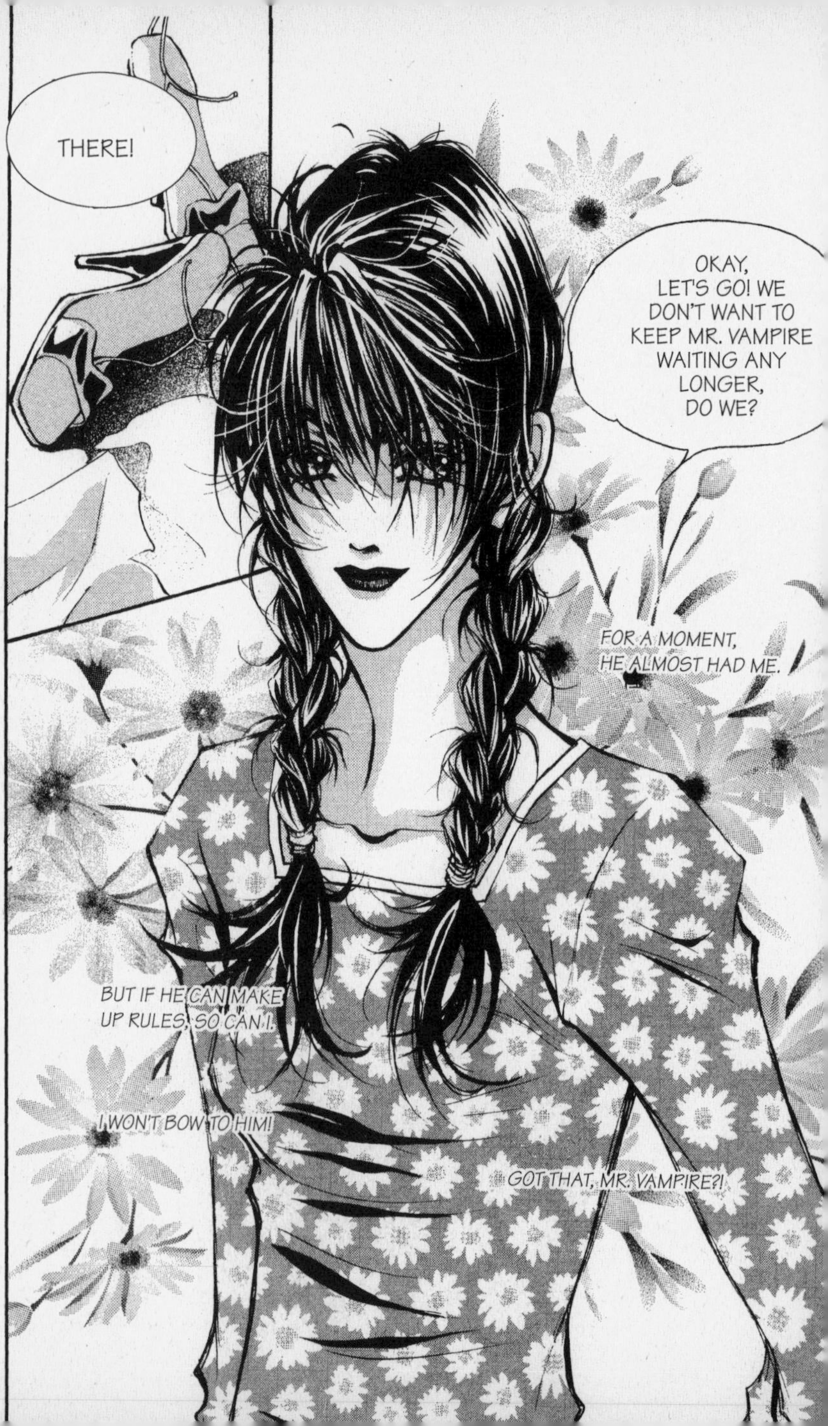
THERE!
OKAY, LET'S GO! WE DON'T WANT TO KEEP MR. VAMPIRE WAITING ANY LONGER, DO WE?
FOR A MOMENT, HE ALMOST HAD ME.
BUT IF HE CAN MAKE UP RULES, SO CAN I.
I WON'T BOW TO HIM!
GOT THAT, MR. VAMPIRE?!

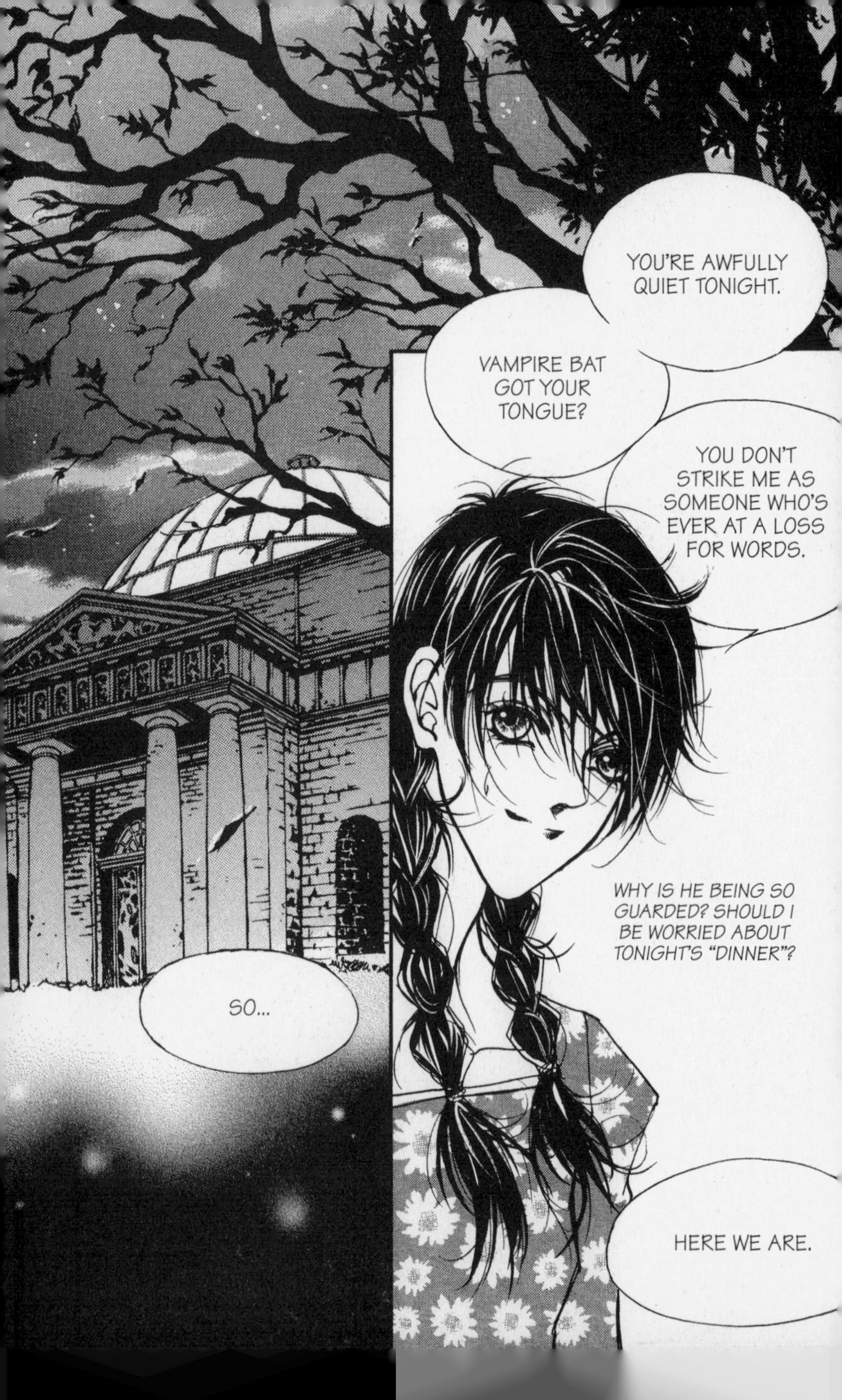
SO...
YOU'RE AWFULLY QUIET TONIGHT.
VAMPIRE BAT GOT YOUR TONGUE?
YOU DON'T STRIKE ME AS SOMEONE WHO'S EVER AT A LOSS FOR WORDS.
WHY IS HE BEING SO GUARDED? SHOULD I BE WORRIED ABOUT TONIGHT'S "DINNER"?
HERE WE ARE.

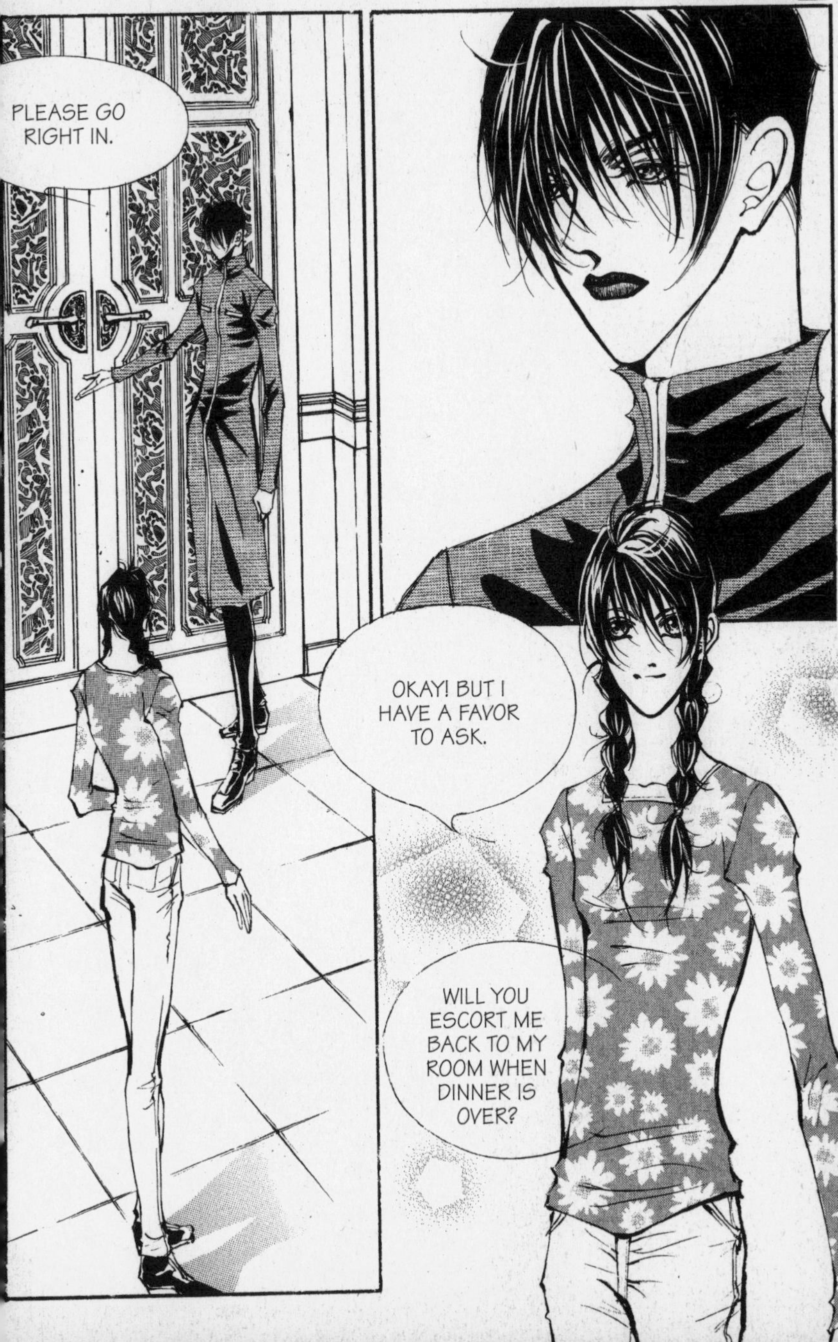
PLEASE GO RIGHT IN.
OKAY! BUT I HAVE A FAVOR TO ASK.
WILL YOU ESCORT ME BACK TO MY ROOM WHEN DINNER IS OVER?

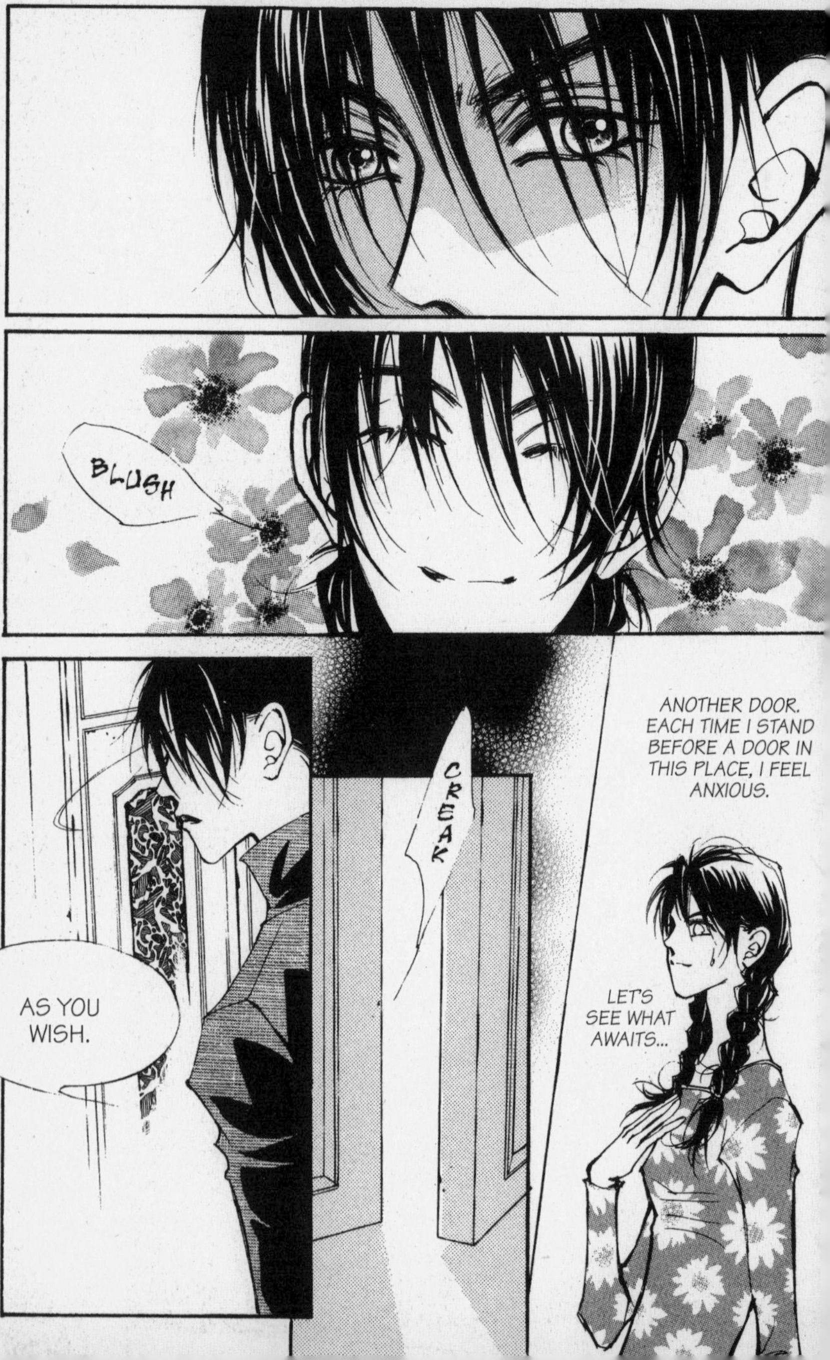
BLUSH
AS YOU WISH.
CREAK
ANOTHER DOOR. EACH TIME I STAND BEFORE A DOOR IN THIS PLACE, I FEEL ANXIOUS.
LET'S SEE WHAT AWAITS...

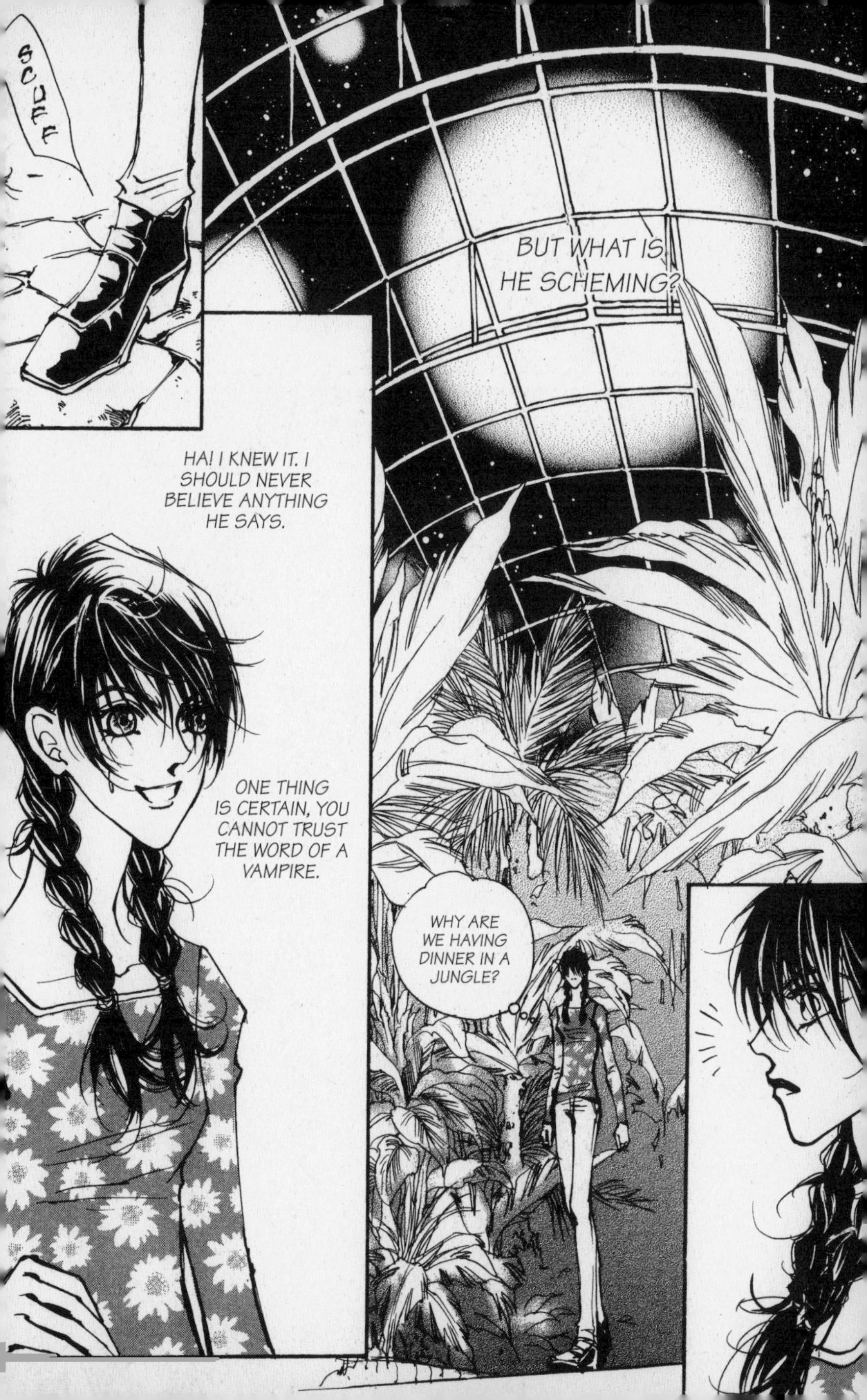
SCUFF
BUT WHAT IS HE SCHEMING?
HA! I KNEW IT. I SHOULD NEVER BELIEVE ANYTHING HE SAYS.
ONE THING IS CERTAIN, YOU CANNOT TRUST THE WORD OF A VAMPIRE.
WHY ARE WE HAVING DINNER IN A JUNGLE?

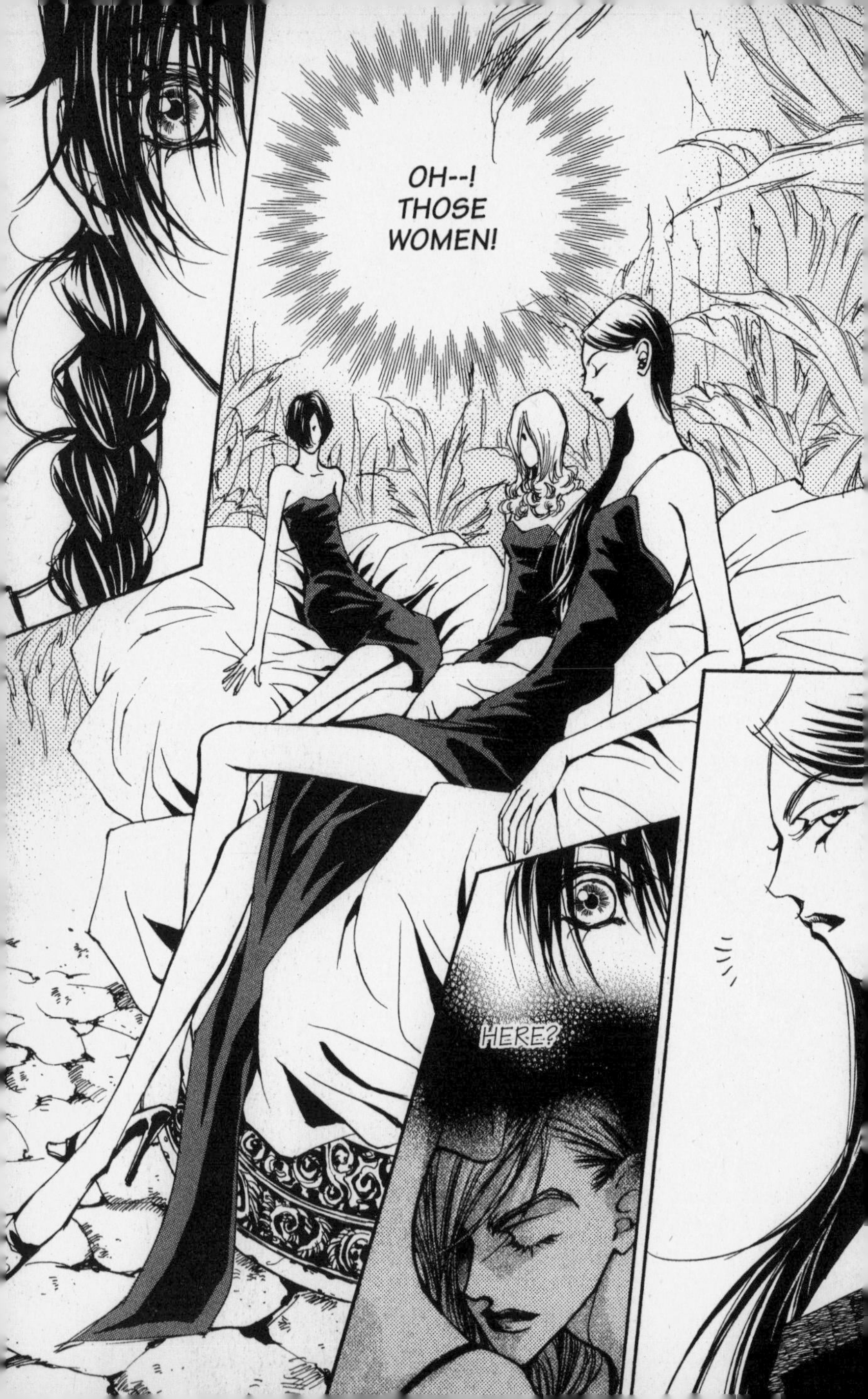
OH--! THOSE WOMEN!
HERE?

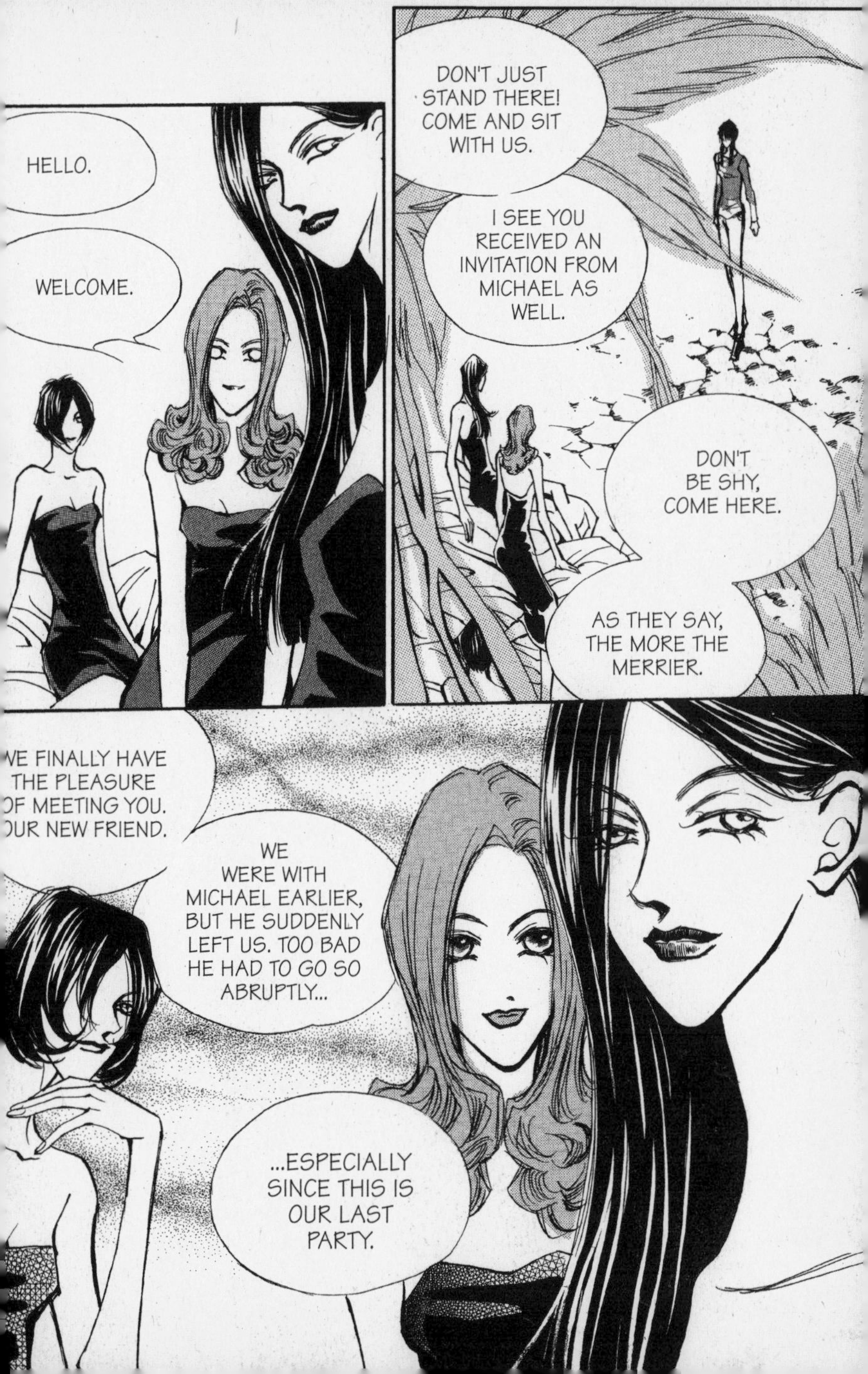
HELLO.
WELCOME.
DON'T JUST STAND THERE! COME AND SIT WITH US.
I SEE YOU RECEIVED AN INVITATION FROM MICHAEL AS WELL.
DON'T BE SHY, COME HERE.
AS THEY SAY, THE MORE THE MERRIER.
WE FINALLY HAVE THE PLEASURE OF MEETING YOU. OUR NEW FRIEND.
WE WERE WITH MICHAEL EARLIER, BUT HE SUDDENLY LEFT US. TOO BAD HE HAD TO GO SO ABRUPTLY...
...ESPECIALLY SINCE THIS IS OUR LAST PARTY.

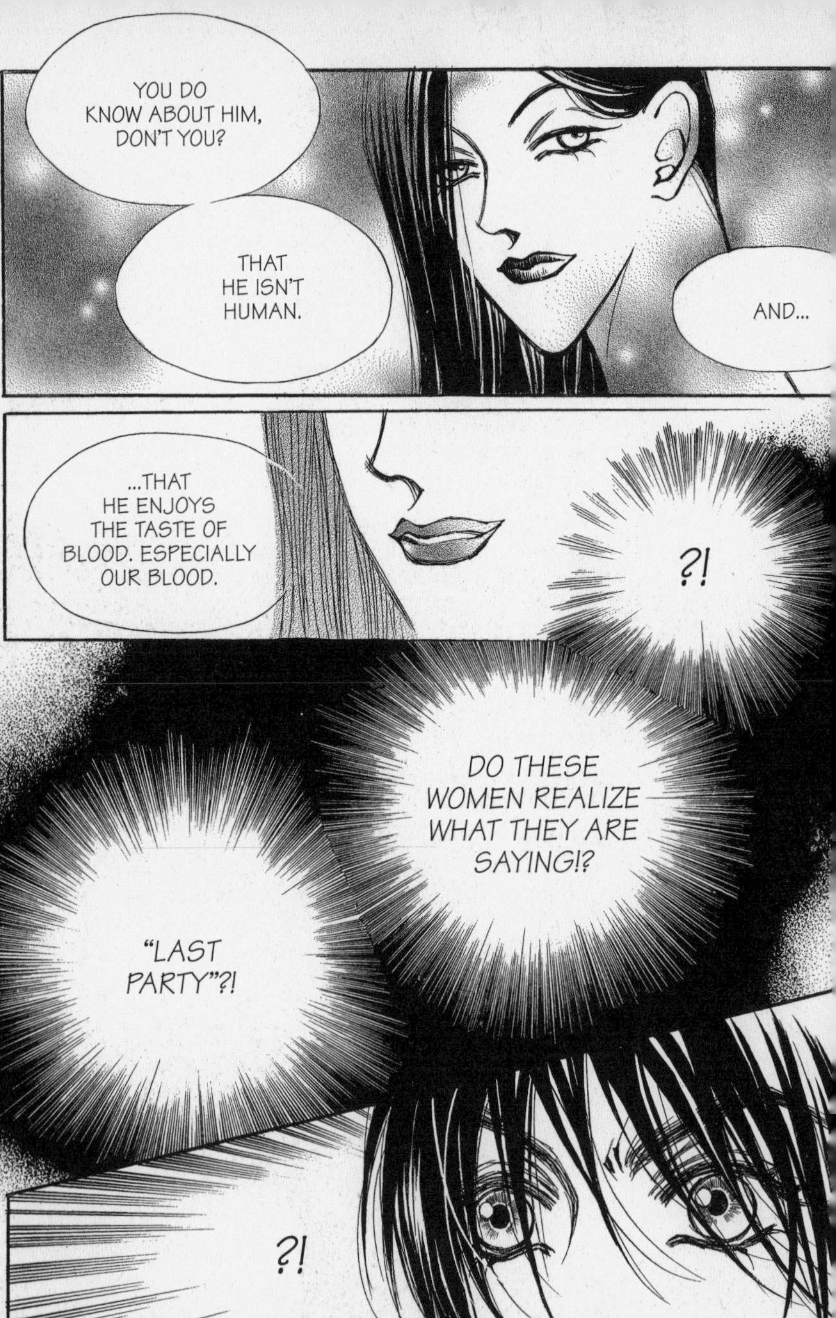
YOU DO KNOW ABOUT HIM, DON'T YOU?
THAT HE ISN'T HUMAN.
AND...
...THAT HE ENJOYS THE TASTE OF BLOOD. ESPECIALLY OUR BLOOD.
?!
DO THESE WOMEN REALIZE WHAT THEY ARE SAYING!?
"LAST PARTY"?!
?!

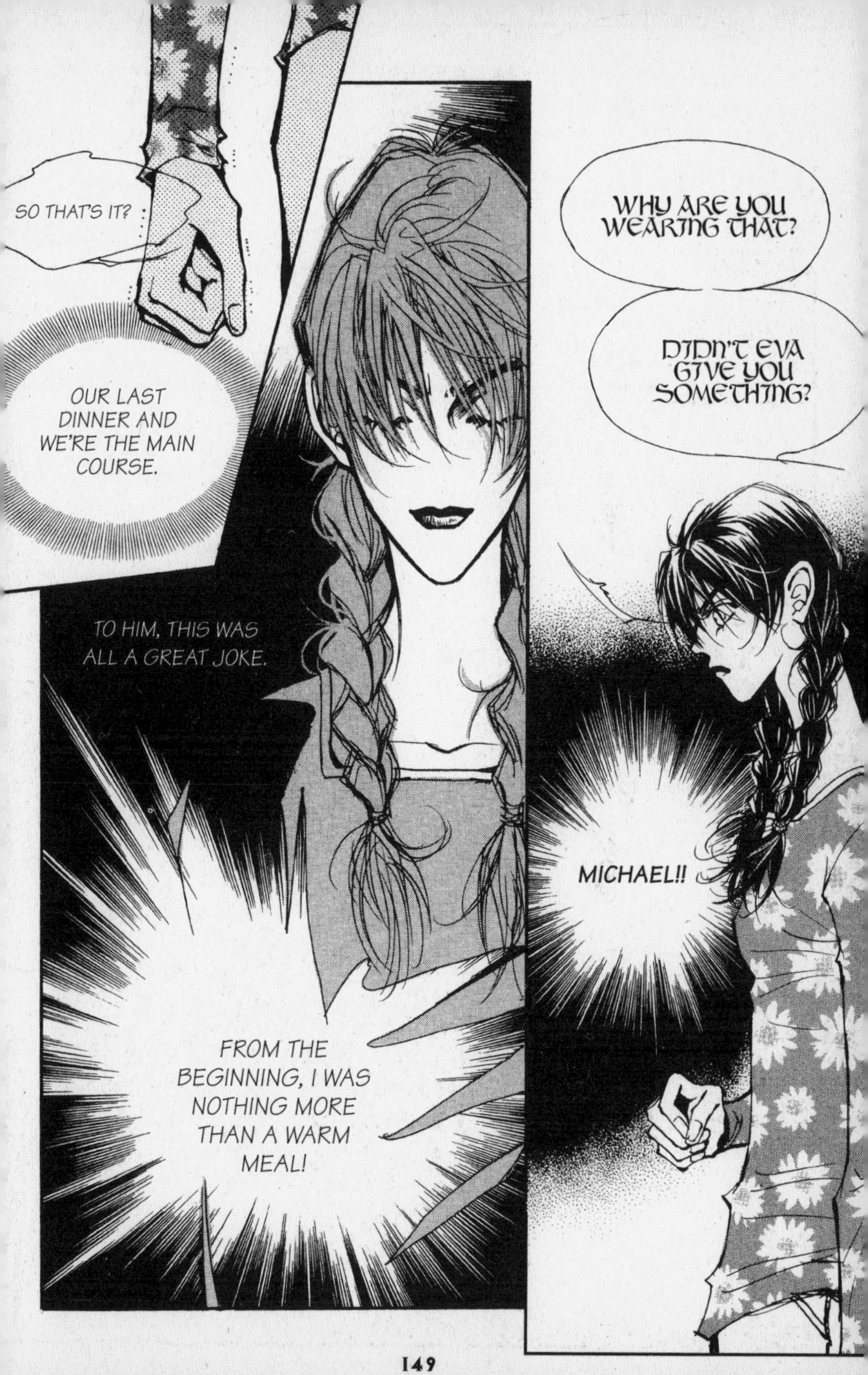

SO THAT'S IT?
OUR LAST DINNER AND WE'RE THE MAIN COURSE.
TO HIM, THIS WAS ALL A GREAT JOKE.
FROM THE BEGINNING, I WAS NOTHING MORE THAN A WARM MEAL!
WHY ARE YOU WEARING THAT?
DIDN'T EVA GIVE YOU SOMETHING?
MICHAEL!!

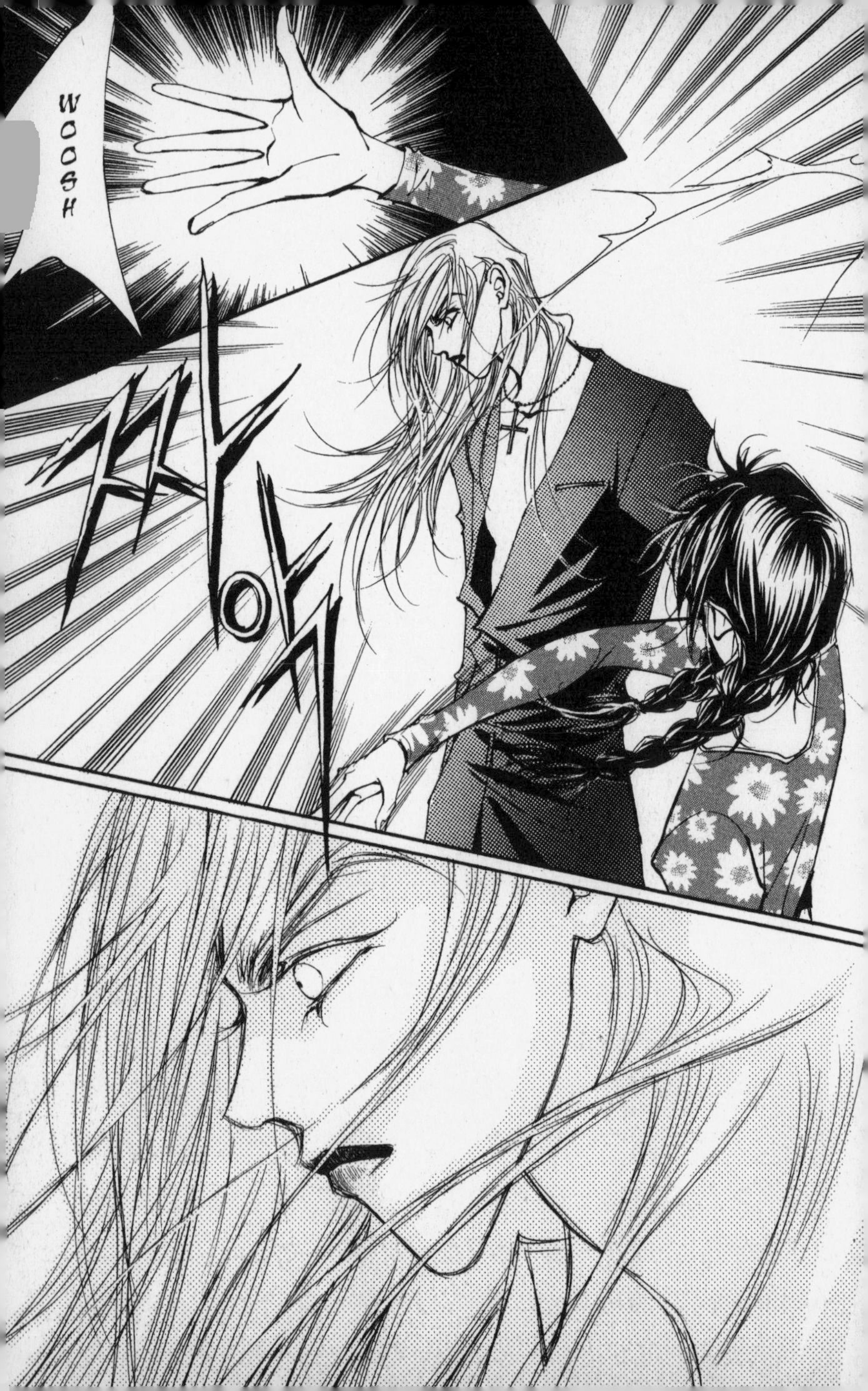
WOOSH

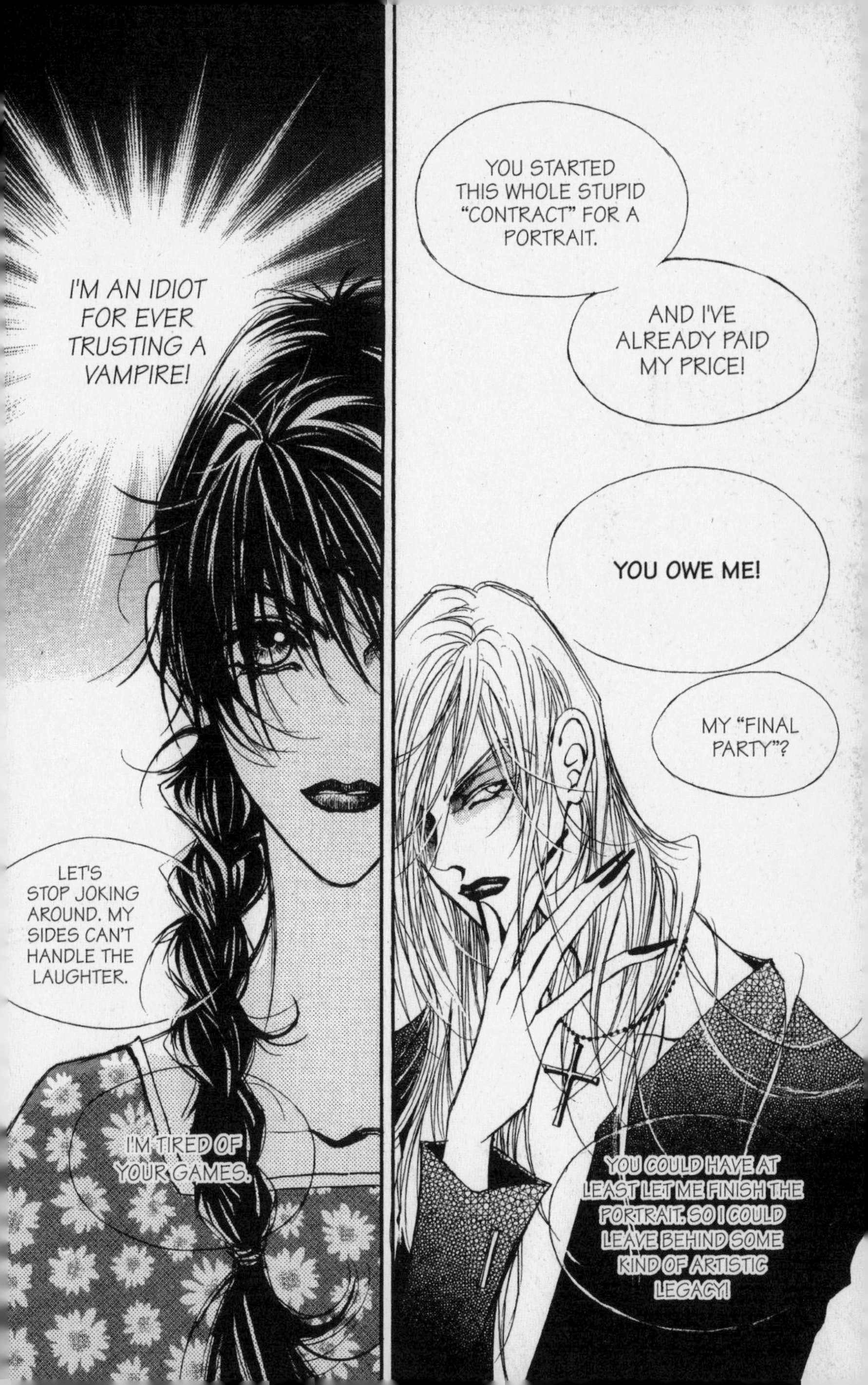
I'M AN IDIOT FOR EVER TRUSTING A VAMPIRE!
LET'S STOP JOKING AROUND. MY SIDES CAN'T HANDLE THE LAUGHTER.
I'M TIRED OF YOUR GAMES.
YOU STARTED THIS WHOLE STUPID "CONTRACT" FOR A PORTRAIT.
AND I'VE ALREADY PAID MY PRICE!
YOU OWE ME!
MY "FINAL PARTY"?
YOU COULD HAVE AT LEAST LET ME FINISH THE PORTRAIT. SO I COULD LEAVE BEHIND SOME KIND OF ARTISTIC LEGACY!

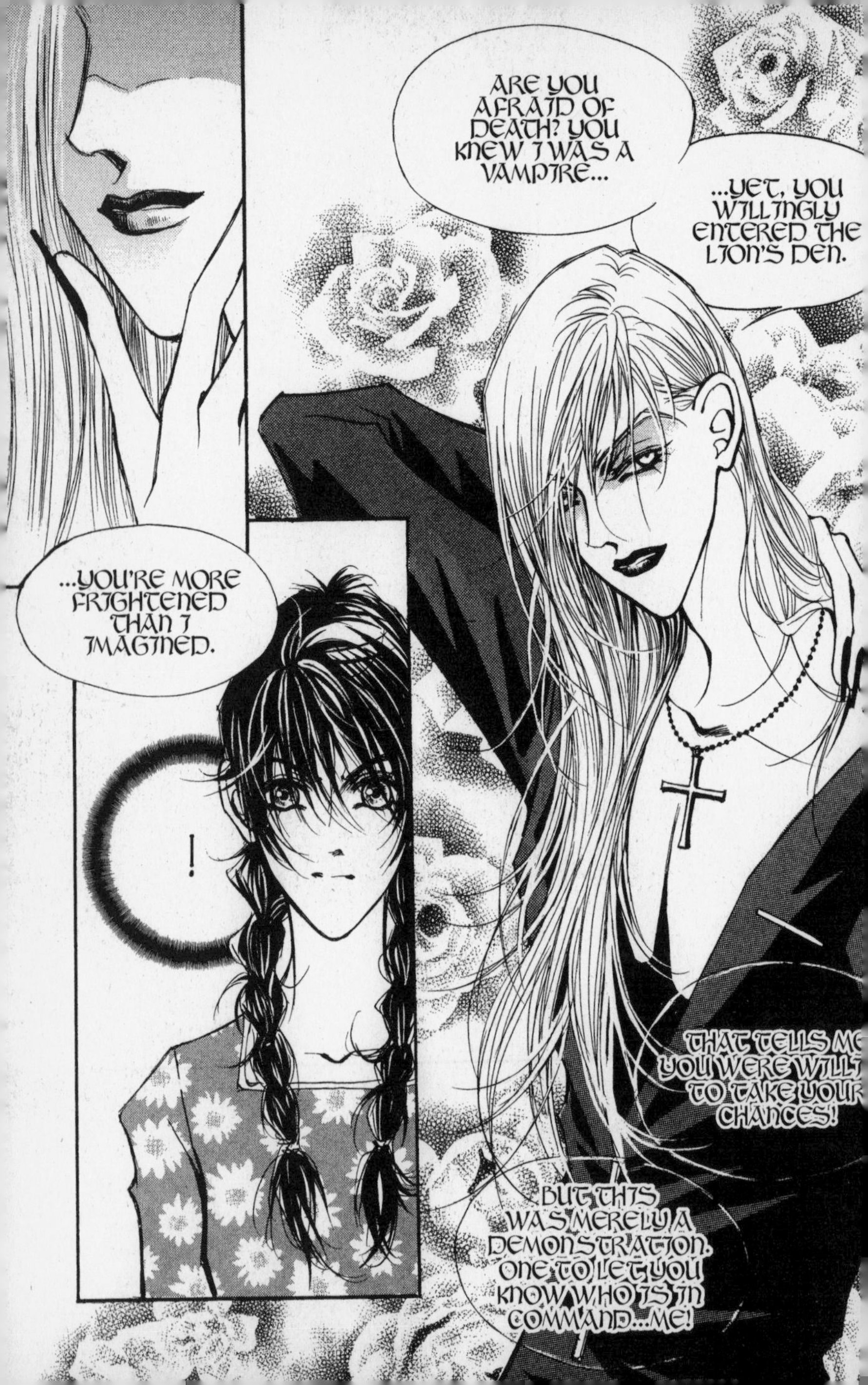
...YOU'RE MORE FRIGHTENED THAN I IMAGINED.
!
ARE YOU AFRAID OF DEATH? YOU KNEW I WAS A VAMPIRE...
...YET, YOU WILLINGLY ENTERED THE LION'S DEN.
THAT TELLS ME YOU WERE WILLI TO TAKE YOUR CHANCES!
BUT THIS WAS MERELY A DEMONSTRATION. ONE TO LET YOU KNOW WHO IS IN COMMAND...ME!

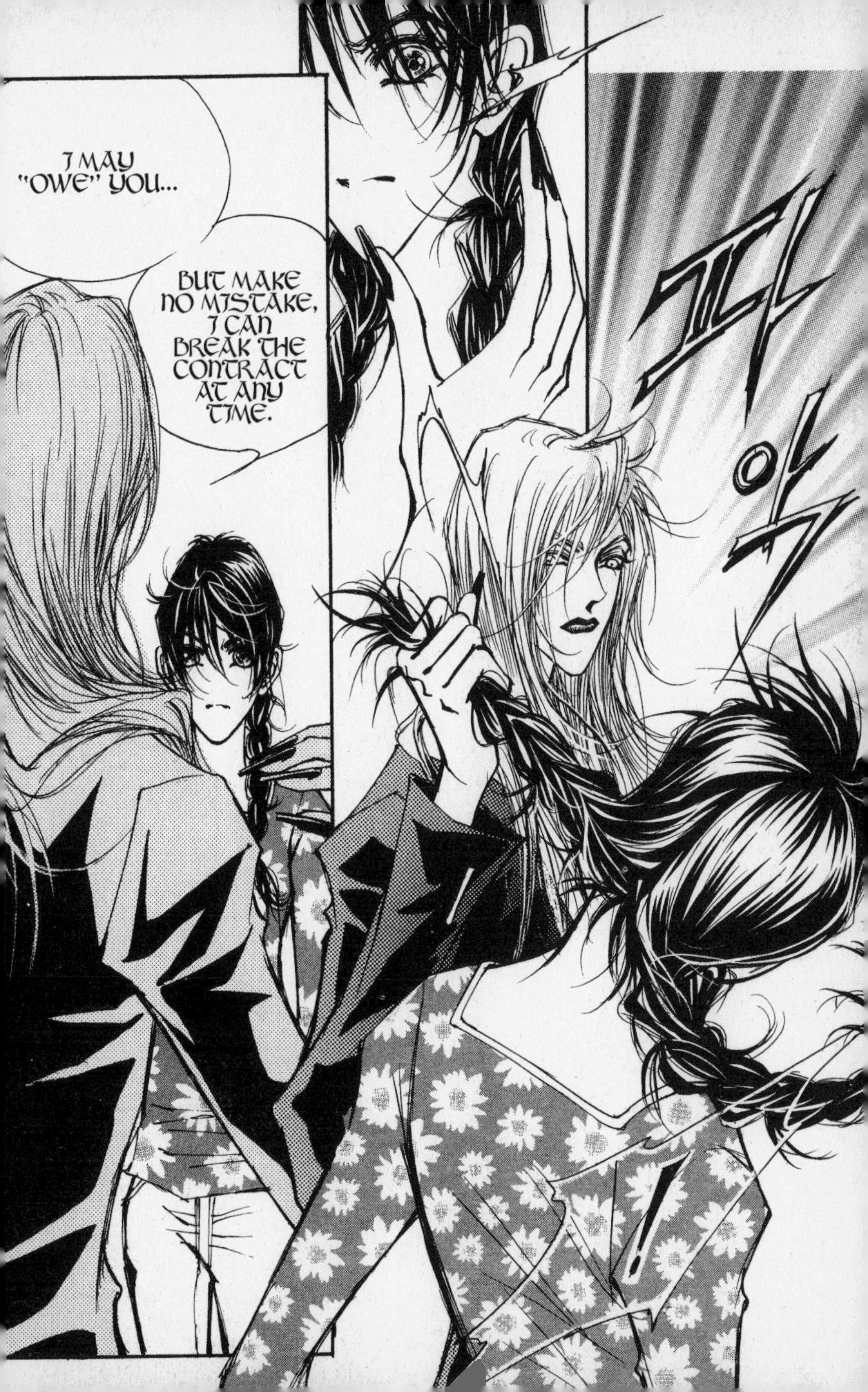
I MAY "OWE" YOU...
BUT MAKE NO MISTAKE, I CAN BREAK THE CONTRACT AT ANY TIME.

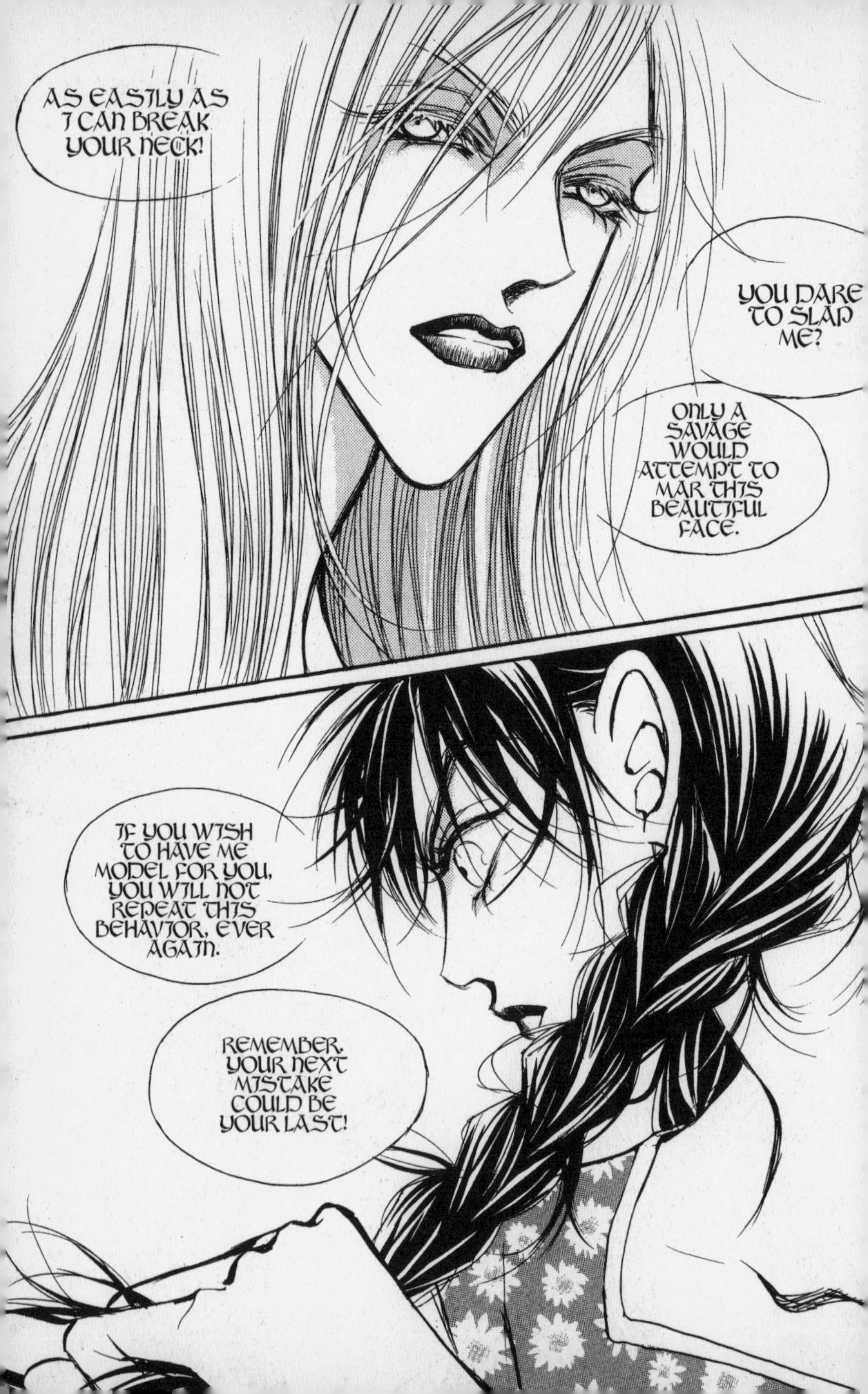
AS EASILY AS I CAN BREAK YOUR NECK!
YOU DARE TO SLAP ME?
ONLY A SAVAGE WOULD ATTEMPT TO MAR THIS BEAUTIFUL FACE.
IF YOU WISH TO HAVE ME MODEL FOR YOU, YOU WILL NOT REPEAT THIS BEHAVIOR, EVER AGAIN.
REMEMBER. YOUR NEXT MISTAKE COULD BE YOUR LAST!

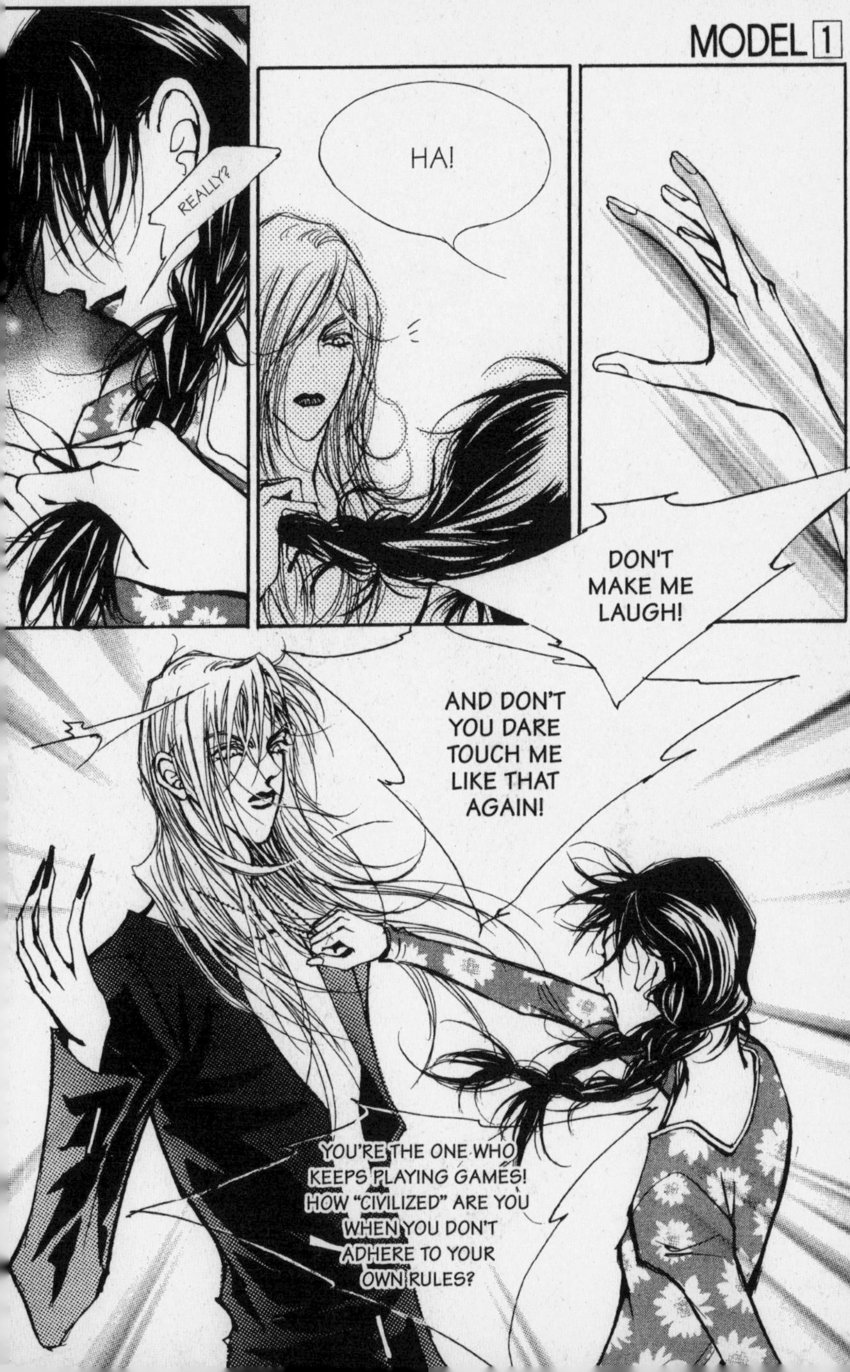
REALLY?
HA!
DON'T MAKE ME LAUGH!
AND DON'T YOU DARE TOUCH ME LIKE THAT AGAIN!
YOU'RE THE ONE WHO KEEPS PLAYING GAMES! HOW "CIVILIZED" ARE YOU WHEN YOU DON'T ADHERE TO YOUR OWN RULES?

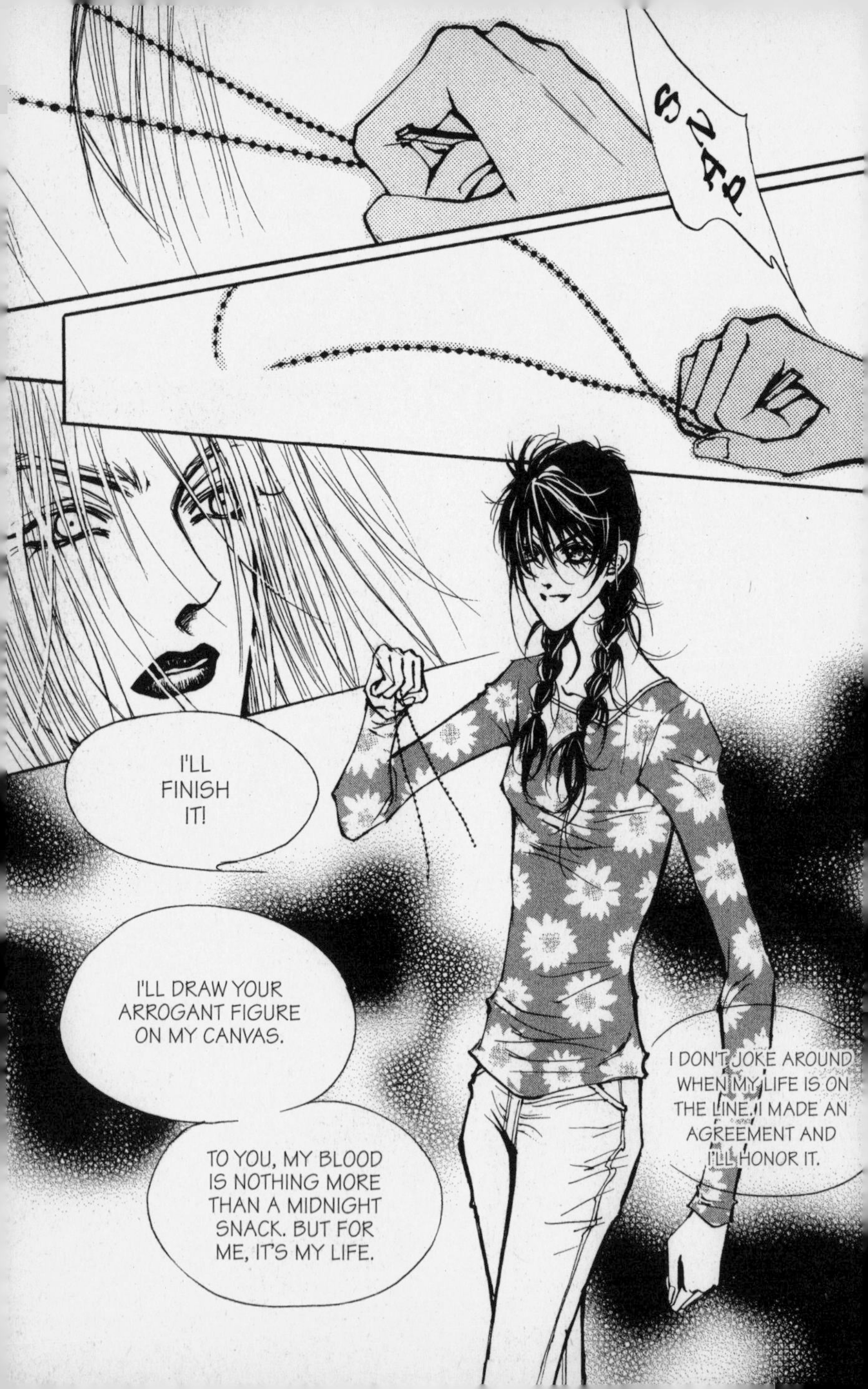
SNAP
I'LL FINISH IT!
I'LL DRAW YOUR ARROGANT FIGURE ON MY CANVAS.
TO YOU, MY BLOOD IS NOTHING MORE THAN A MIDNIGHT SNACK. BUT FOR ME, IT'S MY LIFE.
I DON'T JOKE AROUND WHEN MY LIFE IS ON THE LINE. I MADE AN AGREEMENT AND I'LL HONOR IT.

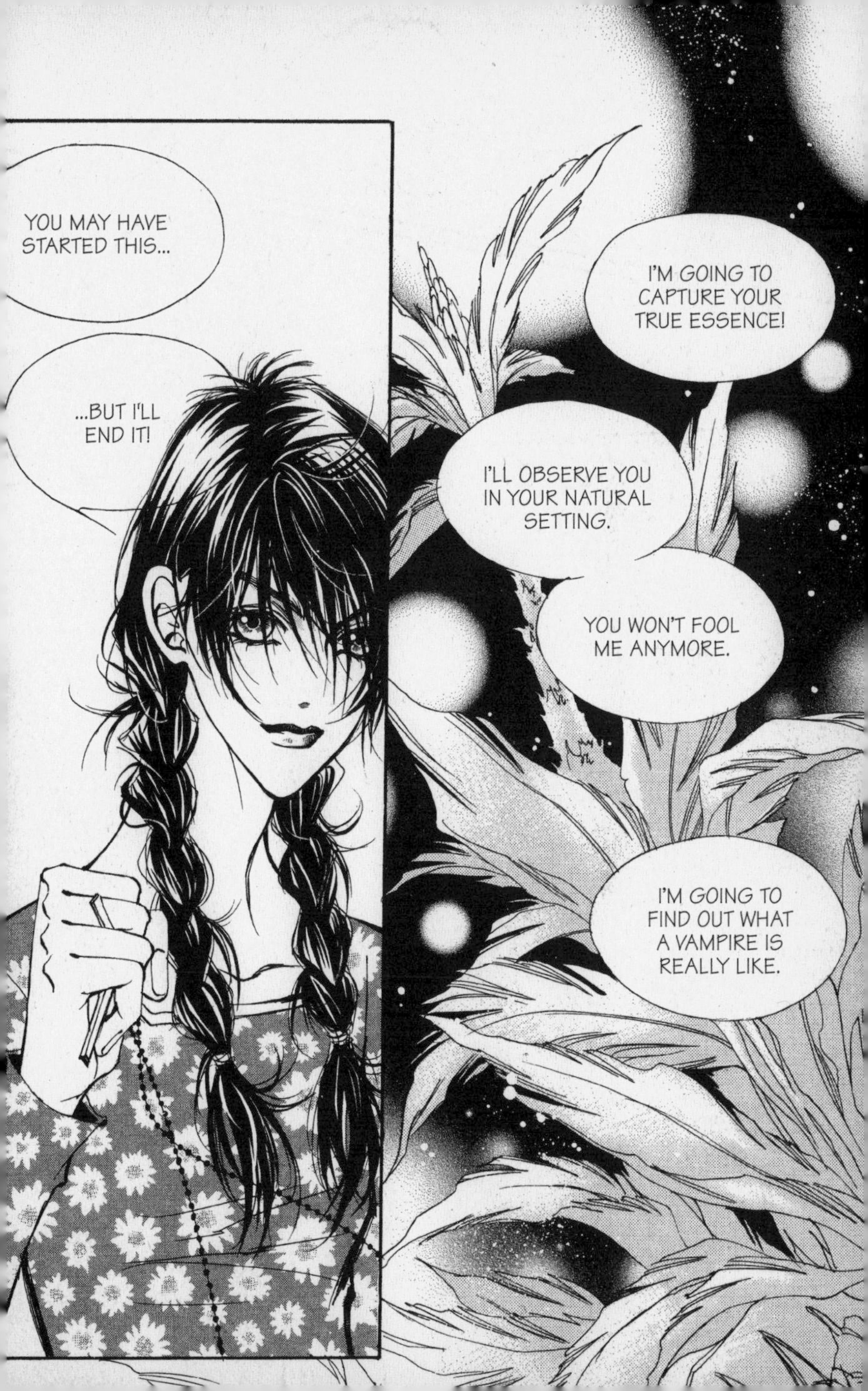
YOU MAY HAVE STARTED THIS...
...BUT I'LL END IT!
I'M GOING TO CAPTURE YOUR TRUE ESSENCE!
I'LL OBSERVE YOU IN YOUR NATURAL SETTING.
YOU WON'T FOOL ME ANYMORE.
I'M GOING TO FIND OUT WHAT A VAMPIRE IS REALLY LIKE.

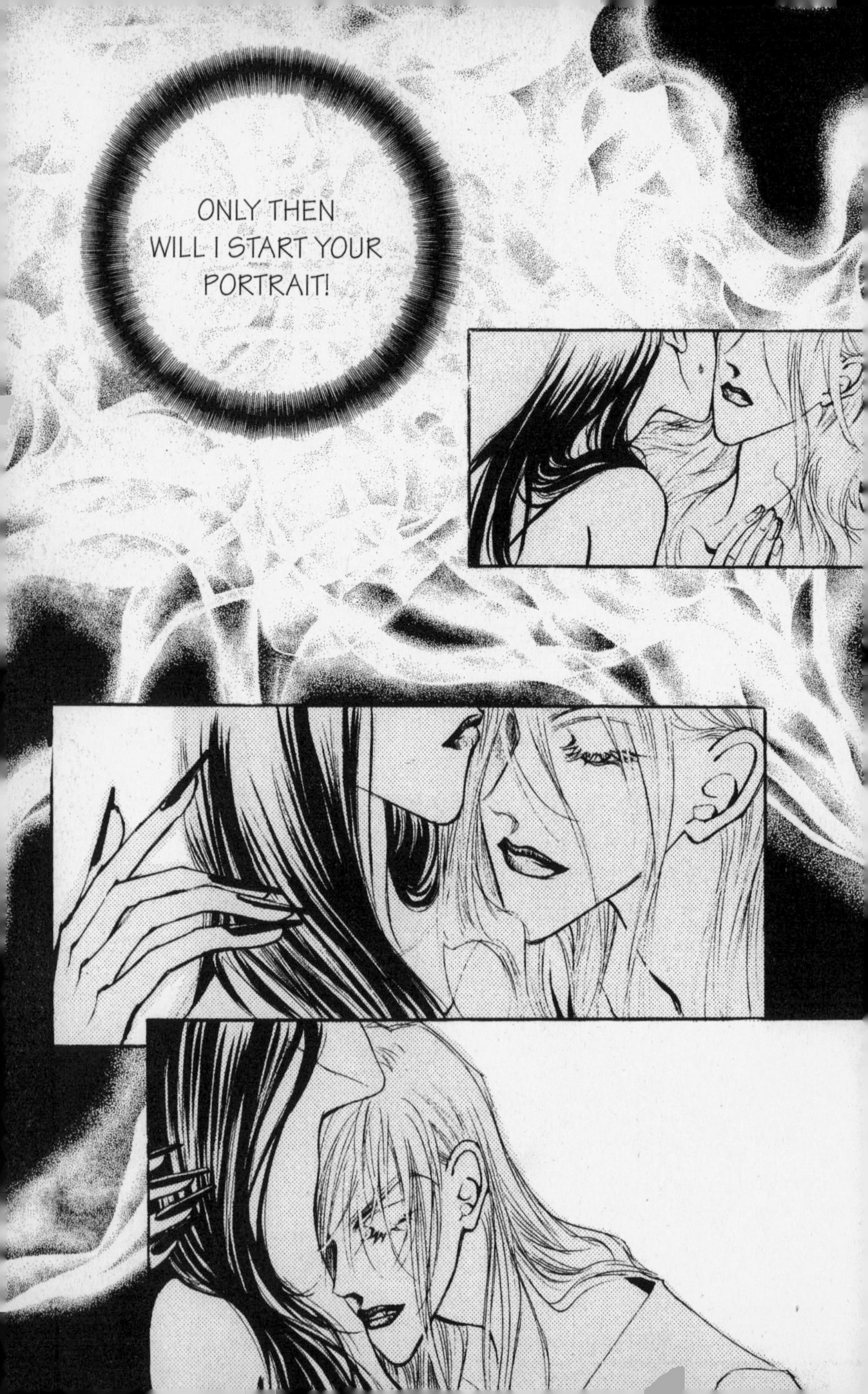
ONLY THEN WILL I START YOUR PORTRAIT!

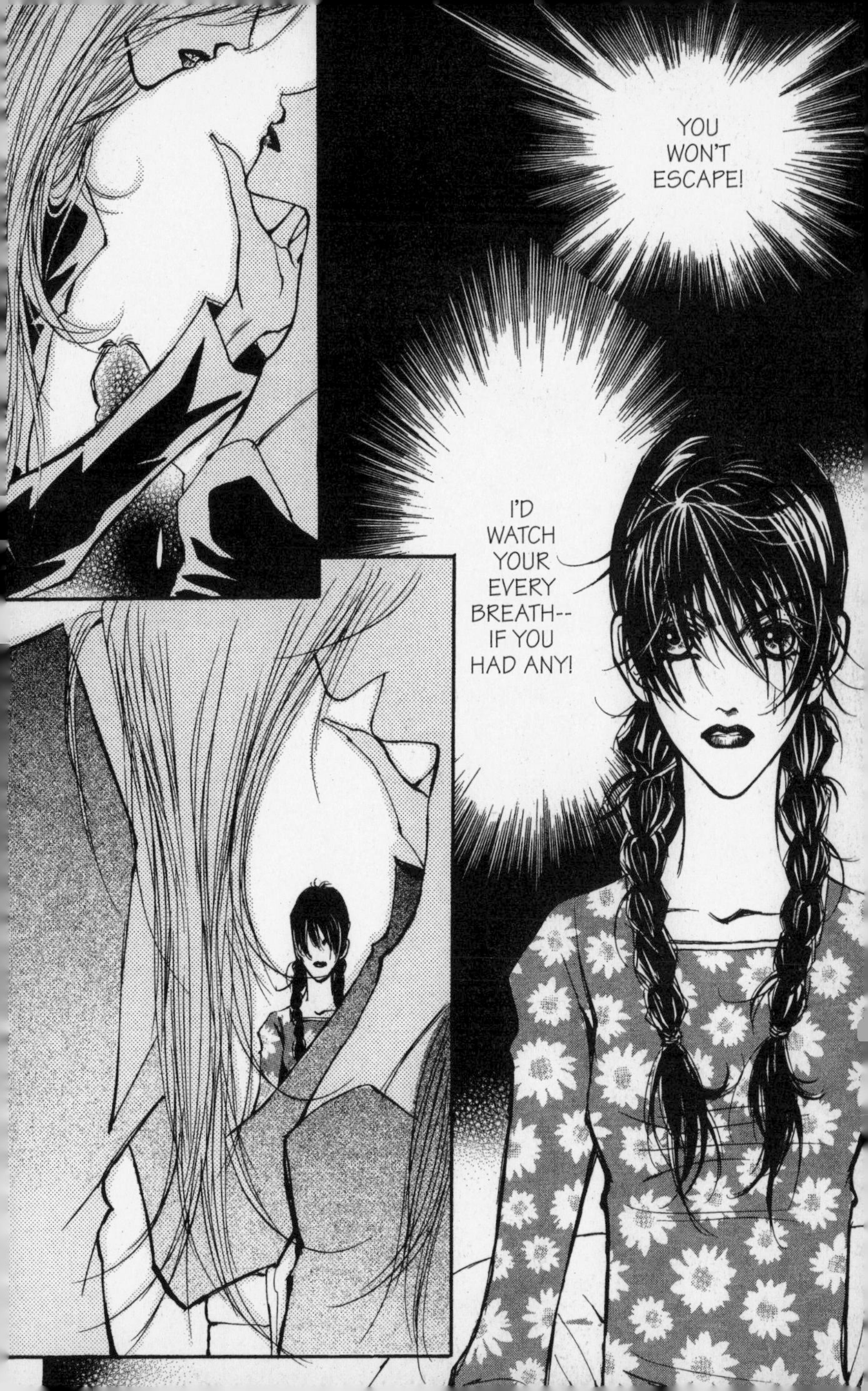
YOU WON'T ESCAPE!
I'D WATCH YOUR EVERY BREATH-- IF YOU HAD ANY!

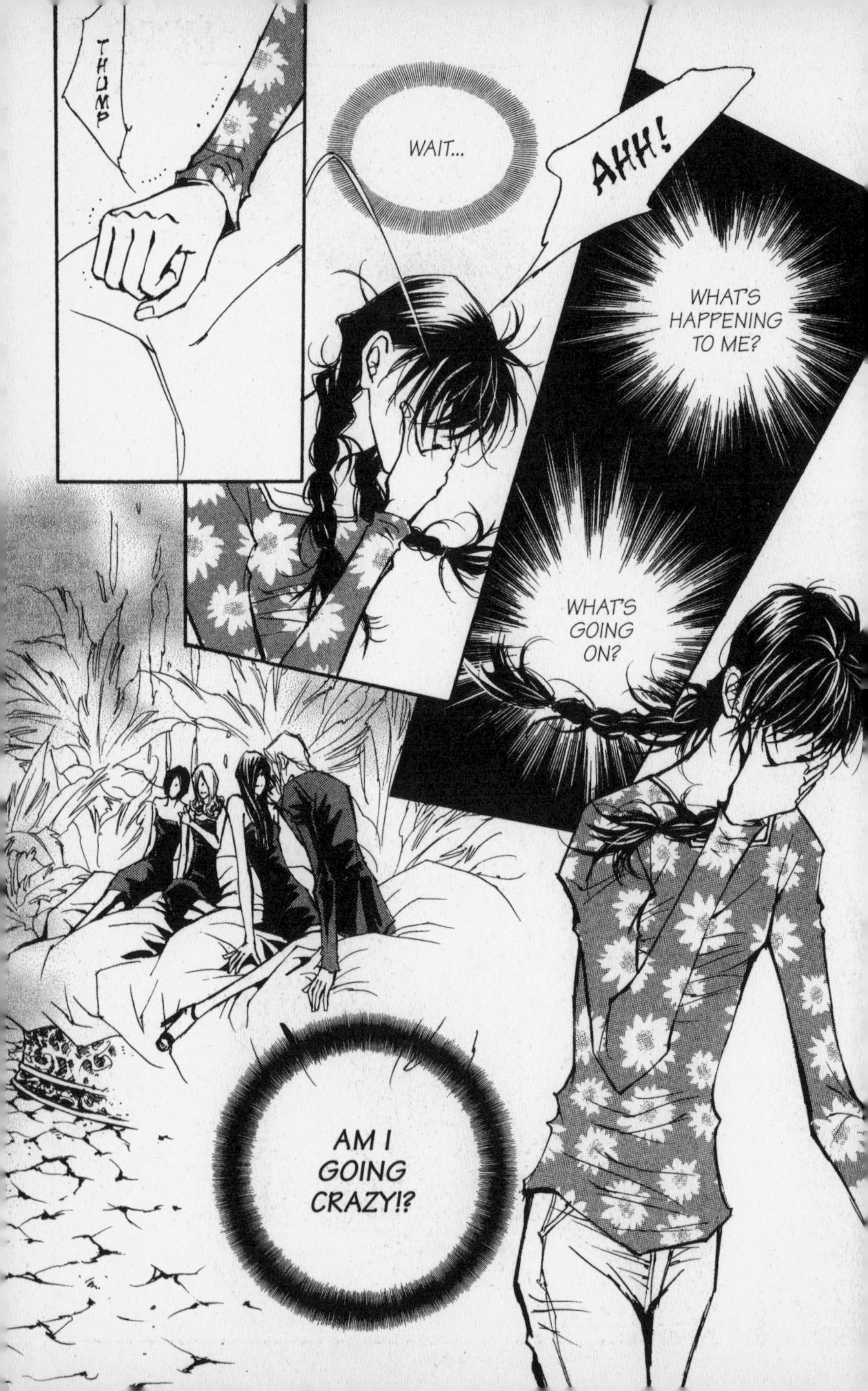
THUMP
WAIT...
AHH!
WHAT'S HAPPENING TO ME?
WHAT'S GOING ON?
AM I GOING CRAZY!?

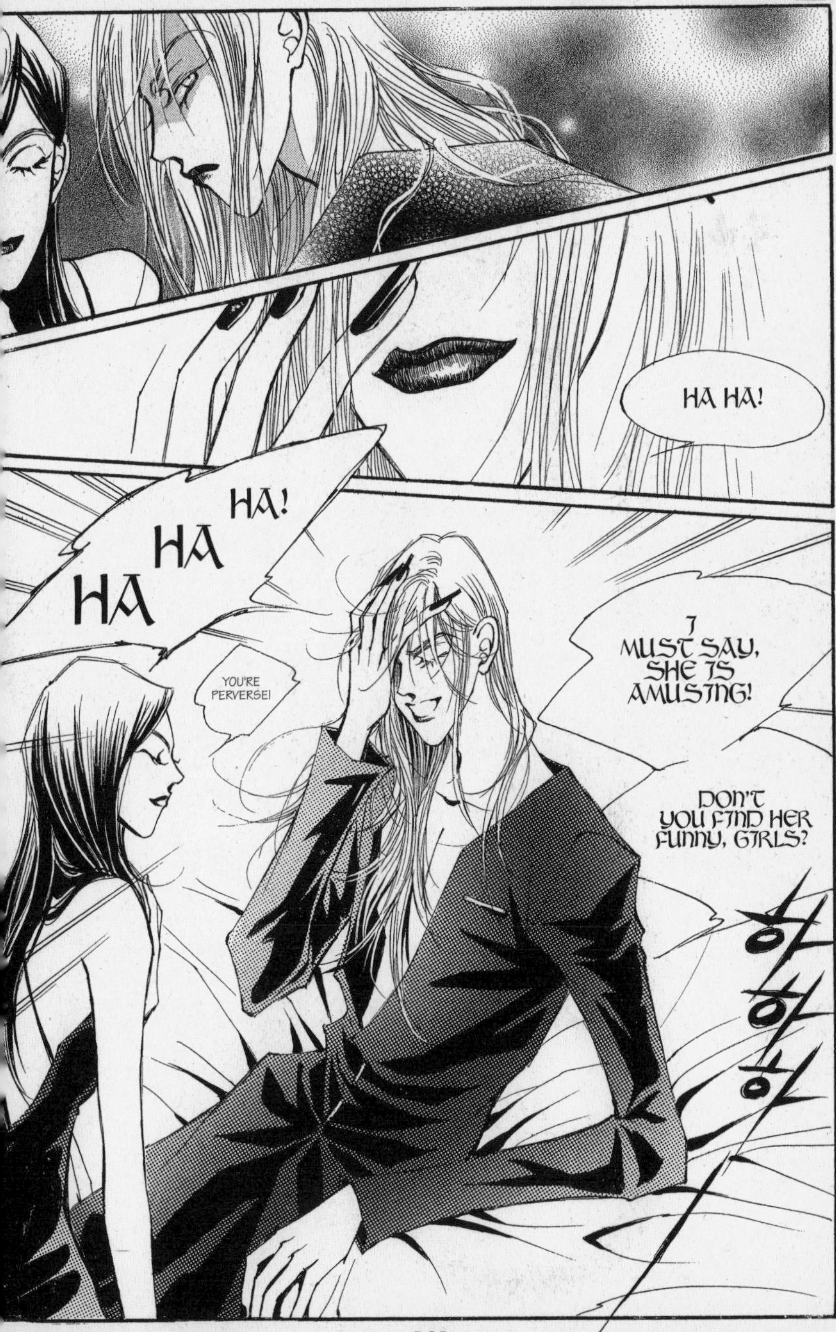
HA HA!
HA HA HA!
YOU'RE PERVERSE!
I MUST SAY, SHE IS AMUSING!
DON'T YOU FIND HER FUNNY, GIRLS?
하하하

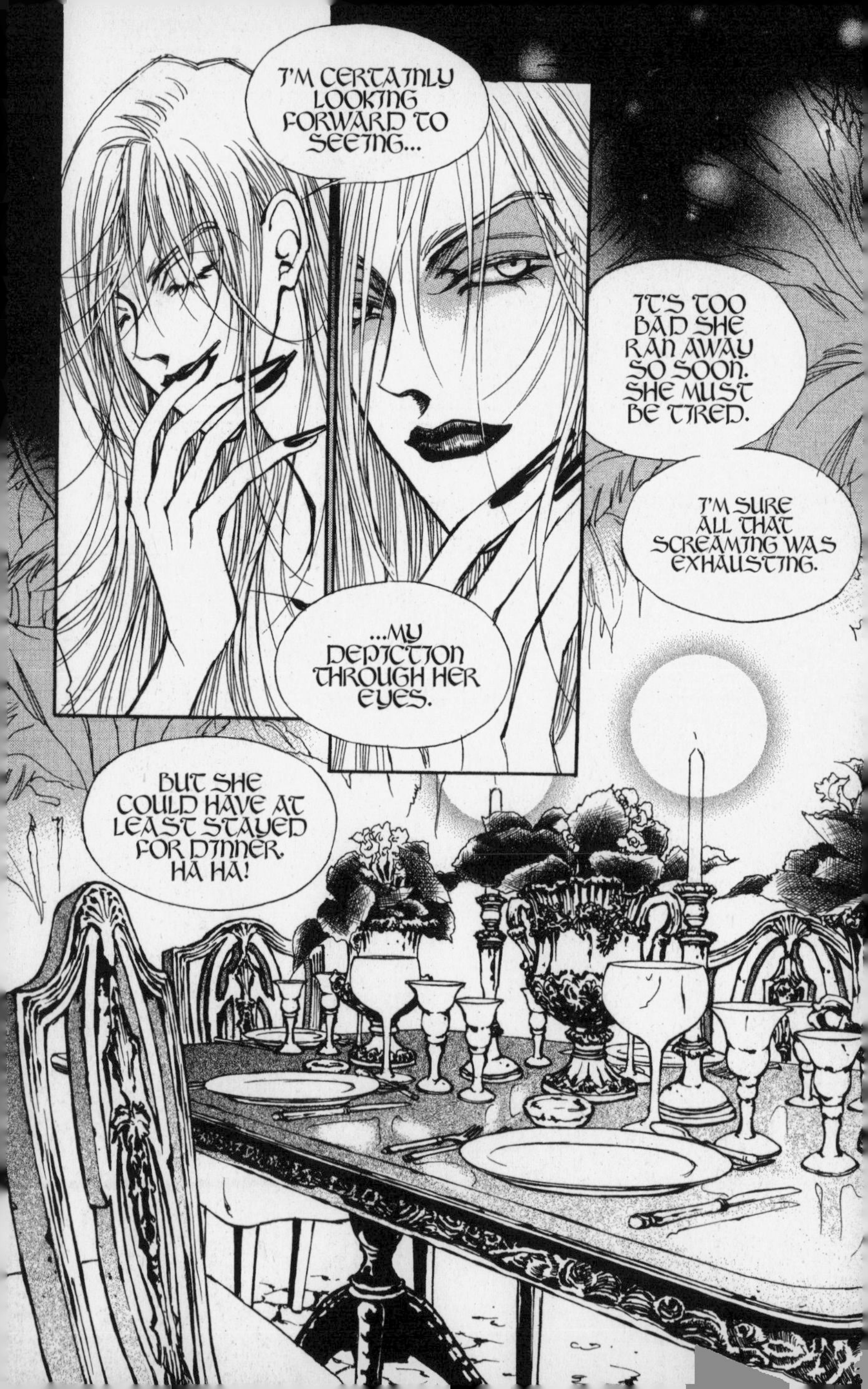
I'M CERTAINLY LOOKING FORWARD TO SEEING...
...MY DEPICTION THROUGH HER EYES.
IT'S TOO BAD SHE RAN AWAY SO SOON. SHE MUST BE TIRED.
I'M SURE ALL THAT SCREAMING WAS EXHAUSTING.
BUT SHE COULD HAVE AT LEAST STAYED FOR DINNER. HA HA!

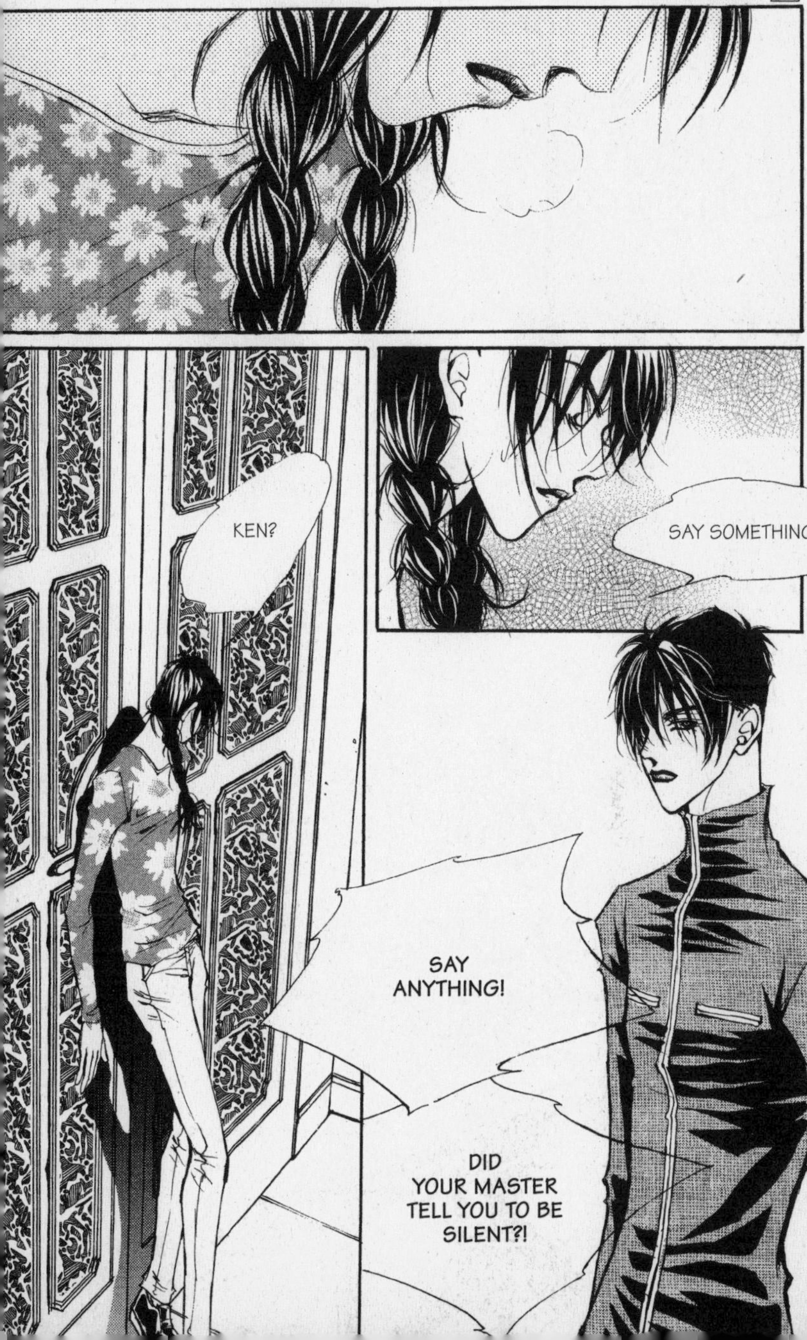
KEN?
SAY SOMETHING.
SAY ANYTHING!
DID YOUR MASTER TELL YOU TO BE SILENT?!

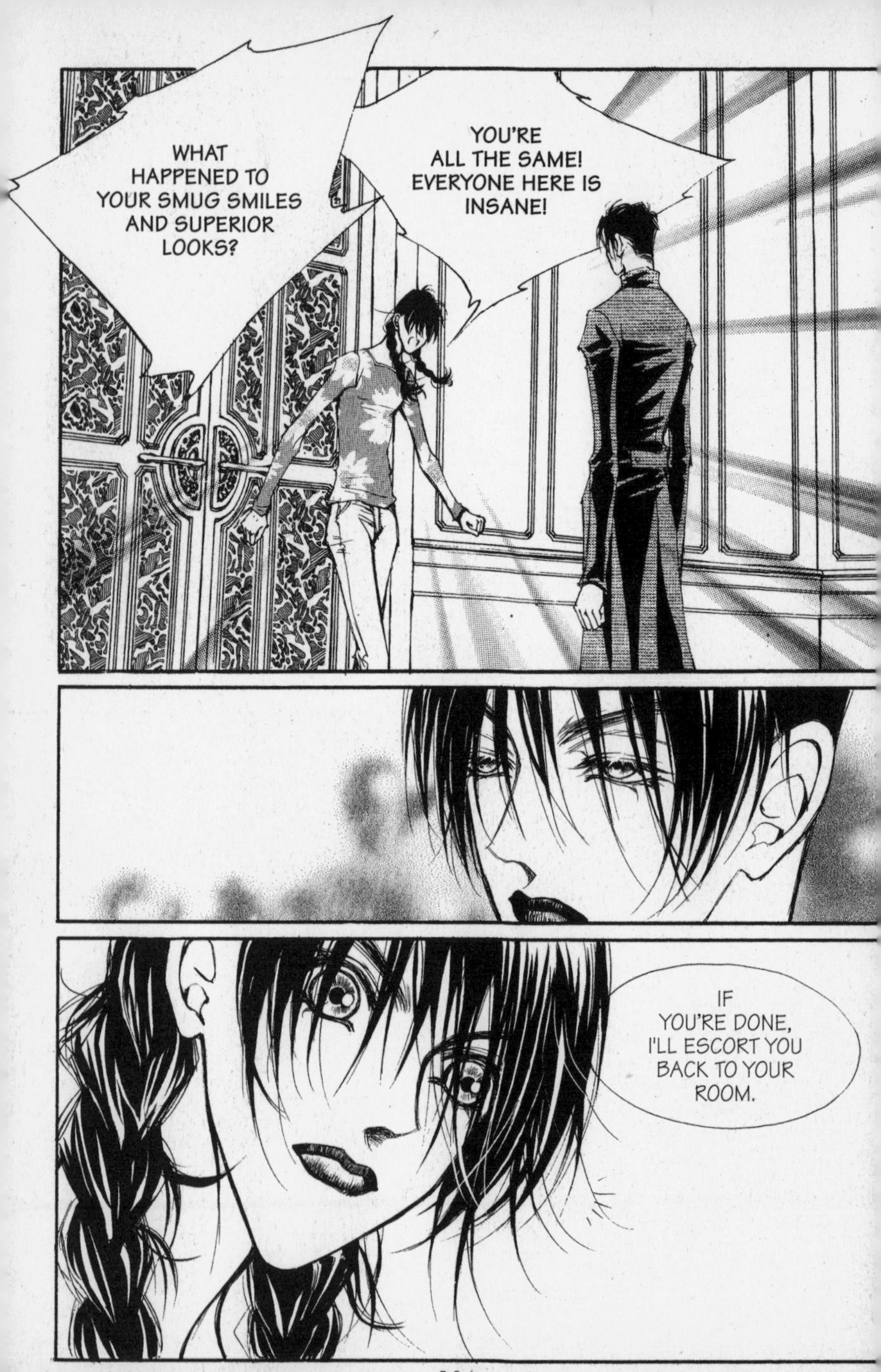
WHAT HAPPENED TO YOUR SMUG SMILES AND SUPERIOR LOOKS?
YOU'RE ALL THE SAME! EVERYONE HERE IS INSANE!
IF YOU'RE DONE, I'LL ESCORT YOU BACK TO YOUR ROOM.

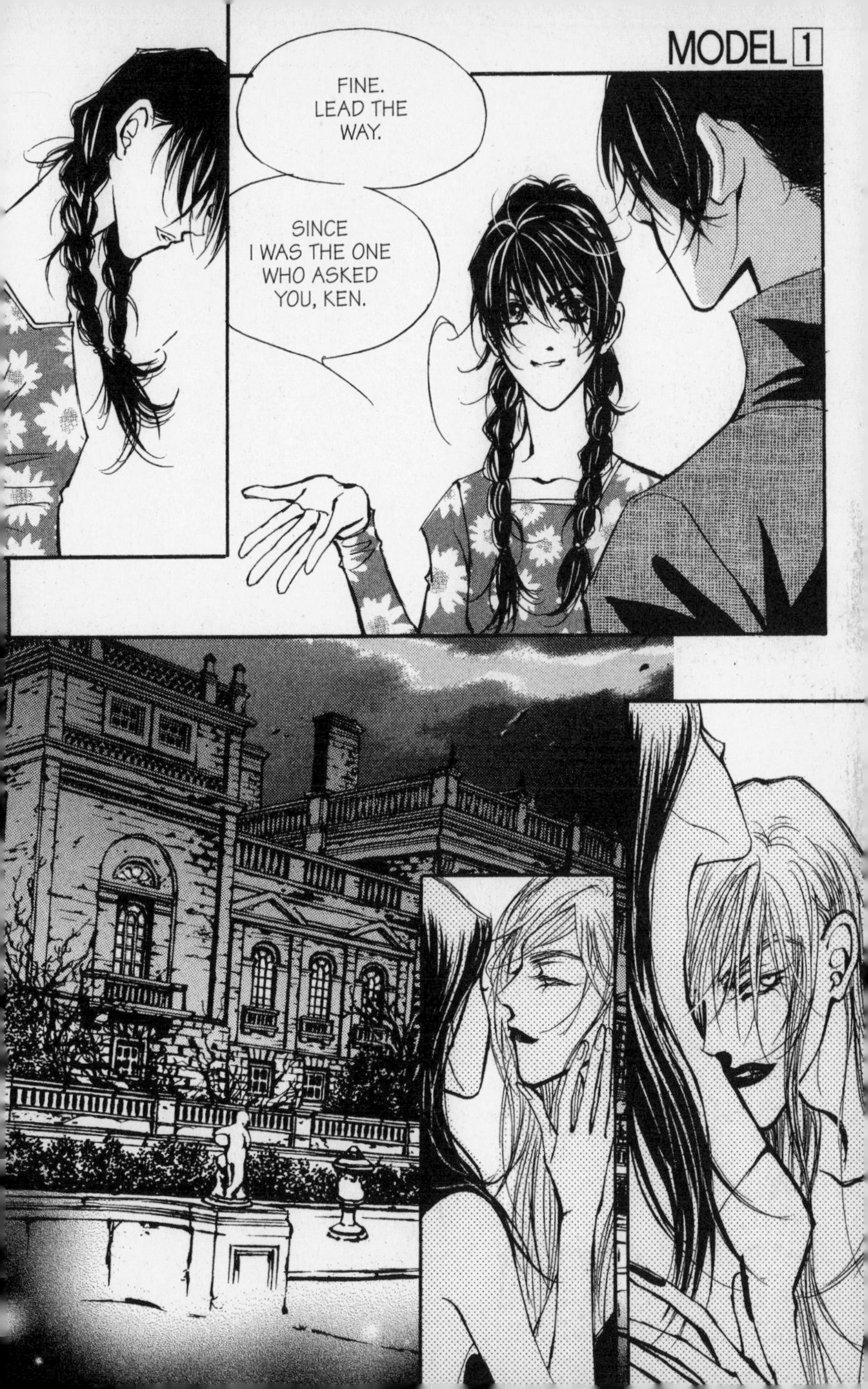
FINE. LEAD THE WAY.
SINCE I WAS THE ONE WHO ASKED YOU, KEN.

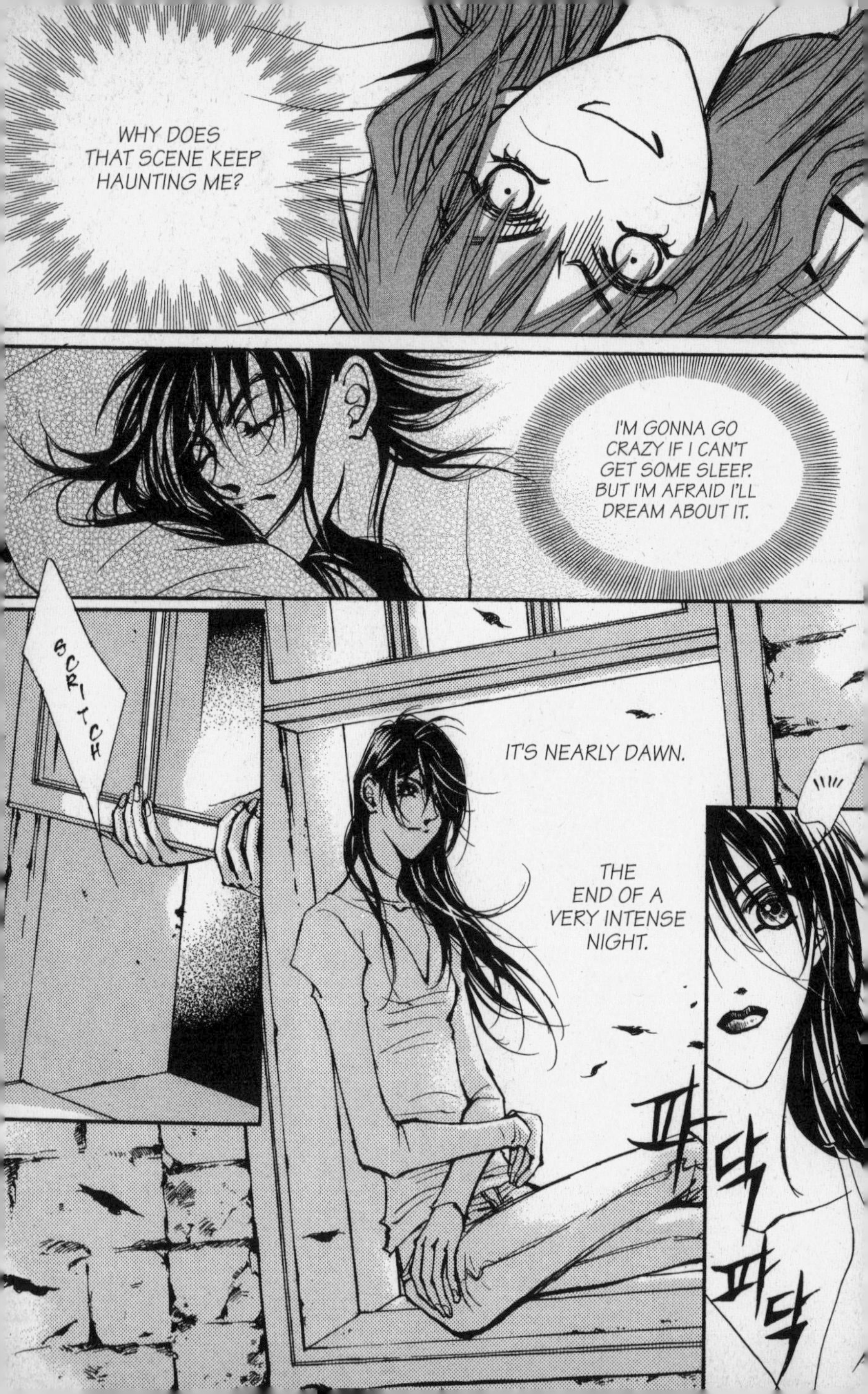
WHY DOES THAT SCENE KEEP HAUNTING ME?
I'M GONNA GO CRAZY IF I CAN'T GET SOME SLEEP. BUT I'M AFRAID I'LL DREAM ABOUT IT.
SCRITCH
IT'S NEARLY DAWN.
THE END OF A VERY INTENSE NIGHT.
파닥
파닥

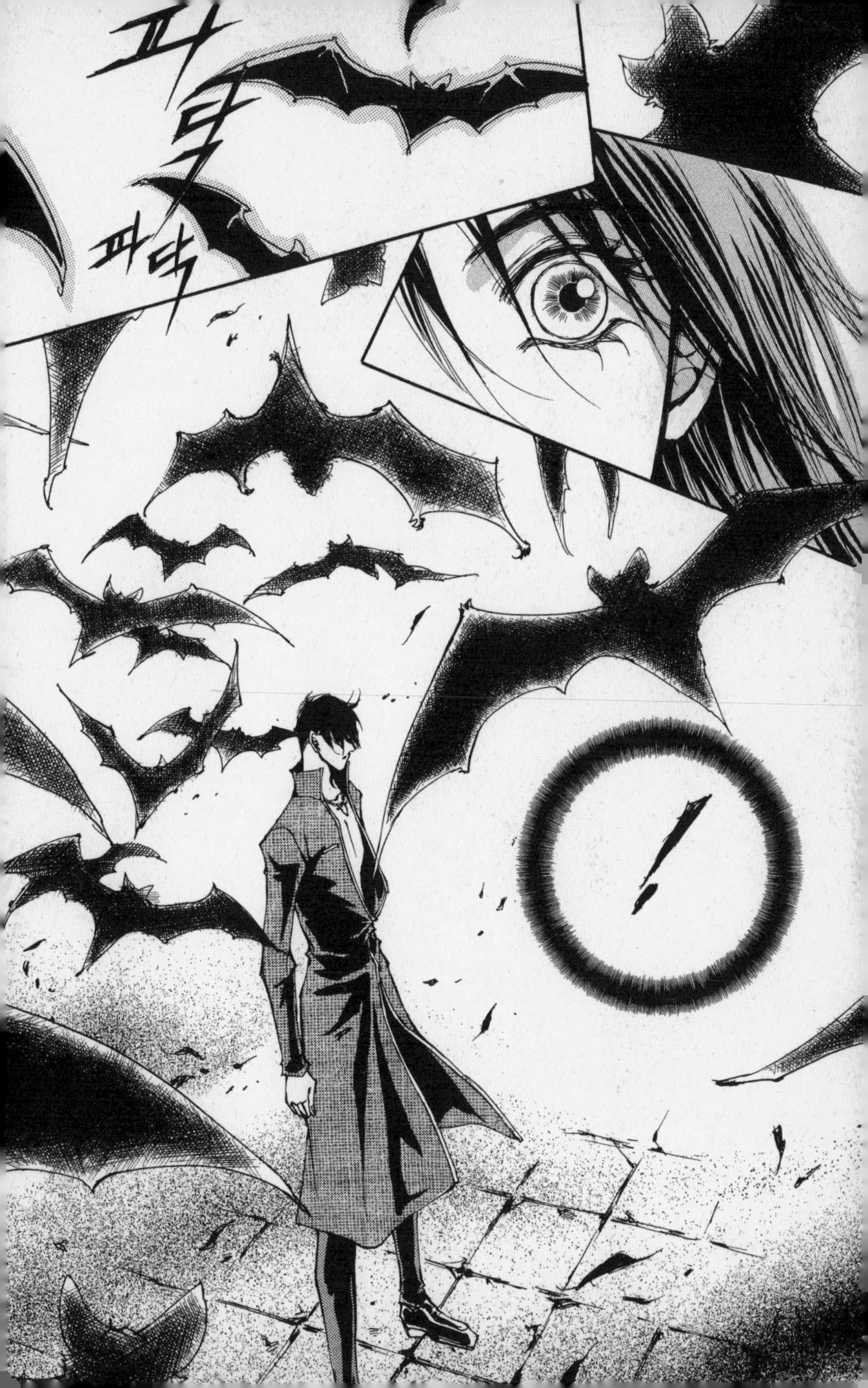
파닥
파닥

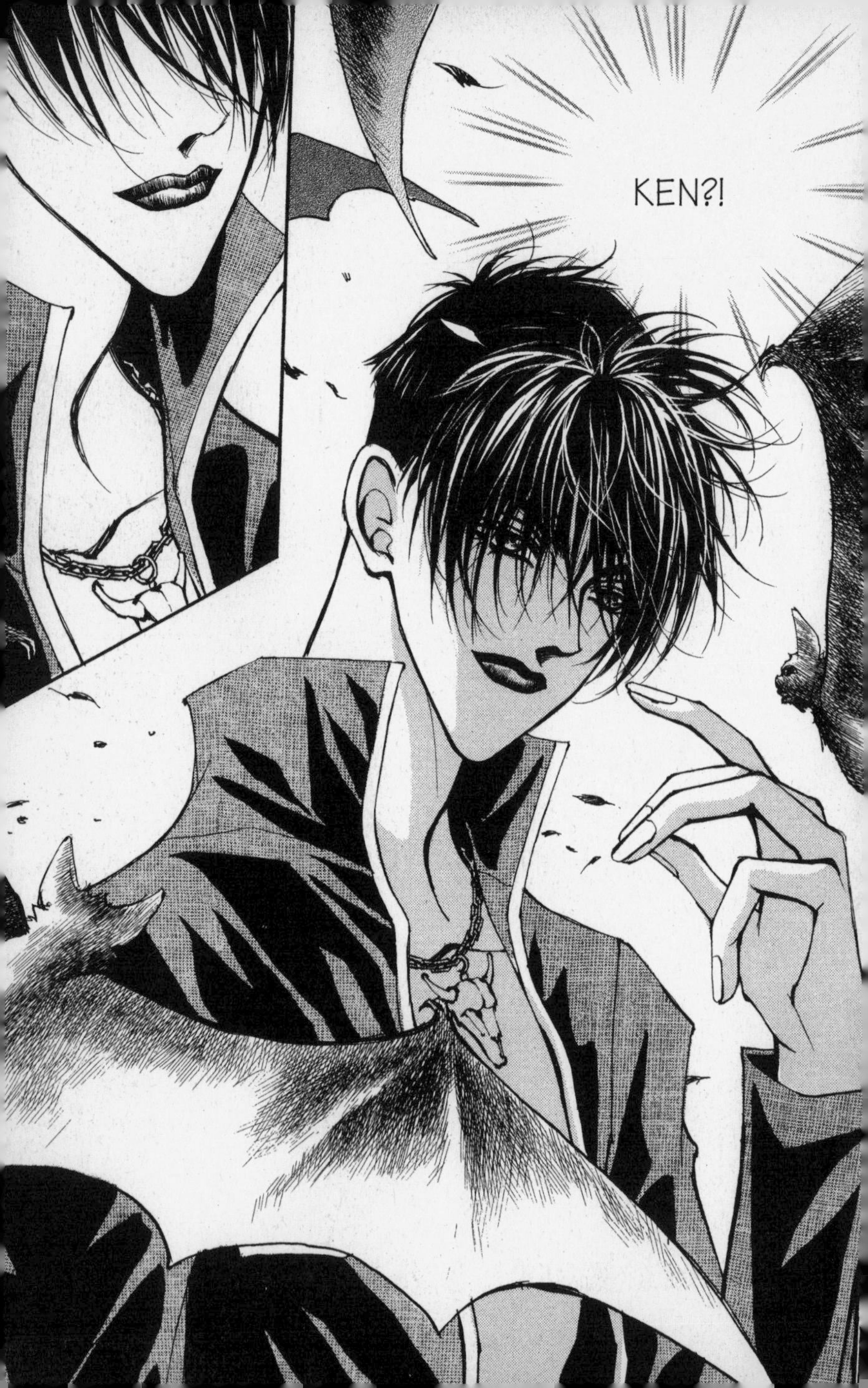
KEN?!

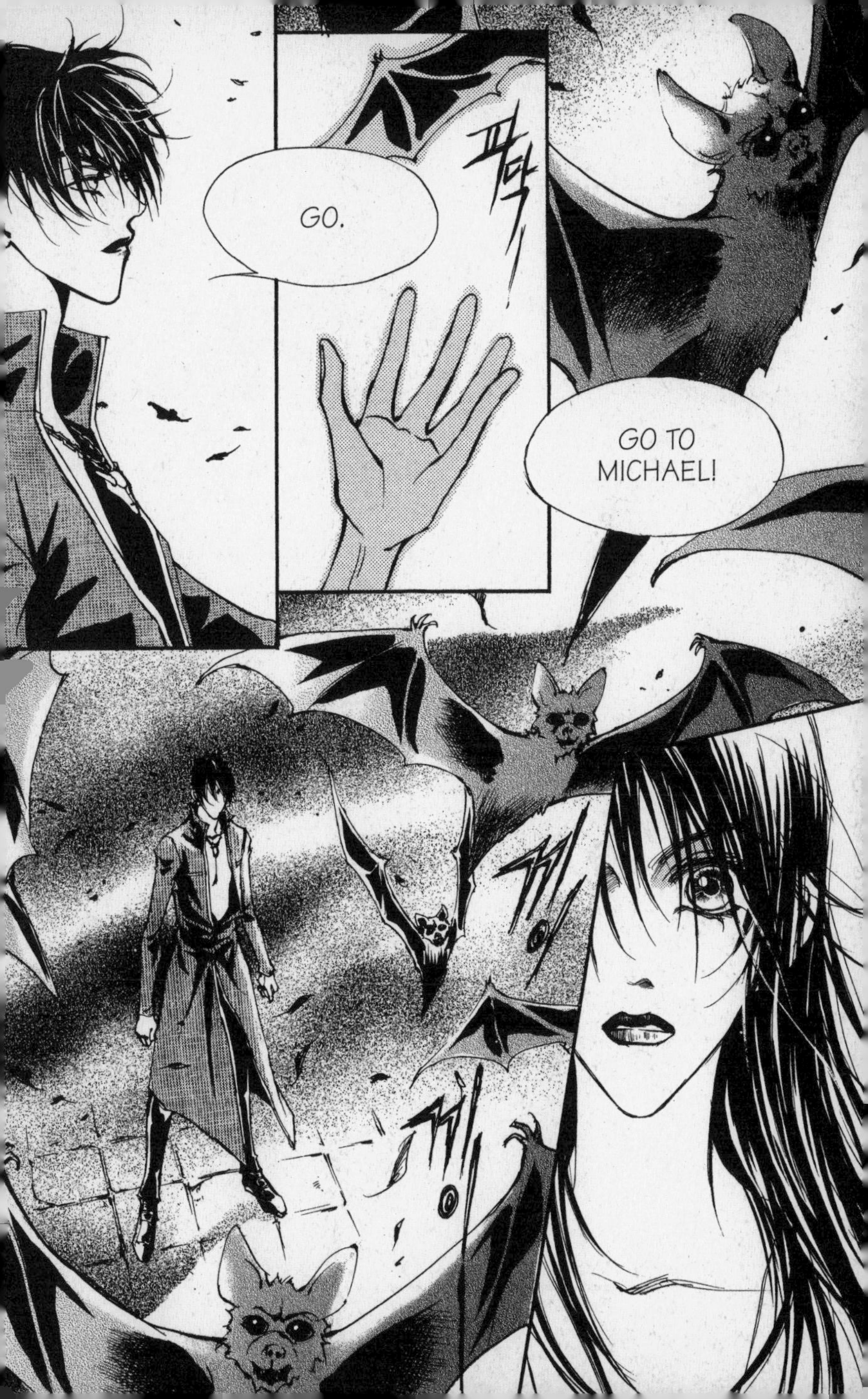
GO.
파닥
GO TO MICHAEL!

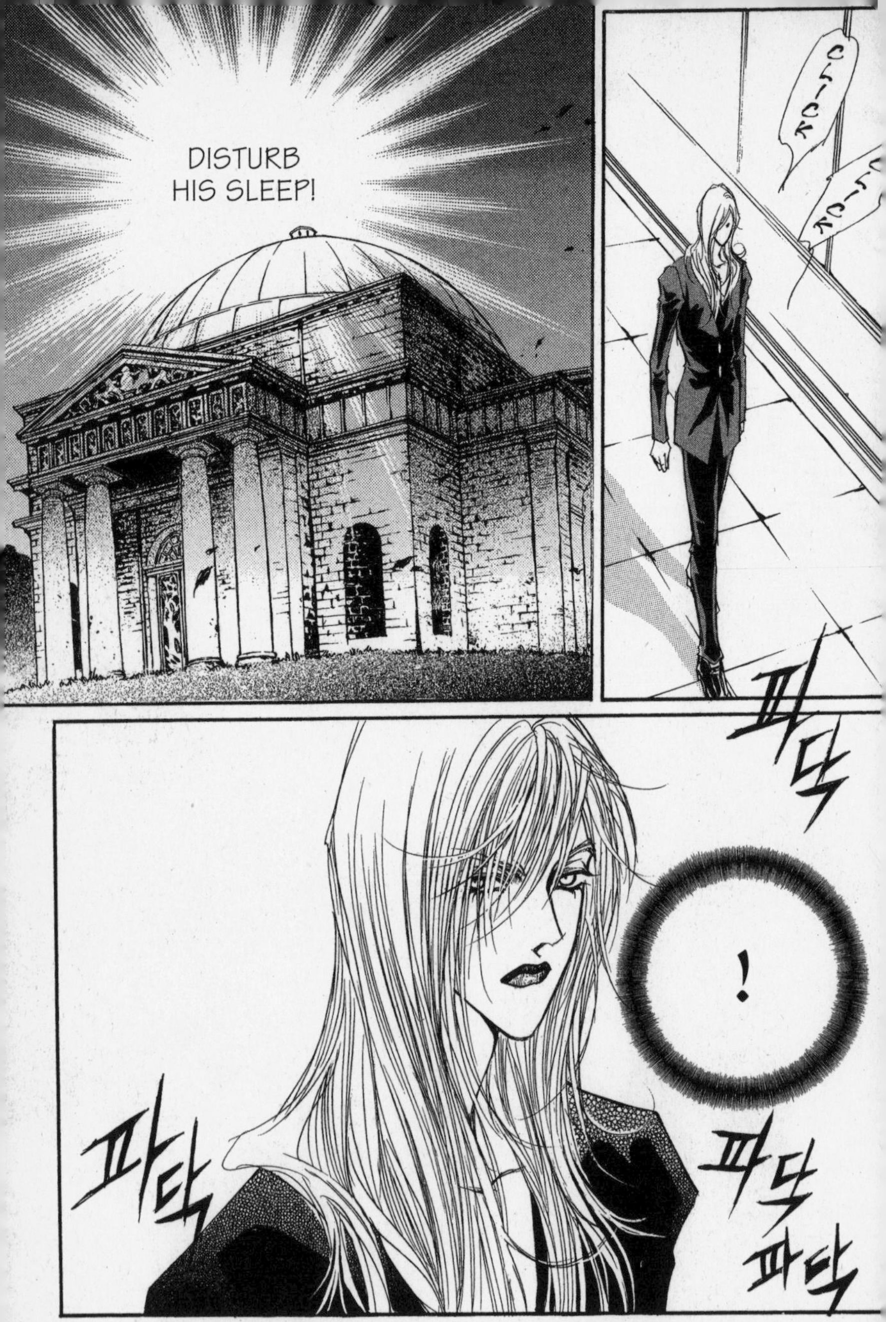
DISTURB
HIS SLEEP!
CLICK
CLICK
파닥
!
파닥
파닥
파닥

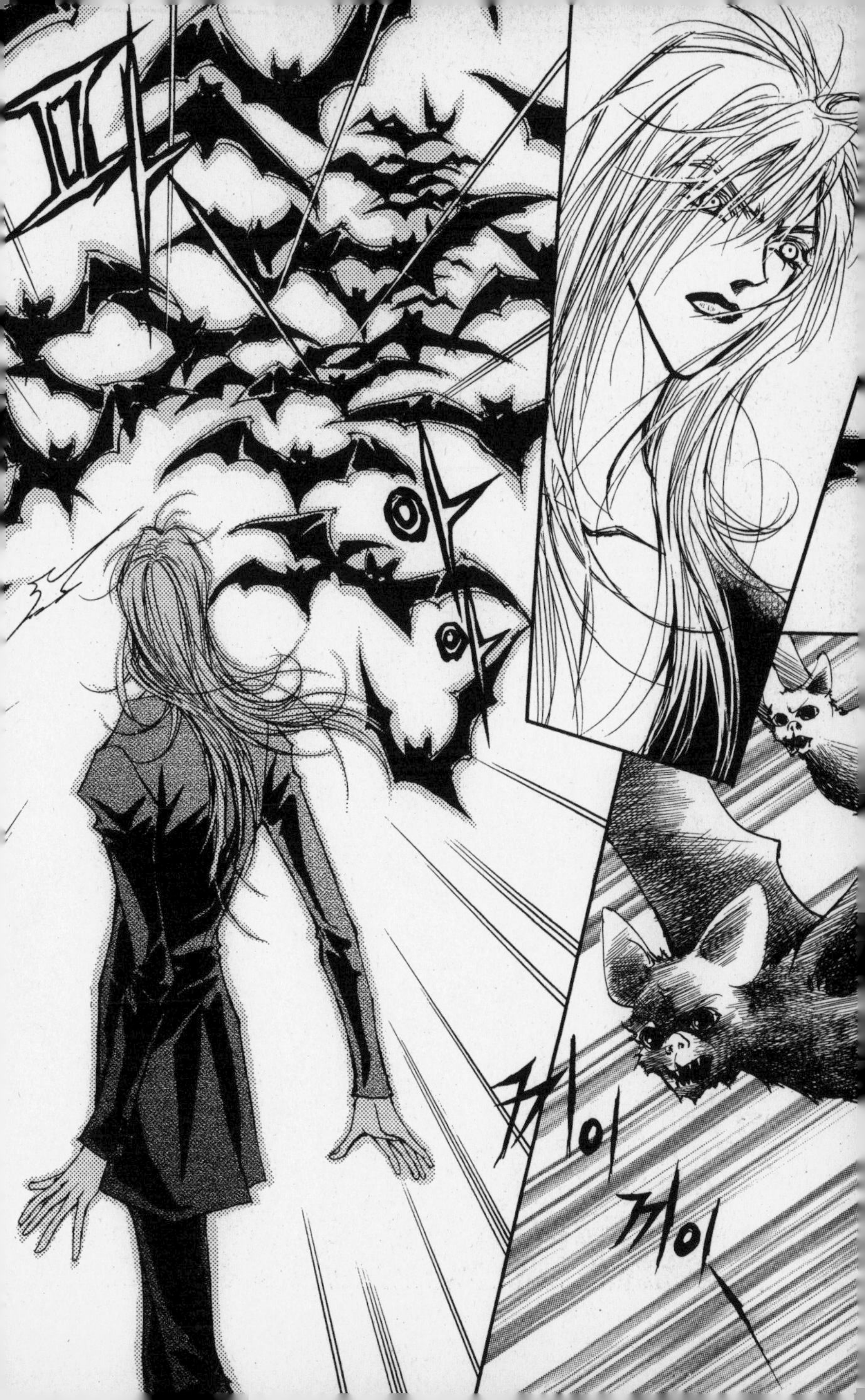
끼이
끼이

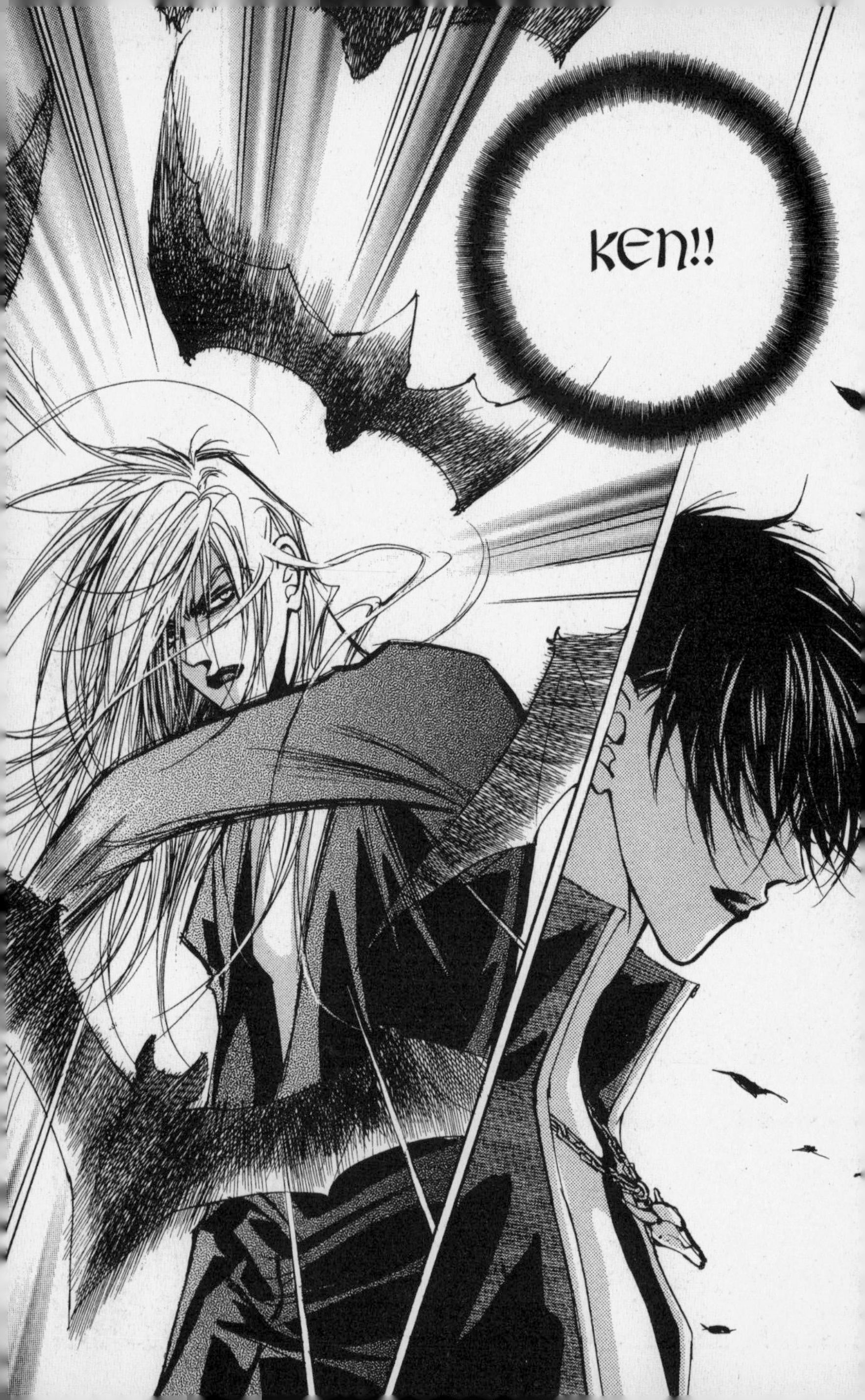
KEN!!

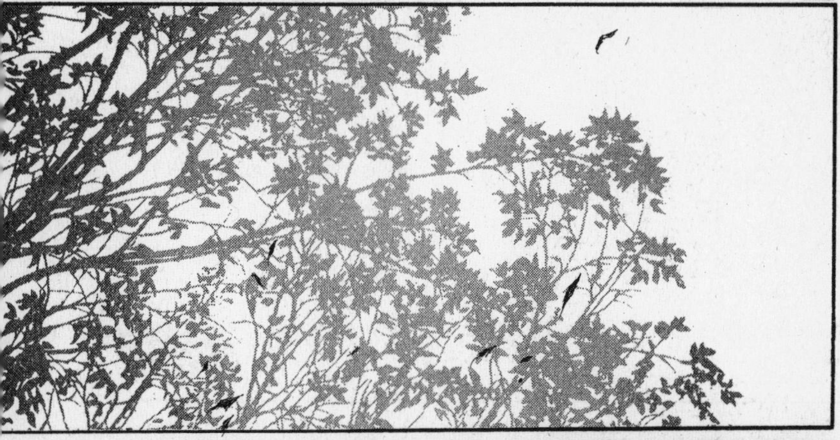

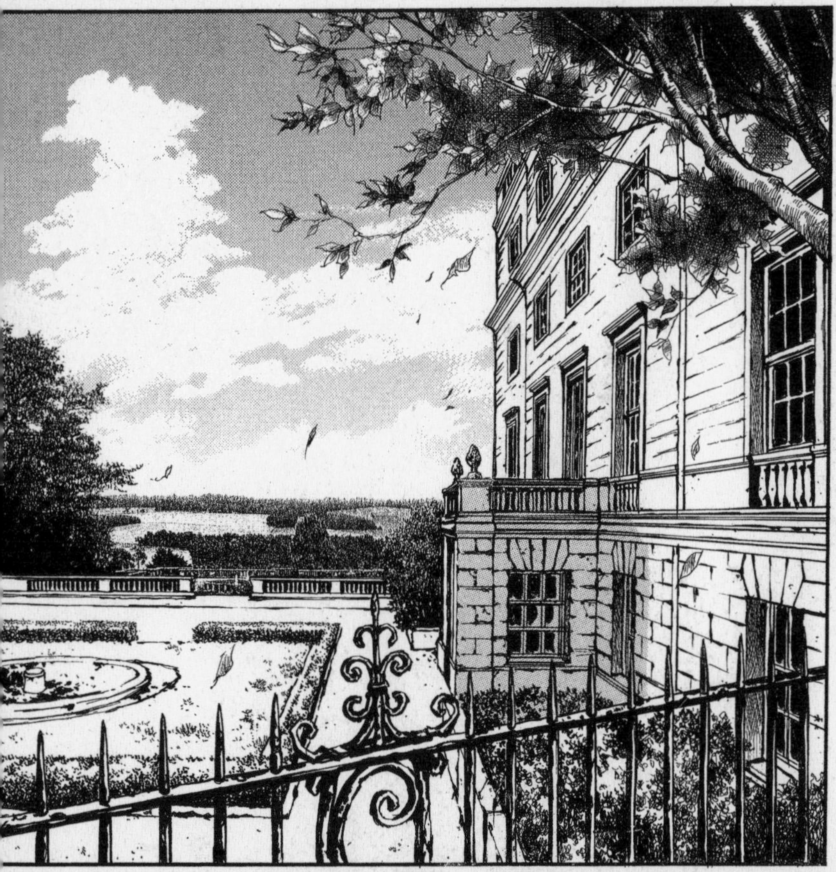

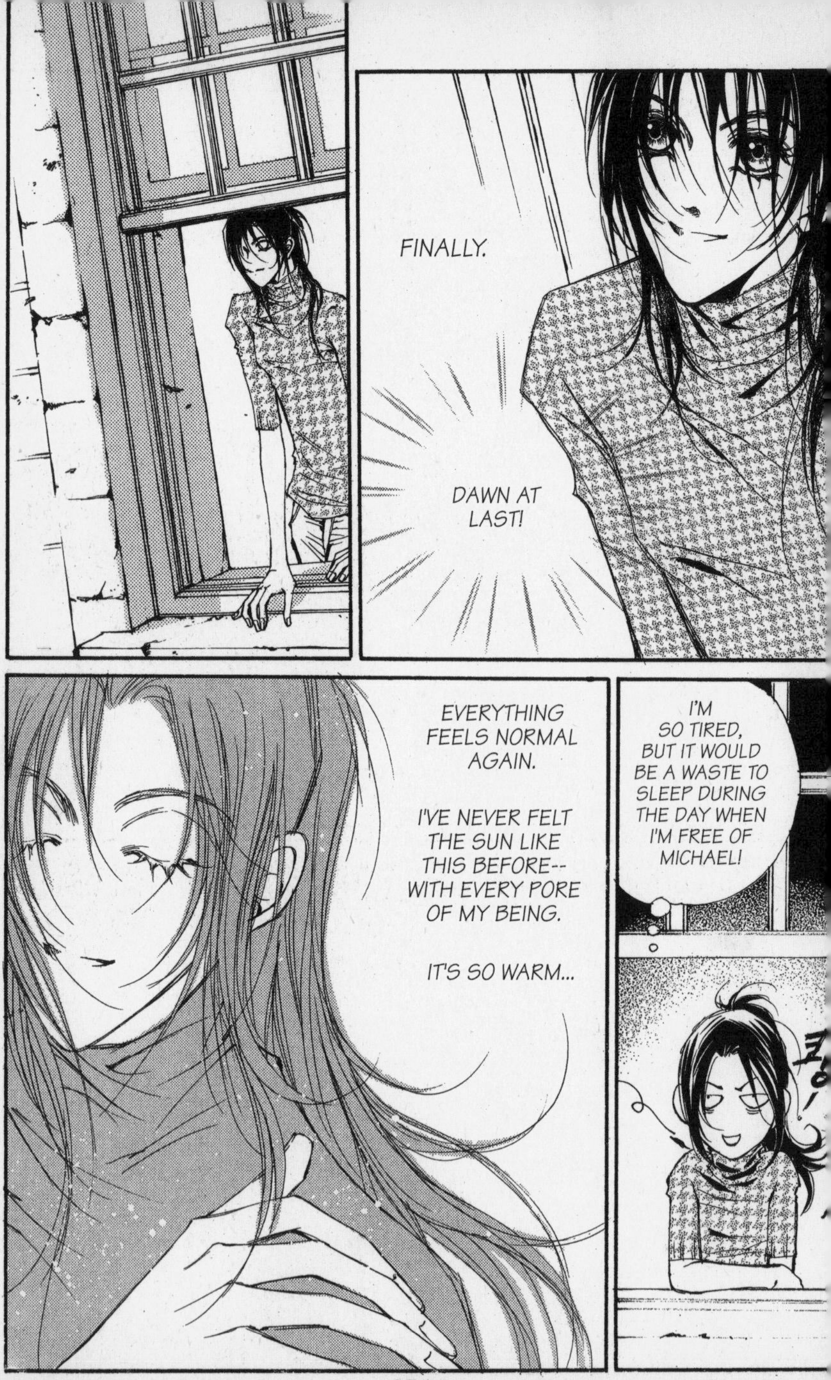
FINALLY.
DAWN AT LAST!
EVERYTHING FEELS NORMAL AGAIN.
I'VE NEVER FELT THE SUN LIKE THIS BEFORE-- WITH EVERY PORE OF MY BEING.
IT'S SO WARM...
I'M SO TIRED, BUT IT WOULD BE A WASTE TO SLEEP DURING THE DAY WHEN I'M FREE OF MICHAEL!

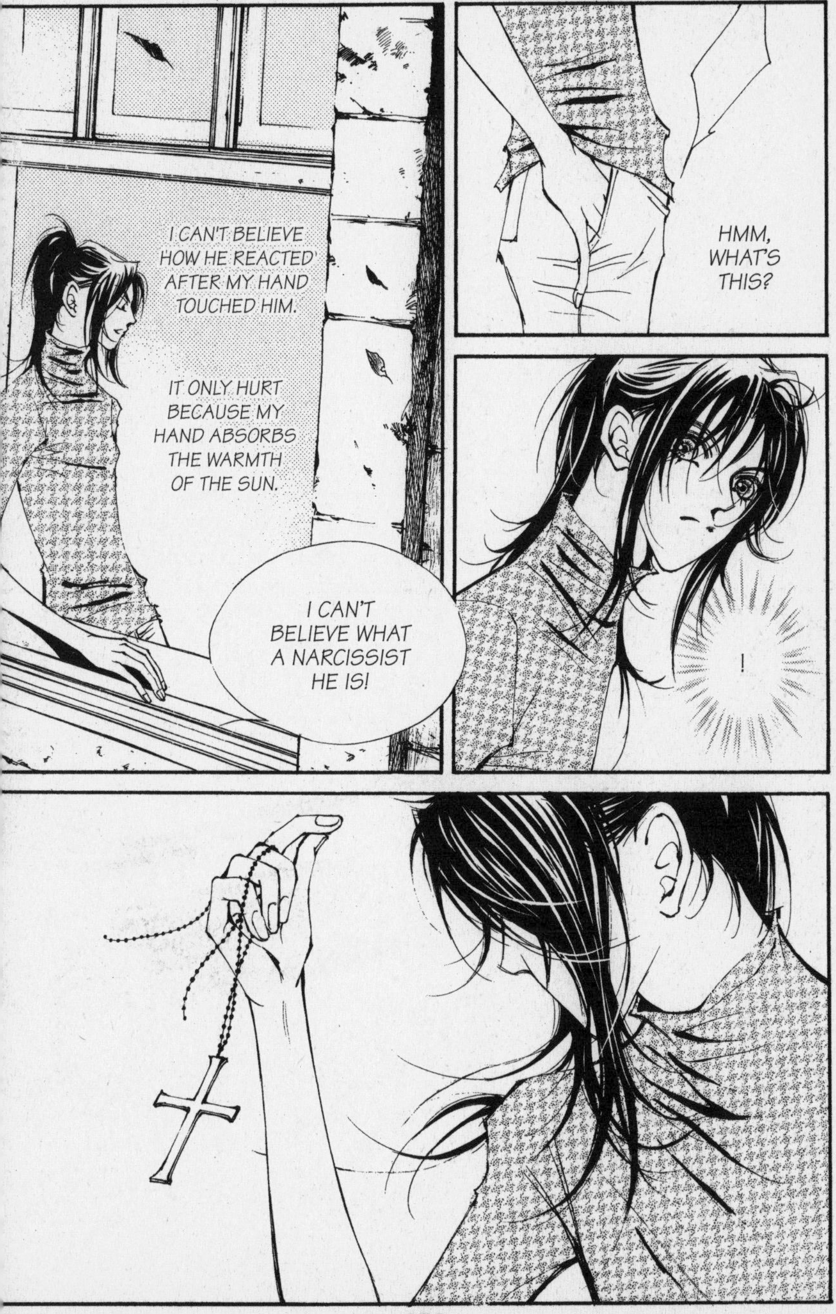
I CAN'T BELIEVE HOW HE REACTED AFTER MY HAND TOUCHED HIM.
IT ONLY HURT BECAUSE MY HAND ABSORBS THE WARMTH OF THE SUN.
I CAN'T BELIEVE WHAT A NARCISSIST HE IS!
HMM, WHAT'S THIS?
!

MICHAEL'S CROSS!

THINK

......

HMM...

I JUST DON'T UNDERSTAND HIM. EVEN IF IT IS THE DESIGN THAT HE LIKES...

...HOW CAN HE WEAR A CROSS AROUND HIS NECK?

IT'S NOT ABOUT THE DESIGN, IT'S ABOUT THE SYMBOLISM.

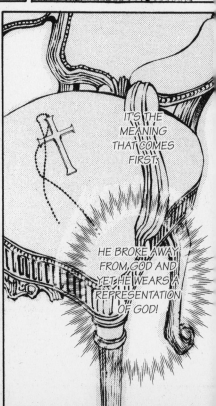

IT'S THE MEANING THAT COMES FIRST.

HE BROKE AWAY FROM GOD AND YET HE WEARS A REPRESENTATION OF GOD!

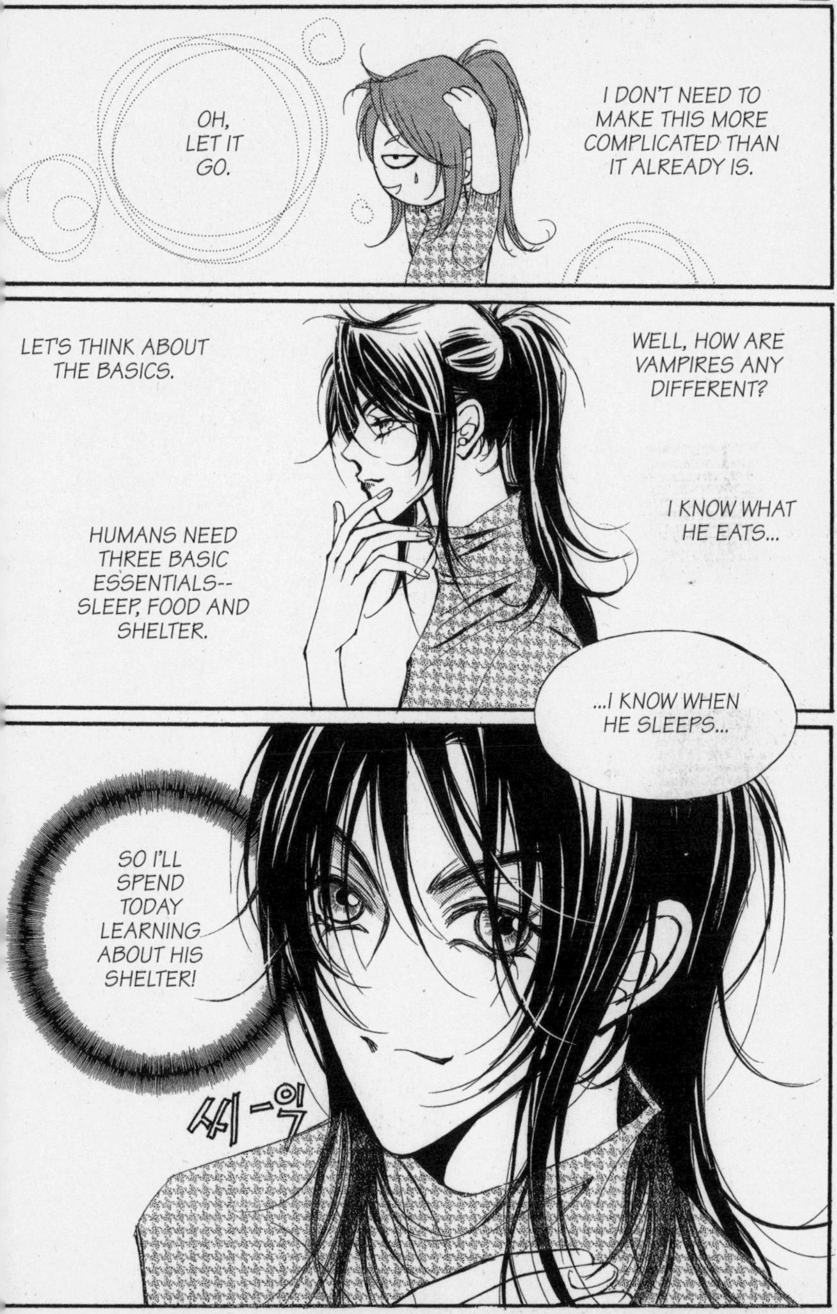
OH, LET IT GO.
I DON'T NEED TO MAKE THIS MORE COMPLICATED THAN IT ALREADY IS.
LET'S THINK ABOUT THE BASICS.
HUMANS NEED THREE BASIC ESSENTIALS-- SLEEP, FOOD AND SHELTER.
WELL, HOW ARE VAMPIRES ANY DIFFERENT?
I KNOW WHAT HE EATS...
...I KNOW WHEN HE SLEEPS...
SO I'LL SPEND TODAY LEARNING ABOUT HIS SHELTER!
씨-익

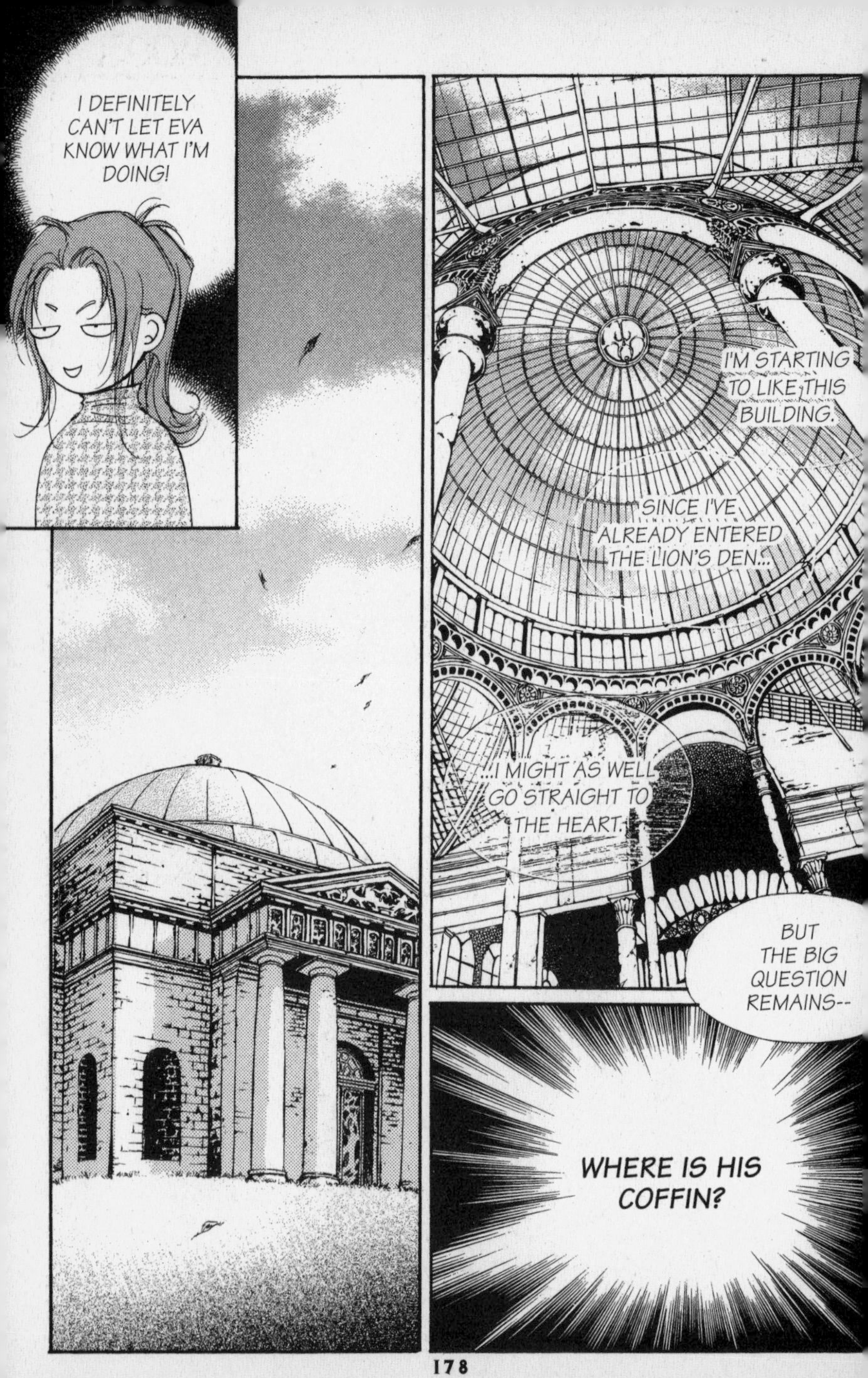
I DEFINITELY CAN'T LET EVA KNOW WHAT I'M DOING!
I'M STARTING TO LIKE THIS BUILDING.
SINCE I'VE ALREADY ENTERED THE LION'S DEN...
...I MIGHT AS WELL GO STRAIGHT TO THE HEART.
BUT THE BIG QUESTION REMAINS--
WHERE IS HIS COFFIN?

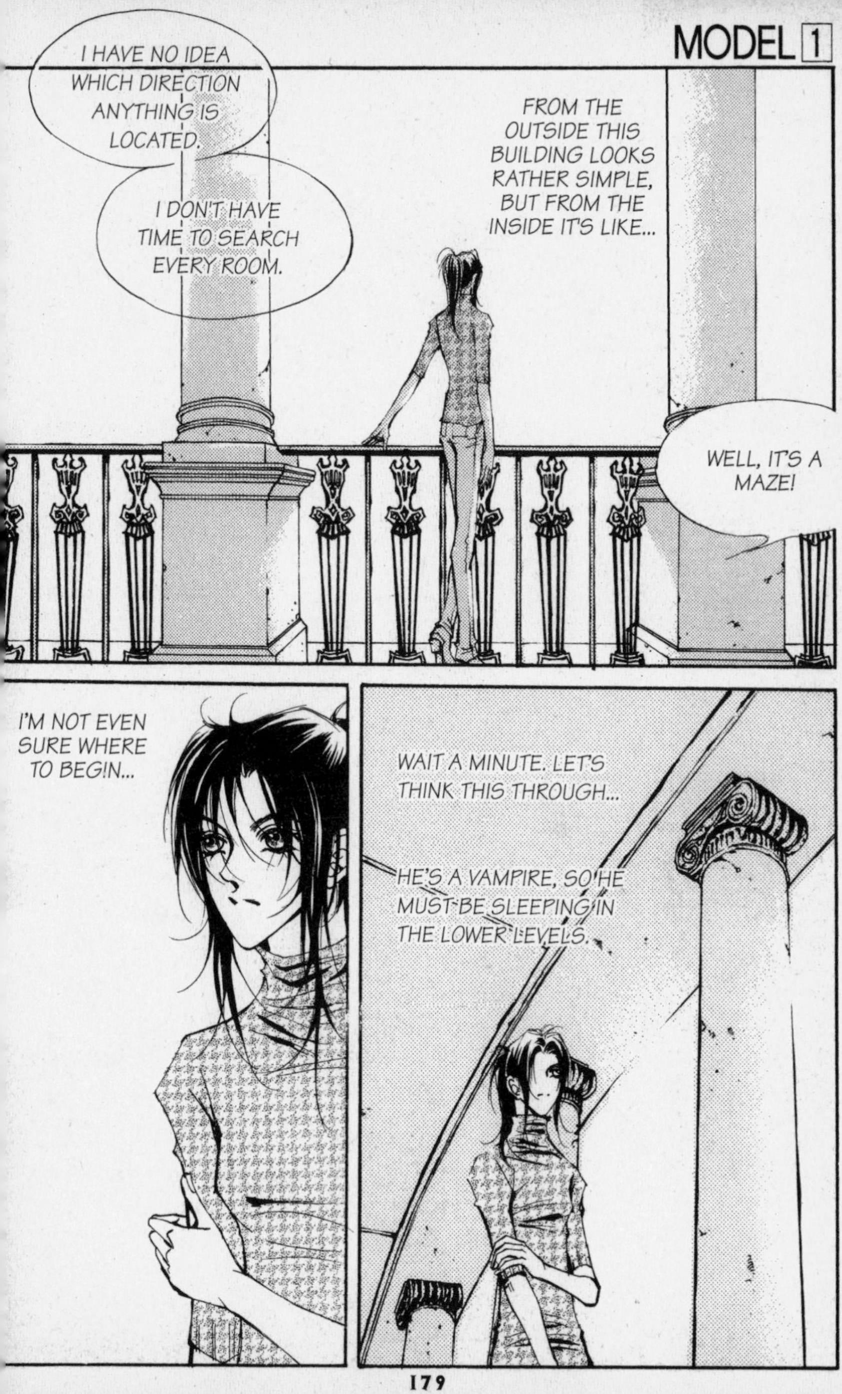
I HAVE NO IDEA WHICH DIRECTION ANYTHING IS LOCATED.
I DON'T HAVE TIME TO SEARCH EVERY ROOM.
FROM THE OUTSIDE THIS BUILDING LOOKS RATHER SIMPLE, BUT FROM THE INSIDE IT'S LIKE...
WELL, IT'S A MAZE!
I'M NOT EVEN SURE WHERE TO BEGIN...
WAIT A MINUTE. LET'S THINK THIS THROUGH...
HE'S A VAMPIRE, SO HE MUST BE SLEEPING IN THE LOWER LEVELS.

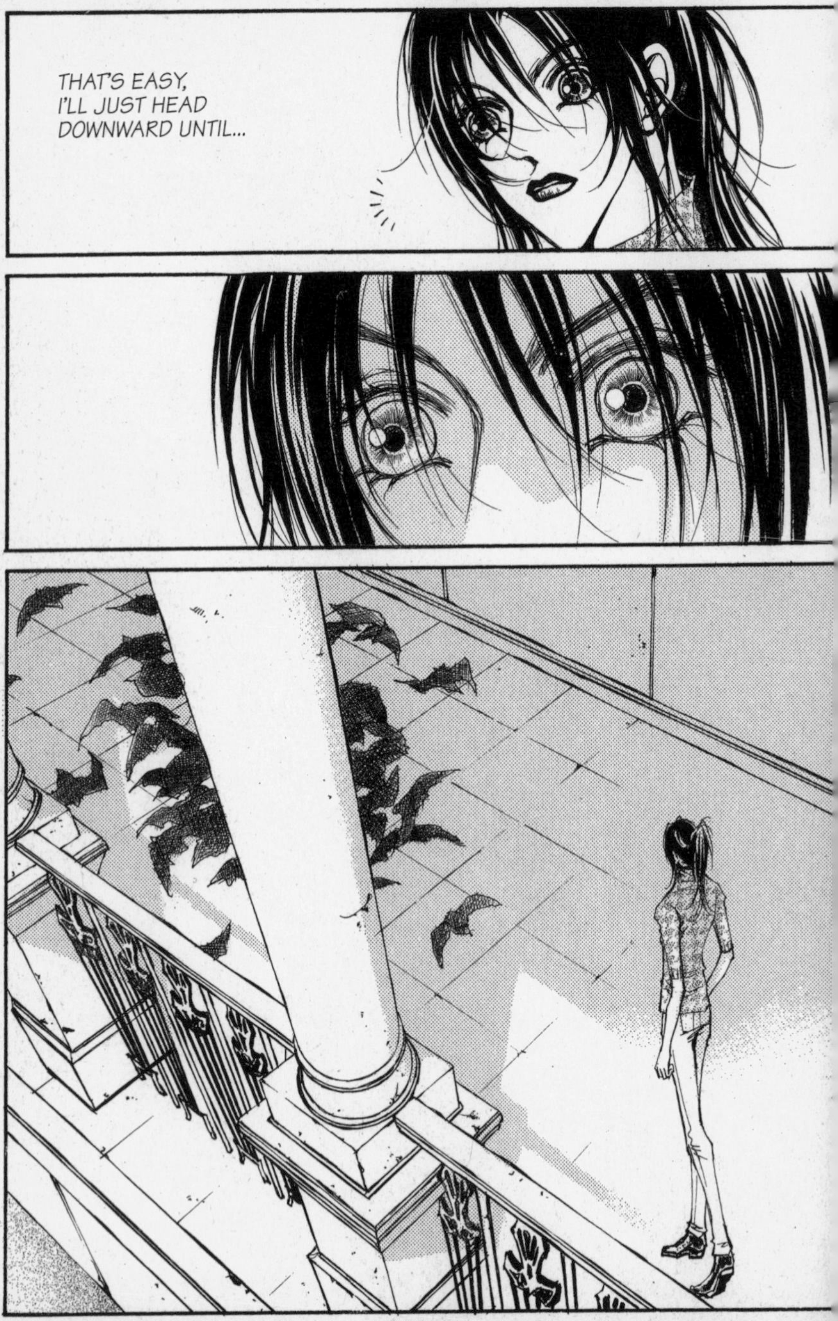
THAT'S EASY,
I'LL JUST HEAD
DOWNWARD UNTIL...

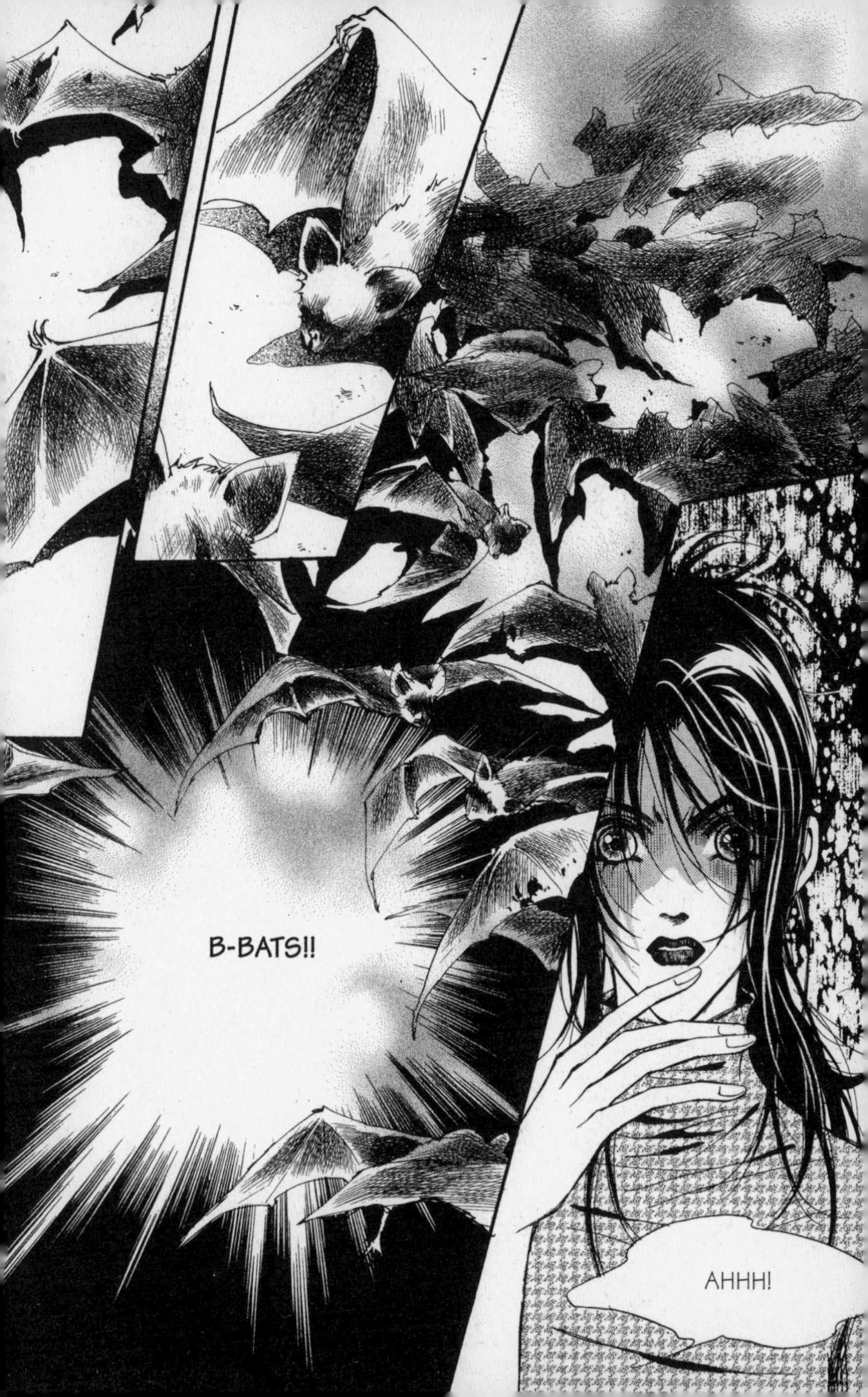
B-BATS!!
AHHH!

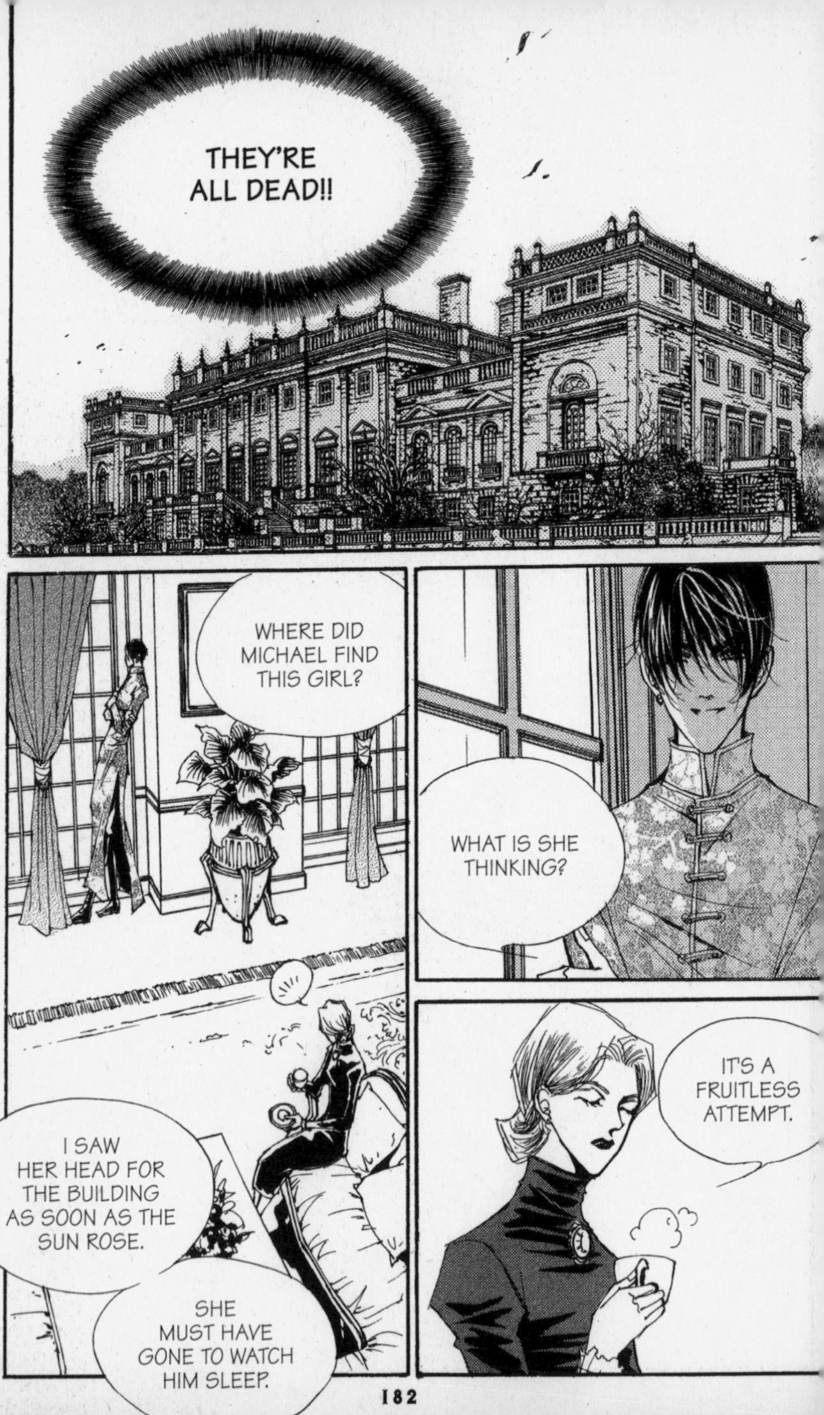
THEY'RE ALL DEAD!!
WHERE DID MICHAEL FIND THIS GIRL?
WHAT IS SHE THINKING?
I SAW HER HEAD FOR THE BUILDING AS SOON AS THE SUN ROSE.
SHE MUST HAVE GONE TO WATCH HIM SLEEP.
IT'S A FRUITLESS ATTEMPT.

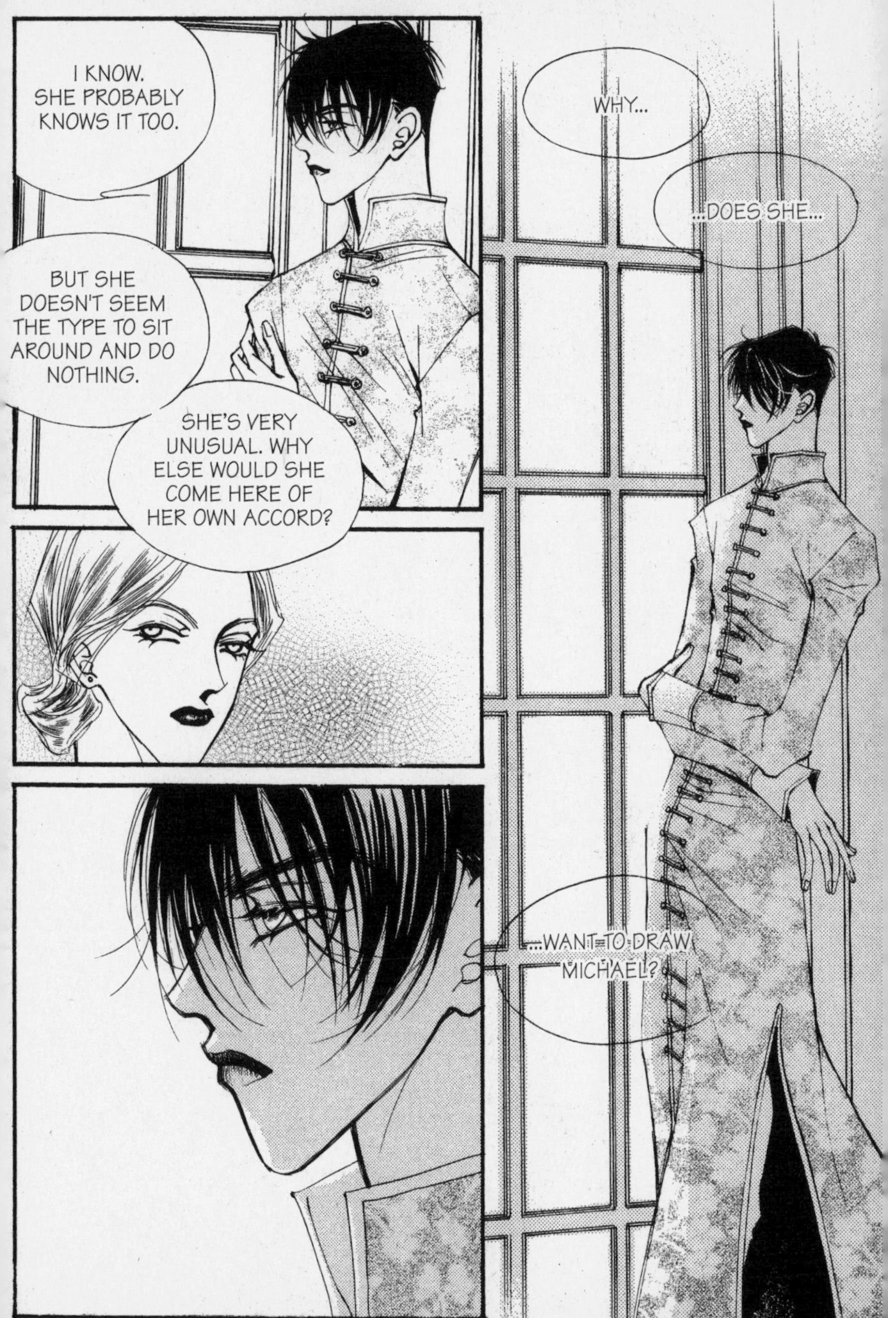
I KNOW. SHE PROBABLY KNOWS IT TOO.
BUT SHE DOESN'T SEEM THE TYPE TO SIT AROUND AND DO NOTHING.
SHE'S VERY UNUSUAL. WHY ELSE WOULD SHE COME HERE OF HER OWN ACCORD?
WHY...
...DOES SHE...
...WANT TO DRAW MICHAEL?

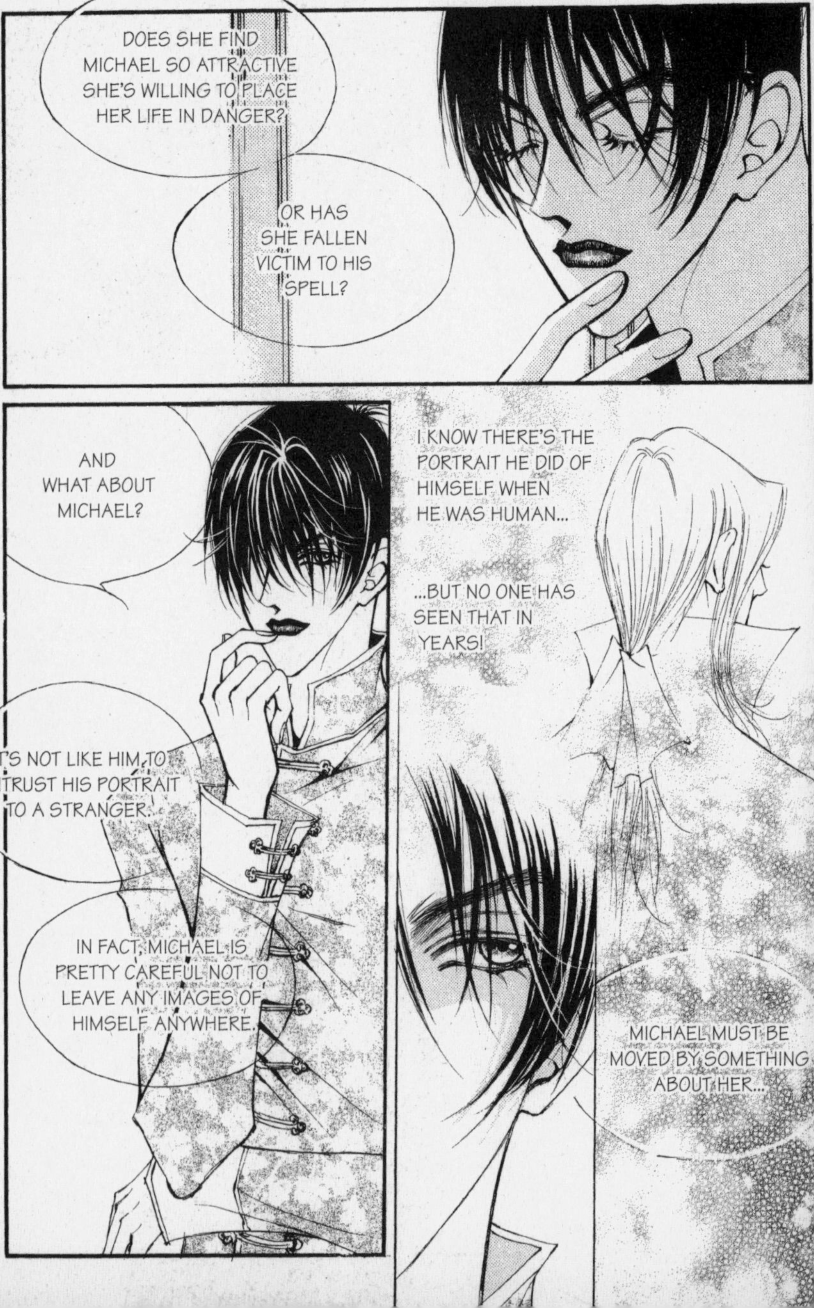
DOES SHE FIND MICHAEL SO ATTRACTIVE SHE'S WILLING TO PLACE HER LIFE IN DANGER?
OR HAS SHE FALLEN VICTIM TO HIS SPELL?
AND WHAT ABOUT MICHAEL?
IT'S NOT LIKE HIM TO ENTRUST HIS PORTRAIT TO A STRANGER.
IN FACT, MICHAEL IS PRETTY CAREFUL NOT TO LEAVE ANY IMAGES OF HIMSELF ANYWHERE.
I KNOW THERE'S THE PORTRAIT HE DID OF HIMSELF WHEN HE WAS HUMAN...
...BUT NO ONE HAS SEEN THAT IN YEARS!
MICHAEL MUST BE MOVED BY SOMETHING ABOUT HER...

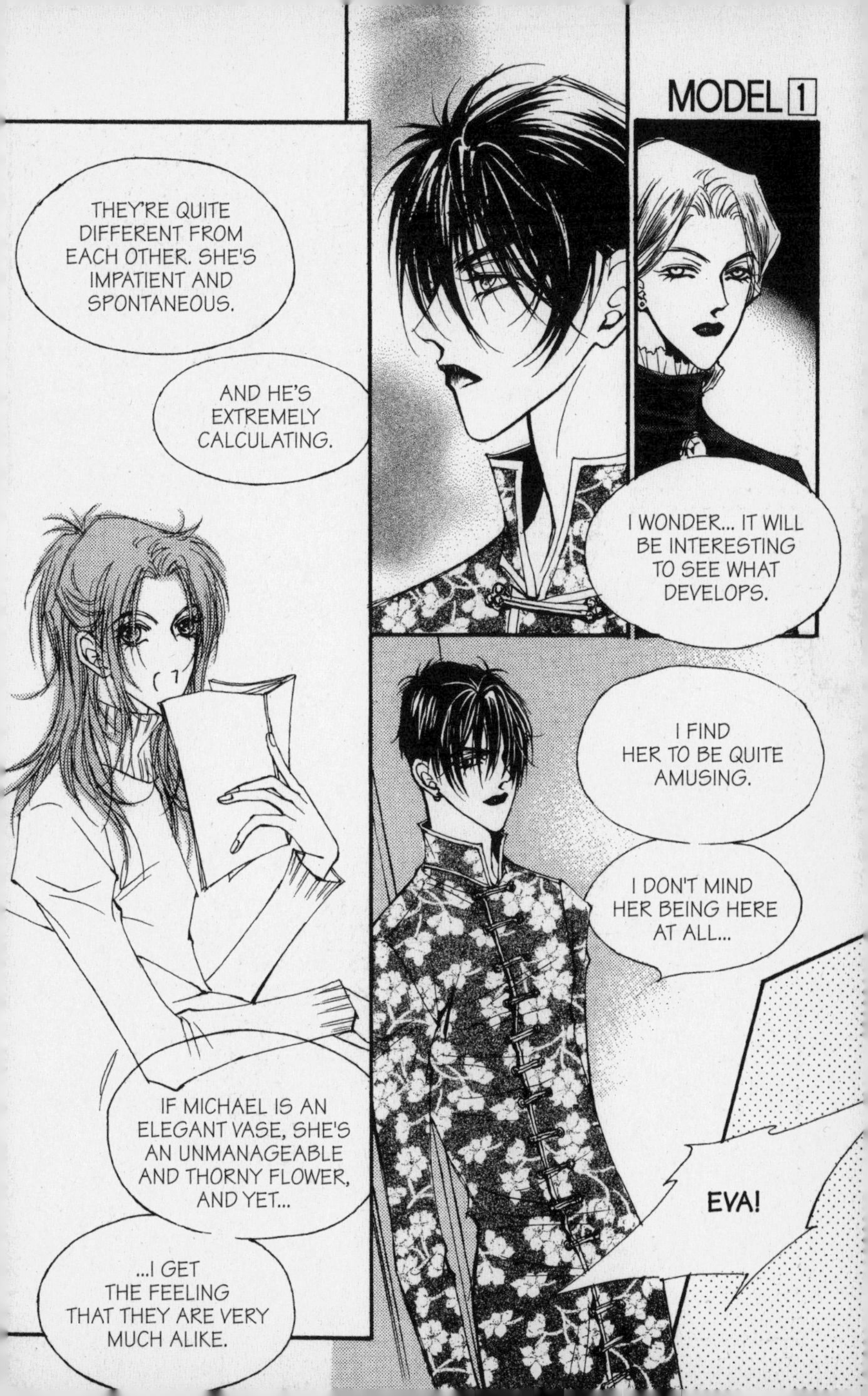
THEY'RE QUITE DIFFERENT FROM EACH OTHER. SHE'S IMPATIENT AND SPONTANEOUS.
AND HE'S EXTREMELY CALCULATING.
IF MICHAEL IS AN ELEGANT VASE, SHE'S AN UNMANAGEABLE AND THORNY FLOWER, AND YET...
...I GET THE FEELING THAT THEY ARE VERY MUCH ALIKE.
I WONDER... IT WILL BE INTERESTING TO SEE WHAT DEVELOPS.
I FIND HER TO BE QUITE AMUSING.
I DON'T MIND HER BEING HERE AT ALL...
EVA!

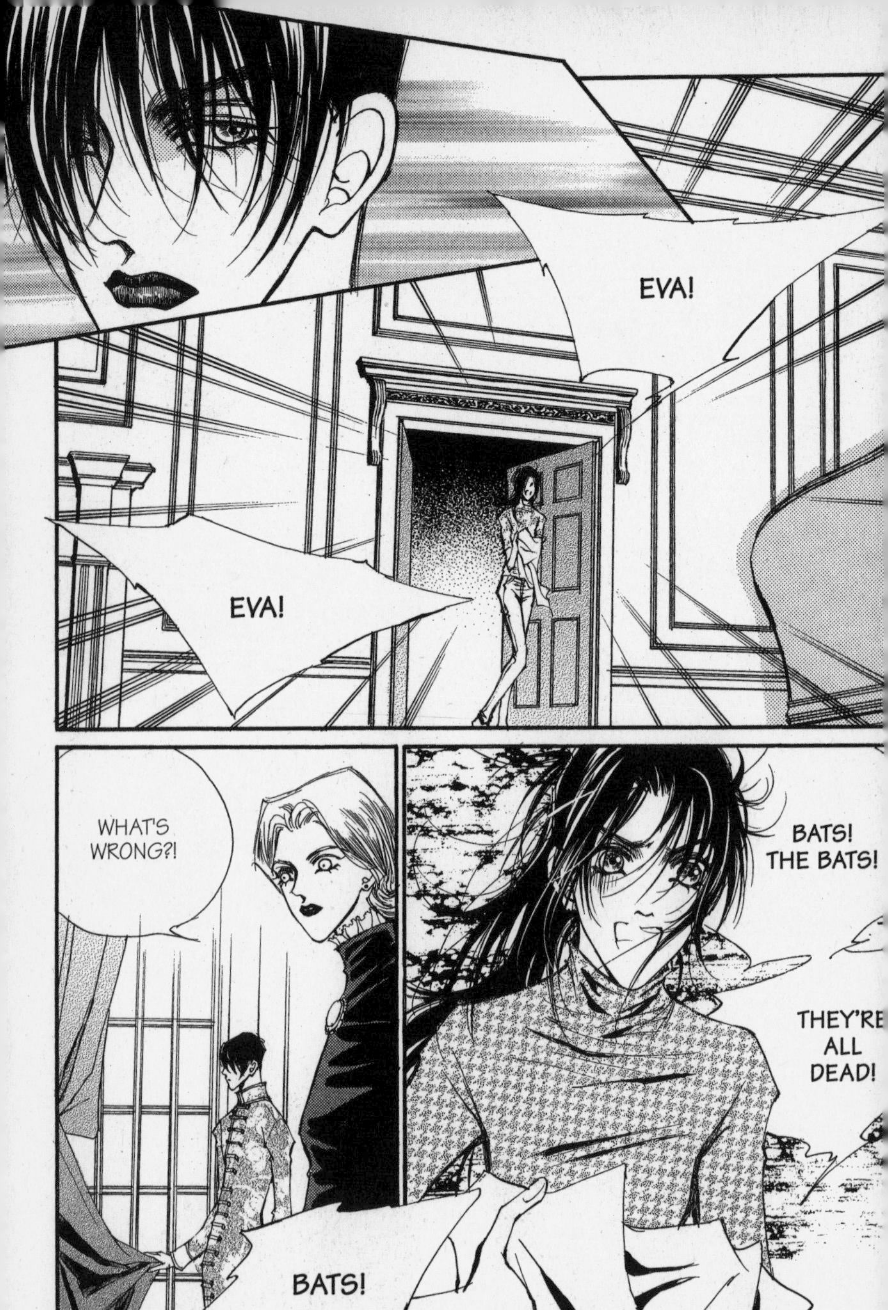
EVA!
EVA!
WHAT'S WRONG?!
BATS! THE BATS!
THEY'RE ALL DEAD!
BATS!

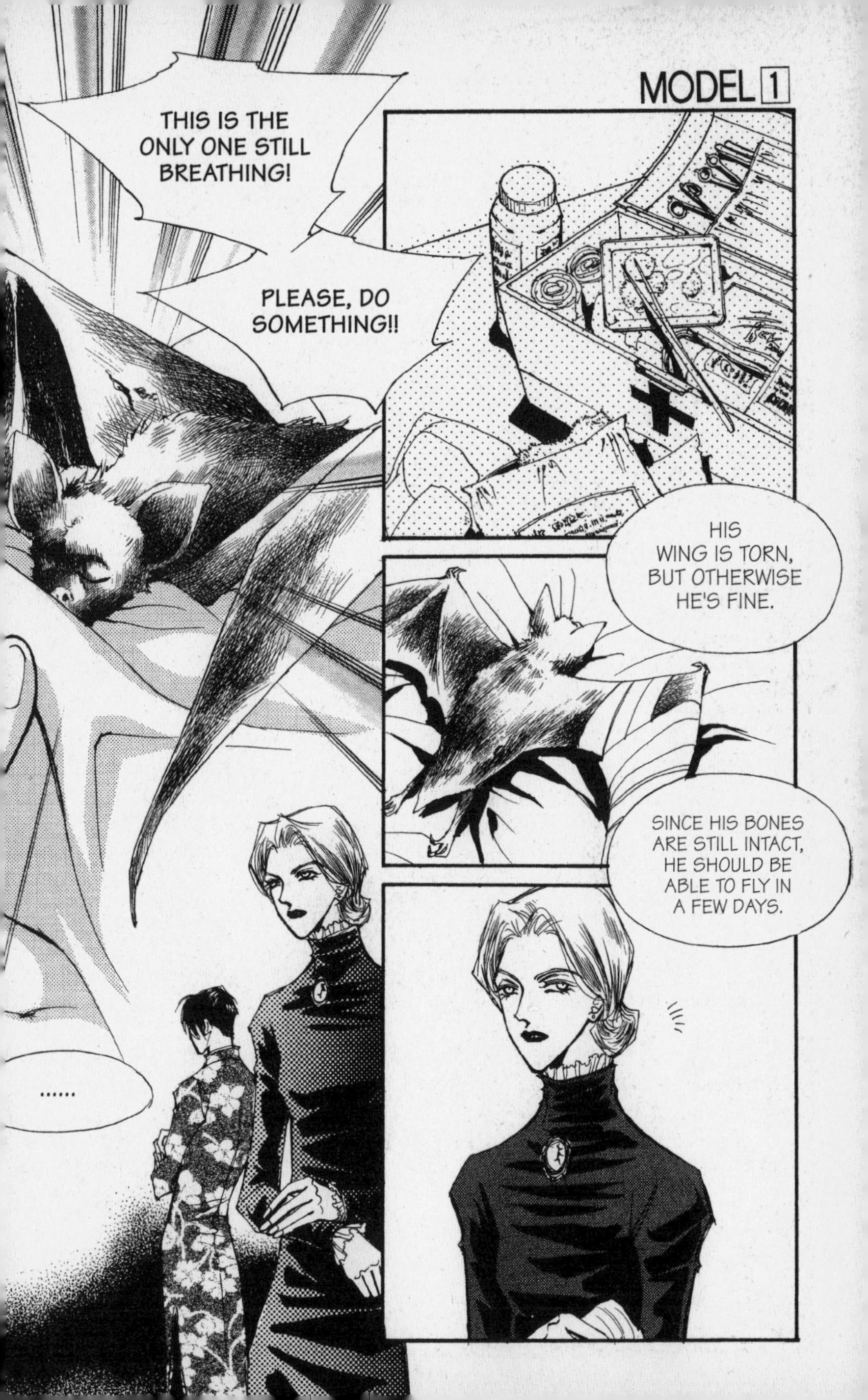
THIS IS THE ONLY ONE STILL BREATHING!
PLEASE, DO SOMETHING!!
......
HIS WING IS TORN, BUT OTHERWISE HE'S FINE.
SINCE HIS BONES ARE STILL INTACT, HE SHOULD BE ABLE TO FLY IN A FEW DAYS.

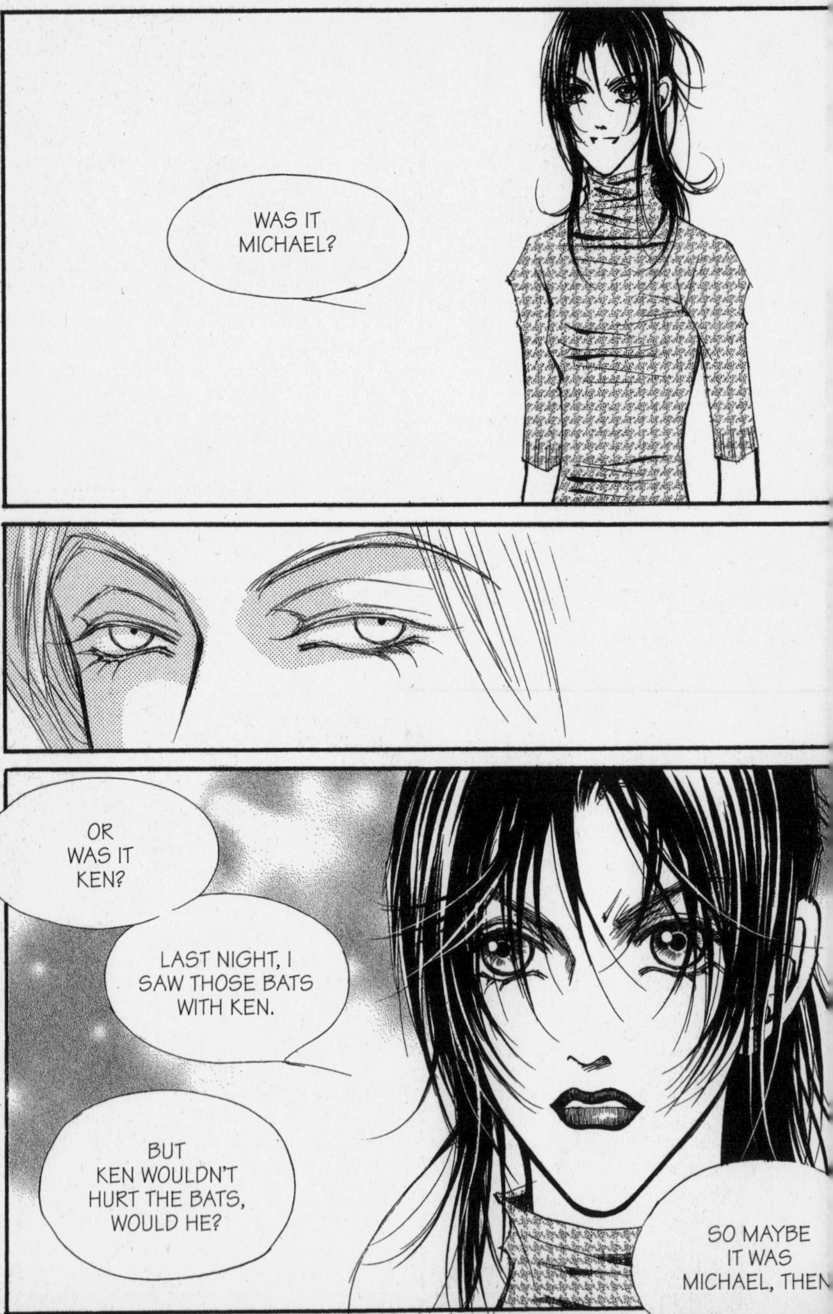
WAS IT MICHAEL?
OR WAS IT KEN?
LAST NIGHT, I SAW THOSE BATS WITH KEN.
BUT KEN WOULDN'T HURT THE BATS, WOULD HE?
SO MAYBE IT WAS MICHAEL, THEN

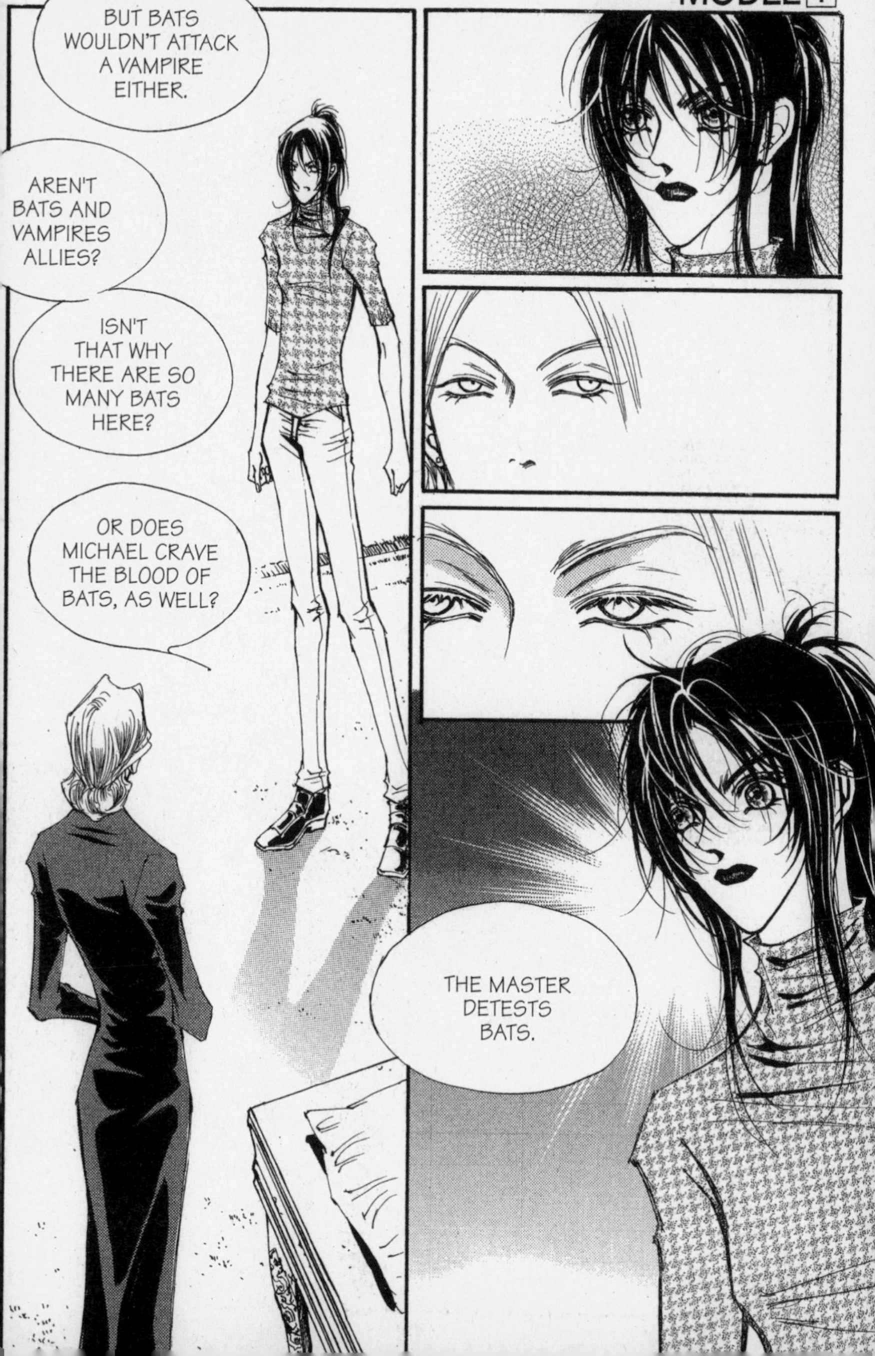
BUT BATS WOULDN'T ATTACK A VAMPIRE EITHER.
AREN'T BATS AND VAMPIRES ALLIES?
ISN'T THAT WHY THERE ARE SO MANY BATS HERE?
OR DOES MICHAEL CRAVE THE BLOOD OF BATS, AS WELL?
THE MASTER DETESTS BATS.

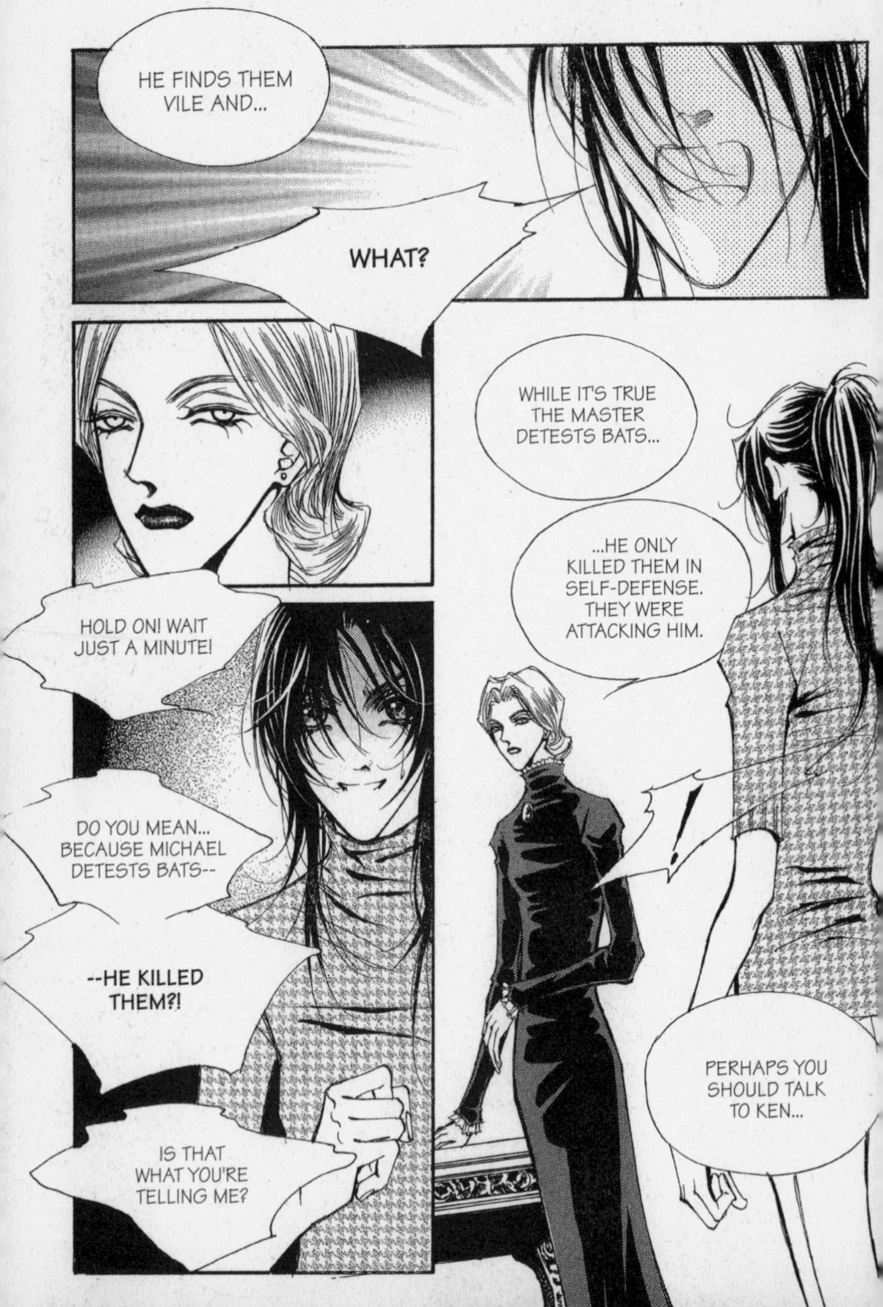
HE FINDS THEM VILE AND...
WHAT?
HOLD ON! WAIT JUST A MINUTE!
DO YOU MEAN... BECAUSE MICHAEL DETESTS BATS--
--HE KILLED THEM?!
IS THAT WHAT YOU'RE TELLING ME?
WHILE IT'S TRUE THE MASTER DETESTS BATS...
...HE ONLY KILLED THEM IN SELF-DEFENSE. THEY WERE ATTACKING HIM.
!
PERHAPS YOU SHOULD TALK TO KEN...

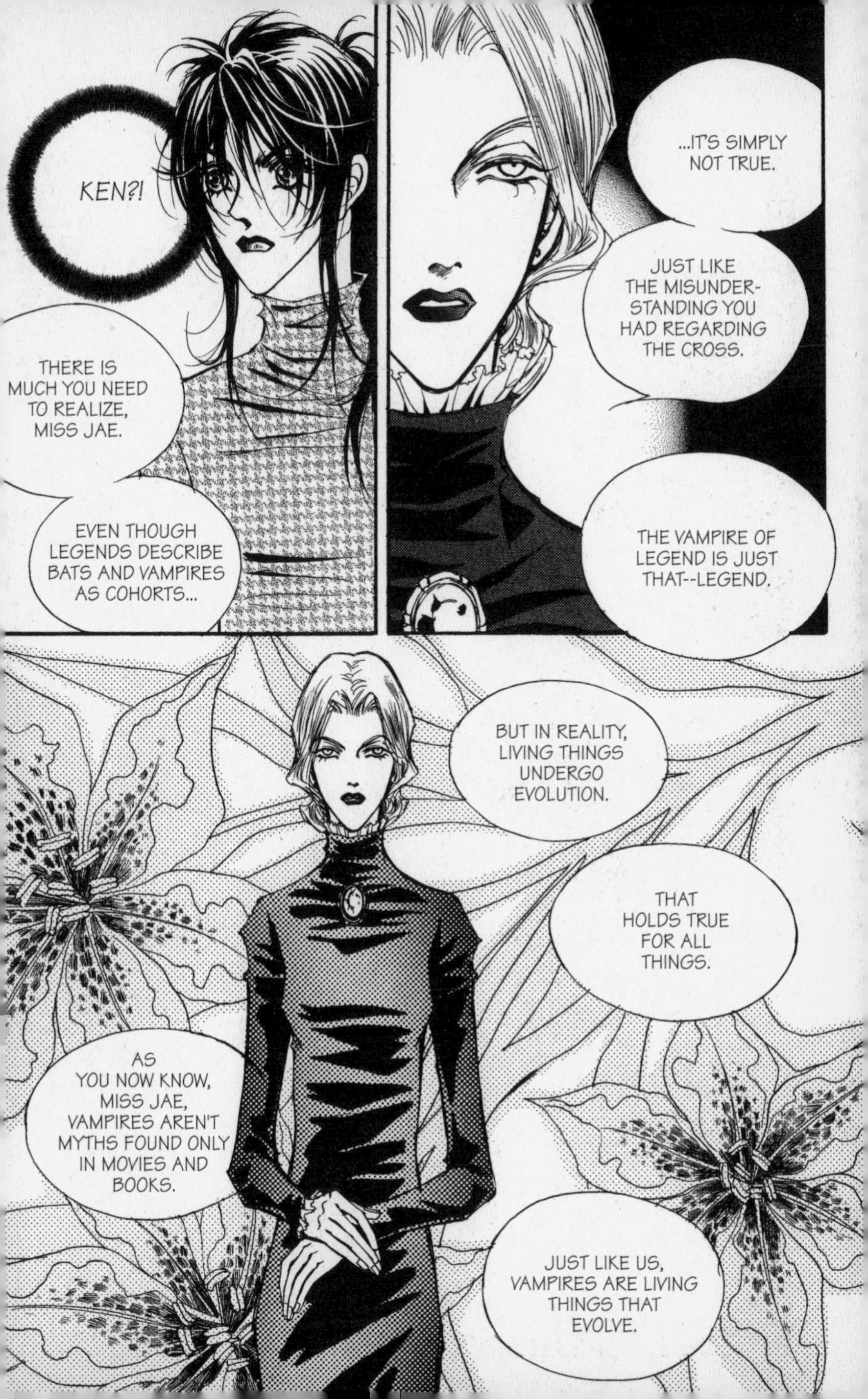
KEN?!
THERE IS MUCH YOU NEED TO REALIZE, MISS JAE.
EVEN THOUGH LEGENDS DESCRIBE BATS AND VAMPIRES AS COHORTS...
...IT'S SIMPLY NOT TRUE.
JUST LIKE THE MISUNDER-STANDING YOU HAD REGARDING THE CROSS.
THE VAMPIRE OF LEGEND IS JUST THAT--LEGEND.
BUT IN REALITY, LIVING THINGS UNDERGO EVOLUTION.
THAT HOLDS TRUE FOR ALL THINGS.
AS YOU NOW KNOW, MISS JAE, VAMPIRES AREN'T MYTHS FOUND ONLY IN MOVIES AND BOOKS.
JUST LIKE US, VAMPIRES ARE LIVING THINGS THAT EVOLVE.

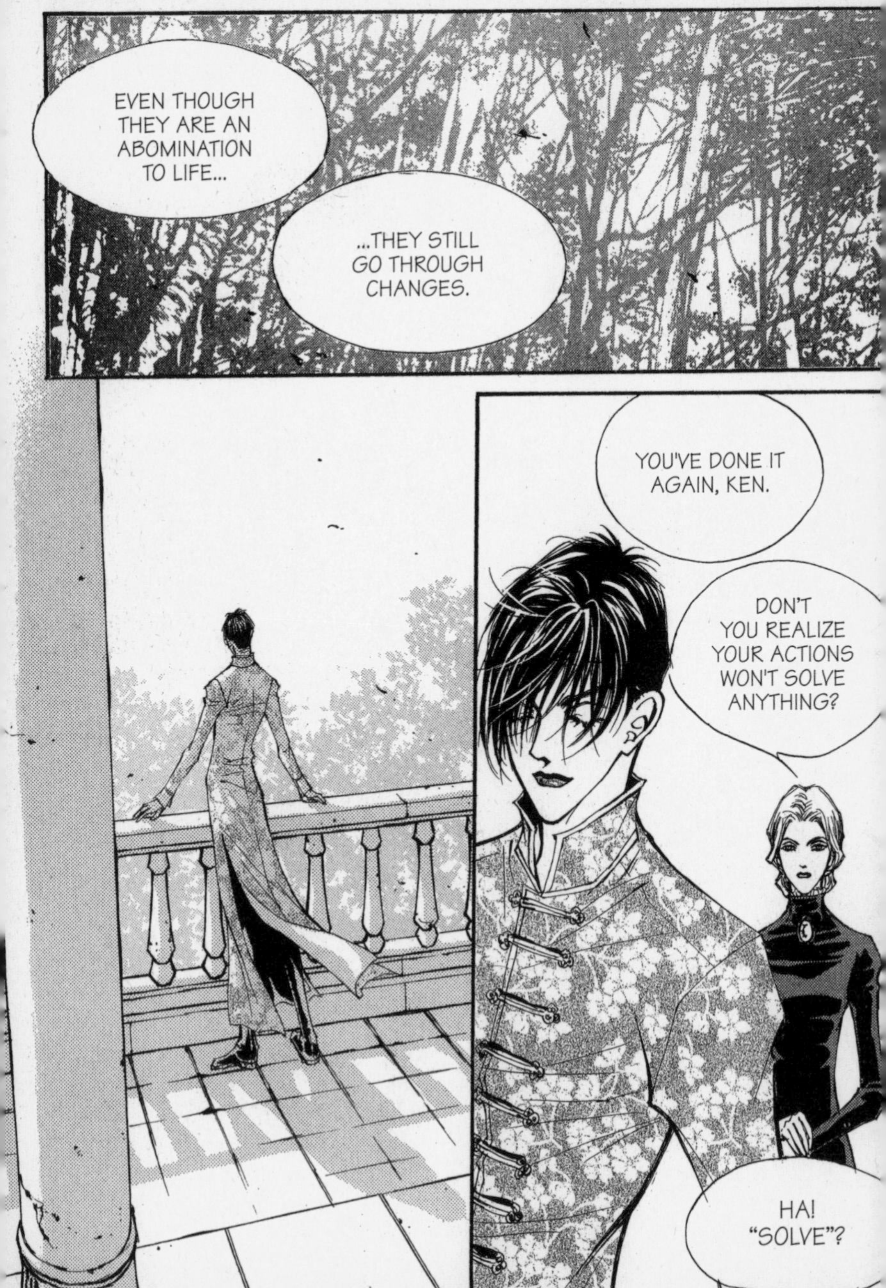
EVEN THOUGH THEY ARE AN ABOMINATION TO LIFE...
...THEY STILL GO THROUGH CHANGES.
YOU'VE DONE IT AGAIN, KEN.
DON'T YOU REALIZE YOUR ACTIONS WON'T SOLVE ANYTHING?
HA! "SOLVE"?

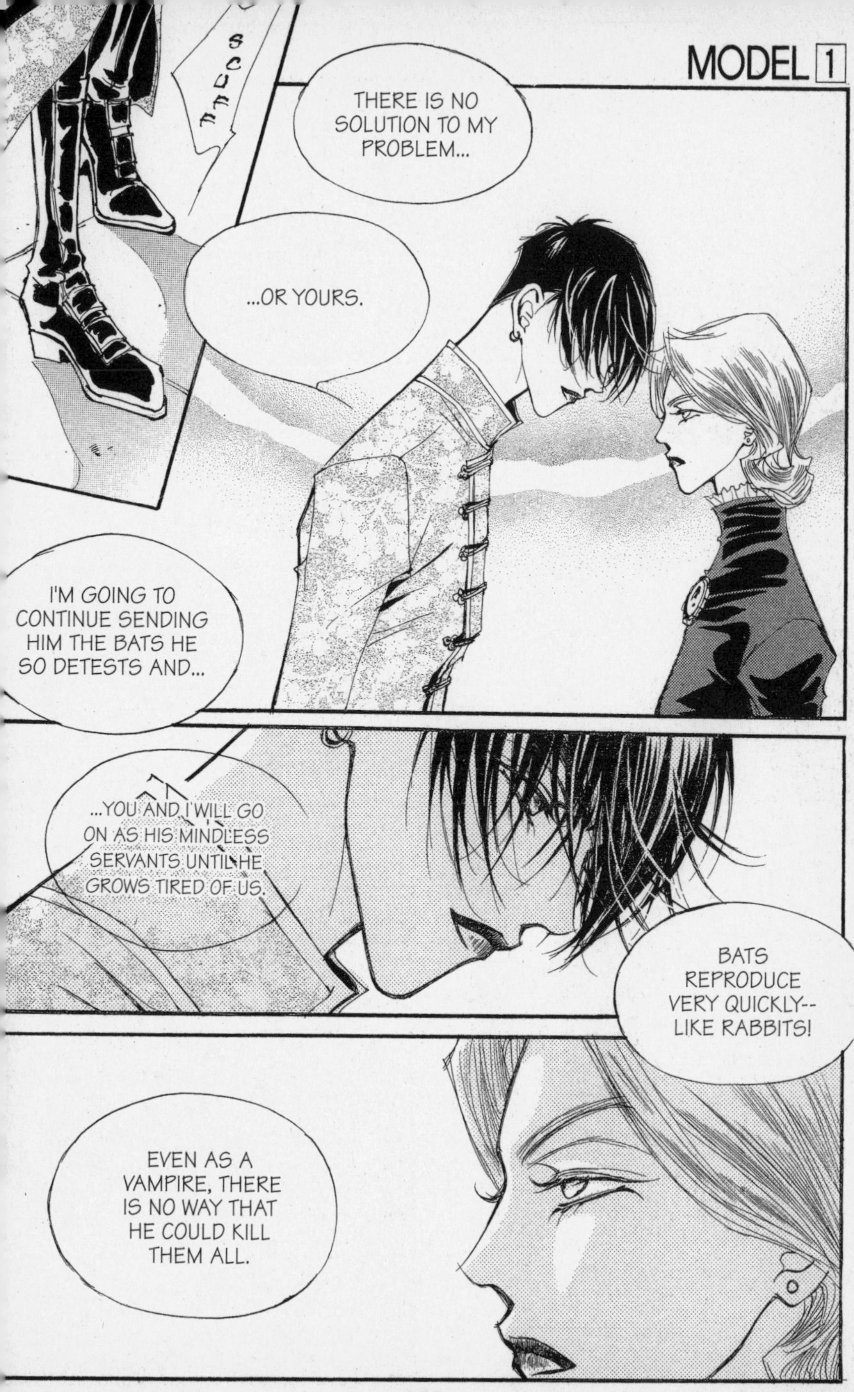
SCUFF
THERE IS NO SOLUTION TO MY PROBLEM...
...OR YOURS.
I'M GOING TO CONTINUE SENDING HIM THE BATS HE SO DETESTS AND...
...YOU AND I WILL GO ON AS HIS MINDLESS SERVANTS UNTIL HE GROWS TIRED OF US.
BATS REPRODUCE VERY QUICKLY--LIKE RABBITS!
EVEN AS A VAMPIRE, THERE IS NO WAY THAT HE COULD KILL THEM ALL.

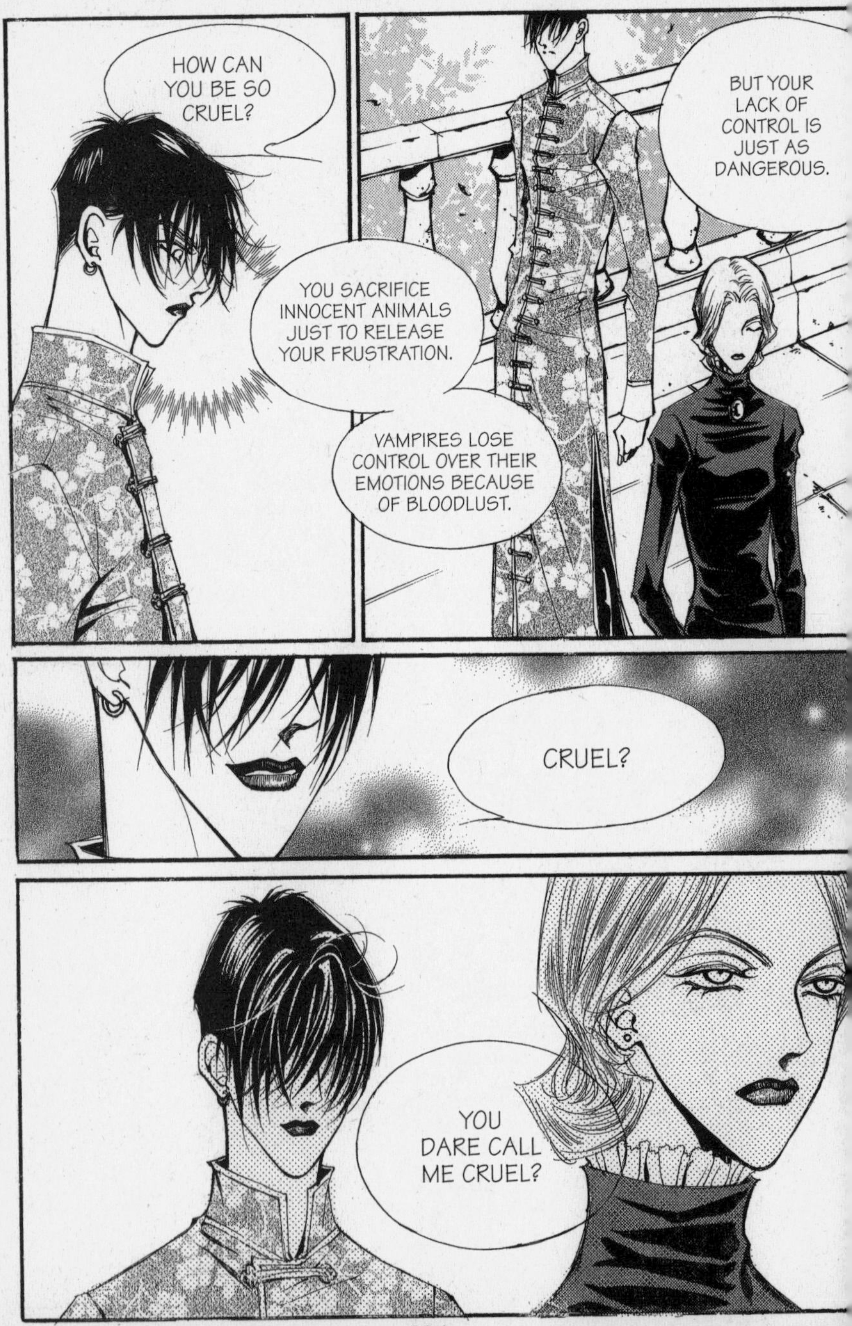
HOW CAN YOU BE SO CRUEL?
YOU SACRIFICE INNOCENT ANIMALS JUST TO RELEASE YOUR FRUSTRATION.
VAMPIRES LOSE CONTROL OVER THEIR EMOTIONS BECAUSE OF BLOODLUST.
BUT YOUR LACK OF CONTROL IS JUST AS DANGEROUS.
CRUEL?
YOU DARE CALL ME CRUEL?

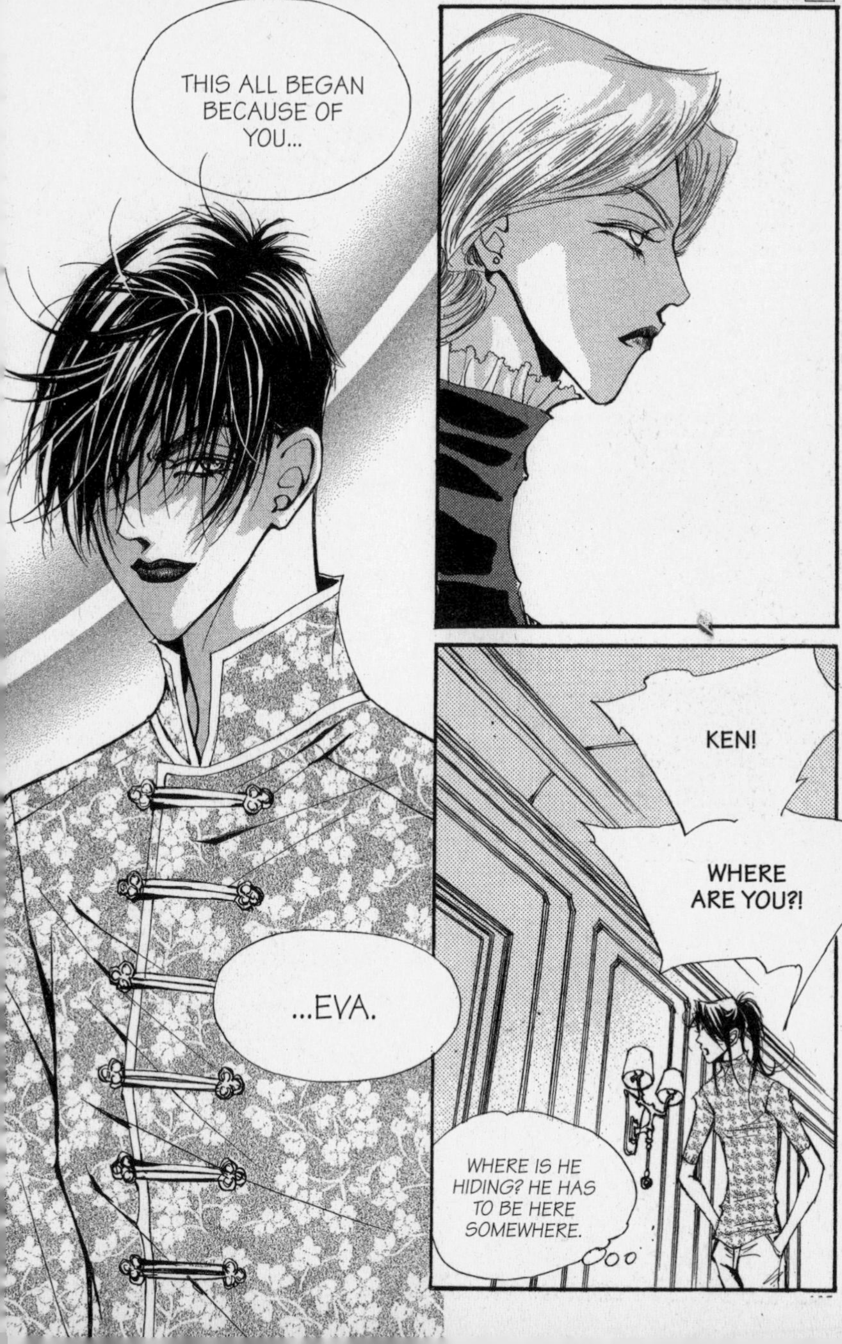
THIS ALL BEGAN BECAUSE OF YOU...
...EVA.
KEN!
WHERE ARE YOU?!
WHERE IS HE HIDING? HE HAS TO BE HERE SOMEWHERE.

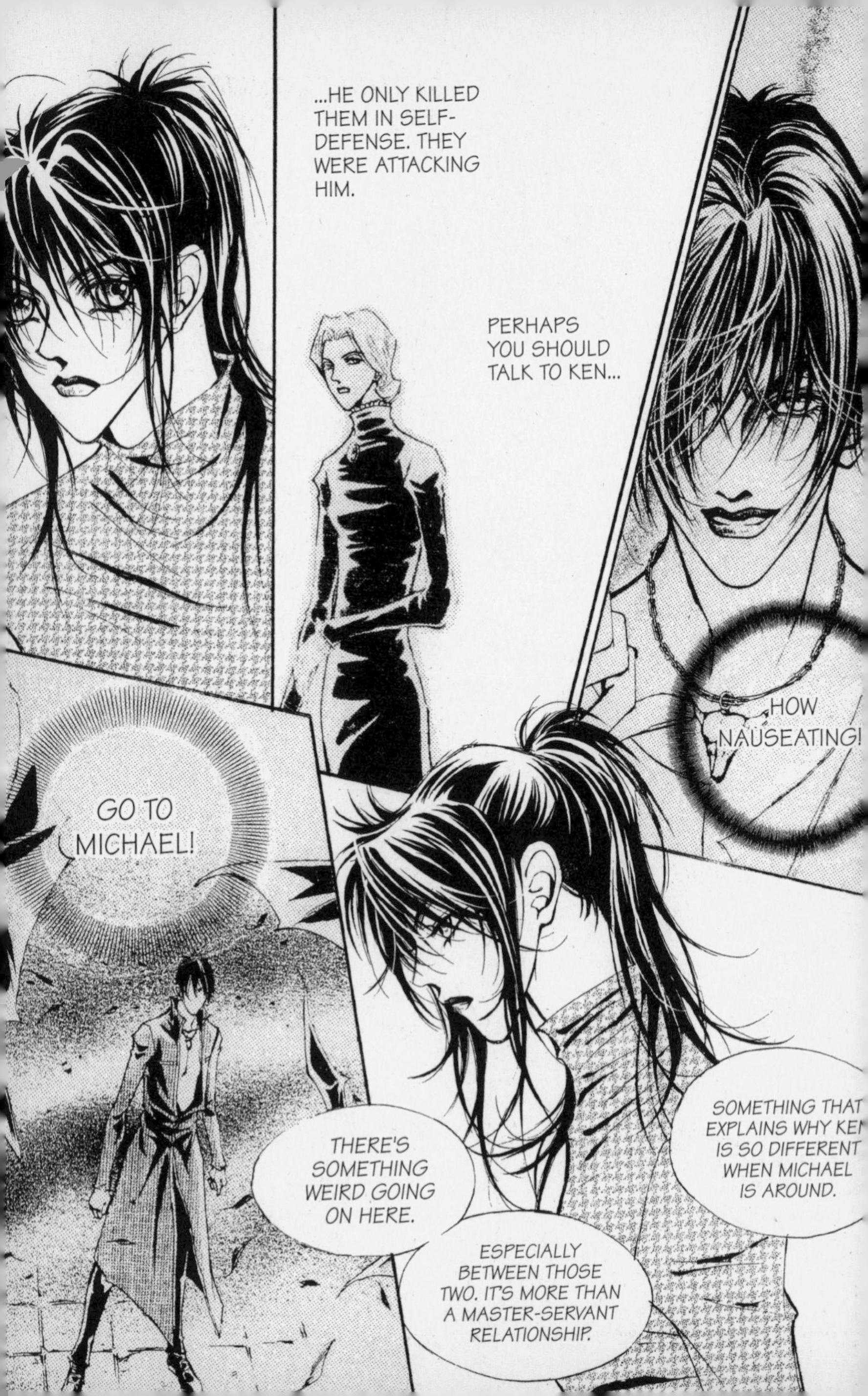

...HE ONLY KILLED THEM IN SELF-DEFENSE. THEY WERE ATTACKING HIM.
PERHAPS YOU SHOULD TALK TO KEN...
HOW NAUSEATING!
GO TO MICHAEL!
THERE'S SOMETHING WEIRD GOING ON HERE.
ESPECIALLY BETWEEN THOSE TWO. IT'S MORE THAN A MASTER-SERVANT RELATIONSHIP.
SOMETHING THAT EXPLAINS WHY KEN IS SO DIFFERENT WHEN MICHAEL IS AROUND.

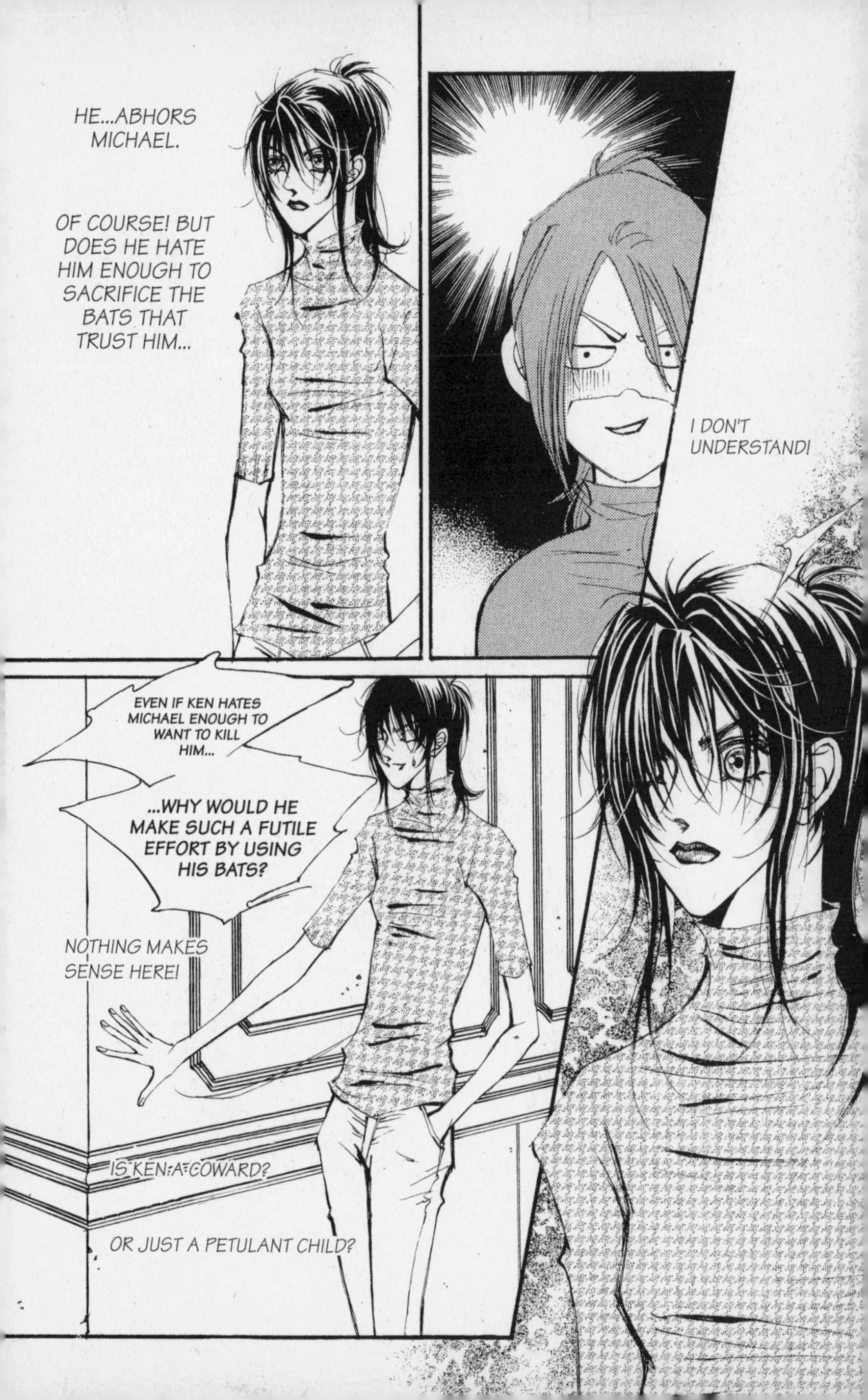
HE...ABHORS MICHAEL.
OF COURSE! BUT DOES HE HATE HIM ENOUGH TO SACRIFICE THE BATS THAT TRUST HIM...
I DON'T UNDERSTAND!
EVEN IF KEN HATES MICHAEL ENOUGH TO WANT TO KILL HIM...
...WHY WOULD HE MAKE SUCH A FUTILE EFFORT BY USING HIS BATS?
NOTHING MAKES SENSE HERE!
IS KEN A COWARD?
OR JUST A PETULANT CHILD?

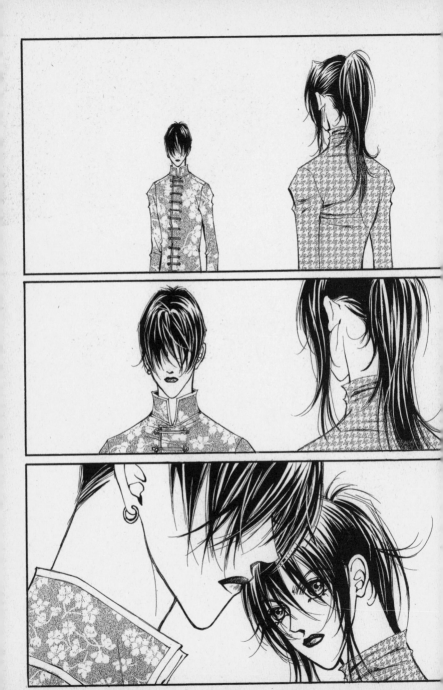

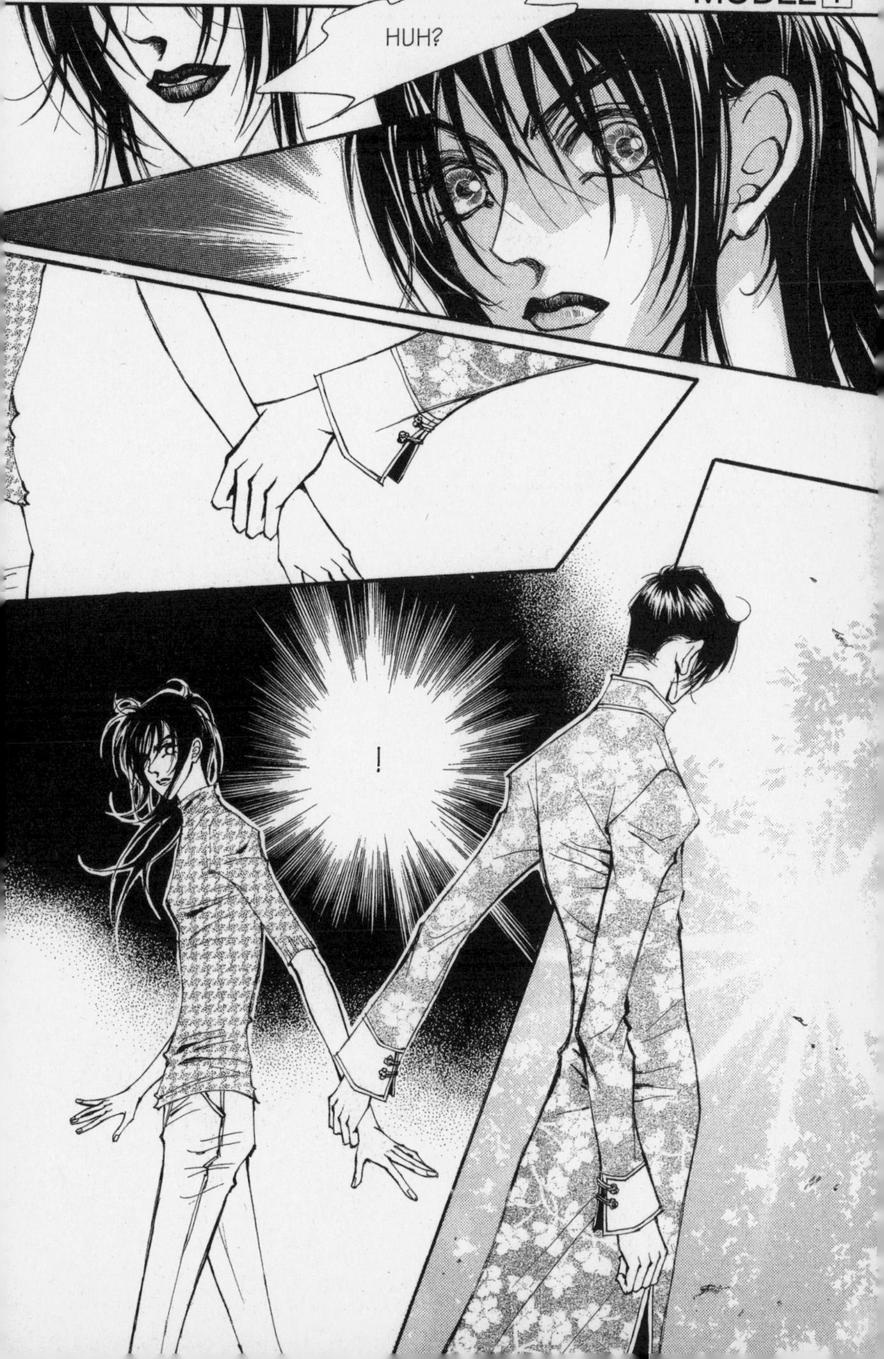
HUH?
!

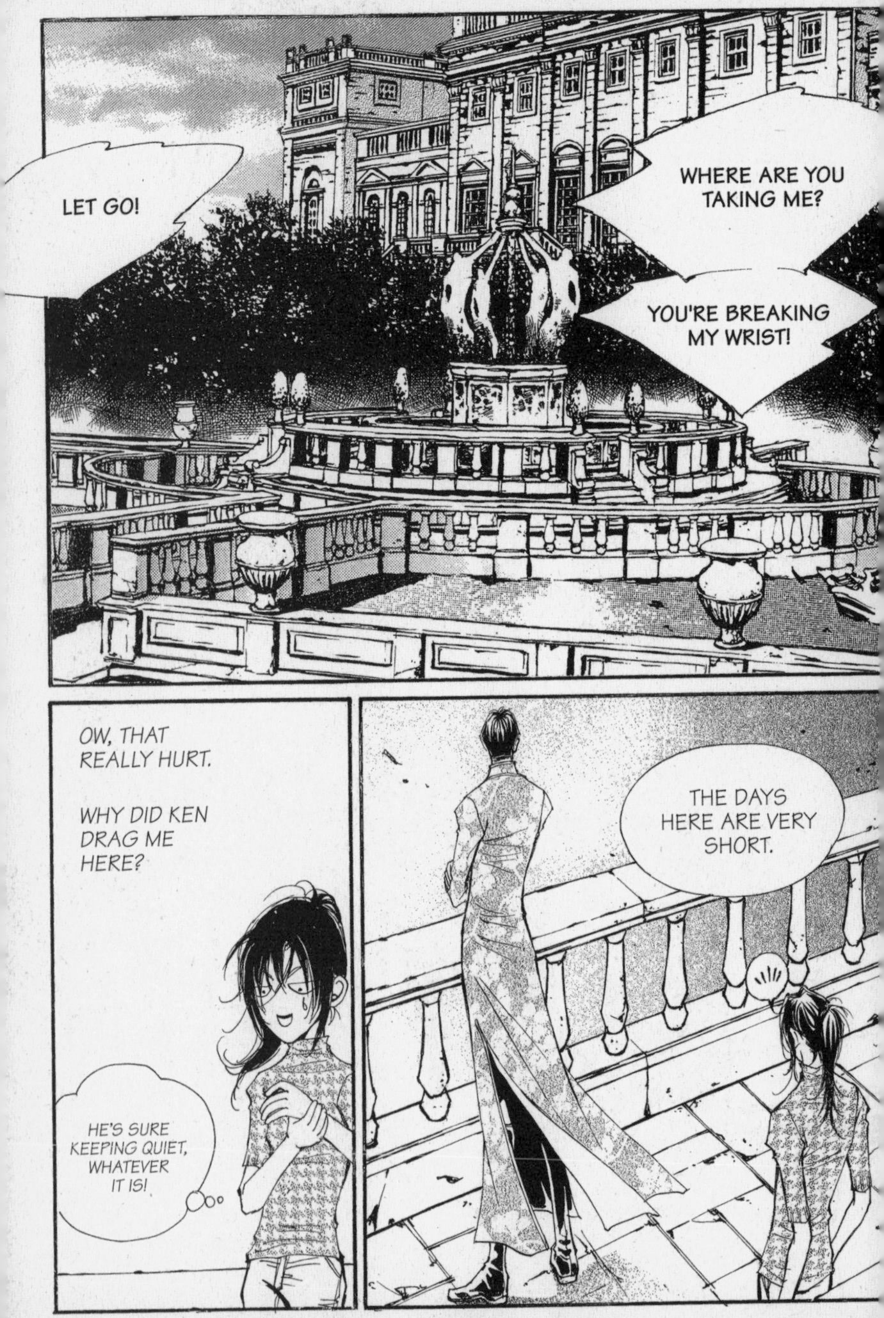
LET GO!
WHERE ARE YOU TAKING ME?
YOU'RE BREAKING MY WRIST!
OW, THAT REALLY HURT.
WHY DID KEN DRAG ME HERE?
HE'S SURE KEEPING QUIET, WHATEVER IT IS!
THE DAYS HERE ARE VERY SHORT.

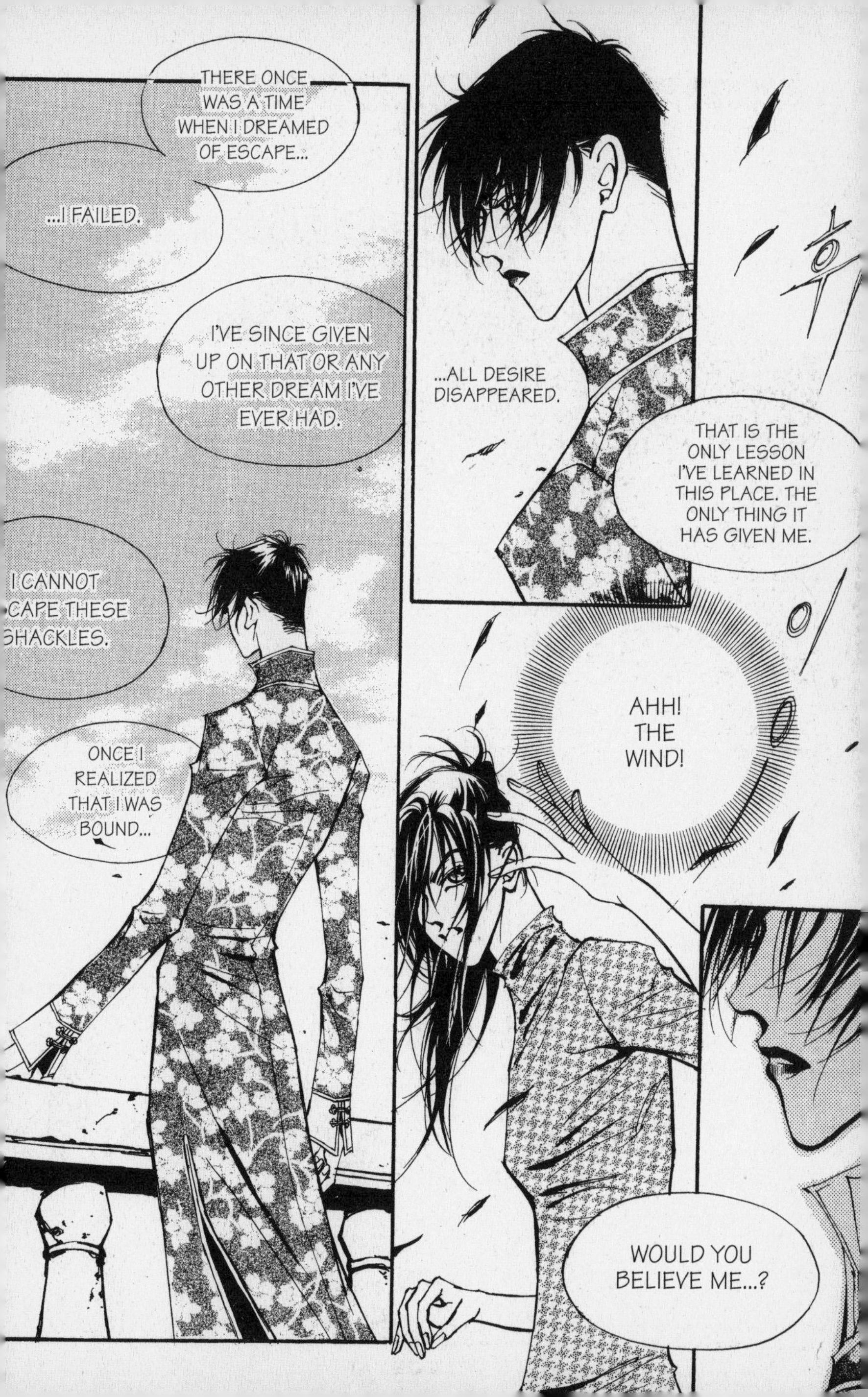
THERE ONCE WAS A TIME WHEN I DREAMED OF ESCAPE...
...I FAILED.
I'VE SINCE GIVEN UP ON THAT OR ANY OTHER DREAM I'VE EVER HAD.
I CANNOT CAPE THESE SHACKLES.
ONCE I REALIZED THAT I WAS BOUND...
...ALL DESIRE DISAPPEARED.
THAT IS THE ONLY LESSON I'VE LEARNED IN THIS PLACE. THE ONLY THING IT HAS GIVEN ME.
AHH! THE WIND!
WOULD YOU BELIEVE ME...?

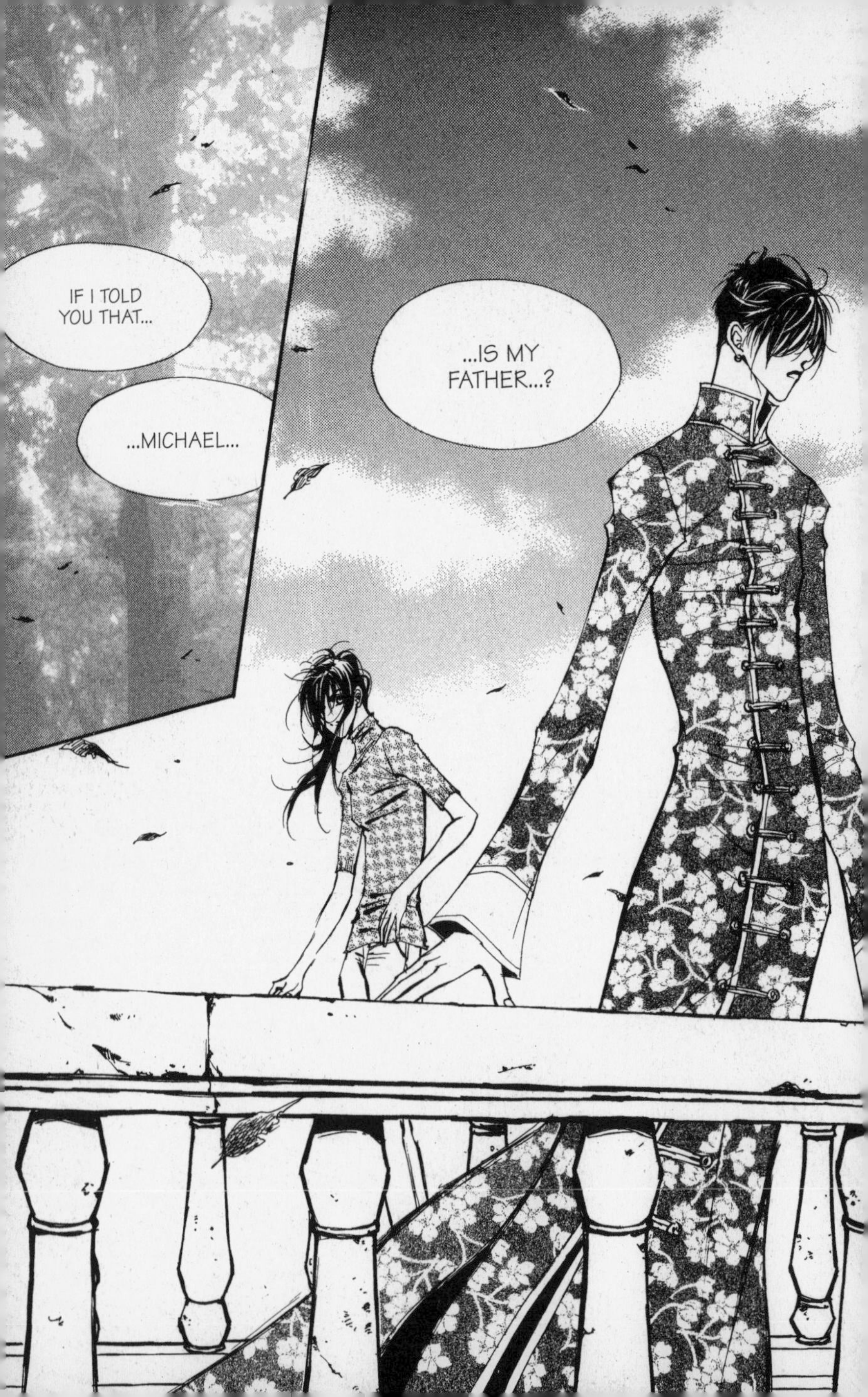
IF I TOLD YOU THAT...
...MICHAEL...
...IS MY FATHER...?

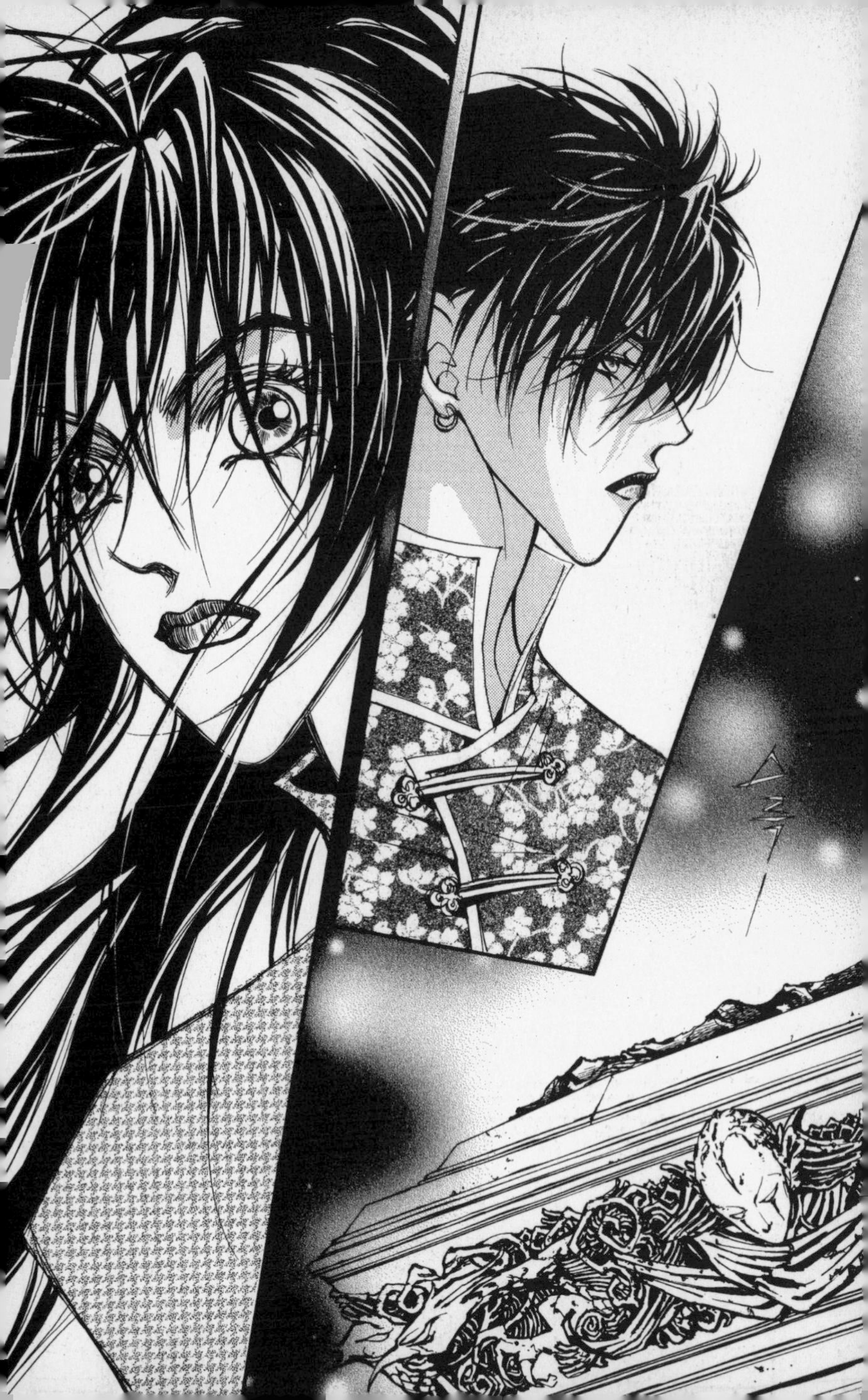

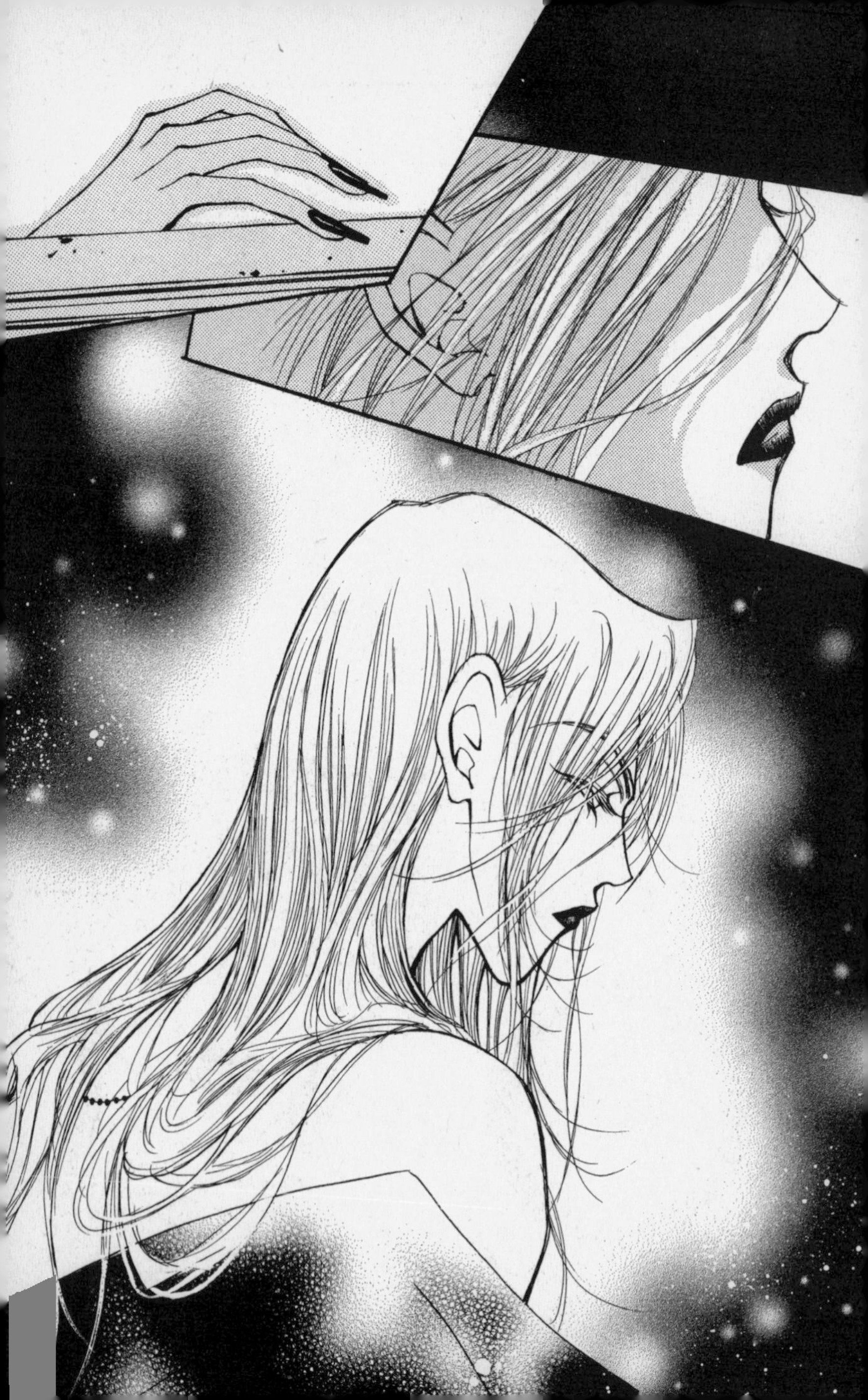

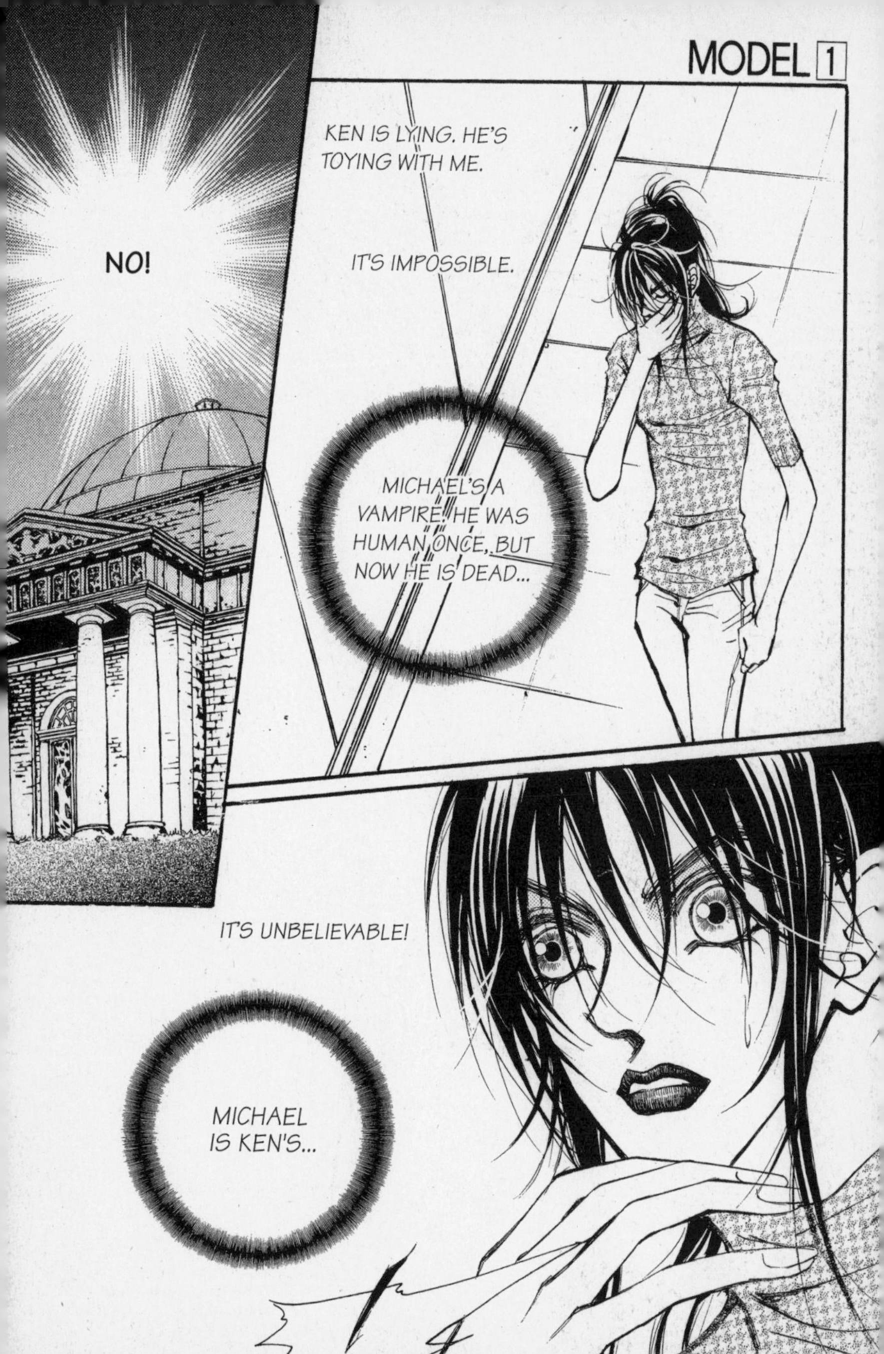
NO!
KEN IS LYING. HE'S TOYING WITH ME.
IT'S IMPOSSIBLE.
MICHAEL'S A VAMPIRE. HE WAS HUMAN ONCE, BUT NOW HE IS DEAD...
IT'S UNBELIEVABLE!
MICHAEL IS KEN'S...

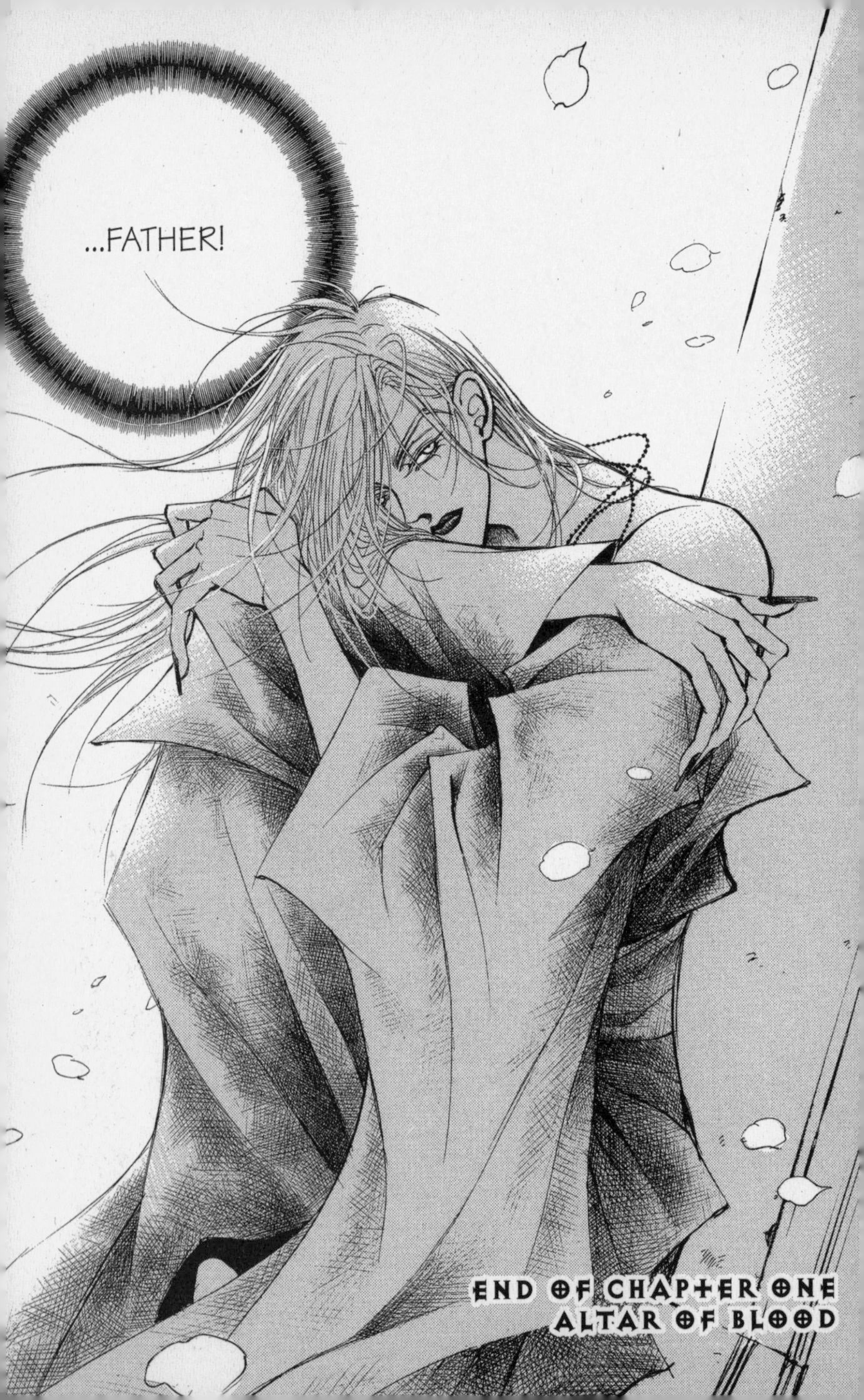
...FATHER!
END OF CHAPTER ONE
ALTAR OF BLOOD

END OF MODEL
VOLUME I

# MESSAGES FROM THE MAUSOLEUM

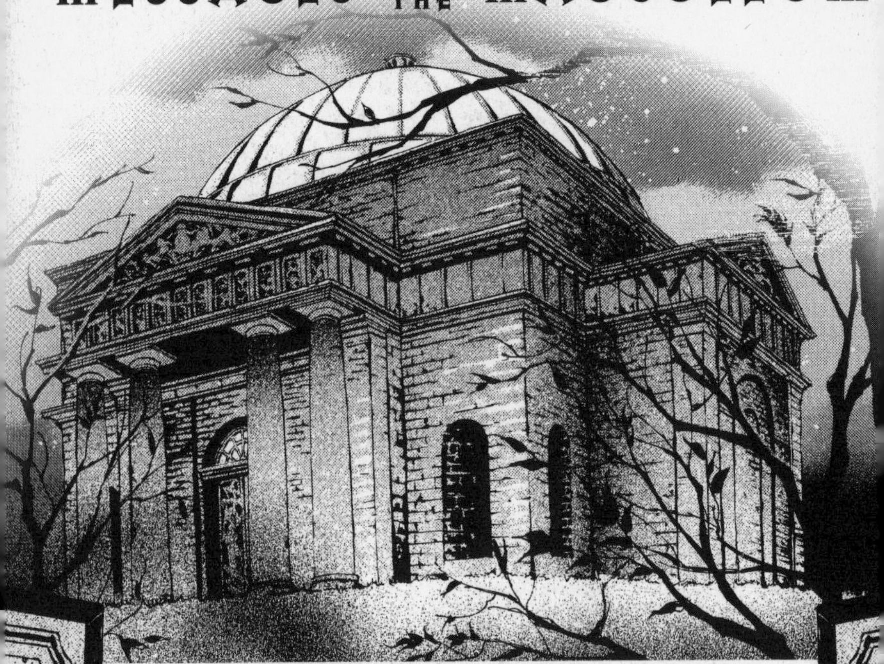

JAE'S NEW LIFE AT MICHAEL'S ESTATE MOVES FROM THE REALM OF THE BIZARRE INTO THE UTTERLY FANTASTIC! AS JAE TRIES TO UNCOVER THE SECRETS OF HER BENEFACTOR'S PAST, IT SEEMS THAT WITH EACH ANSWER COME EVEN MORE MYSTERIOUS QUESTIONS. HOW CAN MICHAEL AFFORD SUCH AN EXTRAVAGANT LIFE STYLE? WHY DOES HE PAINT ONLY THE DEAD AND THE DYING? AND JUST WHO IS THE NEWEST GUEST TO ARRIVE AT THIS MANOR OF THE MACABRE?

UNEARTH THE TRUTH IN **MODEL** VOLUME 2!

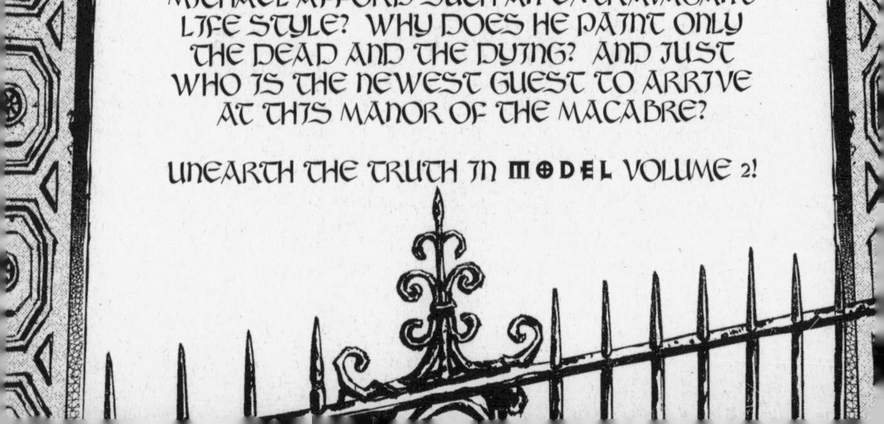

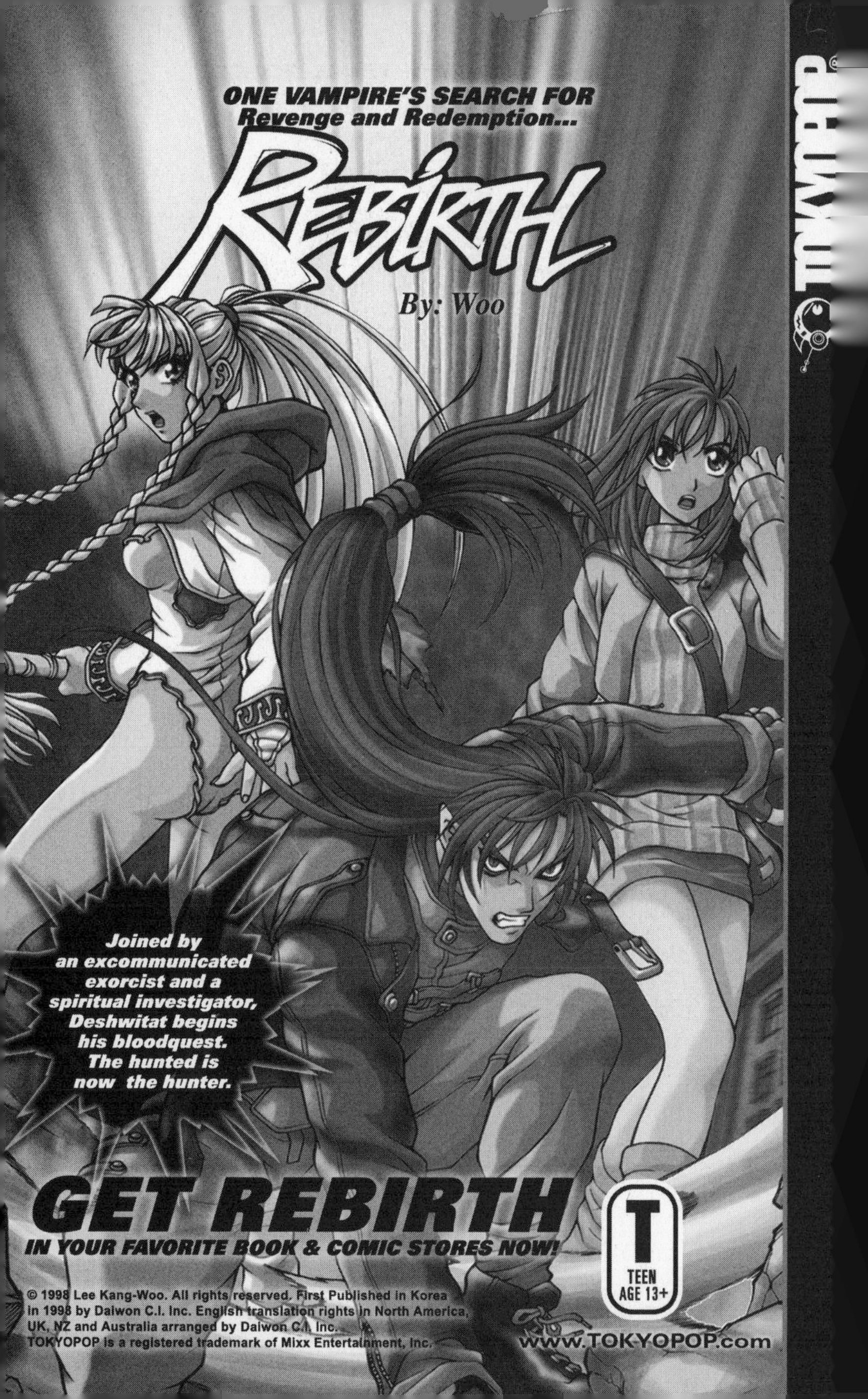
ONE VAMPIRE'S SEARCH FOR
Revenge and Redemption...
REBIRTH
By: Woo
Joined by an excommunicated exorcist and a spiritual investigator, Deshwitat begins his bloodquest. The hunted is now the hunter.
GET REBIRTH
IN YOUR FAVORITE BOOK & COMIC STORES NOW!
T
TEEN
AGE 13+
© 1998 Lee Kang-Woo. All rights reserved. First Published in Korea in 1998 by Daiwon C.I. Inc. English translation rights in North America, UK, NZ and Australia arranged by Daiwon C.I. Inc.
TOKYOPOP is a registered trademark of Mixx Entertainment, Inc.
www.TOKYOPOP.com
TOKYOPOP

# Princess ai

Courtney Love & D.J. Milky
put their spin on celebrity and fantasy.

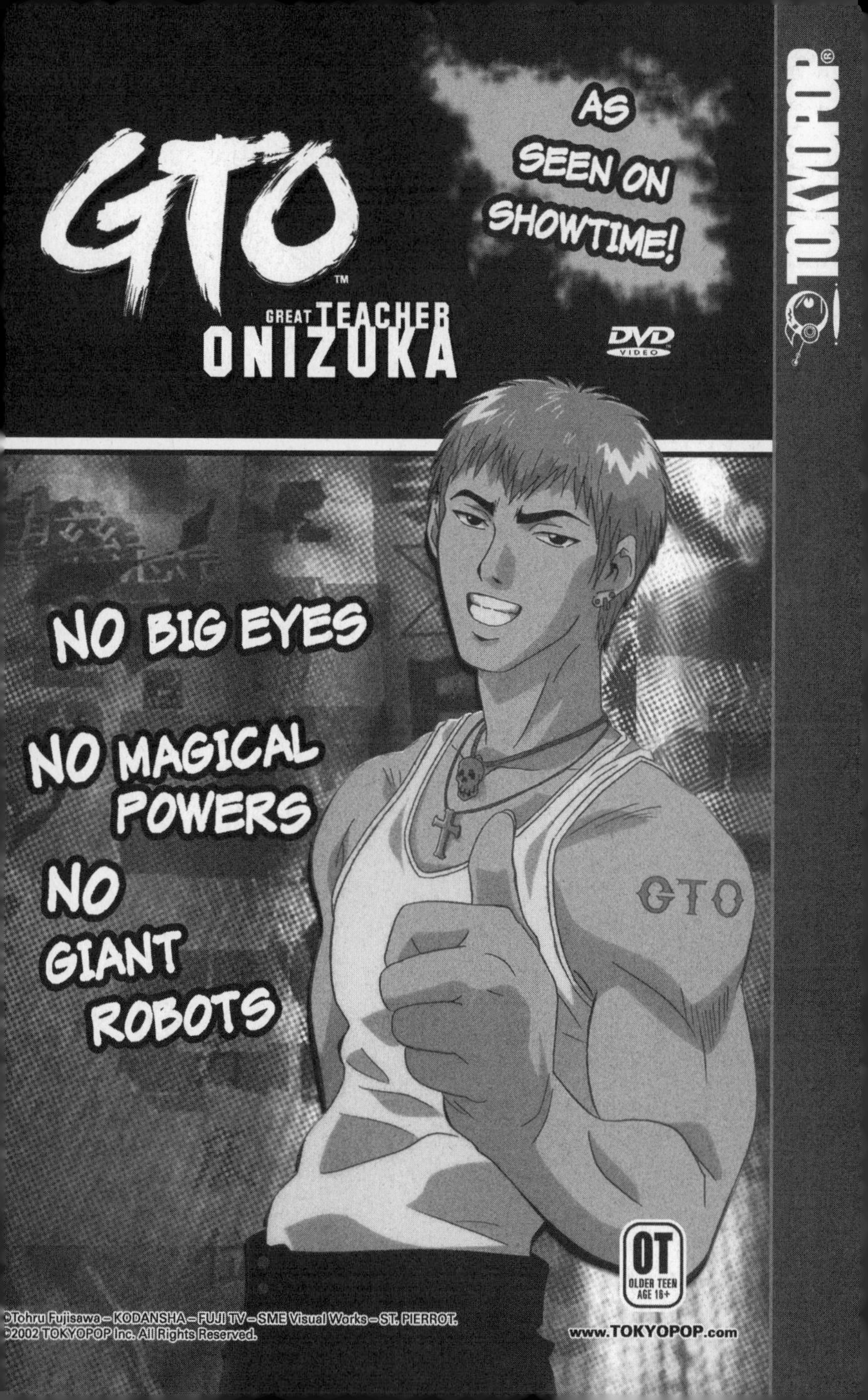
GTO™
GREAT TEACHER ONIZUKA
AS SEEN ON SHOWTIME!
DVD VIDEO
TOKYOPOP
NO BIG EYES
NO MAGICAL POWERS
NO GIANT ROBOTS
GTO
OT OLDER TEEN AGE 16+
©Tohru Fujisawa – KODANSHA – FUJI TV – SME Visual Works – ST. PIERROT.
©2002 TOKYOPOP Inc. All Rights Reserved.
www.TOKYOPOP.com

# LAMENT of the LAMB

SHE CAN PROTECT HER BROTHER FROM THE WORLD.
CAN SHE PROTECT THE WORLD FROM HER BROTHER?

OT
OLDER TEEN
AGE 16+

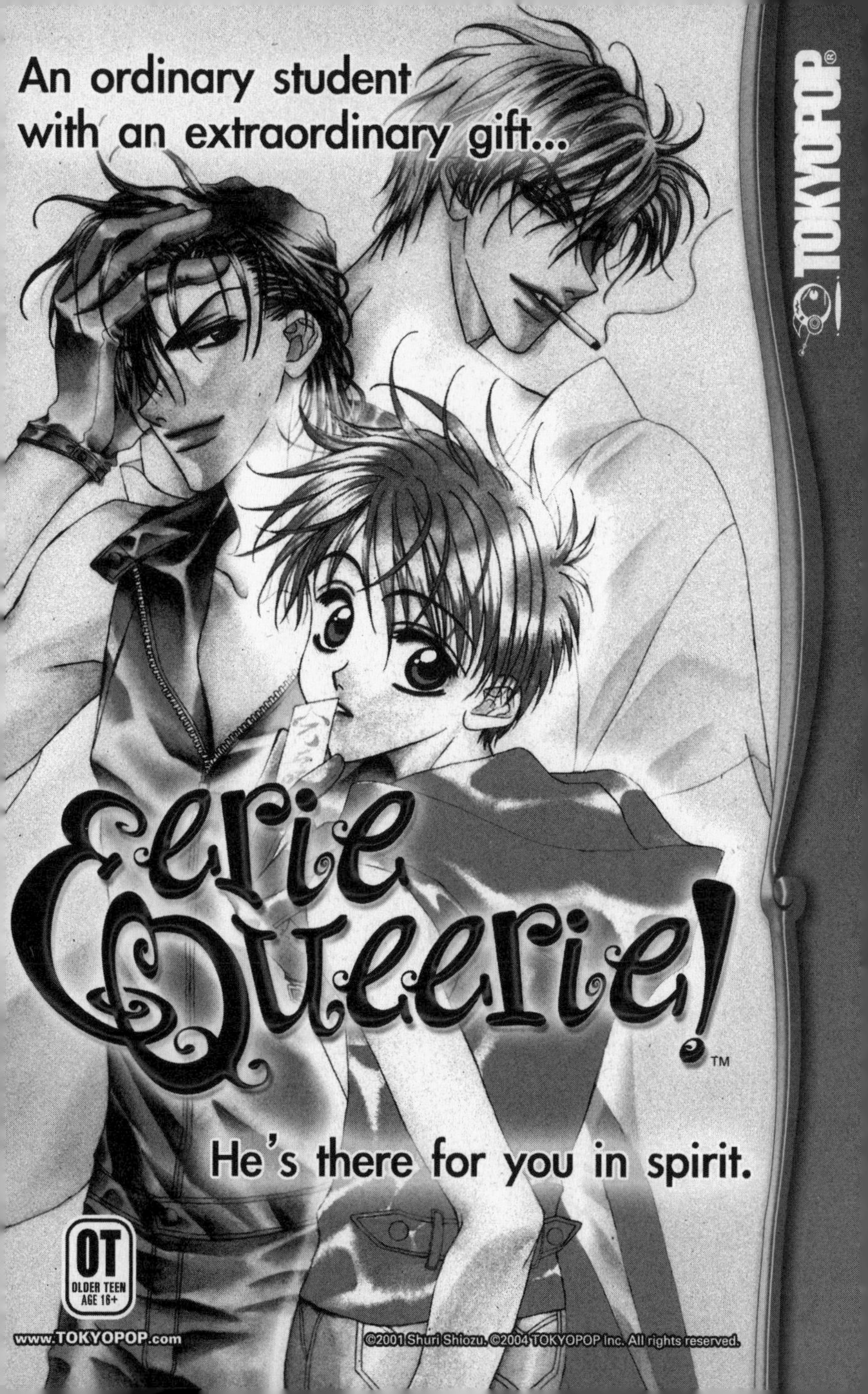
An ordinary student with an extraordinary gift...
TOKYOPOP
Eerie Queerie!™
He's there for you in spirit.
OT OLDER TEEN AGE 16+
www.TOKYOPOP.com
©2001 Shuri Shiozu. ©2004 TOKYOPOP Inc. All rights reserved.

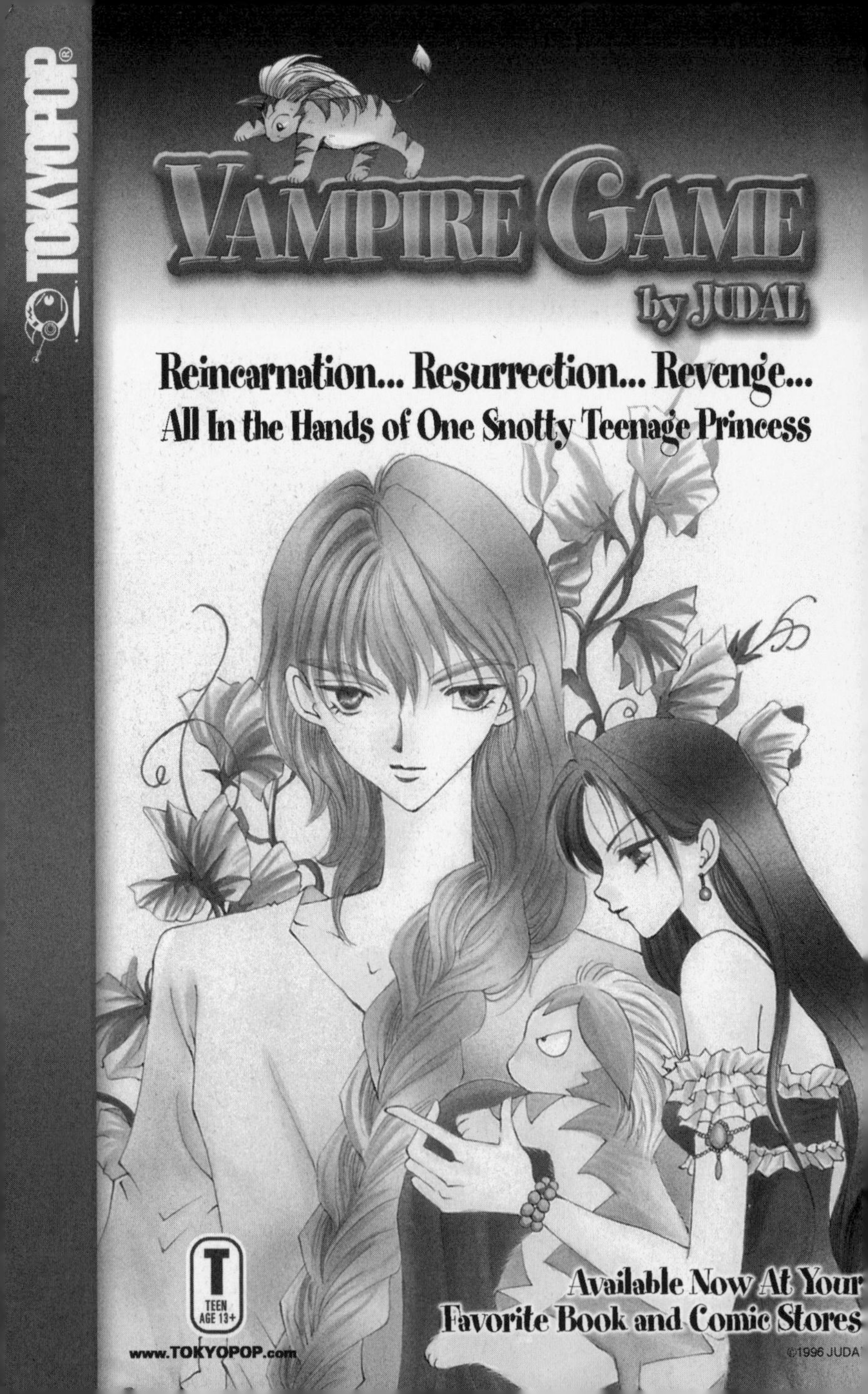
TOKYOPOP®
VAMPIRE GAME
by JUDAL
Reincarnation... Resurrection... Revenge...
All In the Hands of One Snotty Teenage Princess
T
TEEN
AGE 13+
Available Now At Your
Favorite Book and Comic Stores
www.TOKYOPOP.com
©1996 JUDA

# Snow Drop™

Like love, a fragile flower
often blooms in unlikely places.

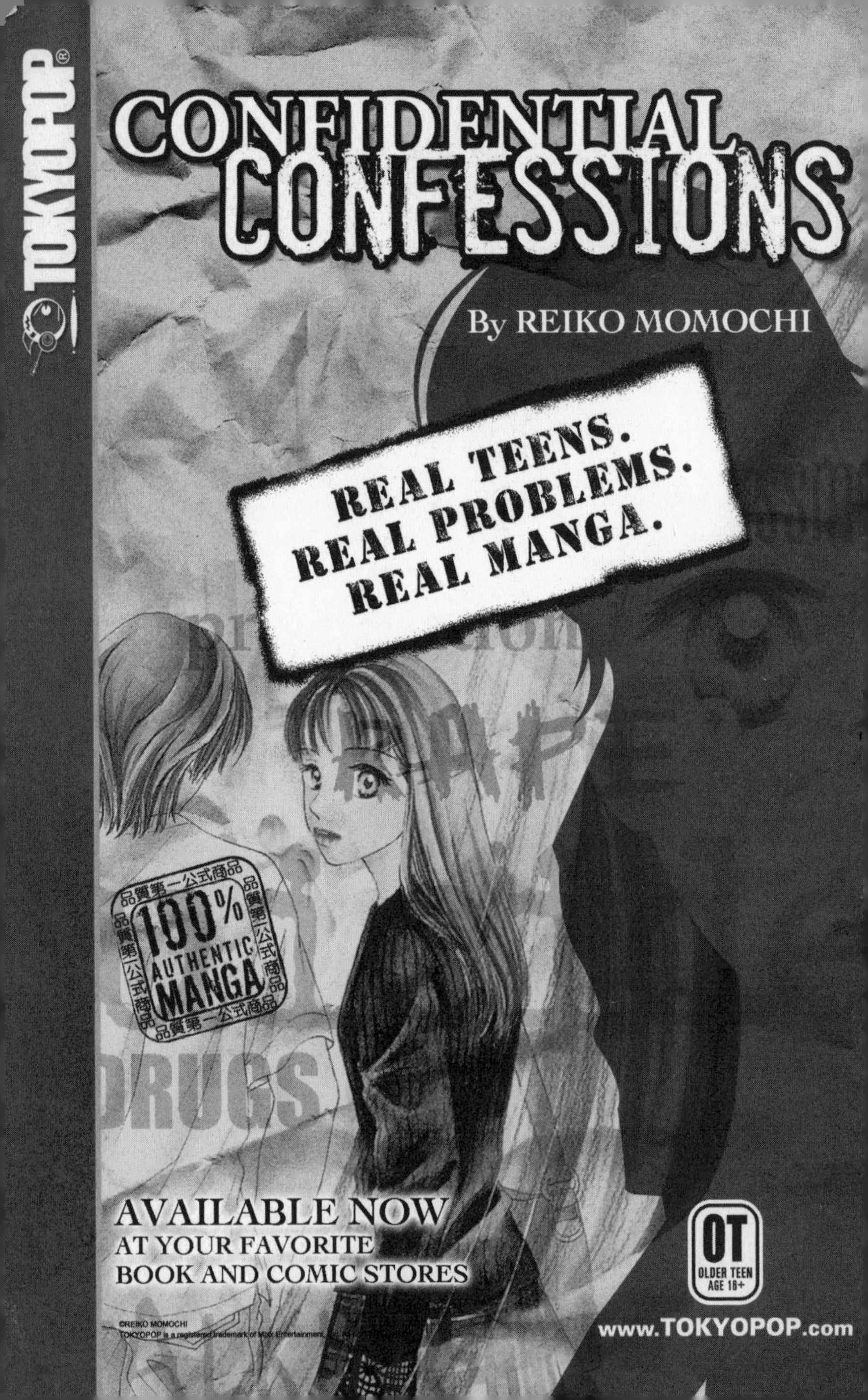